"Little tiger!" he laughed. "You belong in my harem."

Gale fought off Carl's savage kisses, tore herself from his rough embrace and with her free right hand clawed at his face so viciously that he backed out of the room.

She rushed to the window, frantically seeking for a way to escape. There was none; and when the door crashed open again, Carl stood before her, his face bleeding. In his right hand was a whip of the sort she had seen the native drivers use in the caravans—short of handle with a lash eight or ten feet long. Now he let the whip uncurl. He moved forward and lifted it high. It encircled her waist in a fiery embrace of pain. The whip rose and fell again. Now she was on her knees.

"You dare not kill me!" she screamed.

"There are some things," he sneered, "worse than death."

ATTENTION: SCHOOLS AND CORPORATIONS

WARNER books are available at quantity discounts with bulk purchase for educational, business, or sales promotional use. For information, please write to: SPECIAL SALES DEPARTMENT, WARNER BOOKS, 75 ROCKEFELLER PLAZA, NEW YORK, N.Y. 10019

**ARE THERE WARNER BOOKS
YOU WANT BUT CANNOT FIND IN YOUR LOCAL STORES?**

You can get any WARNER BOOKS title in print. Simply send title and retail price, plus 50¢ per order and 20¢ per copy to cover mailing and handling costs for each book desired. New York State and California residents add applicable sales tax. Enclose check or money order only, no cash please, to: WARNER BOOKS, P.O. BOX 690, NEW YORK, N.Y. 10019

Casablanca Intrigue

*A Novel of
Romantic Suspense by
Clarissa Ross*

WARNER BOOKS

A Warner Communications Company

WARNER BOOKS EDITION

Copyright © 1979 by Dan Ross
All rights reserved.

ISBN 0-446-91027-9

Cover art by Tom Hall

Warner Books, Inc., 75 Rockefeller Plaza, New York, N.Y. 10019

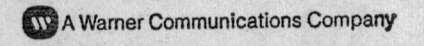

A Warner Communications Company

Printed in the United States of America

First Printing: October, 1979

10 9 8 7 6 5 4 3 2 1

*To my good friends Ron and Venetia Mann
and to a charming critic, Cathy!*

1

Her husband had vanished!

Gale Cormier was filled with fear as she gazed into the main entrance to the Casablanca *medina*, the old Arab quarter of Morocco, where her husband, Paul, had been earnestly conversing with a dark man in a red fez a few moments ago. Now there was no sign of either of them and she was left standing alone in this frightening area of the North African city!

In a flowing white dress, broad-brimmed straw hat, and carrying a white parasol, she was an object of interest for the fantastic gathering of humanity around her. Her pert oval face with lovely green eyes awed these people accustomed to seeing women heavily veiled. And her golden-red hair, alabaster skin, and sensuous red lips might have adorned a creature from another planet.

Frightened by the disappearance of her husband and trembling under the inspection of the many eyes around her, she found herself feeling faint! The blazing sun burned down on her on this June afternoon in 1890, only the second day following their arrival here on their honeymoon. A honeymoon which was also a mysterious business trip! And now, after promising not to move out of her sight, he had vanished!

She was spellbound as she gazed at the curious group circling her. Bearded men, hooded in burnooses, veiled women, ebony blacks with scarred faces from Central Africa, Jewish patriarchs with long beards and skullcaps, whining, ragged beggars. Suddenly, an ancient, wrinkled beggar held out a hand with five stumps whose fingers had been eaten away by leprosy and clamored for alms in a wheezing voice!

"No!" she cried, retreating from the wretched old man.

But he was not to be easily dismissed. As the crowd jeered and encouraged him, the beggar reached out with his other hand to take her pocketbook from her arm.

"That will do!" A resolute male voice cried in English above the clamor, and stepping neatly between her and the beggar was, a pleasant-looking young man in white linen suit and Panama.

The stern rebuff and quick action of the young man was enough to send the old beggar on his way. The show at an end, the group of onlookers sullenly began to disperse.

With a great sigh of relief, Gale told the young man, "I'm most grateful to you. I was in a panic."

"No wonder," he said with a smile and a correct British accent. "That old chap was ugly and that leprous hand would put anyone off!" He gazed at her with reassurance in his brown eyes, which were a shade darker than his lightish brown hair. "My name is Eric Simms. I'm foreign correspondent for the *London Telegram*."

"I'm happy to know you,". she said. "I'm Gale Page, or I should say, Cormier!" She blushed. "I've recently married and I'm not completely accustomed to my new name."

He laughed. "Quite understandable. Are you here on your honeymoon?"

"Partly," she explained. "And also because my husband is an employee of a firm called International Ventures. It does a worldwide business and has an office here in Casablanca."

The Britisher showed interest. "I think I've heard of the company. It deals in a number of things."

"I really know nothing about it," she confessed. She pointed toward the gate to the ancient city. "He went in there a little while ago and met a man in a red fez. He promised he wouldn't be long and that he'd come directly back. But when I looked for him a moment ago he had vanished! Then the beggar came after me."

Eric Simms eyed her good-naturedly and said, "And then I came into the picture."

"I'm so glad you did," she exclaimed. "I was terrified! Now I'm worried as to what may have happened to my husband."

"I'm sure he's all right," the newspaperman consoled her.

She gave him an anxious glance. "You think so?"

"I do," he said. "Casablanca is not all that dangerous. And this is clearly some business confederate he had to meet. They may have had to consult someone else."

"But Paul should know better than to leave me here alone!"

"He may have expected to be out of your sight for only a moment," Simms theorized. Then he asked, "Is that him now?"

She glanced in the direction of the gate and saw that it was indeed Paul and that he was coming toward them at a fast step. Paul was stockier than the newspaperman at her side, and he was perhaps better-looking in a stern, square-jawed fashion. He was dark-haired and almost swarthy and his eyes had a piercing quality.

As he came up to her now, he gave her a sharp, questioning look. "You have met a friend?"

She told her husband, "You might better say I've made one. This is Eric Simms, he writes for a London newspaper. He saved me from a circle of beggars after you abandoned me."

Paul's square face showed annoyance. "I didn't abandon you. I had to go inside a cafe for a moment to speak to someone else. I didn't think you'd be so childishly afraid!"

She blushed. "I was afraid, and I don't think I was being childish."

Eric Simms smiled at her husband. "I will defend your wife, Mr. Cromier. She was being imposed on by a leprous beggar. It was most unpleasant."

Paul eyed him grimly and, with some irony in his tone, said, "I presume you rescued her."

"I had only to order the fellow be on his way," Simms said.

Paul turned to Gale. "I would have thought you capable of that. You were raised to deal with servants."

"This was quite different," she said.

"No doubt," Paul said, rather mockingly. And to Eric Simms he added, "I'm very much in your debt, sir. Thank you."

The pleasant young Britisher said, "Not at all; my great pleasure."

"You will excuse us," Paul said, with a hint of impatience. "We have to get back to our chateau as soon as possible. I'm entertaining one of the officers of my company and his wife."

Gale spoke up, "Why don't you give Mr. Simms our address. Perhaps he might find time to call on us and allow us to repay him with some hospitality for his services to me today."

"It was nothing," Eric Simms protested.

Paul swallowed hard. "We are on the shore," he said. "LeClaire House, a white building. It's on Mohammed Five Boulevard."

She could not help feeling that her husband was giving this information with reluctant annoyance and she worried that Simms might sense this as well. So she quickly added, "We have only just settled in. But we would be delighted to have you call at your convenience."

"Thank you," Eric Simms said, seeming not at all put out by Paul's manner. "I may not be able to take advantage of your offer for a few days, as I'm busy completing a story for my paper."

"Then do come when you can," she said.

"I will," he promised.

Paul was studying him in his humorless way. "Do you find many news stories here of interest to London?"

Eric Simms replied cheerily, "Actually a great many interesting stories have broken here lately."

"Really?" Paul asked, in the same sour fashion.

The reporter went on, "The Sultan's reign has been noted for its corruptness. He is continually trying to best the French and the Spaniards. The feeling is that in a few years Morocco will become a French or Spanish protectorate."

"Interesting," Gale commented, though she knew little of what he meant. But it seemed vital to be friendly in the face of Paul's unpleasant manner.

"I'll tell you more of the local situation when we

meet again," the journalist said. And with a bow he turned and vanished in the crowd.

Paul was regarding his wife with faint annoyance. "It doesn't take you long to make friends!"

It was almost a rebuke and she would have shown resentment if it had not been their honeymoon. Instead, she said, "Believe me, I was in need of a friend. The crowd was closing in on me."

"I told you I'd be right back."

"But you weren't!"

He took her by the arm. "Let us get out of this infernal sun. It's no time to be out and about in any case. This must be our siesta time in future. This sun gets too hot from midday to late afternoon."

He led her along the cobblestoned street with its collection of different-sized buildings. It was a poor area of the city, one which Europeans seldom visited except for sight-seeing. They passed a turbanned man in white robe leading a camel.

They finally emerged on to a wider street where the carriage that had brought them was waiting. Paul raised his hand to summon the open carriage, and the driver flicked the reins of the single white horse and drove over to them. Paul helped Gale into the vehicle and then stepped up beside her. He told the driver to take them back to their chateau.

Settled comfortably beside her, he said, "You must be careful about making new friends in this part of the world. So many of the Europeans here are drifters who failed in their homelands."

She protested, "I'm sure Eric Simms is not one of that type."

"You have only his word he's a journalist," her husband warned her.

"But he wouldn't lie about it!"

Paul's look was disagreeable. "Swindlers lie about anything!"

She couldn't help replying indignantly. "I'm also sure he's not a swindler."

Her husband's smile was taut. "What a child you can be, dear Gale!"

"I am not all that naive," she said. "I did grow up in New York City."

"Greatly protected by your Aunt Gertrude," Paul reminded her. "She was most careful of you."

Gale could not resist teasing, "I don't know! She let me marry you!"

Her new husband showed slight surprise, then managed a smile as he said, "She knew I was the catch of the season!"

"At least you do not suffer from modesty," she chided him.

He laughed and leaned close to her. "Forgive me, my dear. I grow jealous whenever I see you talking to another man. You must forgive my bad humor, it stems from my adoring you."

She looked at him happily. "And I adore you, Paul."

He squeezed her hand in his. "So we have no problem."

They were driving along a wide boulevard now with palm trees lining it and impressive stucco homes along both sides of it. She sighed, "I think we are terribly lucky," she said. "But I would like to make some friends while we're here."

"We have the Waltons," he said.

"But Edmund and Diana are company people," she protested. "We have to be friends with them."

"And Peter Hall."

"He is a traveling representative of the company and only here occasionally," she said.

"Carl Revene will be here to take us on a cruise on his yacht."

"And he is the owner of the company," she said. "The great man himself. So it's all company! Let us have some friends on the outside."

"You'll be seeing Eric Simms," her husband told her. "You've nicely arranged that."

"You seem to resent it."

"Not really."

"And I don't know what to tell people when they ask about your work," she complained.

Paul frowned and picked up on this at once. "Did he ask you what I did?"

"No. I told him International Ventures and he seemed to know something about it."

"What?"

"He didn't say," Gale told her husband. "And I don't know anything. I think you should tell me."

Paul shrugged. "We are in many things. Carl Revene is one of the world's greatest financiers. He has a hand in building railway systems, bridges, great buildings, and he also has many other ventures. He finishes with one and starts another."

"I see," she said, not sure that he had fully answered her, but at least it gave her something to tell people.

They came to a wide boulevard fronting the ocean. Here the buildings were large and imposing. Giant palms and green lawns surrounded the structures. It was an area where wealthy Europeans lived while in Morocco. At last they drove into the courtyard of a white house with high turrets resembling a castle. This was their new home, the LeClaire House.

They went inside and up to the second floor. Paul told her, "I have some paperwork to do. I suggest you try to get a nap before Edmund and Diana

Walton arrive. They will expect drinks at seven and dinner around eight. Then they'll likely stay until late. So you'll need a rest."

"Thanks," she said with a smile and upturned her face for him to kiss her. He did and then left her to go into their bedroom alone while he went downstairs to his books.

Gale put her parasol aside and took off her straw hat and white dress. Then she put on a new dressing gown of pink that had been a wedding present. She went to one of the windows which opened on to a balcony overlooking the ocean. The view made her feel better at once.

She then stretched out on the bed and closed her eyes to rest. But she was not able to sleep. Too much had happened to her in the past few weeks. It had all been climaxed by their arrival in the strange land of Morocco and this white castle by the ocean.

She worried that she had foolishly allowed her nerves to get the best of her earlier and so had annoyed Paul. But the old beggar had been a menacing figure; even now she could vividly recall his ugly, wrinkled face and leprosy-ravaged hand. She had badly needed the help that Eric Simms had provided.

She liked the Britisher and she hoped Paul would get over his resentment of him. It worried her that her new husband had been like this almost from the moment of their marriage. He had seemed anxious to avoid talking to people or allowing her to do so. He had been especially closemouthed about his business in Morocco and seemed to think she should be satisfied with only vague explanations.

He had been very different when she first met him a year ago at a dance in the home of a wealthy girl friend from her boarding school days. The girl had pointed out the ruggedly handsome Paul to her and confided, "That is Paul Cormier! He's a favorite protégé of Carl Revene, the railway magnate. They say Revene is grooming him to succeed him one day."

"He's young but he has a stern look," Gale said, studying him as he waltzed with a laughing dark-haired girl on the crowded floor of the ballroom.

"He can have his pick of girls," her friend had said. "And he's with Harriet! She's such a heartless flirt! I'm going to introduce you to him after this dance and count on you to take him from her."

Gale had laughed. "Why involve me in your plots?"

"Because I think Paul Cormier might be right for you," was her friend's reply. "Anyway, we'll see!"

And so they did. As soon as the music ended, her friend took her to Paul and introduced them. They seemed to have an empathy for each other from that first moment.

Paul said, "You're the Page girl! Your family owns the department store at Thirtieth Street."

"My uncles run it," she said. "My parents are dead. I live with my Aunt Gertrude and Uncle Harry."

"Do you have the next dance free?"

She shook her head. "Sorry! All my dances are promised! My program is fully written in."

"Ignore it and dance with me," he challenged her.

"Do you think I should?" she worried.

"Yes," he said, as she might have expected. And as the music began he whirled her off for a lively polka. And he kept her for every dance for the balance of the evening. At the evening's end Gale found herself facing several irate young men and curious stares from a number of onlookers wondering what her audacious behavior with the good-looking Paul had meant.

He saw her home in his own carriage and before he kissed her good night at the door of the Fifth Avenue brownstone mansion in which she lived, he had her promise to meet him for tea at the Waldorf Hotel on Thirty-fourth Street the next afternoon. Gale went inside with his kiss still wet on her lips and her eyes bright with happiness. She had made a conquest!

But the next day at noon she had to face her aunt and uncle after lunch. The story of her unusual behavior at the dance had already reached her aunt through the mother of one of the other girls who had been there.

Aunt Gertrude, stout and good-natured, told her, "Your ignoring everyone else for that young man was the talk of the party last night!"

"I'm sorry, Aunt Gertrude," Gale said. "It was just that we were having so much fun!"

Aunt Gertrude considered this. "You know he's a newcomer to our set. He has been accepted only because he was introduced by Carl Revene. He seems to take a special interest in this young man."

She nodded excitedly. "It is true. Paul says that Mr. Revene is training him to take over their firm one day."

Uncle Harry, long-faced with gray hair and sidewhiskers, had been silent until this moment. Now, he said, "Some people might wonder what sort of firm it is."

Gale asked, "What do you mean, Uncle Harry?"

"There have been nasty rumors now and again about the source of Revene's fortune. He has interests all over the world. A mine in South America collapsed and a lot of people lost a great deal of money. The story is that Revene sponsored the venture but managed to get out of it without losing anything."

Aunt Gertrude told her husband, "I don't care a

whit for mines in South America, but I am concerned about Gale and her future!"

Gale had protested, "Don't make it seem so serious, Aunt Gertrude."

"I have a feeling, and I'm seldom wrong," her aunt warned her. "I fear you are much taken by this young man and you might even marry him."

"Aunt Gertrude!" she protested, but the truth was she had been considering that very thing all morning. If Paul asked her to marry him, what would her answer be?

Uncle Harry spoke up again, "He has no money of his own, be sure of that. It may take awhile working for Revene to make him rich. You, on the other hand, possess a considerable fortune."

"I don't see that as important," she said.

Uncle Harry gave her a meaningful look. "But he might."

"No!" she said, her cheeks flaming. "We just found ourselves liking each other!"

"That is all very well," Aunt Gertrude said. "Are you planning to see him again?"

She hesitated, then admitted, "Yes."

"So it could be serious," her aunt said.

"Not really," she argued. "I simply want to get to know him better and that probably is why he wants to see me—to learn what I'm really like."

"It could lead to more," her aunt warned.

"Not if I don't want it to," was Gale's answer.

"That is perfectly true," agreed Uncle Harry, tugging at one of his side-whiskers, a nervous habit of his. "And I think you would be wise to let this new friendship develop at a slow pace."

"I promise," she told them.

And she meant it. But she knew better now. She had learned that one doesn't work out the moves in a love affair as cautiously as one does in a game of chess. When she met Paul Cormier that afternoon she felt weak at the knees and filled with an excitement she could hardly contain.

The dining room at the hotel was set up for afternoon tea. A string trio played on a platform at the end of the room. It was an elegant and romantic setting. They gazed at each other across the table as if they were alone in the room. They paid little attention to the waiters or the food. They were lost in a timeless world of their own.

"I was afraid you wouldn't come," Paul said.

"I gave you my promise."

"So you did," he said. And then he asked her, "What do you think of me?"

"I like you," she said.

"I love you," was his reply.

"Paul," she rebuked him. "That is not a thing to joke about."

"It is no joke," he told her. "I'm dead serious. I hoped that you might feel the same about me."

"I may," she said in a near whisper.

"Will you marry me, Gale?"

"We hardly know each other!"

"We know we care, and what else is important?"

She stared at him in happy dismay. "Dozens of things!" And seeing the look of sadness which clouded his face at her statement, she added, "Nothing!"

He reached across the table and took her hands in his. "Then it's settled. I'll get you the finest engagement ring and I'll go to your uncle to ask for your hand."

She smiled ruefully. "He won't be easy to approach."

"I'll brave him," he said. "I'll brave anything to win you!"

That had been the beginning. Aunt Gertrude and Uncle Harry had been reluctant to give the marriage their blessing. But Paul had been persistent. Carl Revene had even gone to her uncle's office, in an unheard-of move for the renowned magnate, and pleaded Paul's case. He'd told her uncle, "That young man has great promise."

So despite Paul's obscure origins and his lack of money, her aunt and uncle finally agreed to the match. The months of the engagement had passed like a glorious dream. The wedding was held in a fashionable Fifth Avenue church and then she and Paul had taken a steamship to Morocco for the combined honeymoon and business trip which had brought her to this elegant chateau.

Paul had proven himself a considerate and loving husband, but the one thing that had bothered her was the mystery with which he surrounded himself and his work. She felt he was extremely loyal to Carl Revene and if the millionaire's deals veered toward the shady, her husband would still support his employer.

The world-renowned Revene was to meet them shortly in Casablanca and take them for a trip on his enormous yacht. It seemed that everything about the financier was on a lavish scale. They were halfway across the Atlantic when she found out that Revene's firm, International Ventures, actually owned the ship on which they were traveling. He also owned fine houses in New York, London, and a string of other cities around the world. No wonder there was so much gossip and speculation about his doings.

She rested until a little after six and then quickly got up and washed and changed into a yellow gown that suited her reddish gold hair. She selected a string of fine pearls as her jewelry for the evening. They had been her mother's.

This was her first attempt at entertaining and she wished it to be a success. She had met the Waltons only fleetingly when they had come to the dock to greet them as they stepped off the boat. She had not paid too much attention to the couple except to note that Edmund Walton was at least twenty years older than his wife, that he had an aristocratic air, and that he walked with a limp so bad that he needed a cane. His wife, Diana, was attractive, golden-haired, and witty. They also lived in Casablanca in a large house supplied by the company.

When she went downstairs she found the Waltons already there. Diana, in a white gown with a low-cut bosom that was extremely revealing of her lithe body, apologized, saying, "You must forgive us! We have so looked forward to this evening, we dressed early! Then it seemed silly not to come on and join you early."

"I'm glad you're here," Gale said pleasantly, hiding her apprehensions about not being able to have consultations with the cook and maids, who were new to her.

"Edmund and Paul are having a drink on the balcony," Diana said. "We may as well join them."

"Very well," she said. "You go on. Excuse me for a moment while I check with the cook about dinner." And she left the golden-haired Diana, to make her way to the kitchen.

The cook was a little man who spoke Spanish better than English but she managed to make her wishes known to him. And he in turn was able to translate her wishes to the two maids who would be doing the serving. Having satisfied herself that all would be well, she went to the balcony and joined the others.

Paul was standing by the balcony wall with a drink in his hand. He said, "I wondered where you were."

"Checking on dinner," she said with a smile. "Are you all making out well?"

"Fabulously," Edmund Walton said, rising from the wicker chair in which he'd been sitting. "Do sit down over there with Diana."

"Thank you," she said, and joined the attractive Diana on a matching wicker divan.

Paul said, "I'll fetch you a drink. The usual?"

She nodded. "Gin with plenty of tonic."

Edmund Walton sat down again, his drink in his hand. His hollow-cheeked, ascetic face was graced by craggy gray eyebrows over keen blue eyes and he had a head of unruly gray hair. He said, "How do you like it here?"

"I'm stunned," she said. "I never expected such an elegant house."

"Mr. Revene does things in style," Walton said, with a thin smile.

"Our own house is lovely but not as fine as this," Diana told her.

Paul came back with Gale's drink and told her, "By the way, Peter Hall is back in the city. I invited him to drop by later."

"Oh?" she said. Peter Hall was another agent of the great company. She had been introduced to him back in New York. He was a short man and very fat with a great stomach and an oval face with a pouting lower lip. His bald head made him look like a fat, sullen baby.

Edmund Walton gave her a sly glance. "You don't like Peter?"

"I hardly know him," she said.

Walton replied, "He's ugly and overweight, but he's clever when it comes to closing a deal. He's respected in the company. When you know him better perhaps you'll feel differently about him."

She protested, "I have no set opinions of him."

"I have," Diana said, frowning. "He doesn't know how to treat a lady. Can't keep his roving hands to himself."

"You must have encouraged him, my darling," Edmund Walton teased her.

"I did not," Diana said angrily. "He's a horrible little fat man. I hate him!"

"My dear!" her husband rebuked her most gently.

"Peter has his place among us," Paul said, draining his drink. He went out to make another.

Edmund Walton gazed out at the ocean and said to her, "Has Paul told you the history of this house?"

"No."

Diana brightened. "You must hear the story. It's terribly exciting."

Walton was looking at her directly now. "It was built by an engineer, who was also very rich. His name was Henri LeClaire. He'd barely had the place erected when he was killed."

"Wasn't that sad?" Diana commented.

"Yes, very," she agreed.

"That's not the end of it," Edmund Walton said with a grim smile. "His grieving widow became strange from living here alone and in a few weeks killed herself by taking poison."

"Shocking!" Gale said.

"And it's such a lovely place," the golden-haired girl at her side said.

"Their deaths gave the chateau a bad name," Walton went on. "It was empty for a long while. No one locally cared to live here. Then Revene came along and bought it for half its value."

Gale said, "He seems to have a knack for taking advantage of situations."

"He is a genius," Walton said. "So we all work for him. We can't all have minds like his."

"I wouldn't want you to!" Diana burst out.

Her husband raised his shaggy eyebrows. "Meaning what?"

She hesitated, and her pretty face crimsoned, "I don't know," she said, flustered.

Her husband laughed softly and told Gale, "Diana means she would rather have a husband with ordinary qualities. Less demanding."

"She is probably right," Gale agreed. But she had the uneasy feeling that was not what Diana had meant at all.

Paul came back to join them; sitting on the balcony rail, he asked, "What is the discussion?"

"Edmund has been telling Gale about the sad history of the people who built this house," Diana said.

"Indeed?" Paul's face was unsmiling.

"We didn't tell her about the ghosts," Diana protested, and then looked ashamed. "I'm sorry! I didn't mean to say it."

Edmund Walton rose and glared at her. "You blundered very well," he said sharply. And to Paul he apologized, "I'm sorry I didn't mean to bring up anything unpleasant."

Paul shrugged. "It doesn't matter. She was bound to hear the story from someone."

"What story?" Gale asked, aware of the tension in the other three.

Paul gave her a stony glance. "About what you'd

expect," he said. "Because of the deaths of the owners the locals at once decided the place is haunted."

"I see," she said in a small voice.

"Of course it's nonsense," her husband went on sharply. "No sensible person would believe the story."

Diana was looking uneasy as she said, "But there have been people who claim they've seen the ghost. The cook for one. Mr. Revene offered the house to Edmund and me, and that is why we refused it."

The tension grew rather than diminished. Paul glanced at Edmund Walton and said, "You didn't tell me that!"

"I hardly thought it important," Walton said.

"Yet you didn't choose to live here," Paul said accusingly.

Walton lamely explained, "That was not because of the supposed ghosts. I don't believe in such things. Especially not when the only one known to have seen the phantoms is a weak-minded Spanish cook."

"But you found another house?" Paul insisted.

"Because it suited us better," was Edmund Walton's somewhat weak explanation. "Diana didn't want to be so close to the ocean."

"The wash of the waves depresses me," the girl said, too quickly.

"We chose a quieter spot away from the water," her husband said. "And that left this place open for you two."

Paul turned to Gale and said, "I'm sorry you had to hear this silly legend. I hope it doesn't worry you."

"Not at all," she said. "I agree with Edmund. I think too much is made of ghostly visitations."

"Well, I'm glad that's settled," Paul said in his stern fashion. "And I suggest we soon go in to our dinner."

The meal went better than Gale had hoped. But

25

all the time her spirits were somewhat depressed at hearing the tragic history of the old house. She wished that Paul had made up his own mind to tell her.

She rose, saying, "We'll have our coffee in the living room."

They were in the midst of their coffee when the fat Peter Hall arrived. Gale thought he looked more grotesque in his linen suit than when she'd seen him in New York. For one thing the linen was somewhat soiled and rumpled and it seemed that, incredibly, he had put on more weight.

The fat man held her hand a little too long as he greeted her and with a roguish light in his porcine eyes said, "I have looked forward to our being better friends."

She tried not to show her revulsion. "We ought to have a good chance here."

This seemed to highly delight him. He repeated it for the others and laughed heartily, his huge stomach quivering. At the same time he sank into the nearest easy chair and demanded that Paul fetch him a whiskey.

"Better for me than coffee," he told everyone. "I've been in the desert for weeks. I've a lot of drinking to catch up on."

Paul quickly obeyed him as if he were his servant. It was more than being the courteous host. He almost seemed afraid of the fat man.

To carry the conversation at what seemed an awkward moment, Gale said, "I'm not too sure about the Moslem faith. But I have an idea they are against hard liquor."

"Dead against it," the fat man said. "And when you're dealing with those fellows you go along with them."

Edmund and Diana were standing together at the other side of the softly lighted room, looking ill at ease. The thin-faced Edmund said, "May I briefly give you the tenets of the Islamic faith?"

"Yes, I'd like to know," Gale told him.

Walton looked pleased and said, "The Five Pillars of Islam are prayer, keeping the fast of Ramadan, almsgiving, the pilgrimage to Mecca, and the profession of faith. The act of embracing Islam is performed only once. The vow is binding for life. Prayer is required five times a day, at dawn, noon, midafternoon, dusk, and after it has become dark. Only the most pious adhere to the full schedule. The hardest requirement is the pilgrimage to Mecca and only the wealthy make it, as it is so far away."

Paul brought Peter Hall his drink and the fat man gulped it down. He then said, "The hardest requirement for any of us is to please Revene!" And he laughed heartily at his own joke.

The Waltons clearly did not enjoy his company, particularly since he continued drinking. They excused themselves as having to rise early and Paul went to see the two out.

Another drink in hand, Hall gazed after them with distaste and told her, "They don't like me any better than I like them!"

She said, "They seem a devoted married couple."

The fat man looked at her and then his head went back and he gave another hoarse burst of laughter. "Married couple! That's all for appearances! They're no more married than you and I!"

This came as a shock to her. "I don't understand!"

He winked at her knowingly. "Plenty of things to learn, my dear! And old Peter is the one to teach you!"

27

Paul came into the room at that point and gave the fat man a scathing look. He turned to Gale and said, "I think you should go to bed now. I'll join you in a few moments. I have a few things to say to Peter in private."

She said, "Very well." She wished Hall good night and he offered her a somewhat subdued good night in return. Then she left the room. She had no idea what her husband wanted to say to Peter Hall but she had an idea he wanted to reprimand him for something.

She was still shocked by the revelation about the Waltons. She mounted the dark stairs and started along the hall to their bedroom. Suddenly out of the shadows a menacing figure took shape. She halted and her eyes widened with terror as she recognized the beggar who had approached her in the street that afternoon. There was a smile on his wizened face as he stretched out his leprous hand to touch her. She screamed and fainted!

2

Gale opened her eyes to find herself on the bed in their softly candlelit bedroom. Paul was bending over her with a troubled look on his handsome, square-jawed face. He said, "Are you all right?"

She reached for him desperately. "That awful man! The beggar! He came after me in the hallway!"

Her husband took her gently by the shoulders and pressed her back on to the pillow, then sat on the edge of the bed and took one of her hands in his. "Be still a moment and let me explain," he said. "The man you met in the dark was simply an elderly native who acts as a messenger for a business associate of mine."

"Why was he lurking in the dark hall?"

"Because he did not wish to intrude on us below. He is used to wandering about the house at will. He was putting in time waiting for me to send Peter Hall home. In the meanwhile you happened to encounter him and have a case of hysterics!"

She began to feel faintly ashamed though she still could not quite believe this explanation offered by her husband. She said, "The hand reached out for me! It was the same mutilated, leprous stump! And the man's face was the same, wrinkled and black!"

"Wrinkled and black," Paul agreed, "but he was not the same man!"

She hesitated, staring up at him, "I don't know what to think."

"Just try to forget all about it."

"You heard me scream?"

"Yes," he said somewhat derisively. "I came running to help you. The messenger, Jiri, is greatly embarrassed. He fled to the courtyard at once."

"And Peter Hall?"

"He is just about to leave," Paul said. "Now if you will relax I'll go down and send Hall on his way and then talk to Jiri about the business which brought him here."

She closed her eyes and gave a tiny groan. "I'm afraid, Paul. I can't seem to adapt to any of it. This place or the people! Peter Hall told me the Waltons aren't married! Everything seems a sham!"

"I'll speak to him for telling you that!" her husband said sharply.

Gale looked up at him. "It's true, isn't it?"

"It's not any of our business!" Paul snapped.

"Don't quarrel with Peter Hall," she pleaded with him. "I've caused enough trouble for one evening. Go down and see the messenger. I'll be all right."

"You're certain?"

"Yes."

"Remain here in our room," her husband told her. "I'll be back to join you as soon as I can." He leaned down and kissed her tenderly on the lips and offered her one of his rare sympathetic smiles. "It has been too demanding a night for you."

He left the bedroom and she lay there filled with troubled thoughts. For the first time she realized she was a long way from the warm protection of her aunt and uncle. Now she was a new bride in a strange, primitive land with a husband who had not too much patience for her plight.

She could not doubt that Paul loved her. But she began to wonder if that love was as strong as his love for International Ventures, if perhaps he was dominated by a grim desire to follow in the footsteps of the legendary financier who employed him. These people whom she had met were all part of the Revene world network of agents. And she could not say that she felt easy with them. She recognized the same mysterious air of secrecy in them which troubled her in her husband. It left her feeling like an outsider.

She had never met Carl Revene though she expected she would soon do so. She hoped the meeting with him might clear up some of the secrecy. Many of the whispered rumors about Carl Revene and his operations were far from flattering, but she refused to accept that Paul was mixed up in anything of a shady nature.

She was still mulling over these things when Paul returned and they went to bed. As if in an effort to make her forget the disturbing evening and also to possess her more completely, he made ardent love to her before they slept. She surrendered to his almost frantic lovemaking. The burst of passion over, they lay close together, ready for deep, exhausted slumber.

After breakfast the next morning he took her out on the sun-drenched balcony overlooking the beach and the blue ocean beyond. Some tiny lizards frightened her; he sent them scurrying and told her, "Try to rest and enjoy yourself for an hour or two. I have some business calls to make."

"I'll manage nicely," she said. "I want to talk to the cook and get to know him better. And I also want to find some way of communicating with the maids."

Paul smiled. "I'm sure you'll manage. Most of

them know some English even if they don't speak it."

She asked, "When will Mr. Revene arrive?"

"His ship ought to be here in a few days. He's coming in from London," Paul said. "The yacht is already here. We'll be boarding it after he gets here and sailing into the Mediterranean."

She smiled. "I look forward to it. By the way, how did you make out with your messenger last night?"

"Jiri?"

"Yes."

"He was wildly apologetic for scaring you. Quite beside himself. His message wasn't all that important and he left shortly after I went downstairs."

She sighed. "I think Edmund Walton's stories about this house, of the owners being killed, and their ghosts haunting it, upset my nerves."

"It was stupid of him to bring it up."

"I'm over the effect of it now," she said. "But he didn't tell me how the original owner, LeClaire, was killed?"

"He was horseback riding and his horse threw him and broke his neck. Nothing mysterious or sinister about it."

"His wife's suicide was more tragic," she said.

"I suppose so," Paul said with some impatience. "I really must be going." He kissed her and left.

She went to the kitchen and spent some time in a rather one-sided conversation with Pedro, the cook. But he was friendly and anxious to be cooperative. In turn he gave her a few phrases to communicate basic orders to the maids and lined the three young Spanish girls up so she might practice the words on them. Gale felt she had made some headway for a first effort.

Pedro had explained that it was almost impossible to hire young local women as domestic help for Europeans. The veiled and heavily wrapped young females were much protected. By religion and custom they would be disgraced if they entered such work.

She was in the living room explaining to one of the maids how she wished things dusted when her caller came. The bell at the door of the chateau tinkled. One of the maids answered the door and ushered in a man of about Paul's build and with a hint of his features. But this man wore a large mustache and his hair was thinning and gray. His linen suit was wrinkled and not too clean and the Panama he held in his hand was battered. He stood before her with a sly smile.

"You must be Gale," was his startling opening remark in a hoarse, whiskey voice.

Stunned, she said, "Yes. Who are you?"

"You can call me Ben!"

She frowned. "But who are you?"

The mustached man gave her a sly look. "I see Paul didn't prepare you for me!"

"I'm afraid not," she said tautly, beginning to wonder if she were dealing with a madman.

"I'm your brother-in-law, Ben Cormier," the derelict said, grinning.

She gasped. "You're Paul's brother?"

"As good as," the man in the soiled linen suit said. "I'm his half brother. We both had the same father. I'm more than twenty years older, of course."

Still astounded, she said, "He has never mentioned you!"

"Doesn't surprise me," Ben Cormier said, twirling his Panama in his hands as he glanced around the room. "Paul isn't all that proud of me. Nice place you have here."

She asked him, "Do you live in Morocco?"

33

"I've been in Casablanca for nearly five years," he told her.

"Then Paul knows you're here?"

The mustached Ben chuckled. "It's the last place he sent me money, so he should know. I have financial problems from time to time!"

"I see," she said. "I'm sorry Paul is out. You've just missed him."

"That doesn't matter," the gray-haired Ben said. "You can give me a drink. Whiskey straight, if you don't mind."

Flustered, she said, "Of course!" And she went to the sideboard to pour him his drink.

When she turned to take him the drink she saw that his eyes were appraising her in a way that made her feel embarrassed. He took the well-filled whiskey glass and downed half of it at a gulp.

He smacked his lips and with a leering smile said, "I must say I approve of Paul's choice of a wife. And I've always been a connoisseur of women!"

Blushing, she said, "Are you also employed by International Ventures?"

Ben laughed. "Me? Not likely! They don't want the likes of me! Wouldn't be a suitable front for them. I'm on my own. I'm an artist. Or at least I call myself that."

"Interesting," she said. "What do you paint?"

"People, scenic views, anything that offers me some cash. I paint in oil. You must come to my studio and see some of what I do."

"I'd like to," she said. Gesturing to a chair, she added, "Do sit down."

"Thanks," he said, sinking into the most comfortable chair in the room and handing her his empty glass. "You could fill that up again."

"Surely," she said. And she went to the sideboard to pour him another nearly full glass of straight whiskey.

He accepted it from her as if it were his due. He said, "I'm surprised Paul brought you here. This country is like a bomb. Ready to explode at any moment."

"Explode?" she echoed him.

"Yes. Revolution is what I mean," Ben said. "The Sultan is a monstrous crook and tyrant. His own people are tired of him and ready to rebel!"

She sat in a chair across from him in the big room. "I had no idea."

"Nasty situation! Two or three insurgent groups ready to try to take over! The streets here could run with blood any day." He took a big gulp of the drink.

She stared at the gray-mustached artist. "If you think it dangerous, why do you stay here?"

"Fair question," he said. "It happens I like danger. I think it might be interesting. And begging your pardon, I have an Arab girl living with me. I couldn't get her to leave Casablanca with me. And I don't want to lose her."

"I see," she said quietly. At least he could be admired for his utter frankness. He had not pretended, as had Edmund Walton. She said, "Do you know Edmund Walton and his wife, or Peter Hall?"

"They're part of the Revene crowd, aren't they?"

"Yes."

He waved them aside. "I don't want to know them. Carl Revene has dirty hands; I wouldn't want to shake one of them."

Gale showed surprise. "But he is famous and very wealthy. Paul seems anxious to follow in his footsteps."

Ben eyed her with sardonic amusement. "That is

Paul, not me! I like to pick the people I work for and admire."

She stared at him with some concern. She said, "You do not admire Carl Revene."

"I admire neither him nor his company," Ben said, draining his glass again. He stared at the empty glass glumly but did not ask her to refill it. Instead, he told her, "You'll find out in time. You'll know what I'm talking about."

"Paul is hard-working," she protested. "He's most dedicated."

Ben put his glass down and got to his feet. "I know he's dedicated, but I wonder if what he's dedicated to is all that worthwhile."

"I certainly hope so," she said.

"So do I," he said carelessly. He went to the balcony and stared out at the ocean again. "Yes, I like this place."

"You must come again sometime," she said. "And bring your lady friend."

He came back into the room and shook his head. "Paul would not approve of that."

"I wouldn't mind, and I'm sure I can persuade him to accept the idea."

"Thanks," he said. "Maybe in a month or two."

She gasped. "A month or two?" Then recovering from her surprise, she added, "I don't expect we'll be here that long."

The artist winked at her knowingly. "You never can be sure," he said. "Now I'll tell you something better. You tell your fine new hubby to come visit me and bring you with him!"

"Bring me?" she said.

"That's right," the gray-haired man said, seeming at last to be thoroughly enjoying himself. "You just greet him with the news I've been here and he'll not know what to do!" He laughed.

"I'll surely tell him."

"You do that," Paul's brother said in taunting fashion. "And you tell him I want you two to come to my place for tea this afternoon. Say I've promised to show you some of my art."

She was on her feet, following him to the door. Puzzled by his manner, she said, "I'll tell him, though I'm sure you realize he may have something else to do. We've only just gotten here."

The man in the soiled linen suit put on his Panama. His dark brown eyes were fixed on her in mocking fashion. He said, "I think he'll find the time. After all, I'm his only brother. He hasn't seen me for a long while."

"Where do you live?"

"In the medina, the old city," Ben said. "It's not all that bad. Lots of chaps like me have studios there."

"Does Paul know the address?"

"He ought to," Ben said. "But if he's in doubt, tell him it's Eel Alley. It's short and narrow, Eel Alley is; you'll be able to find me." He stepped outside.

She stood in the doorway to ask him, "What time?"

"Teatime is usually four to five," Ben said with a grin. "I'll be serving whiskey. But that time will do as well as any."

Feeling she was being mocked, she said, "I'll tell him but I make no promises."

Standing on the steps in the bright sun, he said, "Tell him I'm on good terms with Abdul-el-Krem. That might do it." And with a nod he left.

She went back inside and shut the door, baffled by the strange caller. She was more surprised to know that Paul had a brother of whom he had said nothing.

He must have known that Ben was likely to still be in Casablanca, and yet he'd said not a word.

Her husband returned about an hour later and when she told him that his brother had called, he looked at her incredulously. "What did you say?"

"Your half brother, Ben Cormier, was here to see you," she repeated.

For a moment it seemed that Paul was ready to tell her he had no half brother. Then his face crimsoned with rage and he said angrily, "So he's still on the beach here!"

"On the beach?"

"It means he's stranded here," her husband said. "He's one of the sort I warned you about. A no-good who has landed here along with the other scum from all over the world."

"He seemed anxious to see you," she said.

"No doubt!" Paul told her with sarcasm. "He wants more money!"

She wanted to reprimand him for not telling her of Ben's existence but she saw that he was already in a rage and knew it was not the time. So instead she said, "He's invited us to his studio in the old city. He suggested you bring me today for tea."

"Not likely!" Paul scoffed with an ugly smile.

"I think you should see him," she ventured. "He asked me to tell you that he's on excellent terms with Abdul-el-Krem."

Her husband's mouth dropped open and his mood changed from one of scorn to something close to dismay. In a taut voice, he said, "He told you that?"

"Yes. Who is this Abdul-el-Krem?"

"No one important," Paul said quickly. "Did he say where his studio was?"

"An Eel Alley in the medina," she said.

"I see," her husband said grimly. "I suppose I must show some sort of brotherly interest in him. Be ready by midafternoon and I'll have the carriage take us to the old city gates."

She stared at him. "Then you've changed your mind? You are going to visit him."

"Yes."

"I see," she said. It didn't seem wise to go into this any further. Surely the name of the Arab had been what changed his mind. She would have to contain her curiosity and find out later who this Abdul-el-Krem was and why the mention of his name had made so much difference to Paul.

The rest of the day went by without event. She rested early in the afternoon and then put on a fresh outfit to be driven to see Ben's studio. Since the sun was still strong, she wore her straw hat and brought along her parasol for protection in the open carriage.

Paul was in his usual white suit and sun helmet. He looked austere and handsome as he sat beside her in the carriage. She found the modern area of Casablanca quite like that of a Western city with the exception that many of the buildings were a snowy white and there were a lot of palm trees. But as they reached the gates to the old city it all changed.

Her husband bade the carriage driver, an old, bearded man in white turban and robe, wait for their return. Then he led her along the cobblestoned streets into the medina. Many eyes turned to stare at her, since a female without a veil was not all that common in the old city.

Paul inquired from a seated ancient smoking a pipe as to the location of Eel Alley. Paul used fluent French for the exchange, another talent of which she had been unaware. She was slowly finding out many things about her new husband.

They walked through the twisting alleys of the medina; she felt slightly dizzy from the heat and trying to look in every direction at once. There were more sights, sounds, and smells than she could absorb. Water peddlers carried goatskins full of water slung over their backs. Men drank tea in dingy cafes and played checkers in the street. Children sat by a Moslem school, reciting in unison a lesson from the Koran. Metalworkers transformed empty tin cans into funnels, pipes, and lanterns. Workmen pounded stones into the mud to repair the streets. Smells of broiling food and rotting garbage blended in pungent aroma.

Paul walked swiftly and did not look at her as he stared straight ahead. She gasped, "I have to watch my dress and heels. I cannot keep up your pace!"

He came out of the trance of his own thoughts a moment to glance at her apologetically and say, "Sorry! I'm used to moving along fast! And this is not all that pleasant a walk!"

"I find it fascinating," she said. And it was. Hawkers bellowed their wares and haggled with customers in animated, guttural Arabic. The shops, niches in the walls, were so tiny that the owners could sit in the center of them and reach any object without getting up. All kinds of food was being sold, as well as rags, clothes, empty bottles, tin cans, rope, rusty scrap iron, firewood, and baskets.

They turned sharply into a still narrower street which was hardly as wide as an alley. And then just ahead of them Ben appeared from one of the arched doorways. He was wearing no hat or coat and his shirt was open at the neck. On seeing them, his face lit up.

"So you still do care about me, brother," he said with a smile.

Paul's expression was cold. "What a filthy hole you're living in!"

Ben showed no annoyance. "It's not as bad as you think," he assured his brother. "Come in and you may be pleasantly surprised. Aya has tidied up for this visit."

He led them inside, and as they entered the fairly large room with a mesh-curtained doorway at its rear, they were just in time to see a shapely, dark girl with a transparent veil across her face step quickly through the mesh curtain and vanish.

Ben watched after her and laughed indulgently. "Aya is bashful with strangers."

Light came into the stone-walled room from a skylight above and now Gale was looking around at the many oil paintings stacked along the walls. They were all unframed, done in bright oil colors, and showed a pleasing reflection of the people and general area of the Moroccan city.

She went over to a study of a mosque and held it up. Turning to Ben, she exclaimed, "You're very good!"

The gray-haired man smiled. "I'm modestly talented, which is almost worse than having no talent at all."

Gale protested. "I think you are undervaluing yourself."

Ben turned to Paul and asked, "Do you think that, brother? You heard her!"

"I know your talents better than she does," Paul said sharply. "You were supposed to move on to Marseille if I recall your last letter."

"Yes, I was," Ben agreed. "But things became more interesting here. You must agree or you wouldn't be here."

Paul eyed him angrily. "My business here has nothing to do with you."

"Well, you never know," Ben said in his mocking fashion. "And then there is Aya. She could get on very well without me. She is young and a favorite with many men. But I have reached an age when I can most enjoy one particular female. And Aya is the company I crave."

"We can do without an account of your erotic life," Paul said nastily.

"You might have at least said love life in deference to your wife's feelings. I'm sorry I bored you with the details. But you asked for an explanation of why I'm still here."

"What about Abdul-el-Krem?" Paul asked.

Ben hesitated and then smiled at him. "We'll get to that later," he said. "For the moment I'll invite you and your good wife to sit on these rugs in this corner. I'll bring you some refreshments, which Aya has gone to a good deal of trouble to prepare."

With that he also vanished through the mesh. Gale turned from a study of the paintings to say to her husband, "I think you're being needlessly rude to him."

Paul's face was livid. "You know nothing about it."

She sat on the rug as Ben had requested and glanced up at her husband's handsome face and saw an angry, tortured look. She said, "It seems to me it would be best for you to make peace with Ben. At least while you're in Casablanca."

Paul sat on the rug next to her and in a low voice said, "I had no idea he was going to be here."

Ben came back with a large tray on which were sweet cakes, a pot of tea with cups and saucers and a bottle of whiskey and glasses. He set the tray down before them and then squatted down on the rug.

"You see we are not without hospitality, Aya and I," he said in the same taunting way. And turning to Gale, he said, "I'm sure you'll want tea, and you must try the cakes."

"Thank you," she said.

"Aya made them. She's an excellent cook," Ben went on as he poured the tea and passed the cup and saucer to her. Then he put the pot down and lifted the whiskey bottle to offer drinks for himself and Paul, adding, "I know your choice will be the whiskey."

Paul said nothing but accepted the glass and drank from it. Then he asked Ben, "When did you meet Abdul-el-Krem?"

Ben looked cunning. "That interests you?"

"It does," he said grimly.

"I was introduced to him at the American Consul's house," Ben said. "I'm not a social regular there but I have sold the consul's wife some paintings. I happened to be there when Abdul-el-Krem was seeing the consul. He noticed my paintings and admired them."

Gale spoke up, "So I'm not alone in thinking you are good."

"You are kind, dear sister-in-law," Ben said. "I told Abdul-el-Krem that I had a brother with International Ventures and that interested him a lot."

Paul said, "How dare you trade on my name!"

"I was not trading on you," Ben said. "I merely mentioned it. He asked me your name later, and I gave it to him."

"And?" Paul said tautly.

"He was very cordial," Ben said, clearly enjoying leading the impatient Paul along. "He told me he'd be happy to welcome me as his guest anytime I happened to pass by his desert mansion."

Gale interposed, "Who is this fellow?"

Before Paul could stop him from telling her, Ben winked at her. "Very important man in Morocco, my dear Gale. Leader of one of the insurgent groups of whom I spoke. A strong political leader who opposes the Sultan's government."

Paul said tersely, "My wife is not interested in local politics. There is no need to fill her in with a lot of useless talk."

"I don't think it useless," she told him. And she added for Ben's sake, "Your Aya's cakes are most tasty."

"I shall pass on your compliment if she has not already heard it," Ben said, looking pleased. "These Arab girls have no shame about eavesdropping."

Paul addressed Ben, "Did you accept Abdul's invitation to visit him?"

Ben spread his hands. "What would a poor man like me be doing as guest of an Arab prince? I leave that for the likes of you, Paul. And for the mighty Carl Revene. No doubt he will be visiting in the desert when he arrives."

Paul said, "I have no idea of what Mr. Revene's itinerary will be." He turned to Gale and continued, "I think it is time for us to leave."

"But we only just arrived!" she said, reluctant to leave so soon.

"I have other appointments," Paul said sullenly.

Ben revealed no annoyance. He said, "Do not worry, Gale. I understand. My brother is a busy man. But before you leave I ask one thing. That you select a painting which you would like to own. I shall have it framed and bring it to you in a few days."

She was delighted. "You're too kind!"

"Just pick one out," Ben said, helping her to her feet.

Paul got up and warned her, "We haven't much time. Couldn't you do it another day?"

Ben told him, "When will I be able to persuade you to visit me again, brother? She'd best do it now."

Gale went over to go through a dozen or so of the stacked canvases. As she busied herself studying the various paintings, she was aware of her husband and his brother talking in low tones in the background. She could not hear what they were saying but it did not seem to be too friendly an exchange.

Finally she selected a painting of a street scene in the old quarter with a beggar boy in the foreground. She took it over to Ben and said, "This seems the most unusual."

"You shall have it," he promised, and taking it from her, he put it to one side against the wall.

Paul took her by the arm and said, "You must stay close by me as we walk back to the gate. This is an unlawful section of the city."

"It is as safe as the native district of any large city in Africa," Ben argued as he saw them to the door. "I look forward to seeing you again, Gale."

"Thank you for the painting," she said.

"My great pleasure," he told her and bowed as they left.

He was still standing in the doorway as they walked up the narrow dark alley once again. Paul was holding her firmly by the arm as they moved along.

She said, "You weren't very nice to him and he tried to be friendly toward us."

"You do not know my half brother!"

"What does that mean?"

"It means I do not care to have him at our house. He is not to be trusted," Paul said hotly.

"I don't understand," she told him.

"There is no need for you to. You must take my word for it. He is an undesirable person."

"He seems down on his luck," she admitted. "But that is the worst I think you could say about him!"

"You don't know!"

"I'll admit that," she said. "Because you choose to keep me in the dark. Why?"

Paul turned a corner into another alley, and it struck her that he was more tense than before. That he almost seemed afraid. He glanced at her and said, "There are things I can't discuss."

Just then an old white-bearded man with a fancy silver urn came out and held it up before them. He stood in their way and chanted what was likely the price of the item, over and over again.

"No!" Paul said roughly and shoved the elderly man aside so violently that he fell back against the wall of his tiny shop.

"You needn't have been so rough to him!" she protested, slowing down.

"I've no time to argue about that," her husband said, taking her by the arm and leading her along as quickly as he could.

They'd gone no more than a dozen feet when they confronted a brown man naked to the waist, cross-legged before a circular basket in which a good-sized cobra reared up. The brown man played a mournful native melody on a tin flute and the snake swayed before him and undulated as if it were dancing in time to the music!

She gasped at the unusual sight, and Paul reacted in his usual impatient fashion. But before he could drag her along, the brown man threw aside his flute, lifted up the basket with the snake in it and hurled it straight at her!

Paul let her arm go as she staggered back screaming! The basket and snake struck her and she could feel the smooth scales of the swirling snake as it hit her hands. At the instant of impact she fell back and, losing her balance, scrambled on her knees to put some distance between herself and the snake.

Only then, as the cobra slithered off over the cobblestones, did she realize what was going on. Paul and the snake charmer were locked in a struggle, and the snake charmer had a long, wicked-looking knife in his right hand. Only by using every ounce of his strength and wrestling skill was Paul keeping that gleaming blade from finding a target in him.

Gale screamed and struggled to her feet. As she started toward them, Paul pulled a small revolver from an inner pocket and fired it. The bullet caught the native in the shoulder. He cried out as blood spurted from the wound and with the knife still in his hand wrenched himself away from Paul and ran across the alley and down an opening between two hovels.

Paul fired after him and then followed him. Gale cried out to him to halt as he squeezed through the dark space in pursuit of the attacker. But he paid no attention to her. She was now surrounded by a rabble of the slum dwellers, including some women in veils and long robes. There was hatred on the faces of the men, and one of them spat at her!

She backed against the wall of the nearest building and leaned there, trembling with fear. Suddenly there appeared a man in a dark robe and a red fez. It took her a moment to realize it was the same man Paul had talked with the day before.

In perfect English the man said, "Come with me!"

"No!" She drew back, afraid to move.

"You must!" he said urgently. The crowd around her was increasing and growing more hostile. "You must trust me!"

She pointed to the narrow dark place where her husband had vanished. "My husband, in there!"

"I know," the man in the fez said.

He gave her no chance for further argument but seized her and pushed her along ahead of him. And to her horror she found herself being thrust into the same dark space where the would-be murderer and Paul had gone. The man in the fez was behind her, forcing her on and uttering words of assurance which she could neither listen to nor understand.

The darkness and pitch of the stone walls gave way to open space and light. They were now in another alleylike street. The man in the fez hesitated and looked up and down the street, as if attempting to make a decision.

At last he said, "This way!"

She let him guide her on. She had lost a heel and was staggering drunkenly. Her dress was torn and her hat had disappeared in the moment of collision with the snake and basket.

Two men in robes came running down the steep alley toward them, and the man in the fez cried out in exasperation. He wheeled her around and ordered, "This way!" They abruptly began to race in the opposite direction with the two menacing strangers not far behind them.

Suddenly in the midst of this flight the man in the fez halted and whirled around to face their pursuers. She saw a small pistol in his hand and he fired twice directly at them. One of the men fell instantly and the other bent to kneel by him.

"Keep on!" The brown man said breathlessly and guided her along at a fast pace again.

"Where?" she asked.

"Ahead," he said, and then he belied his words by swinging her into still another alley which went off to the right from the one in which they'd been fleeing.

This was again very steep and the sudden appearance of a goat in front of them nearly toppled them. The man in the fez shoved it aside, almost throwing it to the cobblestones. They raced on while an old man, the owner of the goat, shrilled angry imprecations after them!

Then ahead at the crest of the alley she saw a familiar figure. It was Peter Hall. He was standing outlined against the sky and she could see that he also had a gun and it was pointed straight at them.

"Look!" she cried to her companion.

"We must go on!" the man in the red fez told her.

"He'll shoot us!"

"No!" her companion panted, forcing her forward.

He was right. As they neared the fat man he lowered the gun he was holding and stared at them in consternation. He said, "Where did you two come from?"

"I found her back there," the brown man panted. "What about Mr. Cormier?"

"There in the doorway." Hall indicated a pale, motionless figure slumped against the doorjamb. "If he isn't dead, it's not his fault!"

49

3

"Paul!" she cried, kneeling by him.

His square-jawed face took on an expression of concentrated determination as he roused himself up a little and said, "No need to panic!"

"Are you badly hurt?"

"Stab wound in my arm," he said, indicating his upper left arm where the blood was seeping through his linen coat sleeve.

"You could have been killed!" she said in despair.

"He very nearly was," Peter Hall said, coming to join them. "I'll put an emergency bandage on that arm and then get him back to his carriage as quickly as possible."

She turned to the fat man with a frightened look on her lovely face. "What about the police?"

The petulant face showed a derisive smile. "We're not in New York, young woman! The police here would not be interested in this."

"Why not?" she demanded.

Paul struggled to his feet and stood, looking weak and pale. He told her, "You ask too many questions!" And to Hall he said, "Get this coat off me!"

Peter Hall and Gale carefully removed the jacket

and she was shocked to see that his shirt was soaked with blood. The fat man expertly bound the wound with a fresh, white handkerchief and then draped Paul's coat over his shoulders. While all this was going on the brown man in the red fez and robe had vanished.

She asked Paul, "Who was the man in the fez and where has he gone?"

Her husband frowned at her. "He's a native employed by Abdul-el-Krem. He's probably gone to see if he can catch up with that fellow who attacked me."

"I would consider that a police job," she said.

The fat Peter Hall warned her, "While you're in Morocco you'd better forget about the police. They're little help in any case and they're even less interested in the problems of visiting Europeans than with their own people."

Paul said, "We'd better get to the carriage before something else happens."

"Good idea," Hall said. "Lean on me!"

Paul let the stout man help him and Gale followed after them, confused and terrified.

She could come to only one conclusion. These enemies who had tried to kill him were not the only ones outside the law. It seemed all too likely that Paul himself was involved in some sort of shady business.

They reached the carriage and were driven back to the white chateau overlooking the ocean. A doctor, an elderly Arab, was summoned. He treated the stab wound, pronouncing it minor. Gale noticed that he asked no questions as to how the injury had been inflicted on her husband. He left, well paid for his discreet attitude.

Hall then made ready to leave. The fat man

warned Paul before he left, "I advise you not to return to the medina. At least not unless one of us is with you."

Slumped in an easy chair Paul nodded, "I know."

Hall asked, "What took you down there today?"

"My half brother, Ben, asked me to come see him" He gave the fat man a meaningful glance. "He knows more than he should. He dropped Abdul's name to get a rise out of me."

"That could stand looking into," Hall said with a malevolent look on his big face.

"Nothing rough, please," Paul said wearily.

"I'll handle it personally," he said with some satisfaction. "I'll depend on your wife to look after you."

"I'll do my best," she promised and saw him out.

At the door, in a low voice he warned her, "You've got to talk him out of playing hero or you'll be finding yourself a widow."

She went back to Paul in the living room. He was still seated in the big easy chair, his eyes closed and his face a deathly white. He could be dead. She sat beside him and reached out to touch his good arm.

He started and then eyed her accusingly, "You frightened me!"

"I'm sorry," she said. "But I demand an explanation! We came here supposedly for a honeymoon and for you to meet some of your company people on the side. Everything has gone wrong! I find the house visited by dreadful people, you and I both are attacked! And now that repulsive Peter Hall warns me that I'd better watch you carefully or I'll wind up a widow!"

He listened to her harangue, a gleam of resentment in his keen black eyes. Then he said, "Hall had

52

no business saying that to you. What happened today was a simple case of someone trying to assault and rob us!"

"I can't believe that!"

"You don't understand this country or its people!"

Gale said heatedly, "And you are not being fair or honest with me. What is International Ventures doing in Morocco? Are you mixed up in something criminal?"

He frowned. "What gave you that idea?"

"All that has been happening plus your secrecy."

He sighed. "I'm not up to long discussions."

"You must give me some explanation!"

"We are here on business matters," he said. "It is as simple as that. The company has goods to sell and there are buyers here. When Carl Revene gets here he'll take charge of everything."

"Where does your brother fit into it all?"

"Ben is a fool who talks too much," Paul said with disgust. "He has no part in what I'm doing here."

"He seems to think he knows a lot about it."

"Bluff!" Paul said, slowly rising from the chair. "If you'll excuse me I'm going upstairs to rest a little."

With a sigh she went to a desk in the adjoining room and began a letter to her aunt and uncle in New York. In it she stressed the lovely house and climate without telling any of the bad things which had clouded her honeymoon thus far.

Paul developed a slight fever and she had to call the doctor again that evening. He warned Paul that he must not leave his bed for a couple of days. Paul reluctantly agreed and they had a quiet existence for the forty-eight hours which followed.

Then Edmund Walton arrived and engaged

Paul in a secret session in the closed study. When Walton emerged, leaning on his cane, he looked in good humor.

The lame man told her, "Paul and I will be busy with some merchants from the desert this afternoon. I'm sending Diana over to take you out and show you some more of the city."

She said, "You're very kind. Do you think it safe for us to go out alone?"

Edmund Walton's lined face showed amusement at this. "Of course you'll be safe. Diana goes about on her own a lot of the time. And so will you after you come to know the city."

Paul gave her a glance which indicated he wished her to go along with his friend's suggestion and said, "Edmund is right. You'll be quite safe with his wife."

She thought the remark ironic since Paul well knew that she had discovered the Waltons were not married. But she agreed that Diana should call for her. The two men went off in the carriage and about two hours later Diana arrived in her own carriage.

The attractive blond was wearing a blue dress and blue straw hat which set off her beauty. She kissed Gale on the cheek and then settled into a nearby chair and proceeded to light a fat Turkish cigarette. After she lit it, she asked Gale, "Would you like to try one?"

"Thanks," she said. "I don't smoke."

Diana raised her eyebrows. "I understood all modern young women in New York were smoking cigarettes."

"I'm afraid I'm not all that modern."

"In London I picked up the habit early," Diana said, as she exhaled the smoke with evident enjoyment. She eyed Gale quizzically. "You are a charming innocent to be married to Paul."

Gale stared at her. "Why do you say that?"

"It is true," the other girl replied. "Paul is a man of experience. Versed in the ways of the world. Carl Revene looks on him as his most talented recruit."

"Really?"

Diana puffed on the fat cigarette again and exhaled lazily. "That puts him at the top of the company. Edmund says he has only one trouble."

"What is that?"

"Paul is a little too ambitious," Diana said. "Perhaps you may have noticed that in him?"

She was at a loss what to say. "I think he's dedicated to the company."

"To what he is doing," Diana corrected her. "Paul would like to be as successful on his own as Revene has been."

"Is that wrong?"

Diana smiled knowingly. "It is when Carl Revene is employing you. Edmund fears that Paul may incur Revene's anger by trying to make some deals on his own."

Gale said, "Unhappily, I don't know anything about these deals."

The other girl eyed her without replying for a moment, then she said, "I think you're better off not knowing."

"I disagree," she said. "I think a wife should know about her husband's business."

Diana's face crimsoned. She put out her cigarette in the tray by her and rose from the chair. "All this talk is doing you no good. I have orders to take you out and see you get some air and see some people."

Gale said, "You have orders?"

The golden-haired girl laughed. "Don't be so deadly serious. I just used that term. Don't go around behaving as if you were the central victim in some deadly plot."

"I've found myself wondering about it," Gale confessed.

They went out in the carriage and Diana proved a good companion and conversationalist. Wherever they drove they saw something of interest. Cobblers sat stitching sandals before their tiny shops, tailors sat cross-legged on the ground sewing, while small boys wound the thread. Blacksmiths were noisily at work in their tiny holes in the wall, while boys pumped huge bellows.

They passed an outdoor grain market where merchants sat on the ground amid sacks of wheat and women squatted in groups tossing the grain into the air to let the chaff blow away. A chanting holy man wandered from shop to shop with his incense burner. Butchers sold not only pieces of meat and whole carcasses but such things as sheep and cow heads. Everything from a handful of tea to coal and firewood was purchased by weight on hand scales.

They left this section and drove by the harbor where great merchant ships were docked. Along with the modern there was the ancient. Arabs worked at repairing a barge by pounding pieces of green lumber into the damaged side of the craft. Nails were not necessary. A Frenchman was building a fishing boat alone, by hand. Workmen carried sacks of wheat on their shoulders from carts to the dockside.

Gale asked, "Where is Carl Revene's yacht?"

"The *Siren?*" Diana said. "It's down the harbor

a distance. He keeps it anchored well out, and the crew come back and forth by small boat."

She said, "We are supposed to spend part of our honeymoon on board the yacht."

The golden-haired girl looked impressed. "You see? Revene does think highly of your Paul. Very few of us are ever invited on the *Siren*. It is Revene's home while he is here and he uses it to move from port to port on business."

"No doubt that is the answer," Gale said with a wry grimace. "He and Paul will be doing business most of the time we are on the boat. That would be typical."

Diana laughed. "I'm sure you won't be neglected. And now I'm going to take you to the place where most Europeans meet when they are in Morocco. The Hotel Empress?"

She directed the driver of the carriage to take them to the hotel. Very shortly after, they reached a huge white building surrounded by gardens. Carriages rode up to its arched entrance and most of those getting down from the carriages were from the world outside the African city. Their carriage took its turn and Diana told the driver to come back in an hour or so. Then they both were helped down from the vehicle by the native doorman.

The lobby of the hotel was crowded and hummed with conversations in English, French, and German. Gale even heard some familiar American accents, which made her feel less isolated. Diana guided her along a wide hall to an outdoor dining place in a gardenlike courtyard. They were shown to a table and she ordered tall, cooling drinks.

Then the blond girl said, "I'm going to leave you alone for a moment. I have to speak to the manager about some guests whom my husband and I are expecting next week. I'll only be a few minutes." With a winning smile she got up and left.

Gale was a little startled by the young woman's sudden departure. Even in a place so obviously safe and respectable, it was a little unnerving to be left alone. She was glad when the waiter arrived with the drinks; sipping hers, she felt less conspicuous, as if the drink explained her presence there somehow.

All at once a male voice at her elbow said, "My dear Mrs. Cormier, what a pleasant surprise finding you here!"

She turned and smiled. It was the nice, young reporter, Eric Simms. "Mr. Simms! I'm so glad to see you again."

He stood, Panama in hand, and said, "And I to see you. Is your husband with you?"

"No. A woman friend."

"Ah!" he said. "So you are beginning to make a few contacts in this fantastic city."

"Yes," she said. "Though I confess I'm still afraid of Casablanca. I feel relatively safe here in this Western retreat."

He laughed. "The Hotel Empress! You shouldn't allow yourself to relax. It's a haunt of the worst scoundrels in the country."

"You're joking!"

"Only a little," he told her. "I intend to accept your kind invitation and visit you and your husband at the first chance I have."

"You will be most welcome," she said, knowing this to be true on her part if not on Paul's.

"So we shall meet again," Eric said, bowing and moving on.

Diana returned just in time to see the good-looking English reporter leaving her. The girl gave him a more than casual appraisal, and when she came back to sit at the table with Gale, she said, "And who was that handsome fellow? Don't tell me you picked him up in the short while I was away!"

Gale blushed. "Of course not! He is a newspaperman who befriended me when I first arrived here. Paul has met him."

The other girl gave her a knowing look. "Does Paul approve of your friendship with him?"

She stared at her. "Why do you ask that?"

"I have an idea he doesn't," Diana told her. "Paul is not one to accept people easily."

"No, he is not," she agreed, without offering any more information. She asked, "Did you have your talk with the manager?"

"Yes. Everything's settled," Diana said. "We'll enjoy our drinks and I'll see you safely home."

Paul had still not returned when she arrived back at the chateau by the ocean. She rested for a little and had gone down for the evening meal when one of the maids ushered in a visitor. It was Paul's half brother, Ben, looking as untidy as before, bringing her the painting she had chosen.

"I just finished having it framed," he said. "I hope you like it."

She studied it again. "It's very good. I'm glad I selected it. You are very kind."

"I had to find a wedding present for you," Ben said with a smile on his battered face.

"There was no need," she said. "I'm sorry Paul is still not home. He went away with Edmund Walton to see some people on business."

Ben waved this aside. "It doesn't matter. I can't stay in any event. I have a few things of my own to attend to." He turned as if about to leave, then paused to add, "I understand you had some trouble after you left me the other day."

"Yes. How did you know?"

"In the medina things get around quickly."

"It was frightening."

"I'm sure it was," her brother-in-law said with some sympathy. "The thieves there are always on the lookout for strangers."

"You think they only wanted to rob us?"

"What else?"

"I don't know," she said. "That is why I asked you."

If he had any ideas it was evident he was not going to share them with her. He said, "The trouble is that Paul has the reputation of being a rich man because of his close friendship with Carl Revene."

"He is only an employee of Mr. Revene."

"Not everyone understands or accepts that," the older man said, standing there in his soiled linens.

"It makes me afraid to venture near your place again," she said.

"Come! Don't let yourself be scared," Ben said. "I hope to see a lot of you and Paul while you are here."

"Mr. Revene is due here now," she said. "And when he arrives we are joining him on his yacht. We will be traveling with him for a while."

"I see," Ben said with interest. "I'm working on a portrait of Paul which I intend to offer to him as a surprise one day. It was good to see him again and have the likeness of his features impressed freshly on my mind."

"It's very kind of you to do a study of him," she said.

Ben smiled. "I have long wanted to do it. I shall give it to you."

"I'd treasure it."

"It will be finished shortly," the artist said. "And when I have it ready I'll find you some way."

"The Waltons or Peter Hall should know where we are," she said.

He nodded. "You look a trifle strained. Worried! Is anything bothering you?"

Gale hesitated. "It's only that I find it all so different here."

"Yes, it is very different," Ben agreed, his eyes fixed on her.

She was embarrassed. "I'll tell Paul you were here."

"You can if you like," Ben said. "He won't mind missing me. You know there's no love lost between us."

"I hope that can be changed," was her prompt reply.

"Thank you, but don't count on it," was her brother-in-law's parting comment.

She had one of the servants help her hang the painting in their bedroom where Paul would be bound to see it often. And she had dinner alone in the large, formal dining room that night.

Later she was standing on the balcony in the darkness gazing out at the ocean and the distant lights of some fairly large craft out there when she heard a step behind her. She turned to find herself in her husband's arms. He kissed her warmly and then stood with his arm still around her as they gazed out at the ocean again.

"Isn't that a lovely sight," Paul remarked cheerfully.

She looked up at him in the dark and asked, "Where were you? What kept you so late?"

"It was an important meeting," he said. "Arab chiefs from the desert. They offer a lucrative market for many of the things we have to sell."

"I see," she said. "When you didn't return I almost went out of my mind with worry."

"I'm sorry," he apologized, taking his arm from around her. "I'll try not to have it happen again."

"But it will," she said unhappily. "I'm sure of it. I'm left with the feeling you care a good deal more for this business you're in than you do for me! Why did you marry me, Paul?"

He gasped. "That is a ridiculous question."

"Answer me?"

"I married you because I love you!"

"But when there is a question of the business or me, it is the business which comes first! Don't deny it!"

"Gale!" her young husband said in a pained voice. "You don't understand!"

"Do you think you can make me understand?"

He sighed, and gripping the rail of the balcony stared out at the ocean, not looking at her. "I'll try," he said finally. "I have two or three giant deals going at one time. I'm representing Revene in two of them; one of them is my own."

"Does he know that?"

"No."

"What about Edmund Walton and Peter Hall? Do they know?"

"Not yet."

"You'd best be careful," she warned him. "Only

today Diana said that it was thought that you were too ambitious. That you resented Revene having any hold over you even though he is employing you."

Now Paul stared at her. "Did she say that?"

"Yes. So they must suspect something is going on."

"Let them!" he said bitterly.

"Is it dangerous?"

"Dangerous?"

"Yes. They might interpret this private scheme of yours as a betrayal," she said. "Are they the sort who might exact some violent revenge on you?"

"Of course not," her husband told her, but there was little conviction in his voice.

"I don't like any of it," she told him.

"Just forget we had this discussion," he begged her. "Don't think of what I said. It will be all right."

"I hope so," she said. "Ben was here earlier."

"What did he want?" Paul sounded angry.

"He brought my painting. You remember he was going to have it framed."

"Just an excuse to come here," was Paul's bitter reply.

"You think that?"

"Yes. He's trying to find out what I'm doing in Casablanca. And he's not to be trusted. In the five years he's been here he's picked up a lot of evil companions and been on the fringe of a good many crooked deals."

"I think you're being unfair to him," she said. "He seems fond of you."

Paul gave a short, sour laugh. "He hates me!"

"I hung his painting in our room," she said. "I hope you'll both come around to being friends. It is wrong for brothers to feel as you do."

"He's only my half brother!" Paul protested.

"That is close enough."

"Don't worry about it," he told her. "Revene will be getting here day after tomorrow and we'll be taking off to visit some other places."

She shivered slightly. "I have a funny feeling about it."

"Nonsense," Paul said, placing an arm around her again. "You're bound to enjoy the experience."

Gale was by no means reassured. She lay awake for a long while after Paul had fallen into a deep sleep. Troubled by all the things she was gradually discovering, she realized that unwittingly she had allowed her new husband to lead her into a world of which she knew nothing. Somewhere close to the edge of the unsavory! She was certain of it!

She slept for a little and then woke with a deep feeling of terror! Paul was still asleep as she raised herself on an elbow and stared into the shadows of the room. She was almost certain she saw a ghostlike form standing there. Then as she stared into the darkness the figure evaporated. She lay back with a sigh.

Paul was clearly weary and she did not wish to wake him needlessly. So she forced herself to remain very still and at last fell asleep. So weary was she that she slept well into the heat of the sunny morning. When she wakened, Paul had left and she was alone in the bedroom.

Feeling guilty at not having been awake when her husband left, she quickly got up. It was past midmorning when she went downstairs for a light breakfast, and she was still at the breakfast table when Peter Hall arrived. The maid showed him in and he stood there looking annoyed.

"Where is Paul?" he asked.

"He left while I was still asleep," she said.

Hall frowned. "He was to wait until I came here for him. What about Walton? Has he been here?"

"No."

The fat man took a big white handkerchief from a rear pocket and mopped his perspiring brow. "I'd like to know what's going on," he said angrily. "And Carl Revene will have some questions to ask when he gets here."

She got up from the table. "Questions about what?"

Peter Hall at once looked wary. "It's nothing to do with you."

"But," she said, "anything that concerns Paul has to do with me."

He smiled nastily. "Then you can ask him to fill you in on the details. I won't."

She stared at him. "You resent me, don't you?"

He looked faintly surprised. "What makes you say that?"

"You've been antagonistic toward me ever since I first arrived."

"All right, if you want the truth," the fat man responded grimly. "I think Paul was a fool to get married. This place is not fit to bring a wife to and he hasn't time to give a marriage."

"I think you are wrong, Mr. Hall," she said quietly.

"We'll see," was his reply. "I'm going. You can tell your husband I was here." And he waddled out.

Paul returned earlier than usual and seemed in a better mood. He was almost jubilant, in fact. Gale told him about Peter Hall's call and he ignored it. At the same time he confided to her, "Things have gone well for us today. I'll be having a visitor this evening."

"Who?" she asked.

"No one you know," her husband said. "I will have a short conference with him in my study first. Then I'll have you come down to meet him."

"Very well. I'll go upstairs after dinner and you can come up to get me when you are ready."

Paul's handsome face showed a smile. "If this goes as I hope it does, we may soon be able to leave here."

She brightened at once. "You really mean that?"

"Yes. If this works out I will be able to give Revene my resignation."

"Will he accept it?"

"He'll have to," her husband said.

"But aren't you his right-hand man?"

Paul smiled bleakly. "He'll have no trouble finding someone to replace me. Revene smells of money; it attracts people to him!"

She gave him a knowing look. "But sometimes they are sorry afterward?"

"I know I am," Paul said. "I want out. And I think I have it arranged."

"How soon could we get away from here?" she asked.

"A week or two," he said. "No longer."

"Wonderful!"

"Not so fast," he laughed. "We haven't put the deal through yet."

She asked him, "What sort of deal is it?"

Paul appeared uneasy. "Nothing of interest to you. You don't have to worry your head about it."

"But I will," she told him. "If it's the same unsavory type of thing that Revene is so often involved in, you won't truly be getting away from him. You'll simply be carrying on in his pattern, but on your own."

"That's the important thing," Paul said. "To be on your own!"

"That's only true to a point," she warned him.

He kissed her and said indulgently, "Go on up to our room or go out into the garden and get familiar with the flower beds, I simply can't give you any more time. I'm weary, and I have an important evening ahead."

Paul had her so hypnotized by his charm that she put off asking the vital questions she had intended. But she knew sooner or later there had to be an understanding, and if she found her husband into anything of which she did not approve, she would insist that he leave Revene and this great house in Morocco.

As soon as she finished her dinner she left him and went up to her room to write some letters, including a further note to her uncle in New York, telling him she was not at all happy in Paul's dealings. She addressed it to her uncle's office rather than to the house, where her aunt might share the contents with him and be worried. This way her uncle could use his own judgment whether to keep the troubled account to himself or tell his wife.

She heard a carriage arrive and voices down below, but had no idea who it might be. Some time went by and she began to become weary. She studied herself in the mirror over her dresser and approved of the yellow dress with white lace trim which she had selected to wear for this special occasion. But there were dark circles under her eyes.

Then the door opened, and it was Paul. He was smiling as he stood there in his immaculate white linen suit and told her, "We are ready for you now."

"I would soon have fallen asleep," she said.

"I'm sorry," her husband apologized. "But we had many items to go over."

"And it is all settled?"

"Almost everything," he exulted. "If I get the signatures tomorrow, I can tell Revene I'm through with him when he arrives."

"Who am I to meet?"

"Two men, most important to our future," he told her.

She slowly descended the stairs with him and then they went on to the study. Standing there was the brown-skinned man in the red fez and striped robe who had rescued her several days ago and with him was a black-skinned man in a rich white silk robe and turban. Both men ceased their discussion when they saw her.

Paul introduced her to the black man in the rich, silken robes, saying, "This is my best friend, Abdul-el-Krem!"

The black man bowed and in perfect English said, "I'm most truly delighted to be introduced to you officially, my dear Mrs. Cormier."

Gale stared at him with growing awareness. The black, wrinkled face and the bright, intelligent eyes were all too familiar. "We have met before!" she gasped.

He smiled and bowed. "Several times."

She pointed to him. "You were the beggar!"

"I elect to disguise myself in that role when it is useful for me," Abdul-el-Krem said in his educated voice.

"Your hand! The leprosy!" she stammered.

He chuckled and held up the stump of a hand from the sleeve of silk. He said, "The state of my fingers on this hand came from a gunshot explosion, not leprosy. But it does have the appearance of being eaten away by disease. This gave me the inspiration for my role of leprous beggar!"

"You are so different now!" she marveled. "It is hard to believe."

"Abdul was educated at Oxford," Paul informed her. "And so was his assistant, Jiri."

The man in the red fez bowed also. He said, "I'm pleased that I have also been of some service to you, Madame Cormier."

"You probably saved my life," she said.

Abdul-el-Krem told her, "We owe much to your husband. And if all goes well we will see you many times in the future. I would like to show you more of this great country. Morocco is suffering an unhappy serfdom under a tyrant, but one day soon let us hope the tide will change."

"Allah has deemed it must be so," the man in the red fez said quietly.

Paul turned to her and said, "We have to go to the quarters of Abdul-el-Krem for a short while. I may not be home until late."

She stared up at him with a rising feeling of uneasiness. "Must you go out again tonight?"

"I'm afraid so," he said. "But never mind. I'll be quite safe. You go to bed in case I'm really late."

Gale made a reluctant promise that she would and the two men bade her good night. Paul saw her to the stairs. She could tell by his excited manner and his assured good night kiss that he felt he was on the brink of great success. She was happy for him and at the same time afraid.

The men left in a carriage. From the balcony she watched it draw away from the chateau. Then she went inside and tried to settle down. But she was not ready to sleep so she found a book and read for a long while. The night was hot and there was a veil of silence over the great house that struck her as uncanny. When she became aware of it, she became even more nervous.

She closed the book as she thought she heard her husband's step in the hall outside the door of the bedroom. But when she went to open the door, there was no one there. She began to tremble and did not know why. The atmosphere grew so ominous that she could stand it no longer and left the bedroom to go downstairs. She went to the living room and lit several of the lamps there. Then she began to pace, praying that Paul would soon come home.

She was still pacing when she heard a carriage drive up to the entrance of the chateau. She went to the door and opened it to discover Edmund Walton and Diana as they got down from the vehicle and came toward the open doorway where she was standing. She saw Walton leaning heavily on his cane, and Diana took the lead.

The golden-haired girl eyed her anxiously. She said, "We didn't expect to find you up so late."

This seemed strange to her. If they had not expected to find her awake, why had they made this late-hour visit. She said, "I've been nervous. Paul is out. I haven't been able to sleep."

Edmund Walton limped up the steps to face

her. He looked extremely worn. He said, "You say that Paul is out?"

"Yes," she said, stepping back for him to enter.

Edmund Walton sighed. "I had hoped to find him here. I wished to talk with him."

She said, "He went off with two men to take care of some sort of agreement."

Diana said, "Was one of the men Abdul-el-Krem?"

Startled, she turned to her and said, "Yes. Why?"

Diana gave Walton a significant glance and said, "I think I'd better leave this to Edmund." And she turned away, with her back to Gale.

More alarmed, Gale asked the lame man, "What is it?"

In a taut voice, still leaning on his cane, Walton said, "There has been a bad accident in the harbor."

"Accident?" she echoed in a hushed voice.

"Yes," he went on. "A launch belonging to Abdul-el-Krem was taking a party to a yacht. It exploded en route."

"Oh, no!" she sobbed in protest.

The lame man nodded. "You must be brave. All aboard the launch are reported dead. And from what you have said, Paul was one of the passengers."

4

The room reeled around her. She reached out as if for help, then darkness closed in and she slumped to the floor.

When she opened her eyes she was on the divan and Diana was worriedly bent over her. The golden-haired girl asked her, "Are you all right now?"

"Yes," she said in a small voice.

Edmund Walton came limping over and leaning on his cane told her, "I know this has been a dreadful shock for you. We are all stunned by what happened."

As memory came back she felt the need to hope. Raising herself up a little, she asked, "Isn't there a chance that Paul may have survived the accident?"

"None," Walton said with a dark look on his thin face. "The boat was blown to bits and so were the people in it. No doubt the work of one of the guerrilla groups. Morocco is filled with them, and Abdul-el-Krem had his share of enemies."

"I can't believe it," she said, stunned.

Diana placed an arm around her as she sat

up and tried to cope with this horror. The blond girl said, "At least he didn't suffer. He probably wasn't aware of what happened."

"It took place in a flash," Edmund Walton agreed.

The doorbell rang and when the maid answered it, she showed the stout Peter Hall in. The big man was clearly agitated. He at once went to Walton and asked, "Is it true? Is Paul dead?"

Edmund Walton limped over to him and said, "Paul, Abdul-el-Krem, and his associate were all in the launch along with its operator. The explosion tore both passengers and craft to bits!"

"Gad!" Peter Hall said, consternation showing on the red face under the shining bald pate. "So he was playing games with Abdul and his crowd."

"Evidently," Walton said dryly. "It doesn't matter now."

"Revene will want an explanation of this," the stout man warned.

Walton shrugged. "We will worry about that in good time. I have yet to see you express any sorrow to the widow."

Peter Hall looked guilty and shuffled over to stand before the divan to tell her, "My sympathy, Mrs. Cormier. A bad business!"

"Thank you," she said weakly. "I cannot accept it yet."

"No wonder," Diana said, staying close to her. "You must be brave. We have all lost a friend, but you have lost a husband."

Peter Hall turned to Edmund Walton and asked, "What about the briefcase? Did he have it with him?"

Walton shook his head. "I don't know."

Diana gave Gale a worried glance and asked,

"Do you remember if Paul had his briefcase when he left?"

"I don't know," she said, shutting her eyes. "I must go rest for a little or I'll faint again."

"I'll see you to your room," Diana said.

Once in the room she helped Gale get ready for bed. And when she was safely between the sheets, still numbed by shock, Diana brought her a sleeping potion in water.

"Take this," the girl ordered her.

She drank the potion without protest. In a very few minutes her eyelids became heavy. She lay back on her pillow and, closing her eyes, sank into a deep, dreamless slumber.

When she awoke, it was daylight. Diana was standing by the window, glancing out at the ocean. "Feeling a little better?"

"I'm still in a kind of daze," Gale said.

"That is natural enough," the other girl told her.

"When did you get here?"

"Edmund and I stayed the night here," Diana said. "We sent back to our place for some things. He feels we should remain with you until you have recovered a bit more."

"You're very kind," she said listlessly.

"We were Paul's associates," Diana said. "We have a certain duty in this."

Gale opened her eyes wide, on the brink of tears. "Why?" she asked. "Why would he open himself to such danger?"

Diana sighed. "You may be sure he had reasons. Do you feel well enough to go downstairs?"

"I must force myself," Gale told her. "I cannot spend the balance of my life in this room."

"Why should you?" Diana wanted to know. "I'm certain Paul wanted to make you happy, but I don't think he'd ask that you make a martyr of yourself."

"I don't know what to do! I should let my aunt and uncle in New York know," she said unhappily.

"You can send a cable," the other girl said. "Edmund is downstairs waiting to talk with you."

"It was good of you to remain here this way," she said as she got out of bed.

Diana said, "Carl Revene would expect us to be here."

As Gale washed and dressed, it suddenly hit her that Diana and her supposed husband might be there not merely as friends but to guard her. Paul had been acting for Revene in several highly confidential matters. It could develop that she was a prisoner of these mysterious people. Paul had told her very little about his dealings. But he had let her know he was in at least one venture on his own. Perhaps he had died because he had dared to do this!

These thoughts added a turmoil of fear to her sadness in the loss of Paul. She was weak and still light-headed from the sleeping potion as she hesitantly made her way down the stairs to the living room of the chateau.

Edmund Walton was there to greet her and quickly pull up a chair for her. Then he sat down by her, his thin face showing sympathy. "I trust your sleep was helpful," he added. "I have a few things I must discuss with you."

"Can't you wait until later?" Diana demanded.

Edmund Walton gave her an angry look. "No. I must talk to Gale before Revene arrives."

"I don't agree," Diana said, and turned away from them.

"Diana doesn't understand," the lame man said apologetically. "I dislike having to question you as much as she abhors the idea. But I have a duty to my employer. To Paul's employer, Carl Revene."

She stared at him. "All right. I'll answer any questions I can."

Walton looked pleased. "Good. How much did Paul tell you about his role in International Ventures?"

"Very little," she said.

"Did he tell you where he was going last night?"

"No."

"But you knew who he was with?" the man across from her said.

"Yes. He introduced me to Abdul-el-Krem and an associate."

Walton nodded. "When they left here they boarded the launch. We know what happened after that. But there is a briefcase. Paul's briefcase. It contains many highly confidential and valuable papers. Can you remember if he took it with him?"

"I didn't notice," she said.

Walton was watching her closely and she had the feeling he didn't believe her. "You are sure?"

"Yes."

He gave a deep sigh. "I don't believe he took the briefcase with him. It had nothing to do with his business with Abdul-el-Krem."

"Then he must have left it here," she said. "Must you bother me about it now?"

"I'm afraid I must," Walton said, his tone cold. "I have taken the liberty of searching the study and other parts of the house, and I have not been able to find it."

She stared at him. "You have no right to search our house without my permission!"

"I'm sorry," he said coldly. "I have to protect our company. There are papers in that briefcase so confidential and so important they could cause an international situation. The briefcase must be recovered and the papers returned to our company."

Gale was becoming increasingly fearful of her position. She could see that Edmund Walton cared nothing about what had happened to Paul or her sad plight; he was intent on carrying out the orders of Carl Revene.

She said, "I know nothing about the briefcase."

The thin man was stern. "It could be bad for you if you are concealing the truth!"

Indignantly, she protested, "Do you think I would lie about it?"

Walton backed down and became apologetic, saying, "I'm sorry, but the weight of all this evolves on me. The briefcase must be found."

"What if it were with Paul on the launch?" she asked.

The lame man said grimly, "That would be a different matter. But I have every reason to believe he did not have the briefcase when he boarded the launch."

Again her suspicions were aroused. "How could you know that?"

"You've told me so, yourself."

"I told you I wasn't sure!"

He rose and leaned on his cane. "All right, if I must tell you. Certain people in our organization believe your husband was double-crossing us. He was being watched. The business with Abdul-el-Krem had nothing to do with International Ventures. It was his own project, and it brought about his death."

"You were spying on him?"

"We had no choice," Edmund Walton snapped. "Both Peter Hall and I felt he was getting ready to operate on his own, using our methods and information. We have just been waiting for Revene to arrive to report this to him."

"You are saying that my husband was not doing his best for the company?" She knew full well that he hadn't been, but she did not want Walton to guess how much she knew.

"I've said it plainly enough. He was cheating on us," Edmund Walton said. "So he was being watched. And he had no briefcase with him when he stepped onto that launch."

"I cannot help you," she said.

Walton glared at her. "Perhaps, given time, you'll be able to remember."

Diana moved toward her protectively. She told Walton, "You've found out what you wanted. Why not leave her alone?"

He eyed her furiously. "I don't need you to tell me what to do!"

Diana's smile was sarcastic. "No. Revene does that!"

Walton looked as if he'd like to strike her but then controlled himself, and leaning on his cane, he said, "I will let the matter go for now and hope the briefcase turns up somewhere else. But in the meantime I suggest you search your memory for anything you know about it and be prepared to pass the information on to me."

Gale said, "Is that a threat?"

"Not unless you wish to construe it as one," he said.

"I have other things bothering me," she said. "I wish to send a cable to my aunt and uncle in New York."

He said, "You can give it to me and I'll send it."

She looked up at him in fear. "Am I not allowed to leave the house?"

"I think it best for your own safety that you remain here for another day or two," Walton said. "The same guerrillas who placed a bomb on that launch may be seeking some way of getting at you!"

"I see," she said quietly.

Walton went on, "You may be resentful of my attitude. But believe me, I and the others in the company are your friends compared to those who killed Paul."

"So I must place my trust in you?" Gale said.

"There is no one else," was his chilling reply. "Diana will stay here with you. And we have a few guards outside to watch that no one enters."

"I see," she said, more than ever having the sense of being under arrest.

"Compose your cable and I'll take it to the telegraph office," Walton said.

She wrote out a short cable and he took it with him when he left. In spite of the outside warmth and sunshine the house seemed bleak and threatening. Diana looked unhappy at the task of watching her. And as soon as Walton left, the flaxen-haired girl spoke frankly with her.

Diana sat in the chair which Walton had occupied and lighting a fat Turkish cigarette she inhaled it with satisfaction and then asked, "Do you know anything about that briefcase?"

"No. I told the truth."

"I felt you did but I don't think he does."

"Why should I want it?"

Diana shrugged. "In the right hands it could be a dangerous weapon. Revene and others could be blackmailed for a king's ransom."

Gale said, "Paul told me very little about the business."

"So it seems," Diana said with a wry smile. "You know he was planning on skipping out after making a big deal on his own?"

"Not really."

"Well, he was," Diana said. "That is why they were watching him."

"How could he dare?" she said. "He knew how ruthless you people can be."

"Did he tell you that?"

"It's not hard to know it," Gale said. "Even now you're holding me as a sort of prisoner."

"It's not quite that bad," Diana said. "I won't let them bully you. I'm on your side."

Gale looked at her directly. "You're not Walton's wife, are you?"

The other girl crimsoned. "Who told you?"

"Peter."

Diana shrugged. "Well, what of it? He was right. I don't take any orders from Walton and I owe him nothing."

"Why have you stayed with him?"

"He gives me nice things—and being considered his wife is a kind of protection, you know."

"I think he's a criminal and that International Ventures must be a criminal organization," Gale told her.

The other girl looked perturbed. "Don't say that!"

"But it is true!"

"Whatever is true the thing you need is to get back to New York and to your aunt and uncle," Diana said. "I'll try to help you."

"Why?"

"Because I hate Walton and what his gang are doing," the other girl said bitterly. "And I'm leaving him soon. You remember I went away for a while the other day. I was talking with someone. Someone who is taking me away from Casablanca. Back to London."

"I wish you luck," she said.

Diana ground out her cigarette. "If they don't find that briefcase things could get bad."

Gale said, "Paul had a half brother. He lives in the medina, in a studio there. I'd like to see him and tell him about Paul."

"You'll not get out of here without Walton allowing it," the girl warned. "Even if I let you go one of the guards would stop you."

Gale stood up, anger balancing her grief. She said, "So the guards serve a double purpose!"

Diana stood with her. "You're smart enough to have guessed that!"

The day passed quickly and Walton returned for dinner. They all sat at the big table with the stout Peter Hall joining them at the last moment. Walton was clearly in charge and he did little to disguise that she was under benevolent house arrest.

"Revene should arrive tomorrow," Walton said. "Then I shall turn you over to him."

"Did you send my cable?" she asked him.

"Yes."

"I would like to return to New York if you would find out the first sailing," she said.

Hall leered at her and said, "Don't worry! I'm

certain Revene will take care of all that. He is a generous man and has a lot of connections."

"I'm sure he has," she agreed, with irony.

Diana spoke up, "Paul's half brother is in the old city. Gale would like to go to him and tell him what happened."

Edmund Walton asked Gale, "Is this true?"

"Yes," she said.

"I will take you there," the lame man said. "You realize it is too dangerous to venture there on your own."

"I'm sure all Morocco is dangerous," she said.

"You have seen the bad side of it," Hall informed her. "When you recover from your grief you'll feel differently."

"I doubt it," she said. And she asked Walton, "When can we go to Ben's studio?"

"After dinner," he said. "I'll have a carriage ready."

They left a quarter-hour after dinner. Diana elected to remain at the chateau with Peter Hall, so Gale was alone with Edmund Walton. He knew she would not dare break away from him to face what might be worse danger, but he kept close to her in case she might get such an idea.

The carriage rumbled over the cobblestones of the dark streets. Some of the large buildings were well-lighted, but Casablanca after dark was a frightening place. Dark forms scurried out of nowhere to vanish in the same elusive manner.

At her side Walton said dryly, "In the daylight these old streets harbor no one much worse than beggars. But at night the cutthroats and thieves are out!"

She said nothing, realizing it was a warning for

her not to run away. She had contemplated this but lacked courage.

She thought of Abdul-el-Krem and how he had pretended to be a beggar. And of his associate Jiri, in the red fez, who had come to her aid. She badly wanted to outwit Walton and the others if only because she felt she owed that to her husband. More and more she was beginning to believe that the International Ventures group might have planned his death!

They reached the spot where the carriage had to wait, and Edmund Walton guided her through the gate and along the narrow streets. Now they were lit up by torches set out at intervals, and some of the merchants had small fires before their place of business. The dark, narrow streets were filled with people of the night: men in turbans with patriarchal beards, blacks, villainous-looking men who gazed at her hungrily and openly.

"Walk swiftly," Walton told her. "Pay no attention to them."

"Are we safe?" she worried.

"I hope so," was his tense reply. "Are you sure this is the way?"

"Yes," she said. "It is in a tiny side street over there."

They followed along the path she and Paul had taken and within a few moments were at the door of the studio! It was in darkness!

She said, "No one here!"

"We'll see," Walton said, and he lit a match and held it in the doorway. To her surprise the studio was bare! The spare furnishings and every one of the paintings were gone.

"It's empty!" she gasped.

The match went out, and he gave her a stern look. "Are you sure this is the place?"

"Yes. It is! I know it is!"

Walton impatiently lit another match and went on into the studio. The flame of the match gave the place an eerie light. She stared into the shadows and was dismayed to see that the room had been stripped! There was nothing left, not even the bead curtain at the rear door.

"He's gone," Walton said. "No question of that."

"Maybe he heard about Paul," she ventured.

Walton lit another match from the expiring one he held. And as he did so she gazed through the rear doorway and saw a shadow! A moving shadow!

"In there!" she said excitedly. "Someone in there!"

"Look out!" Walton whispered as he pulled a revolver from his pocket and went to the doorway.

She waited in the shadows, afraid to breathe. Suddenly there was a shriek of fear from the area of the doorway and a crouched figure hobbled out.

"Pity, good sir! Have pity on an old man!" the crouched old creature wailed in accented English.

Walton kept the old man covered with his revolver as he lit another match to reveal an emaciated brown figure in a loincloth and dirty turban. Walton asked, "What are you doing here?"

"Seeking refuge!" the old man said. "I knew it was empty!"

"How did you know?" Walton asked.

"The foreign man who lived here with the girl, Aya, had his throat slit!"

Gale gasped. "Ben, murdered?"

"The girl Aya took everything with her when she left," the old man said.

"You're sure about all this?" Walton asked.

The old man nodded. "It was told to me!"

Walton turned to her. "Well, now you know! Brother Ben is as dead as Paul!"

She asked, "Does he know who did it? Why?"

Walton turned to the old man once more and asked, "Do you know who killed the artist who lived here and why?"

The old man spread his hands. "I only know that it happened."

Walton said, "You can go back to sleep!"

"Thank you, sir, you are a good man! Allah will reward you!" he chanted.

Walton took her by the arm. "Let's get out of here before someone slits our throats too!"

She shuddered. "What a horrible place this is!"

"No better or no worse than most of these Middle Eastern cities," he said. "Violence seethes beneath the surface of all of them."

As Walton guided her through the dark alleys and streets back to the main gate of the medina she thought back to a night when Paul was still alive. He had told Peter Hall that his half brother, Ben, had taunted him about knowing Abdul-el-Krem. Hall had hinted he would deal with Ben, and Paul begged that there be no violence. Could Ben's murder have come about as a result of that conversation? It was possible.

She was coming to believe that anything was possible. They reached the main gate and left the potpourri of sights, sounds, and smells of the old city behind them. Walton squired her to their waiting carriage and ordered the driver to take them back to the chateau.

Walton sat back in the carriage seat and, glancing at her, said, "I wouldn't want to repeat that visit."

She asked, "What do you suppose happened to the body?"

"They remove the dead almost immediately," he said. "No doubt it has been cremated by now."

"You think the old man told us the truth?"

"Why should he lie?"

"I don't know," she admitted. "I guess he gave us the right information."

"Revene will be here in the morning and you will meet him," Walton said.

"What is he like?"

"Like no one you've ever met," the man beside her said in a sober tone. "He'll not be pleased when he hears about Paul and that missing briefcase."

She said ironically, "I imagine the briefcase will be more cause of concern for him than my husband's murder."

"Probably," he agreed.

"I'm not sure I want to meet him!"

Walton smiled bleakly. "You do not have any choice."

The nighttime traffic was heavy. There were even camels bringing loads of produce into the city, their owners marching beside them. Wagons and carriages were so thick that the traffic had to stop every so often before they were able to move on.

Gale studied the many sights and gazed at the people in the streets. They neared the famous Hotel Empress and she gave the entrance door her full attention. All at once her heart leaped. Walking into the lobby with a distinguished, gray-haired man was the British journalist, Eric Simms!

She leaned forward in the carriage seat, all on edge, trying desperately to plan an escape. Simms would help her, she was sure. But how . . . Then another jam in traffic caused the carriage to come to a sudden halt. She deftly jumped down and ran toward the street to lose herself in the crowd of humanity there!

She heard Walton's angry cry as she jumped from the carriage and knew he would try to follow her. She moved swiftly, crouching slightly so as not to be seen, and reaching the hotel, she ran around to a side entrance. She found herself in the lobby but in a different area. Moving on, she reached the desk where the gray-haired man and Eric stood in conversation.

"Mr. Simms!" she called out as she ran toward him.

Astonishment crossed his handsome face as he recognized her. He removed his hat and bowed to her as she joined him. "My dear Mrs. Cormier," he said.

"I have been looking for you," she told him breathlessly.

He nodded. "I'm terribly sorry about your husband's accident."

"I need to talk with you now!"

Eric Simms introduced his companion, "This is Professor Bartleet, the British naturalist, I've just been interviewing him." And to the naturalist, he added, "And this is Mrs. Cormier, a lovely new addition to our English colony in Casablanca."

"My pleasure," the big man beamed down at her. "And now if you will excuse me, I'll be on my way. And you can go on with your talk." He bowed and moved on toward the stairs.

Eric gave her an anxious glance. "You look exhausted and frightened!"

"You won't believe it! I'm being kept a captive."

87

"By whom?"

"The International Ventures crowd," she said. "Edmund Walton and Peter Hall!"

"I have heard about them," Eric agreed.

"They're holding me for the arrival of Carl Revene and they seem to think I have a briefcase of important papers which Paul was holding."

"Do you have it?"

"No. I escaped from Walton when his carriage stopped in traffic." Gale looked uneasily about her. "It's not safe here. He's following me. He'll come in here any moment."

The young reporter said, "I think I can deal with him."

"I want to tell you my story," she went on. "Then you'll know what I must do."

Eric said, "We'll go out into the gardens. They're almost all in darkness at this time of night. And you can bring me up to date without too much risk."

"Fine," she nodded.

They went out a side door, passing a brightly lighted pool with a tall fountain in the center. They reached the gardens and escaped into a dark section.

He faced her in the shadows and said, "Now tell me!"

She did, hurriedly and somewhat incoherently, but he seemed to follow her. Finally she said, "I'm not sure, but they may have arranged Paul's murder and that of his half brother as well."

"I know something about the background of all this," the journalist said. "And you are quite right. Revene's group are a bad lot. He is believed to be smuggling arms on a wholesale basis and selling them to whoever can pay the price. In this case, the rebels who want to unseat the present Sultan."

"They are dangerous," she assured him. "They'll stop at nothing. If they take me prisoner again I may be killed too."

Eric Simms said, "We'll have to try to outsmart them. I can book you a room here in the hotel under an assumed name."

"And I can remain there until I get word from my relations in New York and am able to find a ship to take me home."

"Ships leave here for New York twice a week or more," he told her.

She smiled up at him, tremulously. "I'm so glad I saw you and was able to find you. You're giving me fresh hope."

"We'll get you out of this," he promised.

And as he said this a shadowy figure came up behind him and slammed a revolver butt into the side of his head. He fell to the ground. At the same time iron fingers gripped her and Walton whispered in her ear, "Make no scene! I have a gun pointed directly at you. One wrong move and I shoot you!"

"Not here! You wouldn't dare!" she protested.

"Try me," he said. And the man who had struck Eric stepped out of the shadows. It was the driver of the carriage.

She said, "Are you going to leave him there? He may not be found for a long while and he may be badly hurt."

Walton's lip curled. "Like most reporters, he's hardheaded enough to live through almost anything."

"Let me go!" she demanded.

"Don't make me use this!" he told her, pushing the revolver toward her.

He took her back to the carriage by means of dark, winding streets. Then he made her get up and sit with him. The driver was back in his seat and drove them on.

Walton was angry. "You did yourself no good! Running away and talking to that reporter!"

She said, "He knows about you and International Ventures.

"He'll know you've kidnapped me. When he comes to he'll be after you!"

"Will he?" Walton said with an indulgent smile. "Well, it won't do him any good!"

"He's not a child," she warned her captor as the carriage rolled on.

Holding the gun against her, Walton said, "Nor am I. All you've done is make your plight worse. I'll not be able to take you back to the chateau."

"What are you going to do with me?" she asked in alarm.

"I have only one choice," he said. "I'm taking you to Revene's yacht."

"He isn't here yet!"

"No. He arrives in the morning. But he won't mind when I tell him why I took you there!"

She said, "You can't put me on board a boat without any clothes, or any of my own things!"

"I'll have Diana pack for you and bring a suitcase on board later," was Walton's reply.

"It won't do any good," she warned him. "He'll find me."

"If he turns up on the yacht," Walton said, "we will be able to deal with him!"

"You mean kill him as you did my husband?"

Walton had a jeering smile on his thin face. "Your big problem, young woman, is that you have far too vivid an imagination."

He leaned forward and spoke in the native

tongue to the driver. The man changed his course and she saw that they were indeed heading down to the docks. Her heart dropped at the realization that there was now no hope for her. In spite of her bold front she did not expect Eric to think of the millionaire's yacht as a place where she might be held.

And poor Eric! For all she knew he might be seriously hurt or dead, and all because of her. It seemed she had sealed her fate. A short while ago she had been free and offered help by this young man whom she so respected. Now she was back in the hands of the enemy once more.

The dock was dark and a swift wind had come up. It was the forerunner of a storm. She stood trembling on the dock as the driver left his carriage to find a boat to row them over to the yacht. It took him several minutes and then he waved for them to join him at the dock's edge. His brown face was triumphant as he pointed down to the empty rowboat in the churning waves.

Walton ordered the brown man to go down the ladder to the boat first. Then he pointed the gun at her and said, "Now, you!"

"I can't!" she protested. "I'm afraid!"

"Get down that ladder!"

"I'll fall!" she cried.

"Then you'll drown!" he told her as he threatened her with the gun.

Terrified, she made her way to the wooden ladder on the face of the dock and gingerly placed one foot on a rung. Clinging to the ladder's sides, she gradually let herself down to the swaying boat in the rough harbor waters. She did not dare look down.

She felt the hands of the brown man as he reached up and took hold of her and helped her down into the boat. She lay there terrified. Then Walton came down and sat in the bow while the brown man picked up the oars and began to row them out into the harbor.

The waves grew angrier as they went farther out. She lay still and said nothing. Then she saw the lamps of the yacht loom above them and the golden inscription *SIREN* on her white hull. There was some maneuvering and shouting as the boat was made fast alongside the yacht.

"You first!" Walton said, crouching in the swaying boat at her side.

This time she did not protest. As the yacht dipped down with the movement of the waves she reached up and the hands of the several brown seamen aboard extended to grip her by the arms and drag her up on to the deck.

Walton clambered up on to the yacht's deck next and jabbered in the same foreign tongue to the crew. A man ran ahead of them and unlocked a cabin door. Walton thrust her inside as the little brown seaman touched a match to the wick of a hanging lamp which offered light to the elegantly furnished cabin.

"You'll be comfortable here," Walton told her with a nasty smile. "And in the morning Revene will be here to deal with you as he thinks best."

"This is a mad thing you're doing!" she told him. "You will be made to pay for it!"

"You mustn't worry about that," her captor said with an urbane look on his face.

It suddenly struck her that he had managed all this with great agility. Also, his cane was not in evidence.

She said, "I don't think you're lame at all."

92

His smile was mocking. "I regret I didn't have my cane along. You see, the walking stick conceals a most useful sword. You are right, of course. I'm not lame. I assumed that limp as part of my disguise. Also it gave me an excuse to carry the cane."

She stared at him in consternation. "Your . . . disguise?" Was Walton some criminal? She shook her head, trying to clear it. Of course he was. Probably all the principals in the group were criminals. Paul had thrown in his lot with these desperate men to make a quick fortune. Instead it had brought him an early death!

Outside there was a blaze of lightning and the sound of thunder followed by heavy rain. Her eyes sought out one of the two large portholes and she again witnessed the blue bolt of a lightning flash.

Walton eyed her mockingly. "It would seem we are all to be captives on board tonight. I can't risk going back to shore in this."

"You deserve to drown!" she told him angrily.

"Perhaps, but that doesn't mean I shall," he told her. "And I'll not be able to get your clothes as I promised. So the storm will cause you some inconvenience as well."

She turned her back on him. "I have no wish to talk further with you."

"Nor I with you," he said. "Good night! Tomorrow you will have the unique pleasure of meeting Carl Revene!" There was a menacing undertone in his voice as he told her this.

Then he went out and locked the cabin door behind him. The storm continued and she realized that not only was her head aching terribly but she was utterly exhausted. She saw a decanter of water on a

93

desk and poured herself a drink. Then she threw herself on the wide bed.

So great was her fatigue that she almost at once fell asleep despite the raging storm, which rocked the good-sized yacht like a toy. She lay there in sleep for perhaps an hour when the tossing of the ship brought her awake again.

She sat up in bed listening to the howling wind, aware of the wild motion of the ship. It creaked and groaned as the waves lashed against its hull. Then her eyes wandered to the portholes and she froze in terror as she stared at the second one. For there in the porthole was framed the face of her drowned husband, pale and awful, with seaweed strewn in his hair!

5

She screamed and pressed her hands over her eyes to shut out the horrifying vision. Then, with a shuddering breath that was almost a sob, or another scream, she lowered her hands. The face had vanished from the porthole.

The wind still howled and the yacht swayed at anchor as each board of it seemed to groan with the storm. She lay back on the bed and every so often let her eyes wander to the porthole. It must have been her imagination, she told herself . . . but it had been so hideously *real!*

She fell asleep at last despite her fear and when she woke it was morning. The storm was over and sunshine poured in through the portholes. She got up and found there was a dressing room with water off the main room of the cabin. The place was like a fine hotel suite. She washed and freshened up, then returned to the main room in time to see the door open.

It was Edmund Walton with a breakfast tray for her. His ascetic face showed a thin smile as he put the tray on the desk. "I supervised the preparation of this myself," he said. "I think you will find it all right."

"When can I return to shore?" she asked.

"Not until Revene sees you."

"When will that be?"

"Later this morning," Walton said and started to leave.

She called after him, "What do you hope to gain by this? I know nothing about that briefcase."

"Perhaps a short voyage will help improve your memory," he said. "If not, we must think of some other means."

She sat down to the breakfast in an uncertain mood. She was hungry yet she didn't want to eat. But she finally realized it would be best for her to keep up her strength. To starve herself in rebellion to her capture would only weaken her and make her an easier victim for them.

One of the brown men returned for the tray. He smiled at her and carried it out. She tried to talk with him but he spoke no English. Once again she was left to pace up and down in the cabin and consider her plight. She was as much worried about Eric Simms and what had happened to him as she was about herself. The blow on his head had been a cruel one and she prayed that it had not injured him too badly.

She felt sure he would have found some way to help her if he hadn't been attacked. Just as Ben would have been of some aid, but if the old man they'd found in his studio had told the truth, Ben had been murdered. She gave a tiny shudder. International Ventures was thorough when it came to dealing with its enemies. And at the moment she could only be considered an enemy.

Paul's pale, drowned face at the porthole still haunted her. What did it mean? What had she seen? She went to the porthole nearest her and raising herself on her toes stared out. In the distance she could see the docks and the sprawling white city of Casablanca. Steamships and crafts of all kinds lay at anchor or were tied at the docks.

Everyone assumed that Paul had died in the explosion. But supposing he hadn't. Could it be he had somehow escaped and was still alive? Would that explain the face at the window last night?

He might even be alive and without memory from the shock of the explosion. Hiding out around the docks or on various craft in the harbor. He might even be hidden somewhere on the *Siren,* unaware of who he was or how he'd gotten there. It was almost as frightening to think of him alive in this state as to think of him dead!

If he were alive it could change everything. Especially if his mind had not been damaged. Together they could testify against the criminals operating International Ventures and see that they were properly punished. The very thought of accomplishing this gave her hope!

There were voices outside; then the door opened and Walton came in accompanied by a very tall man in a brown silk suit. The tall man had a hawk face, swarthy skin, bushy black hair with heavy black sideburns, and keen eyes. She did not need to be told that this was Carl Revene, the evil genius of the fraudulent group.

"This is Paul's wife," Walton said. "I leave her in your care, sir."

"Thank you, Walton," Revene said in a languid voice. "I will not need you for a while."

"I'll be forward if you want me," Edmund Walton told him. And to her, he said, "A couple of suitcases of clothing will be here for you in an hour or so."

"I don't want them!" she protested. "I want to leave!"

Revene waved Walton on out and then turned to her with a small smile on his hatchetlike face. "You and I can discuss whether or not you are remaining on board."

"I was brought here a captive," she said.

"Indeed?" he said sardonically as he stood there appraising her with sharp eyes that sent a thrill of fear through her. "Aren't you comfortable here?"

"That's a ridiculous question!"

"Not at all," the tall man said. "I want to help you."

"Then take me back!"

"I'm sorry! That I cannot do," he said with another smile, a smile that had no warmth or pleasantness in it. "You should be content here. I have furnished this yacht more luxuriously than any around."

"I'm a prisoner!"

"It is not urgent that you leave," Revene said, his hypnotic black eyes appraising her. "You need a vacation after Paul's sad death. Say I invited you on board for a few days. You are my guest."

"No!"

"Why not?"

"A friend of mine was violently attacked when I was kidnapped," she told him. "He may be dead, for all I know."

Carl Revene said, "If you are referring to the journalist Eric Simms, he was not seriously injured."

She stared at him, feeling a surge of hope. "How do you know?"

His smile was sinister. "It is my business to know a good many things. Especially about people like

Simms, who make a habit of prying into matters that don't concern them."

She was reasonably sure that the head of International Ventures was telling her the truth. She said, "You know that Paul is dead. I have had enough of all this. I want to return to my family in New York."

Revene's cruel mouth twisted in another smile. "You have a bad habit of jumping to conclusions, my dear. Sit down while I discuss your situation with you in more detail."

"You can't talk me into remaining," she warned him. "You must release me." She sat down in the nearest chair.

He paced up and down before her, turning to glance at her every so often as he made a point. He said, "You were brought here for your own good. During your stay in Casablanca you made some unfortunate friendships, among them Ben Cormier, Eric Simms and Abdul-el-Krem. All people opposed to what my group stands for."

When she said nothing, he went on.

"You think that is my quarrel, not yours. You are wrong. You were married to my most valued assistant," he said. "That could make you a target for our enemies. You are tagged as one of us whether you like it or not."

"I don't like it!" she exclaimed. "And I don't want it!"

He raised a hand to pacify her. "Listen to me! I trusted your husband. But he was not loyal to me or the company. He was dealing on his own and that is why he was killed."

"By you?" she asked.

He shook his head. "No. I did not want Paul dead. Enemies of the people with whom he was dealing killed him. He had not the experience or means of protecting himself that I have. It was a sad mistake on his part."

"So why take me prisoner?"

"For several reasons," Revene said smoothly. "One of them is a briefcase stuffed with the most personal documents dealing with political figures in this part of the world."

"I don't have it," she said. "I've already told Walton that."

"Yet you must know where it is."

"No. I know nothing about it."

"I'm afraid I cannot believe that," the thin man said harshly. "Are you going to be reasonable or not?"

"I can't help you!"

"Won't!" he snapped back.

"I don't think Paul ever had such a briefcase," she told him.

He halted before her, a serious look on his hawk face. "I wish to be your friend."

"You can prove that by releasing me!"

He shook his head. "Not until I get that briefcase."

"Then we're at an impasse!"

He nodded. "I hope you will be comfortable here. You will occupy these quarters, which are mine, and I will take lesser ones. We are sailing for Rabat this afternoon, a port about sixty miles along the coast from here."

She jumped up. "Please!"

"Remember, this is mostly for your own good," he warned her. "Other people are actively seeking that briefcase at this minute. People who would not hesitate to kill you. Utterly ruthless characters to whom your life means nothing!"

"I'd be willing to take my chances," she said.

"I can't allow it. And now if you will excuse me I have some urgent matters to attend to. I will talk with you later." Revene bowed and went out, locking the door after him.

She stood staring at the door and found herself amazed at the kind of man he was. There was no question that he had a hypnotic personality, an authority which made it difficult to refuse any request he might make. He was used to being obeyed and did not doubt that his every command would be carried out. She saw that he was a leader, however ruthless he might be, and she realized this quality was what must have won Paul over.

For all that she knew about him she was shocked to find that she had felt him to be attractive. Physically, he was almost ugly, but the vibrance of his charm came from the keen mind and the scintillating personality. Revene was the sort of man who might have gone far in political life, been a world leader. Instead he had chosen to live on the edge of the law, dealing in all kinds of contraband items, mostly the selling of arms illegally to revolutionaries. As such, he was a threat to the peace of the world.

The day wore on and she moved impatiently about the cabin. One of the Arab sailors brought her a lunch tray. Once again she was faced with the choice of going on a hunger strike or eating the food. She decided she still would do best by taking whatever nourishment was offered her.

As it turned out this was fortunate. When she lifted her teacup from the saucer on the tray she was startled to see scrawled in small black crayon letters in the circle where the cup had rested the message, "Play for time. Help will come! Erase!"

She held up the saucer and read it over and over again, trembling with excitement. So she was not alone on board the yacht! She had a friend who would eventually help her! Again she recalled the pale, phantom face of her supposedly dead husband and once more she had hopes that he might have survived death in the launch explosion. That he might be hidden aboard the *Siren*. If that were so, it was he who had written this message.

She obeyed the instruction to erase the message and finished her tea. At least this unusual communication served to give her new hope. She would follow the advice and try to deal with the menacing Carl Revene until she was rescued. Late in the afternoon there was another development which troubled her.

The cabin door opened and Peter Hall came in breathing heavily and placed two suitcases on the carpet in the middle of the cabin. "Some clothes for you!"

She saw that the bags were indeed hers. And she said, "Did you do the packing?"

He mopped his perspiring brow with a huge handkerchief, then returned the handkerchief to his pants pocket as he glared at her. "No point in your complaining. You're lucky I brought them. I did the best I could."

"You might at least have let Diana pack for me," she said. "Or didn't you want to let her know you were holding me here?"

The small eyes in the large purple face took on an uneasy look. He said, "I packed because I was the only one there to do it."

"Where was Diana?" she asked.

"My wife had an accident," came the cold reply

from Edmund Walton, who had just come into the cabin to join them.

Startled, she told him, "She is not your wife!"

Walton was studying her in a nasty fashion. "Did she tell you that?"

Peter Hall said, "You two can talk this out! I've delivered the suitcases and I'm going!"

Walton told the departing fat man, "I'll join you in a minute. I want to go back to shore before they sail." Then he turned to her again. "I guess we need to have a little chat."

She turned from him. "I want nothing to do with you!"

Walton seized her arm roughly. "You talk too much, Mrs. Cormier. You might wind up dead one day if you don't learn better!"

"Let me go!" She tried to pull away.

He held on to her arm and she reached out with her free hand and struck him across the face. This only resulted in his taking her by the other arm as well. Panting from the exertion of dealing with her, he warned, "Don't go too far with me!"

"You don't dare to really harm me without Revene's consent!"

He said savagely, "I can make you miserable!" And he twisted one of her arms until she cried out.

"Coward!" she sobbed.

"Listen to me," he said in a taut, low voice. "Neither you nor Paul was smart enough to fool the group. Nor was Diana. She told you I wasn't her husband. I suppose she also told you that she was leaving me! Running away!"

"I know nothing about it!"

"I think you do!"

Gale remembered the day in the hotel when the

other girl had gone to meet someone and later had told her that she was planning to get away from Walton and the gang.

She said, "Diana was my friend, but she told me nothing of her plans!"

"You think I believe that?"

"It's true!"

"It doesn't matter," Walton said with a terrifying smile. "No worry about Diana anymore. As I said, she had an accident!"

Tautly, she asked, "What sort of accident?"

"She packed a bag and left the house, intending to meet someone," Walton said. "But a thief saw her alone on the street and followed her."

"A thief?"

"Who else?" Walton asked. "And when she was a good distance from the chateau, in a lonely spot where her cries for help could not be heard, the thief stabbed her and took her purse and bag."

"Oh, no!" Gale cried unhappily.

Walton's smile was grim. "So you see, she didn't get all that far!"

In a half whisper, she asked, "Is she dead?"

"Yes."

She stared at him in horror. Then she cried, "It was no thief, it was you! You knew she was running away from you and you followed her and stabbed her!"

"That is a serious charge," he said, without denying it.

"You're a monster!" she shouted at him and struggled to escape him again, this time freeing one hand.

Walton let out an angry oath and grabbed for her. Instead he caught the front of her low-cut dress and ripped it roughly, revealing her lovely, curved breasts. She lifted her arm in a futile effort to cover her nakedness as Walton drew her close to him, an expression of greedy desire on his thin face.

"I'll have you! Little beast!" he snarled and pressed his thin lips to hers with such vehemence that she felt pain. He held her close as she kept fighting to save herself.

The cabin door flew open and Carl Revene burst in. He crossed to them and grasping Walton by the neck and shoulder pulled him off her and threw him to the cabin floor.

"You fool!" he cried at the cowering Walton.

"She asked for it!" Walton said, still on the floor.

"That's a lie! He attacked me!" she sobbed, pulling the torn shreds of her dress back to cover her bare breasts.

Revene told the man on the floor, "Get up! And get out of my sight! I can't abide fools!"

Walton scrambled up and tried to assume some sort of damaged dignity. He eyed her with hatred. "You'll pay for this!" And to Revene, he added, "I'm going back to Casablanca with Hall in the launch!"

"Go! The sooner you're out of my sight the better it will be for you," Revene told him angrily. And he waited until the crestfallen Walton had slunk out.

The immaculately dressed Revene then turned to her and with his hawk face still clouded with anger, he said, "I trust that I sized this up correctly. That you were the victim!"

Her cheeks crimson, she said, "How can you think anything else?"

"You should learn to avoid arguments with men like Walton," was his advice.

"He's a murderer!" she said unhappily. "I'm sure

of it! He murdered poor Diana because she tried to leave him!"

Revene shrugged. "I have not time to stand here listening to your assumptions. I'm sorry you were disturbed in this manner. I promise it will not happen again."

With this he turned and went out, again locking the cabin. She sank down into the nearby chair and sobbed, partly for herself and partly for Diana.

After a little she opened one of the suitcases which had been hastily packed but did contain a lot of her clothing. She found fresh undergarments and a dark brown gown. Then she placed the bags on a large mahogany case where she could open them and remove items from them with ease.

She had hardly finished this when she heard shouting on deck and the sound of feet padding about. Then from far below, the rumble of the yacht's engines as it was made ready to sail. The cabin door was unlocked and Revene came in.

"You feel better now?" he asked.

Blushing, she said, "Yes."

His sharp eyes were devouring her body. He said, "That dress becomes you. I had not noticed at first, you have a lovely figure."

The reference to her near nudity earlier made her look down. She asked him, "Are you going to let me go?"

"Not yet," he said. "But we are sailing for Rabat. I felt you might like to come out on deck and enjoy the fresh air and sunshine. Also, the harbor and city make an interesting view." Having told her this, he went back out leaving the cabin door open.

She could not restrain her impulse to escape the cabin and followed him out. The little brown men comprising the crew were all busy. An Arab with a huge scar on the left side of his brown face stood at the wheel guiding the sleek white yacht. Revene stood behind him.

Gale remained by the railing on the deck outside her cabin door. She saw the lovely blue of the ocean and the white buildings of the city of Casablanca beginning to move away from them as they headed out of its harbor.

A ferry came by, crossing the harbor with a heavy load of passengers, along with a half-dozen mules, some camels, and two fine dappled horses. She stared down at the upturned faces of the passengers on the much lower ferry as it floated past the yacht. And all at once her throat tightened.

There, near the forefront of the cluster of brown faces, she recognized one. She was certain it was the face of Jiri, the assistant to Abdul-el-Krem. She strained to watch him as the ferry glided by but it all happened too quickly for her to really be certain it was him.

Still, it haunted her! She ran along the deck to catch a last view of the ferry. But it was now well on its way back to the docks. She could not clearly make out anyone aboard it any longer. And the man she had seen had not waved to her or made any sign!

Slowly she moved back to the spot where she had stood before. The yacht was gaining speed now and a cooling wind ruffled her hair and gave some relief from the intense heat. She thought about the incident and could not be sure that it meant anything.

But Jiri was supposed to have died on the launch with Paul and Abdul-el-Krem. Did it mean that the three had not really died in the explosion? That all three were alive and had gone underground, taking with them the briefcase of important papers which Carl Revene was so desperate to get!

She dared not let her hopes build on this theory, but this would mean that Paul was alive and somehow this nightmare in which she found herself would be satisfactorily cleared up. But there was this small glimmer of encouragement which she could not deny. The message on the saucer had advised her to play along for time. This was what she must do.

Now the shore of Casablanca faded in the distance. They were out of the harbor and moving swiftly in the ocean water. She was standing by the railing outside her cabin again when Revene joined her. His manner was more friendly than it had been.

He said, "I apologize for Walton. He is a difficult person to control."

"He practically boasted that he murdered his companion, Diana!"

Revene shrugged. "I do not know."

Unhappily, she went on, "Paul introduced them to me. But I cannot believe that he approved of a man like Walton. He must have known of his cold cruelty."

"Your husband was a competent executive," the man at her side said. "It is quite possible that he would make an effort to get along with someone whom he did not approve because it would be for the benefit of International Ventures."

"That had to be it," she agreed. "Paul may have had some faults but that sort of violence was never one of them."

Revene nodded. "I had great respect for your late husband's talents."

"Then why take me on this cruise against my will?"

He showed an expression of wry amusement. "Must we always come back to that?"

"Yes."

"You will enjoy Rabat. It is not a long journey and it will give us a chance to know each other better."

"I consider myself to be kidnapped."

"Think what you like," he said easily. "It does not alter the facts."

"The fact is I am your prisoner."

He ignored this and said, "We will have a fine feast tonight and entertainment in your honor. We managed to pick up several dancing girls in Casablanca. They will entertain us."

"There are other women aboard this ship?"

"Most certainly," he said, his eyes twinkling. "Did you think you had the honor of being the only lady aboard? I see I must explain. It is my way of celebrating my return to the yacht and to the Middle East. Tonight we will have a feast on board, and these dancing girls will perform."

"Where are they now?"

"In one of the small cabins," he said. "It is not wise to allow them to move about the ship as you are allowed to do now that we have left shore."

"I see," she said. "You think their presence would upset the crew?"

"I know it is better this way," Revene said. "I have given you my cabin and the captain has in turn offered his quarters to me. I invite you to join me there this evening for dinner."

She recalled the message on the saucer advising her to cooperate for a little. So she said, "Very well. But unless I'm given my freedom when we dock at

Rabat I will consider that you've broken faith with me!"

"My object is to protect you," the man in the silken suit said.

"I prefer to look after my own protection."

"Perhaps," he said. "But you may not know what is best for you. The whole problem would be simplified if you could only recall what became of that briefcase."

Her eyes met his. "That is what it is all about, isn't it? The briefcase is what you want."

His hawk face was void of expression as he replied, "It would make things a great deal easier."

He left her to think about this. She really tried to recall when and where she'd seen Paul with this important briefcase, and she couldn't. After a little she went back inside and slept for a while. It was a restless sleep troubled by dreams, and in these weird nightmares she again saw Paul's white face pressed against the porthole. She awoke from this dream weltered in perspiration.

Sitting up in bed she began to wonder if it had been a dream the first time, and she knew that it hadn't. She forced herself to think of other things and to wash and dress for her dinner with Revene. Fortunately in packing her clothing, Peter Hall had included a smart black gown which had ruffled layers of skirt and an interesting, low-cut neckline. She decided to wear this in an effort to charm Revene and win his support.

He came to the door of the cabin at sundown. He had also changed and was wearing a linen suit of faultless white. When he saw her, his usually stern face relaxed and he actually smiled. "You present a most pretty picture, my dear!"

"And you are surely elegant!" was her reply.

"Thank you," he said. And offering her his arm, he asked, "May I escort you to the captain's cabin where the table is prepared for us?"

When they reached the smaller cabin she saw it was also finished in the same antique mahogany. A white-clothed table with flowers and lighted candles was set with fine china, glass, and silverware. The setting was as perfect as any she had known.

Revene helped her into her chair and told her, "We will be in Rabat tomorrow. It is smaller than Casablanca and once was a haunt for pirates."

She smiled across the table at him as he sat opposite her. "What about today?"

He returned her smile. "I'm the only pirate left who pays the city regular calls."

"Would you have been angry if I said that?"

His black eyes twinkled. "Yes."

He rang a bell on the table beside him and at once a middle-aged, bewhiskered man in turban, yellow tunic, and red moorish trousers appeared to wait on them. He was an excellent waiter and the food was as good as any Gale had enjoyed since arriving in Morocco. For a little she almost forgot that she was a helpless widow, the captive of her dinner partner.

He poured out wine and told her, "This is a generally good vintage. It is a *Sidi Lardi.*"

She sipped it and found it full-bodied and excellent. "Very good," she said.

"My chef specializes in Lemon Chicken," Revene said. "So that shall be the main course tonight."

Gale could find no fault with the soup or the main course. The ocean air had made her hungry and she tried a little of all the side dishes offered. The

111

dessert pastries were rich, as was the coffee that ended the feast.

They sat staring at each other after the table was cleared, finishing the wine in the romantic candlelight. She had to admit reluctantly that for all she believed Revene to be a villain, he had a definite charm.

Her face must have betrayed her thoughts, for he said, "You do not find this so bad?"

"In other conditions it would be a charming experience," she admitted.

He smiled at her and said, "Try to think of it in that way."

"You amaze me," she told him.

"Kindly explain."

She sighed. "You both attract and repel me. I find you interesting and likable and yet I'm all the while conscious that you are ruthless."

He arched an eyebrow. "Is that not a desirable combination to attract a woman?"

"I'm very much afraid it is."

He laughed lightly. "You have no reason to be afraid of me. I admire rare beauty too much to harm you."

She studied the sharp face in the glow of the candles and asked, "Will you tell me something?"

"It depends."

"Are you married?"

He shook his head. "No. Why do you ask?"

"Men of your type often are," she told him. "I do not see how you can have escaped so far."

"I have a mistress," he said bluntly. "She would like me to marry her. She has a titled husband and would divorce him if I undertook to offer her marriage."

"But you prefer to be free?"

"Yes. Perhaps that means I do not love her enough," the swarthy man said.

"I'd say it is because you love your shady business deals more," Gale suggested.

He shrugged. "Paul had no other dedication but our business until he met you and married you."

She gave him a rueful look. "I think that even then I took second place."

"Really?" Revene said. "I'm sorry."

"So was I," she said, with a sigh. "So it is only natural that I wish to go back to New York and forget all about my short marriage and the business which cost Paul his life."

"His own double-dealing did that," the man replied. "He staked too much on Abdul-el-Krem!"

She gave him a surprised look. "You can't forgive him for that!"

"He was my most trusted aide," Revene said. "It was a huge setback to me. Especially the loss of the briefcase."

"I sometimes wonder if that briefcase ever existed!"

"I can promise you that it did," Revene said. "And now I think it is time for the entertainment." He rose from the table and helped her out of her chair.

She asked him, "Where is the dancing to take place?"

"On the rear deck. They will have made it ready. There will be chairs set out behind the bridge for us."

A velvet darkness had come down over the blue ocean and the yacht was moving along at a slower speed. The sky was studded with stars and the rear deck of the boat had torches set out at intervals to light it completely in a yellow glow. As they went up and took their places above, she saw the squatted forms of the crew outlined against the glow. All seemed to have gathered on deck. The musicians had struck up their stringed instruments and drums. But the dancers had not yet put in an appearance.

Revene, in a chair beside her, had lit a cigar. She could see its tip glow in the darkness. He leaned toward her and said, "Are you familiar with our Moroccan dancing?"

"No," she said.

"You might call it belly-dancing," he said. "It is a truly erotic art. The Moorish people set high prices on their dancing girls."

"I'm sure they must."

"It is not always possible to have girls perform outside the harem," he went on. "But these young women have long ago discarded their virtue. So they are for hire for entertainments like this."

"I see," she said quietly.

He puffed on his cigar and the end glowed more clearly. "Later, they may entertain those of the crew who wish to pay their fee in other ways. I do not oppose this. It keeps the men in good spirits. In respectable amusement places women are not permitted to dance. Boys of a certain age perform the erotic dances."

"It is a much different culture," Gale observed.

"Definitely," he said. "Great chiefs keep gifted dancers in their harems as symbols of wealth and prestige. When there is some favor wished it is not unknown for a chief to make a gift to the Sultan of his finest dancer."

The drums and guitars sounded out more loudly

114

and three girls emerged into the light. They carried themselves well. The first dancer burst out on the floor in a swirl of veils and glittering anklets.

Her body was as beautiful as any Gale had ever seen. The dancer began to undulate to the music. She swayed and arched and drooped, then in a flash arched again. The head and neck and hips were motionless while the shoulders and breasts undulated. Then the hips and stomach rotated as if there were nothing but muscles beneath the silky brown skin!

Now one of the dancers began to tear off her diaphanous veils, one after the other, and at the same time alternately worked her fingers tenderly over her body. As the music grew wilder she arched and bent backward until her loose black hair swept the deck! Gracefully she became erect once again, her hips thrust forward and her head thrown back, and her teeth bared! She bent her head on her breast and her body became entirely still, except for her small and perfect navel rotating as if a thing apart. Then her head came up and her face took on a sultry expression, while her lips curled in a challenge!

The tension had built to a climax. There was a clash of cymbals and the girl fell limp to the floor in an orgasmic climax. There were a few seconds of hushed silence before the approving cries and applause rang out in the night. The girl rose, gave a brief inclination of her head to acknowledge the applause and then swirled out of sight.

Gale was so much taken up with the erotic performance that she had not realized that Revene had moved closer to her and now his arm was around her.

"Isn't that marvelous?" he asked her.

Uneasily, she said, "Yes. It was very good."

He made no attempt to withdraw his hand as the music began again. He told her, "There will be other more sensual dancing to come!"

She rose, thus escaping his arm, and said, "I have seen enough. I'm rather sleepy after my huge dinner. If you don't mind I'll retire now."

He was on his feet at once. "I'll see you to your cabin."

"No," she said. "You mustn't miss any of the performance on my account. I can find my way easily." And she left him quickly, giving him no chance to argue. The sensual dance had aroused her more than she would have dreamed. I must remember the man is a monster, she told herself, I must keep on my guard. He's a killer, and I am his captive. . . . She shuddered, but it was not with fear.

6

Gale, in a pink silk nightgown with thin shoulder straps, stood by the open porthole and listened to the continuing pounding of the drums and knew the erotic dancing was still going on. She had been in her cabin for almost a half hour and had changed into her night things. The throbbing music and the sounds of castanets and occasional cries of laughter made her tremble slightly in remembrance of the sensual exhibition which she had so recently seen.

She closed the porthole and moved slowly toward the bed. She was about to put out the candle flame, which offered the only lighting, when she heard a key turn in the cabin door. Protectively, she lifted her hands to cover her breasts so visible through the thin silken nightgown.

The door opened and Revene entered in a long black robe tied at his waist by a crimson cord. He closed and locked the door behind him and then stood looking at her.

"How dare you come in here this way!" she said, a tremor in her voice.

His sharp black eyes met hers. In a low voice, he said, "You must have known I would come!"

"No!" She protested, but it was true that she had thought of it.

"Your blood cannot be so cold as not to respond to that music?"

"Please leave!" she begged him.

"No!"

"If you touch me I shall despise you!" she warned him.

He laughed. "I fear I must risk that." The music from the deck went on as he moved slowly toward her.

She took a step back and now she was at the side of the bed with no distance to retreat. Trembling, she whispered, "You must not!"

He reached out and slipped the thin silken straps over her soft, satiny shoulders. Then he seized the gown at the waist and pulled it down slowly over her rosy-nippled breasts, her firm, flat stomach, the golden-red hair of her pubic area, to reveal her slim, straight legs.

All the while his eyes were staring into hers so that she found herself making no struggle against his gentle revealment of her. Her breathing was strained and she was aware of a return of the sensual thrill which she had experienced while watching the shapely dancers.

He whispered, "You are too beautiful!" And at the same moment he untied the red cord and discarded the black robe to reveal his nude body. He was muscled and hairy as she had expected and his maleness was welling up, ready to enter her! He lifted her onto the bed and in a moment he was on her and their bodies had met in ultimate intimacy!

Gale was lost in the ardent lovemaking. He stilled any protests she made by placing his lips over hers. And at last she gave way to her pent-up hunger and lost herself in the peak moments of their togetherness.

Now it was over and they lay naked side by side. Gale realized the music from the deck had ended and all was silence. She turned on her pillow to look at him and say, "So, great gentleman that you are, you raped me!"

He glanced at her, his hawk face weary as he sighed, "I suppose that is technically so."

"I told you I would despise you!"

He raised himself on an elbow and gazed down at her with a tender smile. "No words that you said could discourage me. I have been drunk with your beauty since I first saw you."

She said, "I mean nothing to you! Just another female body to add to your conquests."

"You're wrong," Revene said earnestly. "If I had wanted only a body I could have had that beautiful dancer. All three of them if I so wished."

"Why didn't you?" she demanded with contempt. And tears welling in her eyes, she turned away from him.

He bent and kissed her on the breasts and then on the temple. He smoothed her golden-red hair and said, "You will not believe this. But I have fallen in love with you. I want to marry you. That is something I have never told any woman before."

She glanced at him with a wry expression. "And all you ask from me is that I give you the missing briefcase."

Revene was silent for a moment. Then he said, "You are right. I do want that."

"Is that why you made love to me?"

He frowned. "No. Of course not."

"If so, it is a great joke on us both since I haven't the briefcase."

"But you know where it is."

"You are wrong," she said.

"And you are stubborn," he told her. "But let us forget the briefcase for a moment. Let us talk about us. Will you marry me?"

She stared up at him. "Become a pirate's wife?"

"There are worse things," Revene said. "I understand that Blackbeard and Morgan were admirable husbands."

"I'd rather not risk it," she said.

"I see I will have to prove myself worthy of you," he told her.

"You've picked a very poor way to begin," was her reply.

"Tell me you didn't enjoy our little bout?" he challenged her.

Her cheeks crimsoned and she said, "I'm not proud of the moment."

"That is where we differ," he said, kissing her on the lips. "I am!"

She was about to reply to this when there was a loud knocking on the cabin door. Revene turned to call out and ask what was wanted. A reply came in Arabic. He at once left the bed and donned his black robe. As he secured the red tie around it, he told her, "Business! But I will return soon."

Gale felt it a kindly act of fate that had taken him away. She found her nightgown and put it on and then donned a robe over it. Thus clad, she ventured on deck to see what was going on. She was startled to see that another craft, without any lights, had pulled up alongside the yacht. And this other craft had been made fast to the sleek white *Siren* with heavy ropes.

There was confusion on the rear deck as members of the yacht's crew lugged out heavy wooden boxes and passed them over to the crew of the other ship. Revene stood above them on the upper deck, shouting out commands and directing the transfer of cargo.

She watched from her hiding place and estimated that at least three dozen of the heavy wooden crates were exchanged. She assumed they contained arms of some sort. Then she saw Revene go down and jump nimbly over to the other craft where he was greeted by a man in a brown turban. They went below, presumably to discuss the transaction.

Feeling reasonably sure that Revene would not bother her again in the night she returned to her cabin and tried to sleep. The rumpled bed still bore the odor of Revene's body, not so unpleasant as disturbing—a reminder of those lust-filled moments of such a short time ago. She hated herself for not battling him more and at the same time knew that she had found much about him that was fascinating. Were he not known to be a criminal, she might have found herself falling in love with him. Surely he was not the worst of the group he led!

At last, despite the heat and her upset state, she fell asleep. It was indicative of her turn of mind that she dreamt of Revene. She relived their moments of passion in her dream and woke up with a small, moaning cry! The cabin was shrouded in darkness.

And then she heard the floorboard creak. The sound came from the area beyond the foot of her bed. She sat up and strained to see if there was anyone there. And in the next instant there was a movement in the shadows and she was able to make out a dark figure coming toward her. As the figure came near, she again saw the pale, white face of Paul!

Paul's dark, sunken eyes and the ghastly pallor of his features made him monstrous. As she screamed in terror he reached out for her. She was aware of a sweet odor before his hand closed over her mouth and nose. She tried to fight him off and breathe. But when she fought for breath it was this phantom perfume which filled her nostrils!

She felt herself drift off into the nightmare world again. It seemed that strong arms had picked her up and she was being carried like a child. After this she had the vague awareness of descending, going down a seemingly endless distance. Of dropping into a black nothingness. But every so often there was a jarring motion to spoil the dream. She opened her eyes and saw that dawn was breaking and that she was stretched out in the bottom of a small rowboat.

She heard the rhythm of oars moving and felt the motion of waves. Getting up on an elbow she glanced behind her and her lovely mouth gaped as she saw that it was Eric Simms at the oars. Eric, clad only in rough trousers and a shirt open at the neck.

"Eric!" she cried.

"Right!" the young Britisher smiled. "Don't be afraid. It is all right!"

"How did I get here?"

"Long story," he said as he continued to pull on the oars.

She sat up and saw that someone had placed her robe on her over her nightgown. And in the distance she could see the shore and a familiar cluster of white houses. There were boats by the shore but the ocean around them seemed empty.

She said, "I woke up and saw Paul's ghost! That's all I remember."

"Somebody on board helped you," Eric said, as he strained on. "You were drugged so you wouldn't cry out and then placed in a boat. A boat tied to the rear of the yacht. I was told exactly where I would

122

find you. And sure enough, when I reached the yacht you were in the small boat."

"Who told you where to find me?"

"I don't know," he admitted. "The message came to me after I recovered in Casablanca. It was written on rough paper and unsigned. It told me I'd find you in a boat tied to a yacht which would be anchored a distance from the shore at Rabat."

"And you came to Rabat to find me?"

"Yes."

"It's too fantastic," she said, pushing some golden-red hair away from her face.

Eric nodded grimly. "I took a wild chance rowing out there in the darkness. Once I located the yacht it was easy. Then I started back. We're almost at shore now."

"Was there another boat alongside the *Siren*?" she asked.

"No."

"There was earlier. They transferred cargo."

"No doubt," Eric said. "But that was all over before I arrived. The *Siren* was lying at anchor. I assume they intend to come on in to Rabat some time after dawn."

"Revene will be surprised to find me gone."

"So Revene is aboard. Did he kidnap you?"

"No," she said. "It was Walton and that Peter Hall. So much has happened."

He worked a little less earnestly at the oars as they neared the docks. He said, "I knew when I came to that you were in serious trouble. When I received the message I knew where to find you."

"And you came all the way to Rabat!" she said.

"I'd go a good deal farther than that to help you," he said most gallantly.

They reached the dock and he tied the boat up

and helped her up a wooden ladder to the dock's surface. There he spoke to a native who ran ahead to get them a carriage.

"I'm taking you to the St. George Hotel," Eric said.

She indicated her unlikely garb and said, "In this?"

He laughed. "They won't ask any questions. They expect the worst from Western newspapermen. Especially Britishers!"

The turbanned old man came running back for his reward of several pennies with the carriage on his heels. They got in the vehicle and were driven to the stately hotel. She felt her cheeks crimson as she noticed the surprised stares of the hotel's other European customers as Eric led her to the elevator. He left her in the room, and went out to shop for clothing for her.

Still dazed by her good fortune and also feeling some of the aftereffects of her drugging she rang for a maid. She had a large tin bath installed in her room and was soon indulging in the luxury of a warm bath. After that she lay down for a little and by the time Eric returned with several bundles of clothing for her, she was much rested.

His eyes twinkled as he said, "I had the girl in the city's one large store gather all these things up for me. I just told her your dimensions and asked her to provide me with what she'd expect you to need."

She smiled and took the packages. "I think you've overdone it. You must let me repay you—though heaven knows when that will be!"

"Don't worry on my account," he said. "The newspaper will take care of it. And I'm here to do a story on Revene and his operations. There's no question you can help me."

The clothes he had selected turned out to be excellent. She was impressed by the good taste of the girl, whoever she might be. Wearing a simple blue dress and wide-brimmed hat to match she met the young reporter in the downstairs restaurant of the hotel. On a balcony open to the sun and air, they had a fine view of the harbor and ocean as they dined.

Eric, back in a trim linen suit, told her, "The *Siren* has not docked here yet. I don't know why."

"I've surely been missed by this time."

"Without a doubt," he agreed.

She suggested, "Perhaps he had a rendezvous with another boat and more cargo to dispose of."

Eric's pleasant face registered agreement. "You have probably hit it directly on the head. I'm sure the yacht left Casablanca loaded with munitions."

She sat back with a sigh. "I keep wondering who it was sent you the note and then placed me in the boat where you could find me."

"Someone who wanted to help you."

"Or even a score against Revene."

"That is also a possibility," he agreed.

"Revene and Walton had a bitter argument."

"About what?"

She felt her cheeks crimson. "About me. Walton tried to attack me."

Eric looked angry. "That sounds like him. You know the word is around Morocco that he murdered that girl, Diana."

"He tried to frighten me by telling me that," she said.

"Nice character," Eric said grimly.

"After the quarrel, Walton left and returned to Casablanca," she said.

"So he could have sent the note." He paused. "In that case he must have had an accomplice on board whom he could trust to drug you and place you in the boat."

"I know," Gale said. "But I can't imagine who. I only recall waking up and seeing Paul's face staring at me! A ghostly Paul, so white and tortured-looking!"

"Perhaps the drug they gave you or a bad dream," he said.

"I don't think it could be either," she worried. "I saw the same phantom face of Paul before. And on the *Siren*."

Eric frowned. "Does that mean you think your husband may still be alive?"

"I'm not sure," she said in an anguished tone. "I did see the face twice, at two distinct times. And I also thought I saw that man Jiri, Abdul-el-Krem's assistant, on a ferry in Casablanca harbor. He was supposed to have died in the explosion, you remember."

"Most brown men in a fez look alike," he warned her.

"I think not in this case. Jiri had strong, interesting features. It seemed very like him."

Eric Simms scowled down at his plate. "There were no complete bodies taken out of the water." His eyes met hers soberly. "We might have been tricked. They may never have boarded that ill-fated launch. Others could have been sent in their place while your husband and the two remained in hiding."

Her eyes widened. "You think it possible?"

"Anything is possible in this crazy place," Eric told her. "We have a corrupt Sultan trying to hang on to his throne, and three or four rival groups arming themselves to get rid of him, and war with the others. No matter what happens, this poor country is in for a period of chaos. The French will have to step in and take over."

She wasn't really listening. Suppose Paul were still alive? "But he looked *dead*," she said aloud. "Paul, I mean. I didn't think it was him, I thought it was his ghost."

"Why?"

She hesitated. "Because he didn't seem normal! He didn't speak. His eyes were sunken and his face had a strange pallor. Oh! And there was seaweed in his hair, as if he'd just come up out of the ocean."

"That does sound rather horrid," the young man said, gazing at her with sympathy.

She gave him a troubled look. "Do you believe in ghosts?"

"Not generally," he admitted.

"I didn't until all this began," she said.

"I can't blame you for being shaken by what has gone on," he said. "But I'll keep an open mind on the subject for a little."

"The thing they all seem to want is a briefcase which contained important papers relating to Revene's deals."

He nodded. "No doubt they're afraid of its getting into the wrong hands. Probably Paul had it with him when the launch blew up. In that case it is gone for all time."

"They claim they had spies watching Paul, and he was not carrying it when he boarded the launch."

Eric said, "In that case he might have hidden it somewhere."

"Not at the chateau," she said. "Walton and the others searched it carefully."

"Perhaps when we get back to Casablanca you will think of someplace it might be," the reporter said.

She stared at him. "Are you also interested in it?"

"Yes. My paper could do with some of that information."

"I see," she said. It worried her to know this and wonder if that were his chief interest in helping her. She thought not. Eric had always shown himself to be her friend.

"You've met Revene," he said.

Her cheeks burned a little as she said quietly, "Yes."

"What do you think of him?"

"He's very different from what I expected."

Eric had a look of tired amusement on his tanned face. "You were impressed by him?"

"I suppose so. A little."

"Women always are."

She said, "He has charm. He treated me well enough for the most part. But I was his prisoner. I had to keep reminding myself of that."

"And he'll try to capture you again if he believes you can produce that briefcase."

"I know," she said.

"Revene is not handsome, but there is something about him," Eric went on. "He was doing well in England before he became overly ambitious and started International Ventures. Since then he has grown fabulously rich and has been mixed up in the most dastardly projects."

"Running illegal arms here being one of them," she said.

"Yes. He is bound to get into serious trouble. Two or three world powers now have agents trying to prevent his schemes."

"Do you think they'll succeed?"

"I'm not sure," Eric admitted. "Knowing the man as I do, I'd say he is more likely to die at the hands of some assassin. He has double-crossed so many of these desperate people in deals. Sooner or later one of them will look for revenge."

She said, "He talks like a gentleman and much of the time acts like one."

Eric gave her a questioning look. "Did he try to force himself on you?"

"I'd hardly say that," she replied with caution. For she knew that in that passionate interlude with Revene she had at least been a somewhat willing partner. It stunned her to realize this now but it was true.

Eric seemed to note uneasiness and changed the subject by saying, "When you return to Casablanca you cannot live at the chateau."

"No."

"I suggest the Empress Hotel, named in honor of our Queen," he said with a wry smile. "Not quite up to royal standards, but I have rooms there and I can keep an eye on you."

"I'd like to sail back to New York as soon as possible," she told him.

"I don't blame you for that. You'll be a lot safer out of here," he said.

"What about you?" she asked.

He raised his eyebrows. "Where Revene goes, I go. He is my assignment at the moment and I'm afraid our fates are tied together."

"I don't envy you," she said. "And I'm causing you to sidetrack, since I have you running from him to help me."

"I can get back on the job as soon as you're safely on the way to America," the young reporter said.

"You have become my best friend," she told him. "I shall miss you. I hope I shall see you again."

"As soon as I finish with Revene I will visit you in New York," he said. "It is a promise."

"I'll hold you to it," she said.

He rose from the table and casually glanced over the balcony wall. Then he suddenly took a step back and in a low voice warned her, "Revene is here. I saw him just now coming into the hotel lobby."

She was at once in a panic. "He's after me! What shall I do?"

"Don't lose your head," Eric said, going to her and placing an arm around her. "You're registered here under another name. And tonight we'll take the train to Casablanca."

"When does it leave?"

"Around ten," he said. "In the meantime it will be best if you keep to your room. Revene will likely have his spies searching for you everywhere."

"I fully expect it," she said, worried.

"I don't think we'd better dare the lobby or the front stairway," he said. "We'll find the rear stairs and go up to your room that way."

She fought to keep calm and told him, "I don't know what I'd do without you."

"Probably manage just as well," he said cheerfully.

But she knew this was not so.

She waited in her room. Eric did not join her as soon as she'd expected. As the time dragged on, she became nearly frantic.

Just knowing that Revene had arrived and was in the hotel made her position there terribly dangerous. She had an idea the millionaire would use his spies to search the building for her. Using a false name would be small protection. Sooner or later he would get a line on her.

Eric returned at dinner time and told her, "The yacht is at the docks. And there are rumors along the waterfront that she turned over two cargoes of munitions at sea."

"They likely did," she agreed.

"I passed Revene in the lobby," he told her. "He seemed to be studying everyone who came and went. There's no question he's looking for you. But I have the tickets for our night train and we can leave in a couple of hours."

She gave a tiny shudder. "I won't believe it until I'm on the train!"

"You will be," he said, looking at her fondly. "Don't worry."

She looked up at him. "How can I ever repay you for all the risks you've taken for me?"

"I'm enjoying it," he said. And then taking her in his arms, he added, "And also, I happen to be in love with you."

"Eric!" she said softly.

He kissed her into silence. "We cannot talk of it yet, but the day will come," he promised.

Dusk came and she and Eric had a candlelit dinner in her room. The fare was simple but she had never enjoyed a meal more. Eric told her about himself, his years of school and college in England and finally his undertaking of a journalistic career. She was impressed by his modesty and kindness. And it awed her to think that he was in love with her.

The second declaration of love she'd had within a period of twenty-four hours. Revene's had been very different, but somehow she felt it had been none the less sincere. Revene was cruel and arrogant but he had shown himself to have another side with her. She could not help being somewhat flustered by the knowledge that he'd asked her to be his wife.

Darkness came and Eric took the heavy gold watch from his vest pocket and consulted it. "Time to leave," he said.

"Which way?" she asked.

"I'm afraid it will have to be the rear stairway again," he said. "It's too dangerous the other way."

"Whatever you think," she said.

They left the room, with Eric carrying a bag with his own things and a suitcase he'd loaned her for the clothing which he'd bought her. They waited until the hallway seemed empty before going down all the way to the ground floor. Then they hurried to the street where the carriages for hire stood in line.

Eric had settled their account with the hotel earlier and they used a side door to get to the waiting carriages. As they reached the street she rushed along after Eric, who by arrangement between them took the lead, and she almost ran into the Arab with the scarred face whom she had seen at the wheel of the *Siren*.

The man stared at her a moment and then went on. She was sure he had recognized her.

She ran to catch up with Eric and gasped out, "Someone saw me. A sailor from the yacht."

He eyed her worriedly. "You're sure?"

"Yes. And he rushed into the hotel."

"We'd better not lose any time then," Eric said. "Get into the carriage."

She heard him give the Arab driver some sharp instructions in the native tongue. Then Eric sat with her as the carriage started off quickly.

"I hope there's no trouble," she said.

"We'll have to take our chances," Eric said, looking back at the hotel. "I told the driver to take an indirect route. They may not realize we are heading for the train."

"And we may lose them!"

"It all depends on how soon that fellow finds Revene or one of the others and tells them he saw you. They'll likely try to follow."

The turbanned driver urged his ancient horse on and the wheels of the old carriage creaked over the cobblestoned back streets. The carriage lurched every now and then as it reached a bad spot in the street surface. Lights showed in occasional windows and torches burned in front of small bazaars. Pedestrians, startled at the speed of the carriage, quickly moved out of the way.

Eric glanced behind again and announced, "I think we are being followed!" And he leaned forward and shouted something to the driver again.

Gale was now looking behind and she could clearly see another carriage not too far distant. She said, "It may not be Revene."

"It's more likely to be than not," Eric said, his face drained of color.

"What now?"

"I've asked the driver to hurry and try a new tactic," Eric said. Then he leaned against the back of the seat and taking a revolver from his inner pocket steadied it on his arm as best he could and fired back at the pursuing carriage.

The carriage at once slowed and she exclaimed, "Either you've scared the driver or hit someone!"

He was watching, his weapon still in hand. He said, "I'd say the odds are I've scared the driver."

Now their own driver took an unexpected turn and drove down a steep, very dark side street which was little more than an alley. A woman screamed and ran, holding her baby in her arms as she pressed against a building to avoid being run down. A dog barked wildly and then scampered at the last moment. An old man dropped some sticks of wood and jumped to get out of their way as he howled imprecations at them in Arabic!

"Too bad to upset the citizenry," Eric said. "But we have no choice!"

They came out on another street, the trailing carriage lost far behind them. The ride to the railway station took only a few more minutes. Then Eric was stuffing some coins in the driver's hand and leading Gale in the direction of the station.

The station was dirty, shabby, and filled with a motley crowd waiting for various trains. They were so miserable they barely looked at newcomers and so she and Eric escaped arousing much attention. Eric collared a lazy-looking railway official and with some difficulty extracted the information that their train was on track number three and they could board it.

Within a few minutes they had picked their way across the tracks to the Casablanca train, which looked as small and unimpressive as the station had. A trainman came to greet them and they were shown into a compartment. Eric locked the door.

After he'd put their bags on the rack above he slumped down in the wooden seat opposite her and said, "Well, that was some ride!"

"Yes," she said with a sigh. "Will he find us here?"

"Sooner or later he'll think of the Casablanca train. We can only hope it will be much later."

"I agree," she said.

"Sorry the train isn't more comfortable," he said. "This is one of the better compartments."

"I can manage just so long as the train gets under way," she said.

He produced his pocket watch again. "We ought to be on our way in about ten minutes."

She sighed again. "I wonder if that shot hit anyone."

"I can't think that it did," he said. "The only one I'd worry about would be the driver. He'd be innocent of what they were using him for."

"I know," she said. Strange, she was wondering if the bullet by chance had hit Revene. And thinking what a bit of irony it would be if he should die that way.

The minutes ticked by slowly. The train began to fill with people. A long, sullen parade of men in turbans and women in veils. Some of the women clutched babies in their arms and had other children tagging after them. The men usually carried their belongings in makeshift bags.

Several times, people tried the compartment door and peered angrily through the glass partition shielding it to register protests. Eric signaled to them that the compartment was reserved and told her, "Don't look at them. They'll go away."

And they did. The train moved a little and she thought they were leaving at last. But then after going only the length of a car, it halted with a giant puff of steam. She and Eric exchanged worried glances.

She said, "What now?"

"I don't know," he replied, going to the window and peering out into the darkness. After a moment he said, "I don't see a thing."

He'd barely spoken the words when she heard loud shouts from the other tracks and going to the

135

window caught a glimpse of Revene racing toward the train with a torch in hand to guide his way!

"Look!" she cried.

The train gave another jolt and started moving and this time kept on moving, gaining speed. Eric was jubilant. "We've left them behind! They haven't a hope! We managed to get away just in the nick of time!"

She slumped down in the seat again, her face pale. "I don't believe it!" she gasped.

Eric smiled at her. "In my business you get used to these narrow escapes."

"I don't think I ever shall," she told him.

"You've been wonderful!" was his tribute. "You have plenty of courage."

"I'm beginning to lose my reserve," she warned him.

"It'll be all right now. He can't get another train out of Rabat until the morning. And there's no way he can get to Casablanca quicker than this train."

"How long will it take?"

"Six or seven hours," the young reporter said. "They make a lot of stops at places along the way that are hardly more than a house or two in desert country. And the roadbed is bad, and occasionally there are delays."

She eyed him ruefully. "In other words we are not on the luxurious and speedy Orient Express."

He laughed. "These people have never even heard of the Orient Express."

They settled down on the hard wooden benches and tried to nap a little. But she was not as successful as Eric. Long after he was sound asleep she was still awake. The uncomfortable seat and the motion of the train kept her awake. She was also filled with a confusion of thoughts.

The railway conductor came by and she opened the door and passed him their tickets. He punched them and returned them to her without a word. A short time later they made the first of the many stops. After a while it struck her that the train must go only about ten miles before halting somewhere else. It was discouraging, especially as the compartment was now cold.

She had no idea how many were still on the train. But she guessed that a good many had left along the way.

Suddenly the train halted again. But this time it came to such a violent stop that it jolted her almost off her seat, and a confused Eric came awake on the floor, where he'd fallen. Sleepily and angrily, he got up demanding, "What are they trying to do, disable us all?"

7

Gale stood up and peered out the train window into the vast darkness. She said, "We seem to be at the end of nowhere!"

Eric was now on his feet and he told her, "It may be trouble with the tracks. It happens often enough!"

"Will it take long to fix them?"

"Hard to say," he replied. "I'm going up ahead to take a look. You lock yourself in here and don't let anyone in until I return! Not anyone!"

"I won't," she promised.

Eric gave her a grim smile and a quick kiss on the cheek. "It seems ours is not to be an easy journey," he said, and unlocked the compartment door and went out.

She locked the door after him and then went to the window again to glance out. She could hear frightened shouts from up at the front of the train where Eric had gone and, suddenly, mixed with the cries a series of rifle shots. She froze with terror. Certainly this was no ordinary rail breakdown. More likely bandits of some sort had blocked the train's passage and were now pillaging it!

And what of Eric? He had gone forward to the heart of the melee! Full of fear for him, she turned, thinking to open the door and perhaps follow him. But before she could make up her mind the corridor outside was filled with robed tribesmen in their colorful outfits and carrying rifles. One ugly bearded fellow smashed the butt of his rifle through the glass partition next to the compartment door and reached in and unlocked the door!

Gale screamed as the black-bearded tribesman came in after her. She backed to the window and tried to hold him off but it was useless. Once again she found herself being taken prisoner. Cruel hands bound her hands and feet and someone stuffed a filthy cloth in her mouth and then tied it tightly to gag and almost suffocate her! She fainted as she was carried out of the compartment and off the train.

The cool desert wind in her face brought her around and she realized she was slung across the front of a saddle like a sack. The horse was moving briskly through the darkness and its rider had a hand placed on her back to make sure that she didn't tumble off her precarious perch. It was a most uncomfortable experience, made worse by being bound and gagged. The bindings at her wrist and ankles bit into her flesh and the gag nauseated her.

She was about to faint again when the horse was reined to a halt and the rider dismounted and roughly lifted her off. He carried her in his arms to a blazing campfire and dropped her on the ground. She saw now that the whole company of horsemen had dismounted and were preparing a stop for the night. She could not make out the exact number of those moving within the area of the campfire's glow but she judged there must be more than two dozen.

The ugly black-bearded leader in white headdress and robe came over to stand glowering at her. Then in a harsh voice, he said, "Will you be silent if I remove the gag from your mouth?"

She nodded effusively, ready to promise anything to have the hated, filthy cloth taken away. Then she gazed up at him with forlorn appeal in her lovely eyes.

He grunted and then knelt and took the cloth from her mouth. "It will do you no good to scream. You are miles out in the desert!"

She stared at him. "You speak English fluently?"

His smile was scornful. "I was a servant in the British Consulate until I found myself better employment."

"As a bandit?"

"As a soldier of Sheik Ali," the bearded one said proudly.

"Why did you take me prisoner?"

"You will know soon enough," he said. "I'm taking you to Sheik Ali. He will inform you!"

"Will you untie my hands and ankles? They are hurting dreadfully," she told him.

The bearded one hesitated. "Only on your promise not to attempt any madness such as running away!"

"I wouldn't know where to run!"

He nodded. "You are wise for a female. There is no place for you to run. If you went off on your own you would soon die of heat and thirst! The vultures would pick your bones clean!"

Gale shuddered. "You don't need to enlarge on it. I've told you I won't attempt to escape. But I would like to know why you captured me."

"The man Revene sent out a message on the telegraph that you were to be taken prisoner. The message was not meant for my Sheik. But it came into his hands and he decided that you must be worth taking hostage."

"So that's it!" she said bitterly.

"We knew you were on the train and it must be stopped," he said, kneeling by her and starting to untie her hands.

"Did you harm any of the others on the train? I heard gun shots."

"We only fired our rifles in the air to cause panic among the meek and foolish," he said.

This was comforting news. It at least meant that Eric ought to be safe. And if he were safe he would leave no stone unturned to try to find her. She asked the bearded one, "What is your name?"

"Massabi," he replied. Having freed her ankles he added, "I will bring you some lamb, and wine to wash it down. It would anger my Sheik if I were to deliver you to him in an abject state."

She rubbed her wrists and then her ankles and said wryly, "I'm close to such a state at this moment."

He stood over her gravely. "You will feel better when you have had food and drink."

"Perhaps," she agreed. The smell of the lamb roasting on another nearby fire was appetizing. And she suddenly realized she was both thirsty and hungry.

Massabi motioned to one of his men and gave him some sharp orders in their native tongue. Then he translated for her, "This man will be your guard.

If you go beyond the area of the campfire he has orders to shoot you down. Regrettable, but we cannot tolerate your escape!"

"I'll do nothing foolish," was her promise.

And she didn't. It would have been senseless to attempt escape in the middle of the desert. The armed guard keeping watch over her was hardly necessary. But she knew it would be useless to protest his presence. So she made the best of it by trying to cooperate with her captors.

The feast was a long one. And, after, there was singing and general relaxation among the tribesmen. Massabi came over to her after she had finished her meal. He stood staring down at her.

"You have had enough?" he asked.

"Yes."

"You would be wise to sleep. We travel early on the morrow."

"How far do we have to go?"

"We shall reach Sheik Ali before sundown," he told her. "Tomorrow night you will rest in his palace."

Anxiously, she asked, "What does he want with me?"

The bearded one smiled darkly. "You have been on the side of Abdul-el-Krem. He is our enemy! As evil as the Sultan himself!"

Gale protested, "I have had nothing to do with Abdul-el-Krem."

"Lies will not help you," Massabi told her coldly. "You were on the yacht with Revene and escaped. Revene wants you because you are valuable to him. Which means you must also be valuable to Abdul-el-Krem, since they are evil partners."

"I know nothing of what you say!" she said unhappily.

"I am only a humble soldier in the service of Sheik Ali," he said. "You may plead your innocence to him!"

Massabi left her a single, dirty blanket for a bedroll. She tried to make herself comfortable in it as she stretched out beside the dying campfire. The night was cold, even the stars overhead had an icy glitter to them. The tribesman guarding her sat nearby with his rifle in his lap. She could only hope that when she reached the palace of Sheik Ali she would be able to convince him she was nonpolitical and get him to free her and return her to Casablanca.

At dawn the horsemen were ready to begin the journey again. She had only some water and dry crusts for breakfast. But she did persuade Massabi to let her ride a horse, with the bridle tied to that of his mount on one side and to another rider's horse on the opposite side.

She rode the huge animal sidesaddle and found it a much less trying way of traveling than being carried like a sack. She had no idea in which direction they were going.

The dust of the desert choked her and the sun rose high in the sky and was brutal. She would surely have been in a desperate situation had she tried to get away, for on every side there was barren desert. The horsemen, bred to a life in the saddle, rode on relentlessly.

At last they left the desert for a mountainous area. They halted by a mountan spring and she was grateful to fill her hands and cup the sparkling, cold water to her mouth. The fields now showed green and there were some palm trees. Every so often they passed a small village. She was growing more and more weary, once again filled with a fear of fainting.

She turned to the impassive Massabi as he rode beside her, his head held high, and told him, "I'm exhausted! I cannot go on much farther!"

He gave her a surly glance. "Soon we will be at the palace. We cannot stop."

Nor did they. And her sweat-laden eyelids were almost closed when the village and palace appeared directly ahead. The sight of the whitewashed palace stirred her to life and within a very short while they were being met by veiled women and laughing, naked brown youngsters.

Massabi rode directly to the entrance of the palace with its tall turrets, many shadowed archways, and ornate tile work. He spoke in the native tongue to the burly guards who were on duty at the palace entrance, and she was seized and taken inside.

She staggered along as they marched swiftly, each of them holding her by an arm. They led her along interminable corridors and through murky chambers until they came to a great bronze door guarded by a giant black in a white turban. One of the guards spoke to the giant, who displayed a grin on his black face as he seized her by a wrist. Then he opened the bronze door and thrust her into what seemed at first to be a lovely walled garden with a fountain in its midst. Other black men wearing white turbans and robes with evil-looking swords at their belts were on guard here.

The click of the bronze door closing reminded her that she was a prisoner. The black guards made no move toward her but eyed her impassively. It was then she first noticed a cluster of veiled women on the other side of the fountain, grouped together and gazing at her with intense interest.

The sight of other females heartened her. She felt that surely she might count on them for some understanding and help. She called out and began to cross the flagstoned courtyard to where they stood. But as she reached the fountain the women gave out shrill cries of dismay and fled through a dark archway. She stood staring after them.

Then she continued toward the archway, which seemed to be the main entrance to the palace from this walled courtyard. As she neared it, a lone woman appeared and removed the veil from her face. She alone of the group had apparently found the courage to return.

"Please!" Gale called out. "I need help and friendship!"

"Well, you've come to a bleeding awful place to find it!" commented the woman in a harsh cockney which could not be disputed.

Gale ran up to the girl. "You are British?"

"If being born near Whitechapel makes you British, then that's what I am," the girl said grimly. "Though what good it does me now I can't say!"

"You're a prisoner here like myself," Gale said excitedly.

"You don't have to be bright to know that," the girl said with disgust. She was almost pretty but had a rather weak chin, which spoiled her looks.

"I'm weary and my clothes are a mess," Gale said. "I've been riding for most of a night and day."

"I can see that," the girl said, studying her in a gloomy fashion. "I can fix you up with the same heathen outfit I'm wearing. At least it will be clean and comfortable."

"Anything," she said. "What is your name?"

"Gert," the girl said. "It's good to have someone of my own sort in this place. I've learned to talk with the others but it ain't the same."

Gale glanced around. "It seems so lovely. But these guards. And the women appeared so fearful!"

Gert gave her a wry look. "They have reason to be. We're all in the same boat. Dependent on the whims of Sheik Ali Yusuf."

"This is his palace?"

"This is his harem," Gert said with meaning. "And you are now part of it."

Gale gave a small cry of dismay. "I was told I was being brought here because of political reasons. That the Sheik feels I'm on the side of his enemies."

Gert eyed her wisely. "I can't help what they told you. You're now in here with the rest of us and for the same reason: the pleasure of the Sheik and his friends!"

Gale's panic was increasing every moment. She eyed the black guards with a new sense of fear and turning to the cockney girl said excitedly, "I must get out of here! The Sheik can't keep me here! I'm an American citizen!"

"And I'm a proper loyal party to Her Majesty, the Queen," Gert said acidly. "But that doesn't bother Sheik Ali for a moment. He's the ruler here!"

"It has to all be a weird mistake," Gale said unhappily. "I'm sure as soon as he knows I'm here he'll send for me and make it right."

"If that's what you want to believe, dearie,"

Gert told her. "But first come along with me and get a bath and change into some clean clothing."

Gale found herself moving about as in a nightmare. The sunken bath was luxurious and the cockney girl was helpful. As she lingered in the warm, scented water of the huge oblong tub set in the midst of a tile-floored room with high ceilings of colored glass windows, the other girls in the harem began to emerge from the shadows and stood staring and giggling at her.

Gert, seated on the side of the bath, told her, "Don't mind the poor creatures! They're harmless and friendly! Timid and lonely from being locked up here!"

She stared up at the gathering audience from her bath, and with a wan smile, said, "I seem to be a novelty to them!"

"They want to be friendly," Gert assured her. "Oh, there's an occasional mean one among them. But not many!"

"How long have you been here?" she asked Gert.

The other girl sighed. "Must be nearly four years now. The old Sheik was alive when I was brought here. The father of the present one. He died about a year ago."

"How did you get here?"

"Sold," Gert said, with anger showing on her almost pretty face. "Sold into slavery by a dirty Greek dancer who brought me to Casablanca to entertain. That's what he told me. But he didn't bother to explain the kind of entertainment it would be!"

"You were tricked into this?"

"What else? We had no work and no money

to get back home. He drugged me one night and when I woke up I was on the way here. Not the first white girl to make the same journey, I can promise you. He sold me to the Sheik for fifty pounds. The Sheik told me so. The old man had a sense of humor. He thought I was a poor bargain."

Gale stared at her aghast. "You were forced to make love to this old Sheik?"

"I became his mistress," Gert said without any sign of reserve. "That's what we all are here. Mistresses or prostitutes or whatever you like to call us. Now the young Sheik is our master!"

"Horrible!" Gale said in dismay.

"Not so bad as long as you can stay here," the girl said, offering her a towel. "It's when you are sent away it gets really bad."

Gale stood up in the water and began to dry her shoulders. "I don't understand."

"Better to hear about that later," was Gert's forbidding reply.

Gale stepped up out of the water and Gert went about drying her with huge towels as the other girls watched and made comments in their native tongue. She felt shaken and embarrassed, her cheeks flamed as they made comments on her nude body, even though she could not understand them.

Gert, who was wearing silken trousers of gold with a white blouse, now supplied her with similar trousers in pale blue silk. And the blouse which she helped her put on was of a pale green. She also supplied her with a diaphanous veil of white with a silver band, which all the girls wore.

Gale held up the veil disapprovingly. "I don't want to wear this," she protested. "I'm a Christian! I have no law barring me from showing my face."

"Wear it," Gert advised. "I refused and was beaten for it."

"But it is ridiculous!"

"The Sheik will consider you brazen if you do not wear a veil," Gert warned her.

"Then let him!" she said indignantly, and put the veil aside. "I shall insist on him letting me out of this awful place as soon as I see him."

Gert's eyes widened. "You think he will listen to you?"

"He must! No one sold me into slavery to him! I'm here as a political prisoner!"

"If you think you can manage him so well maybe you can get me free too," Gert said, hope showing on her pert face.

"I shall surely try," she promised. "You have been good to me."

Gert stood up and said, "Let us go out to the garden where we can talk without them watching and listening."

Gale said, "Yes. I'd like that. They make me nervous."

"Wait until you've been shut up with them for a year or two," Gert said with grim resignation.

"I don't even dare think of it," Gale said.

The cockney girl led her out of the room and back to the courtyard. They took seats under a palm tree close by the giant circular fountain, where it was pleasantly cool.

Gert eyed her gravely and said, "I'm not one to show much emotion. But just seeing you and talking to you does my heart good. I'd given up ever seeing anyone of my own kind again!"

"How awful for you!"

"I've tried to be obedient here," Gert went on.

"To be sent away would be worse. So I've a brown son by the old sheik. He's a good little fellow. They took him away from me when he was a year old. But I hear from one of the palace servants he is doing well."

She was shocked by the girl's story. "What about this new sheik?"

Gert smiled wryly. "He is a devoted Moslem. Can't bring himself to mate with an infidel and yet he can't bear to let me go. That's worked out well for me. It may be the same with you!"

Gale was indignant. "He wouldn't dare think of me as one of his harem!"

"That's where you are, my lady," Gert said acidly.

"But I'm a political prisoner."

"Maybe."

"I'm certain of it," she said. "The man who brought me here, Massabi, told me that his sheik was at war with Abdul-el-Krem, a sheik who was a friend of my late husband."

Gert showed interest. "Your husband was friendly with one of the sheiks?"

"Yes. You know there's a revolution brewing. Two or three factions are fighting each other. All planning to overthrow the Sultan and rule Morocco."

"We don't get the daily papers in here," Gert reminded her wryly. "All you say may be true but we don't know anything about it."

"The firm my husband worked for was selling arms illegally to one side or the other," Gale said.

"Sounds like a dirty business."

"It is," Gale agreed. "I didn't know. I'm not really sure about it now. But I'm almost certain. I met a young man working for the *London Telegram* who told me a lot."

"The *Telegram*," Gert said with a deep sigh. "What I wouldn't give to hear Big Ben chime just once again."

She found herself feeling sorry for the other girl. "You will," she said. "I'm sure you will!"

"Don't put any bets on it!"

"I'll make the sheik release us both," she said. "He must know he can't get away with this!"

"Don't fool yourself!" Gert said, her pert face suddenly dark with despair. "Have you any idea how many other white girls have made this trip, or how many others will?"

"I don't understand!"

"White slavery," Gert said. "It's common enough spoke of. This is the real thing. When a white girl gets this far from Europe she's finished. The sheiks want only the best. If your looks begin to go or you catch a disease, and there's plenty of that, you're sent on down the ladder."

"Down the ladder?"

"To be a common prostitute in some village!"

"No!"

"Yes," Gert said. "And then if you survive that, there's the last step. The aisle of cages in the medina. You're offered in cages like animals for the lowest castes and the beggars. No man is so diseased, blind, or maimed that he cannot afford you there!"

"Horrible!" Gale said in a taut voice.

"And then it's death," Gert said. "And that's the only escape. I know this is true because I have heard it from the others in here."

Gale was sickened. "No one can be so inhuman!"

"But they are, I promise you," Gert said. "So

be careful how you conduct yourself with Sheik Ali!"

"I'll be found," she said, panic-stricken. "I'm sure a search party is looking for me now."

Gert eyed her sadly. "What do you think the odds are of their finding you?"

"They're bound to!"

"Not likely!"

"What do you mean?"

Gert leaned closer to her. "This is an underground world. You are a prisoner. As soon as they hear that someone is coming for you they will spirit you off to some other hidden harem. I tell you this is a lost world. We are all phantoms!"

"I can't give up hope!"

"Don't," the other girl agreed. "But don't close your mind to the odds against you."

Their conversation was interrupted by the appearance of the black-bearded Massabi in the garden. He went to Gale and said, "I see you have recovered from your journey."

"I've bathed and changed my clothes."

"Good," Massabi said. "I am to take you to Sheik Ali Yusuf. He chooses to dine with you."

She stood up. "It is time I talked with him."

Massabi gave her a stern look. "You will treat him with proper respect. Where is your veil?"

"I will wear no veil," she said defiantly.

Massabi warned, "The sheik will be angered."

Gert turned to her. "He is right. You'd best put on the veil."

"No," she said, indignation taking priority over discretion. "I have been brought here as a prisoner and treated disgracefully. I will bow to your master no further."

The bearded man shrugged. "Then you will accompany me as you are."

Gale turned to the cockney girl and said, "I'll speak for you."

"Good luck!" Gert said, looking worried.

Massabi led her out of the garden and through the bronze doorway to another maze of corridors. Gale lost track of their wanderings but at last they emerged into a large, ornate room. Standing waiting for her in the room was a handsome young man with a black mustache and Van Dyke beard. He wore a yellow turban and a colorful robe of red, yellow, and white. He epitomized all the romantic drawings she had seen of desert chieftains.

Standing amid carpets and tapestries of great elegance, the floor covered with cushions of many sizes and shades, he fixed his eyes on her.

"So you are Madame Cormier," he said with a hint of French accent.

"Yes," she said, facing him boldly. "And may I ask why you had me taken prisoner and brought here?"

He smiled and his tone was silken. "Surely, you must know!"

"I do not."

Young Sheik Ali seemed gently amused by this. "But surely you know your husband supplied my adversary Abdul-el-Krem with arms. That he and his employer Revene have been selling such supplies to any who can pay their prices."

"I know nothing about it!" she protested. "I demand you release me!"

"Mr. Revene would very much like to have you turned over to him," the handsome sheik told her.

"I know Revene is an evil man and he means me harm," she said. "I am in no way on his side."

"Naturally not," the silken voice went on. "Since your late husband double-crossed Revene and sold the munitions to the despicable Abdul-el-Kreml"

"I know nothing of that," she said. "I'm innocent of any knowledge of those deals."

"I see," he said, with a hint of sympathy. "You expect me to believe this?"

"Yes. It is true!"

"You can convince me by telling me where a certain briefcase is hidden and have it turned over to me," Sheik Ali told her.

She was startled. The briefcase again! Here in this desert outpost the briefcase was still the prize everyone wanted. She said, "I can only tell you what I've told Revene and the others. I haven't seen the briefcase."

Sheik Ali looked disappointed. "You are a stubborn young woman."

"I swear I'm being perfectly honest with you," she said.

His handsome face showed sour amusement. "Come now, you do not expect me to believe that!"

"I do," she said. "And I demand you release me and send me back to Casablanca. And the English girl, Gert, along with me."

Sheik Ali laughed, not unpleasantly. "You are making demands of me?"

"I ask for justice."

"You are now a member of my harem," Sheik Ali informed her calmly. "I paid a good price for you and you are my slave. Just as the English girl is."

"That's a monstrous lie!"

154

"You are not wearing proper attire," he said coldly. "What about your veil?"

"I wear no veil!"

"That is brazen indecency," the handsome sheik said. "I have asked you to dine with me and you appear without a veil!"

"I wish only to be released."

"First, we must come to terms," he said. "That may take time. So you will in the meanwhile remain in my harem. Do not fear my touching you; I will not take an infidel into my bed. I cannot defile myself as my late father did. He was a man of lust for the flesh while I lust for a different sort of power—political power."

"You are going about it in a poor way," she warned him. "The American government will not be pleased to hear my story."

"Ah!" Sheik Ali said in his smooth manner. "But you are a long way from telling your story."

She made a desperate bid for help from him by saying, "If you let me go I'll try to get the briefcase for you. I promise!"

He clapped his graceful hands in mock enthusiasm. "Excellent! We are making a start!"

"I give you my word!"

"I'm sorry," he said. "But I cannot think you are being truthful since I'm convinced you know where the briefcase is now. So we must be patient until your memory returns. In the meanwhile you remain in my harem. Perhaps I can offer you to some other sheik who is not as delicate as I am about consorting with an infidel. We must keep you amused!"

"You are threatening me!" she told him.

"You are completely in my power and so you will remain," Sheik Ali informed her. "Now you will dine with me. And since you are so brazen as to refuse to wear a proper veil it is my order that you discard all your clothing and dine with me in the nude. I shall feast my eyes on your beauty while we mutually share a feast of the table!"

"No!" she cried, stepping back.

"Massabi!" he ordered the black-bearded man who had been standing silently in the background.

Silently the big man came forward and roughly tore the blouse from her and then the silken trousers, leaving her naked and wretched before the amused Sheik Ali.

"What a pity you are an infidel," the sheik mourned. "You have so shapely a body."

Using her hands in an attempt to cover her nakedness, she begged him, "Let me retire! You have shamed me! Is that not enough?"

"I fear not," he said. "Seat yourself and join me in food."

She hesitated and then realizing that he would not give in, she knelt down and sat on a pillow, arranging another to give her additional covering. Servants entered and began passing the many gourmet dishes. She had lost all appetite and made only a pretense at eating.

Sheik Ali seemed to be thoroughly enjoying himself. He told her, "I have seldom had so lovely a sight to adorn my dining area."

She looked down. "You are a savage! A bully!"

"We believe in the domination of the female," he went on airily. "I could be much more cruel to you. I'm merely trying to teach you a lesson."

"So you have humiliated me," she said.

"If you wish to think of it in that way," he replied. "I regard it as punishing a child in a gentle manner."

There were tears in her eyes. "How long must I sit here like this?"

"Until we have dined," he said. "It was my wish to have you dine with me."

"In torment?"

"The torment you have brought on yourself," Sheik Ali said. "And I may say the longer I admire your lovely body the less vile the thought of sleeping with an infidel seems to me. It could be that my lamented father was right and I will come around to his way of thinking."

"Do me no favors," she retorted bitterly.

"This would be a favor for myself," he said with a smile on his handsome face. "You may rise and leave."

She stood up at once and turned to go. But he restrained her, and seizing her by the arm, swung her around and took her in his arms. He kissed her greedily and then his lips wandered to her breasts as she tried to push him away. At last he let her go.

His breathing was heavy and his face flushed as he stared at her in admiration and said, "Yes. I may decide to abandon my scruples and have you!"

She ran from him and out into the corridor where the stern Massabi was waiting for her. He held a cloak which he gave her to cover herself. They began the walk back to the harem.

"You were warned," he said.

She glanced at him. "About the veil? That was only an excuse! He meant to bully me anyway. And you helped him my ripping off my clothes!"

The man marching at her side said, "I had no choice. I am an officer of the sheik. I must obey him."

"You will regret it!" she said. "He has mad ambitions. He will never succeed."

"You are hardly in a position to judge that," Massabi warned her. "You had better give him the information he wants if you wish your freedom."

"I haven't the information," she maintained.

Massabi gave her a troubled glance. "I wish to be your friend. But you wish no help or advice. It is difficult."

He escorted her to the bronze door and again she went into the harem area of the palace as a prisoner. Gert was waiting by the fountain to greet her. And when she saw that Gale was naked but for the cloak she stared at her in astonishment.

"Don't tell me he's already had you!" the cockney girl exclaimed.

She shook her head grimly. "Not yet!"

"But why?"

"Why are my clothes gone?"

"Yes."

"He had them ripped off me! Forced me to dine with him in the nude!"

Gert's eyes widened. "That's a new one, I must say!"

"It was his method of humiliating me, breaking my spirit," she said.

"He's a wizard at that!"

"He used the missing veil as an excuse."

"I told you to wear it!"

"He would have found an excuse to punish me anyway," she said.

"So what happened?" Gert wanted to know.

"I suffered through dinner and then he let me go. But he took me in his arms before I left and

158

hinted that he might abandon his aversion to infidels in his bed!"

"His father coming out in him," Gert told her. "He was one who liked white flesh!"

"I don't know what I shall do," Gale said, looking at the other girl in despair.

"While you're here you'll do what he wishes!"

"I'd kill myself first!"

"Even that isn't all that easy," Gert said. "We had one girl hang herself last year. But they almost found her before she'd stopped breathing. They don't like to lose anyone, it gives the others ideas."

Gale sank down on a bench. "There has to be some way."

"I thought you said you were a political prisoner and that he'd release you because of that."

"He will if I give him certain information."

"What information?"

She shook her head wearily. "Something about a briefcase. Others have been after it. They claim my husband had it. But I have never seen it."

"That puts you in a bad spot," the cockney girl said with awe.

"We'll just have to hope that a rescue party gets here," Gale said.

"I wouldn't count on it."

"There's nothing else to hope for," Gale said.

Gert gave her an odd look. "There may be one other way."

She stared up at the other girl. "You mean it?"

"Yes," Gert said. "I've been planning it for a long while. But I've been afraid to try it. Now that you're here I'm willing to take the chance."

8

"Tell me!" Gale cried.

Gert gave her a knowing look and in a low voice said, "Massabi!"

"Massabi?" she echoed. "I thought he was completely loyal to the sheik!"

Gert smiled wisely. "In everything else. But he has a weakness for me, you might say! He's suggested we run off together. Up until now I've been afraid to try it. Sure the sheik would come after us and murder Massabi and send me to the low brothels of Marrakesh."

"Why have you changed your opinion?" Gale asked.

"Having you here gives me courage," the other girl said. "If there is truly a search party looking for you we might make contact with it. Have a better chance to escape."

"I'm sure Eric Simms is doing something," she said. "And no doubt Revene and his gang are also looking for me."

"We'd have to leave at night," Gert said. "Set out across the desert. If we survive the scorching heat of the daytime sun and the sheik's men, we might manage it."

"Surely it is better than waiting here and allowing Sheik Ali to do as he likes with us," Gale said.

"What do you make of him?" the cockney girl asked.

"He's incredibly handsome and suave and perhaps the most cruel person I've ever encountered," she replied.

Gert nodded solemnly. "So you have an idea of what might be in store for us if he catches up with us."

"I still say that we should make an escape if possible," she said.

"It will take a little time, a few days or a week. I must first discuss a plan with Massabi and then he will pick the night for our attempt."

Gale said, "I can find the courage to wait as long as I know there is some hope."

"I will see Massabi tomorrow night," Gert said. "He bribes one of the guards and comes to my room after midnight. I should have some news the next morning."

Gale retired to the small room which had been assigned her. It led directly off the communal room with the giant bath in which the harem women gathered in the daytime. Gert's cubicle of a room was farther down the corridor from her.

The cockney girl's news that an escape was possible filled her with a new optimism. She lay on the hard mattress in the dark cubicle and considered the problems which might face them. She had a great deal of confidence in Massabi's intellect and felt he could be depended on to plan things in the best possible way. And she also had a feeling that Eric must have discovered by now who had derailed the train and would be on his way to the headquarters of Sheik

Ali Yusuf. With this comforting thought she dropped off into exhausted sleep.

The following day she kept close to Gert and came to better know the other members of the harem. Most of the women were young, and attractive in their own fashion. And as Gert had told her, they were childishly friendly and interested in any newcomer to their ranks. When they got over their awe of her they came close and rippled their brown fingers through her radiant golden-red hair.

Gale looked mildly amused as she said, "You're a true novelty for them. Not many fair beauties turn up here."

"I'm beginning to feel like some animal on exhibition in a zoo."

"It is a kind of zoo at that," the cockney girl said.

"You will see that person tonight," Gale said in a low voice after the others had left them for a little.

Gert nodded. "I will have to depend on his views," she warned her. "If he thinks it is no longer safe he may not want to risk it."

Gale said, "Tell him when we reach Casablanca I will pay him well in American dollars."

"American dollars aren't much good if you have a slit throat."

Gale's tensions increased as the hours went by. And then, in the early evening, one of the black guards came to her and led her from the harem back to the main palace. She once again found herself standing in the presence of the suave Sheik Ali.

The handsome Arab bowed his head and waved a delicate hand for her to be seated on some pillows opposite him. She obeyed him, all the time trembling.

His smile was mocking. "You seem nervous. Surely you are not afraid of me."

She looked at him evenly. "You know I am."

Sheik Ali laughed softly. "You need have no fears. I find myself strangely enamored of you."

"Please release me!" she begged him again. "A search party will come and the American government will indict you when they learn you've been holding a citizen captive."

The handsome face wore a jeering smile. His delicate brown hand with its jeweled fingers dismissed this with a wave. "You will never be found unless I will it."

Her throat tightened, but she tried to bluff it out. "I must warn you that you are playing a dangerous game."

He leaned forward and in a voice full of confidence said, "I have camel loads of the finest weapons on the way."

"You are a fool if you think your camel loads of weapons will make you strong enough to defy the Western powers."

"I shall be the new Sultan!" he declared angrily. "What do you know about it?"

"I know that France is planning to take the country under its protection. It is common talk in Casablanca!"

"In the cities!" Sheik Ali jeered. "What do they know of the strength of desert people?"

"You are deceiving yourself," she said.

He spread his jeweled hands. "One does not discuss these things with women!"

"You'd be wise to listen to me."

"I'll gladly listen if you will tell me where that briefcase is hidden," he said. "Has your memory improved at all since last night?"

"No."

His handsome face displayed annoyance. "In my grandfather's time you would already be on the torture rack. Congratulate yourself that I am a civilized man."

"I'd hardly call you that," she said with disgust. "Your views of the worthlessness of women are shameful!"

Sheik Ali replied, "I place a high value on you."

"Because you think I can supply you information you need."

"I also find you physically desirable," the handsome young Sheik told her. "I still have a vivid picture of your naked body as we dined together last night."

"That was evidence of your savagery," Gale told him, her cheeks crimson.

He laughed softly. "You do not seem to understand. I can do with you what I like."

"And you consider yourself a man of honor?" she asked with scorn.

"I am a person of integrity," he assured her. "Were this not so I would have savored your body by now."

"I consider myself fortunate that you are a Moslem, in that case."

He moved nearer her and said, "But I have solved this dilemma."

"I can't think how."

"Simple," he announced grandly. "You have only to take the Islamic vow and you can be mine!"

The audacity of his offer was stunning. Angrily she rose and told him, "I do not wish to remain here and be insulted."

He got to his feet. "I can wait," Sheik Ali told her. "I am a patient man. And perhaps at the same time you will remember something about the briefcase. If you could offer me that I would gladly free you and send you back to Casablanca under safe escort."

"I cannot help you," she said firmly.

"You weary me," he said with a sigh. And he waved to the black attendant. "Take her away!"

Back in the harem Gert was waiting anxiously for her. As soon as the guard retreated the cockney girl came to her and asked, "What did he want?"

She smiled bitterly. "A small thing. He suggests I embrace the Moslem faith so he can rape me without betraying his good conscience!"

"What a bleeding nerve!" Gert gasped.

"I refused him and then he brought up the briefcase again. He seems to want it as badly as the others."

"What do you expect is so valuable about it?" the cockney girl wanted to know.

Gale frowned. "I'm not certain. All I've been able to learn is that the case contained important papers incriminating to a lot of the officials here and perhaps some of the foreign colony as well."

"Maybe you should pretend you know where it is," Gert suggested. "Tell them where it could be."

"You mean send them on a wild-goose chase?"

"Why not?"

"I'm not sure I'd gain anything by it," she said. "They'd not release me until they had their hands on it."

"It could buy you time."

Gale gave her an approving glance. "That is true. I might make up some story about it being hidden in the chateau."

"The chateau?"

"A house where my husband and I lived when we first came to Casablanca," she said.

"That would sound right," Gert agreed.

"I'd tell them some story about it being hidden in the cellar there," she went on improvising. "Perhaps stuffed in the back of an empty wine keg."

Gert's face was bright with approval. "Blimey if you're not a proper liar!"

"I can manage if I have to," she said modestly. "But is there any point of trying this with the sheik?"

"Not if Massabi can get us away tonight," Gert said.

"In that case I won't need to stall for time," she agreed. "Do you think there's a good chance he will act at once?"

"I think he must," Gert told her. "The longer he hesitates over it the less liable he is to take the chance."

"How will I know?"

"He'll come to me soon after midnight," Gert said. "And if we agree to leave then, I'll make my way to your room."

"I'll remain awake and waiting," she promised.

Gert warned her, "Don't count on it. He may change his mind and turn me down."

"Not judging from what you've told me."

"We'll see," the other girl said gravely. "I can't wait to get beyond these walls. I'll even risk the desert and whatever Sheik Ali may try to do!"

The hours passed in an agony of tension for Gale. She could think of nothing but the planned escape. All the past seemed wiped from her mind as she lived through this uneasy time.

She went to the small cubicle assigned to her and lay waiting on the hard mattress. She snuffed the candle out so there would be no glow of light in the tiny room to reveal a visitor, or her leaving. The night grew cool as it always did, and she waited and prayed that all would be well.

A heavy silence had fallen over the harem, broken only by the unearthly baying at the moon of some animal in the far distance. She was aware of the taut beating of her heart and her very breathing. Then suddenly the silence was broken by a footstep.

Gert was bending over her in the shadows. "It is all arranged," the girl said.

"When do we go?" she whispered.

"Now! You must come with me now!"

"I'm ready," Gale said, rising from the mattress.

"Follow me," the cockney girl instructed her.

She did. They went out into the corridor and, staying close to the harem walls, made their way around the garden to the bronze door. When they reached it Gert tapped on it three times and the door swung open. Massabi was there waiting for them.

"Come!" he whispered hoarsely.

They followed him out to the courtyard and to the stables beyond. Once a guard appeared on his rounds, and all three had to shrink into the shadows by the wall. They waited until he was safely out of the way and then Massabi beckoned for them to continue.

He led them to trees behind the stables where three fine horses were tethered. He assigned Gale a dappled gray mare and he mounted a fiery black stallion, while Gert was given a chestnut of milder temperament. He rode off quickly, the hooves of the great stallion sending up dust as they vanished into the darkness. Gert followed on her mount and Gale prodded her mare to keep up. It would be all too easy to lose the others in the black wilderness.

They rode on without a break until she was aching in every part of her body. The journey appeared to be endless, but as dawn began to break they came to a small village. Massabi reined in his horse and they rode up to him.

"This is Tardit, an oasis village," he said. "We shall pause here for a little to refresh ourselves and the horses. We need supplies of water."

"Is it safe to stop?" Gert asked worriedly, although she was weary-looking and caked with the desert dust.

"We have no choice," he said. "The rest will be mostly desert."

Gale pushed a straying strand of hair back from her face and said, "Have we a good enough start on Sheik Ali?"

The black-bearded Massabi shrugged. "Who can say? I think we managed a good start before they knew we were gone. It all depends."

"If we have no choice, we have no choice," Gert said stoically. "I'm parched with thirst and so are the horses."

They crossed the flat field to the village. It consisted mostly of mud huts, and the few people who appeared stared at them as if they were visitors from another planet. Massabi acted as liaison and talked with a white-bearded patriarch. Soon great jugs of water were brought to them along with some food. The horses were tethered in the shade of some straggly palm trees.

Massabi told them, "Another day will take us across the desert. And then it will be only eight or ten hours to the coast and Casablanca."

"I wish we were there now," Gert said.

"Can we ride that far?" Gale worried.

Massabi said, "We must. We have made our choice. There is no turning back!"

"I'm only afraid of Ali's men catching up with

us," Gert said, looking over her shoulder uneasily in the direction from which they had come.

"I do not know," the bearded Massabi said impassively. "If we reach Casablanca he will not dare follow us into the city."

"Cool!" Gert exclaimed, her weary face brightening. "It will be good to see the ocean again."

"I shall find work as an interpreter there," Massabi told them proudly. "I speak four languages!"

Gert nodded. "And when we've saved enough money we'll leave this heathen place and sail back to England."

Gale smiled. "I think we're getting ahead of ourselves."

"True," Massabi agreed, getting up from where he'd been resting. "We must begin our journey again. To remain here any longer would be laughing in the face of fate!"

Gale asked him, "If Sheik Ali's men come looking for us, will the villagers tell them we have been here?"

"Can't you bribe them to keep quiet?" Gert suggested.

Massabi shook his head. "I have nothing to bribe them with. And even if I attempted that, it would be bound to fail. At least one voice would speak of our being here, and it all would have been to no avail. We must take our chances!"

They rode away from the tiny village and into the flat, blazing desert. Even though they now had jugs of water with them, it was a journey fraught with danger. Gale wondered if they could actually make their way to the verdant coastal area beyond. It was endless miles away now.

Most of the time they rode in silence. But occasionally a few words would pass between them.

Gert rode up beside Gale with a woeful expression on her pert face and said, "This is worse than hellfire!"

Gale said, "It must be worse on the horses than on us."

The other girl watched Massabi, who was riding a little distance ahead, and said, "He must really care for me or he wouldn't have brought this on himself."

Gale gave the woebegone Gert a reassuring smile. "Of course he loves you! He is risking his life to save us."

"I keep thinking it's unfair to him," Gert worried.

"You mustn't," she admonished her. "Massabi is here because it is his wish. He wanted you free and for himself. This is the only way he can manage it."

They continued on, pausing only for an occasional water break for themselves and their horses. Gale had plenty of time to ponder grimly the devious behavior, the acts of criminal cunning and greed that had brought her to this pass. She had given her heart to a man who had brought her to this primitive country and then abandoned her in his lust for quick riches!

She remembered her uncle's warning about her husband before her marriage and wished she had listened to the old man's advice. Now she was finding that all the things he'd said were true. Paul had sold himself to Revene and, then, not satisfied with the profits from Revene's dealings, he had set out on his own. That had been his downfall. And when he'd lost his life in the wild gamble for a fortune, she had been left to the not-so-tender mercy of a choice group of criminals.

They rode on, with the village far behind. An endless expanse of rock and dirt, sun and sky, and little else. The horizons stretched away to the ends of the earth. Suddenly Gert called out happily.

"Look ahead!" she said, spurring on the chestnut horse.

Massabi turned in the saddle to raise a restraining hand and warn her, "Do not be a fool! That lake and those trees are a mirage! They do not exist!"

Gert's face dropped. "It can't be!"

Gale gazed at the lake and trees in the shimmering heat and knew what Massabi said was true. The pleasant oasis was nothing more than a cruel fantasy!

Later, a caravan of traders with a group of plodding camels passed them. The only living creatures they saw all that day. The traders considered them, then moved silently by, as aloof as their camels.

Night came, and still they rode on under the stars. The cool was welcome and they went as far as they dared. The mare Gale was riding developed a limp, and it seemed wise to stop to enable all the horses to rest.

Massabi examined the mare's hoof and could see no sign of injury.

"What now?" Gert asked.

Massabi glanced around. "We shall light a small fire and rest here for the balance of the night. Tomorrow we should pass the edge of the desert."

Massabi stood watch while Gale and Gert attempted to sleep. It was hard for Gale to rest on the ground with only the horse's blanket for a pillow. She was filled with visions of Casablanca and her return to New York as soon as it could be arranged. She was sure she would find Eric there somewhere and he would help her.

She was asleep, suffering the recurring nightmare of Paul's white, tormented face coming to her in the darkness. She awoke with a tiny scream and looked across the fire to see that Massabi had risen to his feet and seemed to be listening intently.

"What is it?" she asked.

He raised a hand to silence her and listened some more. Then he quickly turned and said, "Horses! Coming toward us! I'm certain!"

His words roused her completely. She scrambled up and asked, "What will we do?"

"Douse the fire and get on our way," he said, at the same time beginning to stamp out the small fire.

Gert sat up sleepily, "What is it?"

"Horses!" Gale said. "Likely the sheik's men coming after us!"

"Gor blimey!" the cockney girl exclaimed. She got up, took her blanket, and hurried over to where the mare was tethered.

Gale ran with her and said, "Our horses are restless! They hear something, too!"

Massabi was with them, mounting the stallion and crying out, "Ride like the wind! They draw nearer every minute!"

The three of them rode off at a gallop, but it was a pace they knew their tired mounts could not maintain. The animals were exhausted, and it was only a matter of minutes before they began to lag noticeably. Massabi tried to spur his mount on but to no avail.

As they rode along, Gert cried, "What now?"

Massabi shouted, "I have a rifle and a sword. I will not be taken without a battle. Nor will I submit alive!"

Gale said, "Perhaps it is another party! Not the sheik's men."

"I do not think so," Massabi said.

They rode along across the flat desert under the stars. There were no convenient mountains in which to hide. They were nakedly exposed on this vast expanse of wasteland. Fear was choking Gale as she pictured what might happen if they were captured!

The sheik would show them no mercy. A quick death would be the best they could hope for. Gert had earlier painted a picture of what it could be like to be sold into the brothels and treated worse than any animal.

"They're coming!" Gert cried. She was riding in the rear.

Gale turned and saw that the cockney girl was right. She could see the dust and hear the pounding of the hooves of their pursuers' horses. She made a desperate effort to urge the mare on. Massabi reined in the stallion and rode back to be beside the lagging Gert.

Then there were wild shouts, and shots rang out in the night. Terrified, Gale turned to see that Gert had suddenly fallen forward in her saddle. Massabi executed a masterly feat in lifting her from the mare onto the saddle in front of him. Then he urged on the stallion and rode abreast of Gale.

"Press on!" he cried.

"I will!"

The two rode on with the cries and sounds of the horses growing louder as their pursuers drew closer to them. Their own horses were thoroughly fear-stricken now with shots ringing out around them and bullets biting into the ground. They ran on with the renewed vigor born of terror!

Then Gale's mare suddenly whinnied—it was more like a human's scream—and reared up before it toppled over on to the sand. A bullet had found its way to the noble creature. She struggled to free herself and not be caught under the weight of the fallen animal.

She was left standing, facing the oncoming

horsemen, quite defenseless! Then she was aware of Massabi riding up beside her and sliding out of the saddle. He placed Gert gently on the ground and stood over her with his rifle upraised.

He shouted, "Send the stallion on its way!"

She obeyed him, turning the frightened animal around and striking it on the haunch to send it running off into the safety of the darkness. But at the same time she knew it left them without any means of transport—with the enemy bearing down on them!

Massabi took careful aim and fired, and the nearest of the approaching riders threw up his arms and fell from his horse. The riderless horse went madly past them and Massabi fired again and caught another of the enemy and sent him toppling to the ground. Then the rifle jammed. He worked at it futilely, and after a few seconds flung it angrily away and drew out his sword and held it ready!

The dozen or so horsemen fired a few more shots and then surrounded them. Gale and the brave Massabi, with Gert outstretched on the ground at their feet, were in the middle of a circle of desert riders—led by the handsome young sheik Ali Yusuf!

He dismounted and walked toward them with a scornful smile on his handsome face. He said, "So, all your effort has ended in defeat!"

"Not yet, Master," Massabi said, breathing heavily, his sword still upraised.

"Fool!" Sheik Ali spat out. "The woman you risked your life for is dead!" He glanced down at Gert and then at Gale. "And this one has used you for a weakling!"

"It is not true!" Massabi said huskily.

But Gale knew at least part of it was so. Kneeling by Gert, she saw that the unhappy girl was dead. She looked up at the sheik and said, "Your bullets killed her."

Sheik Ali smiled. "She committed suicide when she tried to escape."

Massabi cried out in grief mixed with rage and in a quick motion swung the sword at the arrogant Sheik Ali. The shining blade flashed across his throat. The startled sheik staggered back with blood spurting from his nearly severed neck. His handsome face wore a look of numbed surprise as he slumped to the ground!

The killing of their leader stunned the desert men for a long moment. Massabi took advantage of that precious moment to grasp Gale by the arm and race off into the night with her struggling to keep up with him. Their moment of relief was all too brief. The horsemen recovered and came after them once again.

As they ran, the ground around them sprayed by bullets, Massabi cried out, "Ahead! A bonfire!"

Gale strained through sweat-drenched eyes and saw that this was so. Not too far in the distance was a bonfire. "I see it!" she gasped.

"Run on!" Massabi said, as he suddenly began to falter.

She turned in alarm. "They've hit you!"

He lifted a hand, "Run!" he ordered her, and then he fell forward on his face.

It made no sense but she ran on! It was the climax of a hideous nightmare! Both Gert and Massabi dead and she like a terrified fox being run down by a group of relentless hunters! She had no chance, and she should have been struck by a bullet just as the others, but fate had spared her and she still struggled on.

Before her appeared a stout apparition in pith

helmet and thick glasses. The apparition in the khaki uniform cried, "Mademoiselle! What is this?"

She fell into the stout man's outstretched arms and gasped, "Gale Cormier! Desert bandits after me!"

Another figure came running to join them and even in her near collapse she saw it was Eric. He lifted her up in his arms and shouted something to the stout man as they ran from the approaching horsemen.

She was too confused and exhausted to think clearly. She only knew that she was in Eric's arms and they were trying to escape from the dozen or more armed horsemen. She heard Eric shout something and was aware of being rudely dropped to the ground.

Then the night was filled with a loud clattering, and there seemed to be explosions everywhere. She was dimly aware of Eric and the stout man crouched behind a mounted apparatus that was making the clamor as they aimed it at the approaching horsemen. Then she blacked out!

She opened her eyes by the campfire. Eric was bending over her; he said quietly, "It's all right! You're safe!"

Memory returned, and her eyes widened in terror. "The horsemen?"

"The ones we didn't kill are routed," Eric said. "I don't think there were more than two or three got away!"

"How?" she stared up at him.

"Gatling gun," he said. "We came armed with one. Mighty useful in a situation like this."

"You did come for me?" she said, staring up at him.

"I've been hunting for you for days," he said. "Myself and Professor Leduc."

The stout man in the khaki uniform and pith helmet now came to stand over her. "My congratulations, Mademoiselle. You are most brave!"

Eric said, "This is my friend, Leduc. Perhaps the most acclaimed balloonist in the world. I found him here doing work for the French army and I enlisted him in my search for you."

She said, "Massabi and Gertl!"

Eric frowned. "Who are they?"

"A Moroccan and an English girl who helped me escape. They were both shot down. She's dead, but he may be alive."

Eric said, "We can look for them in the morning."

"We could still be in danger," she said.

"I think not, we killed many of them and gave the others a bad scare," Eric said.

"The horses are gone," she lamented.

"We won't need them," Eric assured her. "Where were you held captive?"

"In the palace of Sheik Ali Yusuf," she said. "Massabi beheaded him last night when they met."

"Good!" Eric said. "That is one less of the rebel leaders to deal with. But you can believe me there are plenty more of them."

"What about Revene?" she asked.

"He is still in or near Casablanca," Eric told her. "He and the rest of his gang."

"The police should do something about him!"

"You ought to know better than that by now," Eric said grimly. "Try to get some rest. We must be on the move early."

She had a few short spells of sleep and then it was dawn and she had her first glimpse of the wonder which had so miraculously brought Eric to her rescue when she needed him most. Anchored to the ground nearby was a huge balloon with a large basket for travelers and supplies. It loomed above her, glistening and triumphant.

"A balloon!" she cried in excitement.

The stout Professor Leduc came up to her and bowed. "It is the latest and most efficient for weather observation, Madame. I have been conducting experiments for the French government until I was called upon by my friend Simms to help in your rescue."

"What a wonderful idea!" she said.

The stout man with the round face and heavy glasses looked pleased. "It was possible to cover a great deal of country. We were sure to come on you sooner or later."

Eric came up, with a smile on his tanned face. "You approve our means of transport?"

"I'm sure you would never have reached me without it," she said.

"That's likely so," he agreed. "And the Gatling gun would have been difficult to transport by any other means."

Professor Leduc nodded. "The rapid-firing gun saved the day for us. Or I should say the night."

Eric said, "You mentioned two comrades. If you wish, we will look for their bodies now."

It was a gruesome task which she had asked them to embark on. They walked back past the fallen bodies of the desert men. They lay in unreal postures, and Eric and the Professor checked each body to be sure they were leaving no one alive to suffer under the desert sun. The sight of the several dead horses was especially pathetic, victims of human aggression of which they could have no possible understanding.

Then they went a distance further before finding the body of Massabi. Gale knelt by him and felt a special tenderness for the ugly bearded man who had hoped to reach Casablanca with his beloved Gert and become an interpreter.

She said, "Gert cannot be far away."

"What about Sheik Ali?" Eric asked.

"His body should be a distance ahead," she said. "We ran a little way after Massabi beheaded him."

"Let us see if we can find the girl," Eric suggested.

They went on and came to the spot where the sheik had been slain by the sword of Massabi. The sword still lay on the bloodstained ground. But the body of Sheik Ali was not there. The survivors among his men must have spirited it away.

"It would be considered a dishonor for the body to fall into our hands," Eric explained.

"Let us go on," she said.

They walked a little distance more and found Gert. Eric asked, "What now?"

She said, "We can't take the bodies in the balloon with us, can we?"

Professor Leduc displayed embarrassment on his round face. Ruefully, he said, "There would be room, Madame. But it would not be practical."

Eric explained, "Bodies decompose quickly here. This poor girl's body is already showing hints of this."

She stared at the dead girl in despair. "I can't leave her here like this."

Eric said, "We'll bury her as well as we can. By using rocks and as much earth as we can scrape up, we should be able to make a respectable grave."

Gale glanced at him. "She should not be alone."

Professor Leduc said, "Madame is of a sentimental nature."

"Let us bury them side by side. It is the way they would wish it."

Eric looked slightly surprised, and then he said,

"If that will make you feel better, I guess we can manage it."

Professor Leduc nodded. "I'll help you carry the girl back. It will be easier to move her than the man."

"That's certain," Eric said. "Well, let us get about it and then be on our way back to Casablanca."

The men carried the slim body of Gert back and then carefully made the best grave they could and placed the two lovers in it side by side. At Gale's request, Professor Leduc spoke a few words of the burial service. Then they reverently covered the bodies and started back to the balloon. Gale was still in a state of depression as they walked along and so said nothing to the two men.

They were within a short distance of the balloon when Professor Leduc suddenly let out an angry oath! Gale lifted her eyes and saw why. Riding full tilt toward the balloon with a flaming torch in his hand to destroy it was one of the sheik's riders.

9

It was a moment for quick action and Eric lost no time. Rushing ahead of Gale and the Professor he drew out a pistol from inside his jacket and fired. The bullet found its mark. The horseman straightened in the saddle just as he reached the balloon, the torch fell from his hand to burn on the ground next to the basket of the balloon, and he toppled down beside it.

Eric rushed forward with the pistol still in hand and ready to use. He lifted up the torch and hurled it away where it would offer no danger to their aircraft. The horse had taken flight and was far away as Eric knelt to examine the fallen member of the sheik's riders.

"He's finished," he told Gale as she came up to him. Then he covered the dead man's face with his robe and stood up.

Professor Leduc looked shaken. He stared at the still-burning torch and said, "That was a very close thing, my friend."

"Too close," Eric said sternly. He glanced around. "There could be others still somewhere around."

"It is time we left," the stout Professor said.

Gale agreed, "I'm sure the sooner we get away from here the better."

Eric moved the body of the dead rider over to the shade of some rocks. Then he came back to her and asked, "Have you ever been in a balloon before?"

She shook her head. "No."

"Exhilarating, Madame!" the stout man in khaki and pith helmet said.

"Perhaps a trifle frightening," was Eric's warning.

"I don't care!" she told him. "Anything to get safely away from here."

Eric eyed her skimpy harem costume and said, "I have an extra jacket in the balloon carriage. You will need it. The air can be alternately cool and hot up there."

Professor Leduc was already examining the divots to which the large balloon had been tied. He entered the basket and checked the various controls. Then Gale and Eric joined him and helped him pull up the several sandbags by the divots. Finally, the ropes holding the airship secure to the ground were cut and it began to rise up and glide with the wind currents in a dizzying fashion.

Gale clung to the guy ropes and refused to look down. Eric stood close by her with an encouraging smile on his bronzed face. In the meanwhile the fussy old Professor was busy at the controls.

"The Professor has only a certain amount of control over the airship," Eric said. "The rest depends on winds favorable to us."

"How long should it take us to reach Casablanca?" she asked, as her golden-red hair was blown by the wind.

"A few hours if we are lucky," the young newspaperman said. "Longer if we're not. The balloon was still my best way of reaching you."

"You've proven that," she said.

He asked, "Are you sure Sheik Ali Yusuf is dead?"

"Yes," she said with a tiny shudder. "I saw it. His head was almost severed from his body."

"At least that is one less of them."

"There are more?"

"Several factions. One led by his brother Sheik Abdul Numen, but I hope we shall not have trouble from that quarter."

The basket of the balloon lurched wildly and Eric gave her support. Clinging tightly to the guy ropes as well, she now looked down and saw the ground seeming to waver one way and then the other. She knew it was just the movement of the balloon, but it made her dizzy.

With a wry smile for Eric, she said, "You are right. It is a frightening experience."

"But the best way to cross the desert," he assured her.

Professor Leduc turned to her from his instrument panel, and with a smile of childish pride, told her, "You need have no fear. This airship is entirely of my own design and I have safely flown it many, many miles."

"I have every confidence in you," she told him.

She held the jacket Eric had given her close around her as the wind currents hit the balloon. Glancing back at the brown, barren desert she thought of the hopelessness of her fate until Eric had arrived in this curious vehicle. She would always regret that Massabi and Gert had not lived to join her in this final phase of the escape.

Eric pointed out interesting sights below. Once

they passed over a tiny village with its huddle of dark, mud huts. On a hill beyond was a shepherd with a flock of sheep grouped near him. Further on a camel train wended its way.

The newspaperman gave her a grave smile. He lowered his voice and spoke close to her ear, "The Professor is conducting his experiments here with the support of the French military. It is supposed to be a weather mission but I'm sure it is for use when the time comes for revolution. French authorities deny it, but they are preparing to take this country over."

She said, "I was questioned constantly by Sheik Ali. The briefcase was on his mind."

"On the minds of more than one," Eric said with a frown. "When we return to the city perhaps I should accompany you to the house in which you were living and make another search for it."

"I'm sure the house has been thoroughly ransacked by now," she said. "But it might be worth trying."

"Were you harmed in any way?" he asked. "I see you were put in native clothes."

"Harem dress," she said. "That is where I was held a prisoner."

"You must speak to the American Consul about that," Eric said angrily. "He should know what is happening to his nationals."

"Out there in the desert is a long way from Casablanca," she said. "They have their own law."

"Still your story must be told and reported as a warning to others," Eric worried. "I shall file a story for my paper and see that some of the American reporters do the same."

"Won't that expose everything? My late husband's connection with the arms runners and the other illegal business of International Ventures?"

"The story is beginning to break anyway."

"Revene ought to be exposed," she agreed.

The basket of the balloon gave another uneasy lurch and the stout Professor came to them apologetically. He said, "I'm sorry. We are encountering unfavorable winds and they are taking us off our course."

"Far off?" Eric asked.

Professor Leduc's round face revealed concern as he nodded. "I fear so. We are now edging toward the mountainous area."

Eric asked, "Will that make our trip more dangerous?"

"There is always more risk," the Professor admitted. "But we ought to be able to keep our altitude. That is the main thing. And perhaps the winds will change." With this said, he returned to his post of guiding the airship.

Eric glanced below and said, "We are in a different area."

Gale confirmed this by looking down also and seeing the rugged, hilly terrain with some of the hilltops rising incredibly high.

"Did you come by this route?" she asked Eric.

"No," he said, still studying the terrain below. "We followed the desert route almost all the way from the shore."

Eric went to confer with the stout Professor who now seemed busier than ever at the controls. Gale stood alone clinging tightly to the ropes and the edge of the basket and studying the area over which they were floating.

She knew they were thousands of feet above the ground, and some of the summits were reaching close to them, so they must have drifted into a mountainous country. There were wild valleys and intensely blue lakes and occasionally a fertile green plateau.

Then they passed over a wilder area with deep forests of cedar and pine trees, which reminded her of paintings she had seen of Switzerland. Suddenly the basket lurched violently and she was almost thrown to the floor.

Eric came quickly and helped her regain her place at the side of the basket. "Are you all right?" he asked.

"Yes. What happened?"

"I expect a bad down-draft," Eric said, looking troubled. "The Professor has suddenly become silent. He won't tell me anything."

"Something must be wrong," she said, gazing up at the great shining circle of the balloon above.

Eric also gazed upward and his look of concern increased. He said, "I may be wrong but I think we must be losing gas. I'm going to ask him!"

But before he could do this the balloon lurched badly once more, almost throwing them off their feet. Then the Professor went to them, his chubby face pale. The eyes behind his heavy glasses were frightened. "I do not know how. But we are losing our gas. I do not know how long I can keep the craft in the air!"

"Is there any danger of an immediate crash?" Eric asked.

"I think not," the Professor said, holding on to the edge of the basket and looking shattered. "With good luck we may be able to make a landing."

"Where are we?" Gale asked.

"Somewhere in the mountains," was his troubled reply. But then he quickly added, "But I'm sure we're along the trade route. I have seen a road straggling below us at various moments."

Eric was quickly assessing their precarious situation; the expression on his young face was alert and indicated keen concentration. He said, "Then our best hope at the moment is to land somewhere near the trade route where we may be found by a passing caravan and taken on into Casablanca."

The Professor nodded. "That is what I must now try to do."

"There is no chance of making Casablanca on our own?" Eric ventured.

"None!" The Professor was emphatic and looked up warily. "I can see we have lost a lot of our gas already. The problem will be to keep above the mountain peaks. We could smash against one of them."

After this grim news he returned to the controls. Eric remained at Gale's side for a few moments, and it was fortunate that he did, for there was another great tilt of the basket. This time it was apparent that they had lost a great deal of altitude.

"I'm sorry I got you into this," Eric told her.

"I'm the one who took you out to the desert," she said.

Eric put his arm around her protectively. "I have every faith in the Professor," he told her. "But with the equipment broken down there's little he can do."

"Perhaps he will manage to get us down safely," she suggested.

The Professor shouted to them, "I see a road below. In the valley between the mountain peak and the river. I'm going to try and set us down gently in the water."

"Hold on," Eric said and clutched the basket tightly himself.

The Professor now began accelerating the drop of the aircraft, releasing the balance of gas in the balloon in a slow, scientific fashion, and at the same time attempting to direct it over the river.

The drop through the air was alarming. The basket whirled about in an insane fashion. It seemed to Gale that the earth was slamming up toward them rather than they were dropping gently toward it. And the descent was not even but wildly confusing, so that at one moment the river was a blue line on their right and in the next, they were swirling away from it!

The Professor shouted out some sort of warning which they could not hear for the rush of air. Then Gale screamed as the craft dropped like a rock and in an instant plunged into the river! The basket went deep into the water with the ropes and weight of the collapsed silken balloon bearing down on it and covering it. They were lost in a confused watery blackness.

She struggled to escape from the wreckage and felt Eric tugging at her arm as she swam under the water. She followed his lead and a long moment later they both bobbed their heads above the water.

"This way!" Eric called, still staying by her.

Together they swam to the rocky shore and dragged themselves up, soaking wet and still stunned from it all. In the river the wreckage of the balloon floated as a gloomy reminder that they were stranded in this wild, mountainous area.

She pushed back her wet hair and asked Eric, "The Professor! Where is he?"

Eric was on his feet now, dripping wet, and exhausted-looking. He gazed at the wreckage and with a grim glance at her, he said, "I'm afraid he must have died in the crash!"

"Surely not!" she protested.

"He would have surfaced by now if he hadn't," Eric said. "He likely was caught down there and wasn't as lucky as we were in getting away from the wreckage."

"Is there nothing to be done?"

"I can dive in again and see if I can locate the body but it will do him no good, and I might not make it myself this time."

The possibility of losing Eric brought on new panic. She struggled to her feet. "No! No! Don't do that! If you're sure he's drowned, there's no use your risking going back in the river again."

Eric surveyed the scene sadly. "There's no question of it."

And she knew he was right. The pleasant old man had to be dead. Even though she had seen more violence and death in the past days and hours than in all her life before, she deeply felt the loss of Professor Leduc.

"It's hopeless," she admitted. She was beginning to feel chilled and uncomfortable in her wet clothing. "What now?"

Eric fumbled in his trousers pockets and produced a small metal match box. He said, "I've lost our weapons; that Gatling gun helped drag us down, but unless this box has leaked we have some matches. We'd best gather some brush and dry our clothes and warm ourselves and pray that someone will see the fire and come along."

Together they gathered enough dead branches to make a good-sized fire. They kept close to it and their clothing dried fairly quickly.

Eric told her, "The Professor was right. There is

a rough trail up above us a little. It must get some use."

"It ought to lead to a village," she decided. "Perhaps if we walk along it we'll find someone."

"I think so," he agreed. "I'd like to get someplace before dark. I don't relish the idea of being out here alone after daylight has ended."

She didn't ask him why. The facts she already knew were unpleasant enough without her wishing to hear more. They made their way laboriously up the hillside to the rough trail worn by the passage of wooden wagon wheels and the tracks of men and animals.

She had been in her bare feet since her escape from the harem and now the abuse she was giving them was beginning to tell. The rough roadway was especially hard on her and she found one foot so tender that she began to limp.

Eric noticed and asked, "Is it bad?"

"No," she said. "I can go on."

"You're sure?"

"I'll tell you if it gets worse," she said.

"We'll rest awhile when we make the turn ahead," he said.

She protested. "We shouldn't. It will mean more loss of time!"

"We won't be able to move at all if your foot really gets bad," he pointed out.

"Don't worry about it!" she insisted.

But it was extremely painful. She didn't dare let him know how badly it was hurting, since she could picture him trying to carry her in his arms. He came close to her.

"Lean on me for support on that side," he ordered her.

"It's not necessary," she protested. But at the same time she was grateful for this small assistance.

As they trudged on through the mountainous, wooded land so unlike the desert they had left behind, she said, "What a country of contrasts this is!"

"Very much so," he agreed.

"I imagine the French authorities will be very upset to hear of the death of Professor Leduc and the loss of the balloon."

"They are bound to," Eric said with a sigh. "And I feel sorry for his daughter."

She gave him an interested glance. "He has a daughter?"

"Yes. An only child. She is in Morocco. She came with him. Her mother is dead."

"How old is she?"

"Madeline must be eighteen," he said. "I don't relish the idea of telling her that her father is dead."

"How dreadful for the poor girl! What will happen to her now?"

"I imagine the French will send her back home."

They rounded the turn and came to several huge boulders suitable for them to rest on. They sat together on one of the large, flat rocks and gazed across at the sun sinking behind a distant mountain.

She said, "It would seem we're going to be stranded out here after all."

"I know," he agreed. "Are you frightened?"

"Not as long as I'm with you," she said with a small smile.

"You are a brave young woman," he said quietly. And he took her in his arms and drew her close. His lips caressed hers and she cooperated willingly. She knew that she felt more for this man than she had for any in the past. Not even Paul had meant as much to her. The kisses over, he still held her close.

"I love you, Eric," she told him.

"And I love you," he said in return. "If we ever get out of this I want to marry you."

She gave him a warning look. "You forget?"

"Forget?"

"Yes," she said. "Paul, my husband, may still be alive."

Eric frowned. "We've been over this before. It's possible. But I think he died in that explosion of the launch."

"We can't be sure," she pointed out. "If he wasn't on the boat I'm still a married woman," she said.

"To a man who has placed you in grave danger."

"I realize that."

"A man who loved you so little he brought you here to cover up his illegal dealings," Eric went on angrily.

"I have to face that as well," she admitted.

"And because they think you have that all-important briefcase, you will continue to be threatened."

"I agree."

"Would you go back as wife to such a man?" Eric wanted to know.

"I couldn't," she said. "Especially after finding out I truly love you."

"Gale!" he said gently, and touched her cheek with his hand.

She took his hand in both of hers and studying him with loving eyes, told him, "You have become so precious to me. But we must not do anything scandalous! I must rid myself of Paul in proper fashion if he is still alive."

"I don't care a shred for scandal," he said. "I

want to let the world know of our love!" And he took her in his arms again for another long embrace.

Darkness was settling over the forbidding countryside and they had started to painfully make their way along the trail again when she heard the muted sounds of voices and the creaking of wagon wheels from behind them.

She halted and said, "Listen!"

He did and at once cried with delight, "Wagons coming along the road back there."

"We are in luck!" she enthused.

"We may as well wait right here until they catch up to us," he said.

And they did. Then out of the shadows came the first of the wagons. It was like a covered wagon of the American West with a driver seated in the front handling the two horses. Eric shouted and waved his arms to catch the driver's attention.

Gale listened to Eric and the wagon driver exchange talk in a language she did not understand. She judged it was one of the Moroccan dialects. She noted that there were at least five wagons in the group.

Another native in a white robe came up and joined in the conversation. After a little, Eric returned to her looking worn-out.

He said, "They are not exactly delighted to see us. But I've promised them money when we reach Casablanca and I've given them all I had in my pocket. They've agreed to let us ride in the last wagon."

"Thank goodness," she said. "Are they taking produce into the city?"

"I don't know. We'd better go back and climb in the wagon before they change their minds."

"You're right," she agreed. Her anguished feet were not equal to any more walking.

The men regarded them with deep suspicion as they made their way back along the wagon train to the wagon in the rear. It was partly empty and driven by a graybeard who had only one horse to manage. He grumbled aloud at their increasing the load for the animal to drag up the steep mountain trail.

As they climbed up into the back of the wagon and took their places, Gale whispered to him, "The old driver is no more delighted to see us than the others."

"We can't stand on welcomes at this time," Eric told her.

The wagon rode roughly and it was only just a little less trying than walking. She said, "Do caravans like this often travel in the night?"

"No," Eric said. "It could be they are afraid their produce may spoil and want to reach Casablanca in a hurry."

"So do we."

"We'll not arrive before dawn," he warned her.

"I'm so tired," she sighed.

"Lean against me and try to get some sleep," he told her.

She did as he suggested and in spite of the unlikely conditions, she soon fell into a light sleep, filled with a mad montage of dreams. She was back in the harem, seated naked before handsome Sheik Ali as he dined and commented on her infidel beauty. Then she was riding across the desert; someone was shooting, and a bullet struck Gert, and Massabi cut off the head of the cruel sheik!

Then she was falling and moaned aloud in her terror. They were all back in the basket of the balloon again and it was hurtling to earth. She was sick with terror and she had a glimpse of the chubby face of the startled Professor Leduc mirroring her own horror!

She cried out in terror and woke up in the wagon in Eric's arms. She gave him an apologetic look. "Sorry, I've been dreaming!"

"Having nightmares, judging by your moaning," he said.

"Yes."

She noticed that it was almost light. "I must have slept longer than I thought."

"Yes. Dawn has broken," he said. "I expect they'll be making a stop soon for some food and a rest."

"I'm hungry," she admitted.

"So am I," he said with a smile. "Basic needs!"

The wagon train did stop a short while after and she and Eric were able to join the drivers in some native food and drink. Though the fare was foreign to her she enjoyed it through sheer hunger. When the wagons were ready to resume they were roughly ordered to go back to the rear one again.

As they sat in the back of the last wagon, she asked Eric, "Did you get a look at what they're carrying?"

His pleasant face was suddenly sober. "Yes."

She stared at him. "Is something wrong?"

"I'm afraid so." He hesitated. "It might be better if you didn't know. They don't want us to know."

"Tell me," she begged him.

He gave her a sober look. "Ammunition," he said. "These wagons are loaded with wooden cases of ammunition."

"It can't be!" she protested.

"It's true; the whole country is seething on the

edge of revolution. Dozens of different parties are arming themselves. We've just happened to run into another one of them!"

"Will they kill us?"

"I don't think so," he said. "Not if they are friendly to Westerners!"

"The caravan has grown," she said in disbelief.

"You're right!" he exclaimed, seeing that there were now at least three wagons in the string behind them.

A man in a turban rode up to the rear of their wagon, reined his horse, and shouted. His horse reared, and several others came riding up. And Gale had her first good look at the lead rider. It was the native with the deep knife scar along his cheek who had been at the wheel of Revene's craft!

Before she could tell Eric, the scarred man spoke up sharply in broken English, "Madame Cormier!"

The scarred one grinned as he covered her and Eric with his rifle. "It is most fortunate that we should meet!"

Eric was bewildered. "You know this fellow?"

"He's one of Revene's men," she said.

Eric groaned. "So our luck hasn't changed!"

The scarred one shouted out orders in a native tongue, and before she could barely utter a protest she and Eric were taken roughly in hand by the riders. Eric shouted angrily and fought back; she joined him in her own attempts to get free! The end was inevitable and the same in both instances. She and Eric were bound at the ankles and wrists and thrown back in the same wagon in which they'd been riding.

The wagons were rolling again, only this time they were captives. Eric let out a miserable, "Damn!"

"Revene again!" she said, trying to wriggle her body closer to him.

The back cloth of the wagon had been closed, covering them so that now they were in shadows. He said, "No hope for us now. We have to be close to Casablanca!"

"They won't dare take us in prisoners in this way," she said in dismay.

"Why not? No one will see us," he replied and groaned again. "They've broken my lip and I think I may have a tooth missing. What about you?"

"They weren't as rough with me as they were with you!"

"You probably didn't give them as much trouble," Eric said.

"What do you think they'll do to us?"

"Take us wherever they're taking the munitions."

"Likely somewhere in the city," she ventured.

"In the medina somewhere," he told her. "The ancient part of the city is the center for the rebels."

"I'm sorry," she said.

"Quiet," he told her. "Rest while you can, no matter how uncomfortable you are. And listen! What we hear may be our only guide to freedom. We can't see anything from this dark wagon."

She knew that what he was saying was the truth. The bonds at her wrists and ankles hurt as much as the ones she'd suffered previously. The wagon bumped along as much as it had earlier, and it seemed her whole body was one aching mass. They had come full circle and were back in the hands of Revene's gang.

The wheels of the wagon turned with a different sound and there were voices everywhere. The air was warm and she was sure they were within the city.

Eric must have felt the same thing, for he said in a low voice, "We can't have far to go now!"

"We've left the road for the city streets."

"I hear every sort of dialect spoken," he said. "I'm sure we're in the medina."

The wagon suddenly halted. The curtains were clumsily pushed apart and rough hands hauled them out into the open. They were in a narrow alley, and their captors, big men in brown robes, dragged them through a dark, arched doorway.

It was some sort of ancient building, filled with stale and not too pleasant odors. As they were shoved along she had a glance at Eric's bruised and bloodied face and felt a surge of sorrow for the young man who had so valiantly befriended her. She did not dare to imagine how she must look with her skimpy clothing disheveled and her own face dirty and sweaty, her golden-red hair in mats.

They were thrown through another door like sacks and a gate of iron bars closed on them. It was a makeshift prison with a damp, stone floor. Their captors locked the barred door and walked off in the shadows arguing loudly with each other in their own tongue.

Eric's back was to one wall, his bound hands behind him, his knees slightly drawn, and his ankles bound. Gale lay on the floor on her side and struggled to get herself up in a sitting position so she could use the wall opposite him in the narrow stone chamber for support.

He said, "At least they've found a place for us!"

"I feel like a caged animal!" she moaned.

"That's about what we are for the moment," was his reply.

She wriggled painfully and finally reached a sort

of sitting-up position on the floor across from him. "I wish they'd do whatever they intend to do with us and get it over with," she said in distress.

"I imagine they have more pressing duties first," the young reporter said.

"Meaning?" she asked.

"Those wagonloads of munitions," he said. "That is what this is really all about. We just happen to be mixed up in it."

"They have to see the loads safely somewhere before they deal with us?"

Eric nodded. "I would expect that scarfaced one would feel safe disposal of his cargo the first duty."

"I'm near collapse," she told him. "My throat is parched and my body is a mass of pain!"

He said, "Still, we are alive!"

They sat there in the silent shadows of the rough prison for perhaps an hour before footsteps could be heard coming through the room to them. She looked and saw it was Scarface and two others with him. One of the men carried a tray on which there might be food and drink she thought weakly.

The scarfaced one ordered an underling to unlock the iron-barred door, and when it was open he came in and eyed them with disdain.

"So?" he said in heavily accented English. "You do not count for much now?"

She cried, "What have we done to you? You've no right to keep us here! Let us go!"

Scarface laughed harshly. "You ran away from Revene and now you'll go back to him."

"Not even Revene would treat us like this," Eric said angrily. "We are parched for drink and starved."

Scarface showed a mocking smile on his brown

face. "You do not do me justice. I have come here to revive you with some fine food."

He commanded the first robed man to untie their hands and then stand over them with a rifle pointed at them. Then he had the other serve them steaming bowls of a fragrant soup. It took them moments before they could even hold the bowls in their numbed hands. When they were finally able to manage, they drank the liquid greedily. Eric held his bowl out to be filled again. Scarface jeered at this but ordered it filled.

Gale was afraid to take more than one bowl of the nourishing, warm liquid. Her stomach was in such a state she felt she might throw up and lose it if she drank too greedily. She handed the second man her empty bowl.

Scarface showed surprise. "No more?"

"No," she said weakly. "I feel ill."

"You will recover as soon as the food helps you," was her jailer's prediction.

Eric looked up from the bowl he had half-finished and asked, "What do you want from us?"

"Some information," Scarface said. "This girl was a prisoner of Sheik Ali. I would like to know how she escaped and why he did not capture her and take her back?"

She spoke scornfully, "He tried, and he was killed for his troubles!"

Scarface snarled, "You lie, infidel woman! You are a soiled thing filled with untruths!" And he lifted his hand to strike her across the face!

10

At that instant Eric leapt up and seized the scarfaced man around the neck and brought him to the stone floor of the prison. As Eric choked him, the other guard took hold of Eric and tried to drag him off his leader. In a moment the two would have the advantage over Eric whose ankles were, like her own, still bound.

In a frantic gesture she took the huge clay container with the remains of the soup in it and brought it down on the man's head with all her might! It knocked him out and left Eric free to choke the scarfaced one into unconsciousness. When his victim lay limp with no sign of struggle in him, Eric let him go.

"Is he dead?" Gale asked.

"I don't know and I don't care!" Eric said tersely. "Get your ankles untied." And he went about removing the bond from his own.

As she worked with the thick cord, she asked him, "What now?"

He was already free and on his feet. He stamped them for a few seconds to restore circulation. "We'll lock them in and then somehow try to get out of here," he said.

She finished with the ties at her ankles and he helped her stand up. She said, "I'll be all right in a moment."

His young face was somber. "No time to lose," he said, picking up the keys to the barred door which the henchman to the scarfaced man had dropped.

They left the prison room and locked the barred door after them, leaving Scarface and his helper locked inside. Then with Eric leading the way, they slowly crossed the big room outside and went along a hallway. In a sideroom a number of the caravan drivers squatted on the floor, eating, drinking, and making merry. They were having such an uproarious time they neither saw nor heard Eric and Gale as they made their way by the door and then on out into the street.

They were in a narrow alley of the medina. It was a dark night and there were no lights in any of the nearby buildings. Eric took her by the arm and led her along. They found another alley, which gave access to a slightly wider street. It held a number of small shops and each had torchlights set outside.

They came to a potter's souk. The old man wore a turban wrapped above his fez, a superstructure so high it seemed to press his beak nose down to meet his sharp chin. Crouching among his tiers of basins and pitchers, he worked with calculated speed. One sure hand turned the neck of the jar, while a finger of the other, first dipped in a pot of black paint, swiftly sketched on a geometric pattern. Ten seconds was all it took, and the jar joined a line of others on a shelf.

Eric spoke to him in Arabic and the ancient stared up at him a moment and then replied. He used a bony finger to indicate the route they should take.

Eric thanked him and they were on their way again. This time, at least, they were going in the right direction to escape the old section of the city.

There was an angry shout and a bullet zinged from the street behind them. "Keep your head low," Eric gasped. "They're after us!"

"What can we do?" she gasped as she ran at his side over the descending cobblestoned street.

"In here!" he shouted and dashed into an open doorway.

She followed him and he pushed her behind him in the shadows and then stood watching out the doorway from the hiding place. A few moments later Scarface and three of his henchmen came rushing along the street, still in pursuit of them. Unaware that they had taken shelter in the house, the quartet continued down the street.

She whispered, "At least you didn't kill him!"

"I'm sorry about that," he replied.

"And now?"

Eric surveyed the narrow stairs and said, "I think up there is our best move. We daren't go down into the street for a little. They'll be on the lookout for us!"

"I'm sure you're right," she said.

Cautiously he advanced up the rickety, shadowed stairs and then a second flight. There was no sound from the closed doors they passed on the landings, so she assumed the house must be deserted. They finally climbed a small ladder which took them to the rooftop. The houses were so huddled together they were able to move from one rooftop to another.

Once they were forced to make a short jump between the rooftops of two ancient buildings. Eric went first and nimbly sprang across, then he held his hands out to catch her. "Come along!" he said.

She was fearful of attempting it. From the dark chasm below, lit by an occasional torch, came the sound of voices murmuring like a distant surf. She quavered, "I can't!"

"You must!" he told her, his hands outstretched to receive her.

She lifted her eyes from the chasm and tried to draw on any small reserve of courage she might still have. And then, her eyes fixed on Eric, she made the leap. He caught her as she trembled on the edge of the rooftop and took her in his arms for a moment.

In the warmth of his embrace she got over most of her fear and told him, "I'm sorry!"

"No need to be," the young reporter assured her. "That was a dangerous jump."

They moved on to another house, which was in a state of ruins. This rooftop had collapsed in places and they had to move over it gingerly; several times Gale felt the surface of the roof sag a little as she stepped on it, and she uttered small cries of fear. She glanced down through an opening in the roof and saw the hollow heart of the house.

They moved to the next building and crossed a parapet which took them to the edge of a courtyard. Below was a busy scene. Leaning over and staring down into the courtyard, Eric told her, "Those are dyers at work. They are working by torchlight so must have some rush order."

She glanced down and saw earthen vats scooped out of the ground, each with a gaping mouth filled with some violent color. And each sending up a quantity of steam.

Figures moved about the clay vats, their forearms and their legs below the leather aprons permanently stained. In the swirling steam they looked like creatures in a Dantean inferno! The dyers stood on narrow catwalks between the vats and stirred the mixtures with long poles, every so often lifting out the poles to inspect them. The dye coursed along their arms and streaked their perspiring faces. Boys bent double under a load of hides on their backs as they moved along the slippery catwalks. Every so often they dumped hides into an empty vat. The scene was macabre—wraiths of steam, gleaming surfaces of dye, and straining, dye-stained flesh.

A boy glanced up and saw them and shrilled something to his coworkers. At once they became the center of attention as they peered over the edge of the rooftop.

Eric drew her back, "Time to move on! They might be bold enough to come after us. Visitors aren't welcome in some areas of the medina."

Gale needed no urging to go. They left the roof hastily, going down several flights of stairs in another house. This one was not deserted. They heard voices on every floor and almost bumped into an old woman on the lower flight of stairs. She screamed bitterly at them as they left her and hurried down to the street and out.

The street appeared deserted at this point. And again Eric led the way. They moved hastily, and within a short time she was delighted to see the gate leading from the medina to the modern city.

"We've made it," Eric said breathlessly as they ran toward the stand where carriages stood in line waiting for passengers.

They found one and Eric had a difficult time persuading the driver that he would be paid on arrival at the Empress Hotel. The bearded worthy wanted his money first but at last gave in and allowed them to drag their weary bodies up into the carriage. It began to roll through the wider streets of the new city.

Gale gave Eric a relieved glance. "I didn't think we'd manage it."

"There were times I wasn't sure," he admitted with a weary smile.

"I've been a dreadful nuisance to you," she apologized.

"Not at all," he said. "The Revene story is my present assignment. You are part of it. I'm carrying out the business I came here for in the first place."

"That makes me feel better," Gale said. And she glanced down at her thin, torn harem costume and asked, "Do you think I will be allowed into the hotel dressed as I am?"

"I'm hardly in evening clothes," Eric said, indicating his soiled linen trousers and torn white shirt.

"At least you're wearing proper Western garb," she said ruefully. "I'm dressed like a fugitive from a harem, which I happen to be!"

"I'll arrange everything," he promised. "I have your bags with the clothing you bought before going on the train. I salvaged them when you vanished."

"Good!" she said. "Then I'll have something to wear."

"All at my room at the Empress," the young man said.

"You will have to get in touch with Professor Leduc's daughter," she reminded him.

"I know," he agreed. "One thing at a time. First let us get safely to the hotel."

Their entrance at the dignified Empress Hotel caused a number of heads to turn. The fact that their bad-tempered driver was on their heels screaming at them in a manner which he must have reserved for villains of the deepest dye didn't help. They crossed the huge lobby before a host of astonished eyes and to the accompaniment of shocked gasps.

Eric tried to quiet the complaining driver but it was useless. The driver went on telling all earth and Heaven of his bad treatment. They made a weird trio as they presented themselves at the desk with the angry driver behind them.

The clerk was a tall, balding man with an impressive mustache. He first stared at them with annoyance, and on recognizing Eric, showed signs of immediate apology.

"My dear Mr. Simms," the upset clerk said. "Where have you been and what has happened to you?"

"Never mind," he said. "Just pay this booby!"

"Certainly, sir," the clerk said. He fished in his cash box and gave the man some silver. The driver clutched it eagerly and then retreated muttering, leaving them alone at the counter, the object of interest of the bellhops and other hotel employees as well as the guests who were in the lobby.

With typical British coolness Eric behaved as if they were both in the most proper dress. He said, "I will have my keys and my friend, Mrs. Cormier, will require a room on my floor and as close to mine as possible."

The bewildered clerk looked properly troubled and made a show of checking the rack of room keys on the wall behind him. He finally selected two and gave them to Eric.

The clerk said, "This is your key, and this will be

the lady's. The room is directly across the hall from yours, with a view of the square."

Eric took the keys. "Thank you. The view doesn't matter at all as long as they are conveniently near."

Gale's cheeks were burning as she stood there in her scant and tattered harem costume and heard this exchange. She was aware of further exclamations of surprise from the onlookers as Eric passed one of the keys to her.

The clerk was not finished with them. He shoved the large hotel ledger toward them and stuttered, "Do please sign our register, Madame!"

"Yes, of course," she said, taking a pen from its stand on the counter and shakily signing the register on the proper line.

The clerk looked relieved. "Thank you, Madame," he said. "I trust the room is suitable."

"Bound to be," Eric assured the man with crisp dignity. "This young woman, a newspaper person like myself, has just escaped from the headquarters of a rebel leader after enduring imprisonment and torture. Any room will be welcome."

Murmurs went around the lobby as Eric made this explanation in a sufficiently loud voice. The clerk at once looked approving and said, "I might have known. My pleasure at seeing you again, sir. And you, Mrs. Cormier, welcome to our hotel!"

"Thank you," Gale replied, blushing.

The clerk smartly tapped a bell on the counter and summoned a brown boy in turban and uniform with gold-colored buttons. He ordered the youth, "Take Mr. Simms and Mrs. Cormier up to their rooms."

The boy led them across to the elevator while

the onlookers now regarded them with proper respect. Gale could feel that the hostility had vanished and they were now being looked on as representatives of civilization in a corner of the earth where it was not too well-represented. A matter of good Englishmen sticking together.

As they rode up in the elevator with the boy standing by them impassively, she said, "Well, you surely handled that like a veteran."

He smiled. "Do you think so?"

"I do," she told him. "I first feared we were going to be evicted. But we wound up as heroes. I could feel the atmosphere in the lobby change within a few minutes."

"Old colonials," he said. "They always have sympathy for one of their lot in trouble."

"We've surely had our share of that," she sighed.

They got off on the fourth floor and the boy padded down a carpeted hall and showed them to their rooms, which were, as Eric had requested, almost across from each other.

Eric told the boy to wait and then promised her, "I'll bring out your bags of clothing at once." He let himself into his room and emerged within a moment with her bags. The boy took them and delivered her and the bags to a comfortable room with a lamp on the dresser. The boy lit the lamp and the room took on a cheery appearance.

She told the lad, "Thank you. And now will you bring me hot water for a bath?"

The boy nodded soberly and rushed off. Eric came out of his room to join her and ask, "Everything all right in here?"

"Yes," she said. "It's wonderful! I've sent the lad to fetch me water for a bath."

"Good idea," he said. "I'll have him get some for me as soon as he's brought yours. Here is some money for his tip." He handed her some coins.

She smiled. "You think of everything!"

"Not hard now that I'm back at headquarters," he said with his usual modesty. "I have some money and everything I need here. I hope you will find enough in the suitcases to do you."

She glanced at them. "I haven't looked. But I know I will. I packed them before we boarded the train."

At that moment the youth returned carrying two pails of hot water, followed by another with two pails of cold, and a third lad, dragging a large tin bathtub. They set the pails of water and tub down in the middle of the room. The youth then bowed to her.

"Do you need assistance?" he asked in his almost perfect English.

She blushed furiously and thrust some coins in his hands. "No, thank you. Divide this among the others."

The lad bowed his thanks. Then Eric told him to get him the same things as he'd brought her. And the three lads went out chattering loudly in Arabic among themselves.

Eric smiled at her. "Well, I'll leave you now. Perhaps you'll join me for something to eat downstairs a little later on."

"I'll be ready in a little while," Gale told him.

"Good," he said. "I'll knock on your door."

She nodded. "I can't believe we're alive and safe."

"It is something," the young reporter agreed. He kissed her tenderly on the cheek and said, "I'd better

210

get back to my room or my bath will be there ahead of me."

Gale luxuriated in the huge tin bathtub. She lathered her hair as well as her body and felt clean for a change. She had enough hot water to keep her comfortable for a reasonable time. And she emerged from her bath to towel herself thoroughly, leaving her skin tingling and fresh feeling.

Fortunately she had a good selection of clothing left from the things which Eric had bought for her in Rabat. Now she donned a white taffeta dress with blue lace trim. It was a luxury to wear normal clothing again. She rolled up her harem outfit to be thrown away. She wanted to forget the entire ugly experience. Her only redeeming memories of the interlude were the friendships she made with Gert and Massabi. Both of them now dead.

She gazed in the mirror as she brushed her gold-red hair into a suitable coiffure and decided she was among the most fortunate of people to be back in Casablanca safe. But how long would she remain safe? She was certain the only solution for her was to take a vessel back to America as quickly as possible.

There was a knock on the door; she inquired, and then opened it. Eric looked especially handsome in a suit of fresh white linen. His facial injuries showed only as slight bruises on his cheek, and the broken lip was hardly noticeable, although swollen a trifle.

He smiled as he stepped inside. "You are truly a treat for the eyes," he said.

She laughed. "You'd think I'd look good in anything after what I've been wearing. And you look yourself again."

"I've arranged with the dining room for a late dinner," he said.

"Good. I'm famished," she told him. "That soup we had in the medina wasn't all that sustaining."

"It seemed like nectar when I first tasted it," the young reporter admitted. "But I'm sure the Empress dining room can do better."

They went downstairs and were shown to a corner table in the big Palm Tree Room. It had many windows, which in the daytime gave a view overlooking gardens, and there was a bandstand on which a violinist and pianist offered pleasant melodies reminiscent of England.

Both Gale and Eric ordered roast beef and they then sat back to enjoy the music while they sipped at the excellent wine Eric had chosen. There were only two other late diners in the big room, but a number were seated at tables and at the bar in an adjacent area.

Eric smiled over his wine. "Do you suppose Scarface is still searching for us in the medina?"

"I rather think not," she said. "He has probably reported to Revene about us by now."

"That's likely so."

She gave him a knowing look. "And it won't take them all that long to trace us here."

"True."

"And once they locate us the trouble will start over."

Eric frowned. "You're not optimistic."

"Not any longer. I think I should get away from here as soon as I can."

"But how can you go, not knowing whether your husband is alive or not?"

She sighed. "That does complicate matters. But surely it is up to the authorities to find that out."

Eric looked at her with concern. "I don't want

to keep you in needless danger. But I hate to see you leave at this time."

"Why?" she asked.

"I have an idea you might help us end some of this evil business by remaining here," he told her.

"Because I'm still a target for the illegal munitions people?"

"Yes."

"They still think I have that briefcase with whatever information it contains."

"Without a question," Eric said. "That is why Sheik Ali Yusuf kidnapped you. He wanted to get ahead of the others. Unfortunately for him, it cost him his life."

"He was terribly arrogant and cruel."

"I can promise you his brother, Sheik Sidi Abdullah, is more ruthless."

"Is he older or younger than Sheik Ali was?"

"Older. They were sworn enemies of each other and of Sheik Abdul-el-Krem, with whom we must assume your late husband was associated."

"If he truly is my late husband, and not alive and in hiding somewhere."

"That will be found out," Eric said. "To get back to Sheik Sidi Abdullah, he is a large man, more than six feet tall. And he has only one hand. His right hand was cut off in a vicious duel when he was a young man. He wears a steel hook in place of it. And he can use that hook on an adversary with terrifying results."

She opened her eyes wide. "You make him sound even worse than Sheik Ali!"

"I think he is," Eric told her. "All three of these powerful tribal leaders aspired to overthrow the Sultan. To the best of our knowledge both Sheik Abdul-el-Krem and Sheik Ali Yusuf are dead. Which means the chief rebel leader left is Sheik Sidi Abdullah."

"And no doubt Revene was supplying illegal arms to them all."

"No question of that," the young reporter said. "And there is some other shadowy figure in the same game. Perhaps your husband."

She sighed. "You may be right. He confided to me that he meant to go on his own and rival International Ventures."

"An interesting ambition," the young man across the table from her said dryly.

Their dinners came and the conversation was dropped for a time. She enjoyed the excellent food and the music proved soothing. She was gradually lulled into a feeling of false security.

It was over their tea that Eric suggested, "I'd like you to meet the American and British consuls. And I think I can get them together for a short time tomorrow to hear your story."

"If you can arrange it, of course I'll talk with them," she said. "I can use the opportunity to have the American Consul help me get passage on a ship bound for New York."

"He's the one who can help you most," Eric agreed.

"You can let me know in the morning, then."

"I may not be able to set the meeting until the afternoon," he told her. "But I'll advise you as soon as I arrange it."

They finished dinner and left the table just as the musical duo was playing a nostalgic waltz. Eric, with a smile, took her out onto the bare floor where dancing was sometimes enjoyed, and they danced in solitary bliss to the lovely music. When the music ended, the violinist bowed to them, and there was applause from the bar area.

They walked on to the lobby with Gale saying, "I could never have predicted tonight."

"Could you have predicted any of it?"

"No," she admitted.

He said, "Wait here a moment and I'll see you safely up to your room. I want to ask the desk clerk if the American Consul is in his room. He's a bachelor and lives here. I'll be only a moment."

Gale remained near the elevator while he went across the lobby to the desk. There were several others ahead of him, so he had to wait before being able to question the clerk. In the meanwhile she studied the lobby and its people. It was late now and most of the older residents of the hotel had gone to bed. But there were still some rakish-looking young men and fashionable young ladies to be seen at various spots in the big room.

Glancing to the outer lobby, she saw the big glass revolving door turning, and emerging from it was someone she knew! Jiri, whom she had met through her husband. Jiri came toward the main lobby until he saw her. Then he froze where he stood and after a brief delay he quickly turned and hurried out through the revolving door again.

Impulsively, she quickly crossed to the outer lobby and made her way through the door to the outside in pursuit of him. The doorman, standing outside in uniform, gave her a respectful nod.

"Does the lady wish a carriage?" he asked.

"No," she said, studying the empty street with troubled eyes. "I'm looking for a slight brown man in a red fez. He came out the door a moment ago. Did you see which way he went?"

215

The doorman looked wryly amused. "My deep regrets," he said. "But there are thousands of men in Casablanca who wear a red fez and have brown skin. One becomes blind to them!"

"Really?" she said, doubtfully. She could not imagine the doorman not seeing the fellow. Yet he might be telling the truth. Familiarity with the type could make him unaware of any particular individual.

A worried Eric came out the revolving door to stand on the hotel steps by her. He said, "I couldn't imagine where you'd gone. Then one of the bellmen said you'd come out here."

She turned to him, taut with her discovery. "I saw him again, Eric!"

"Saw who?"

"Jiri, the brown man," she told him. "He was coming into the lobby, when he saw me. He turned quickly and fled."

Eric frowned. "Why would he do that?"

"Because he wouldn't want me to question him about Paul!"

"I don't know," the reporter said doubtfully.

"I'm sure it was Jiri," she insisted.

"And you risked coming out here alone in an attempt to catch up with him?"

"Of course."

Eric shook his head in discouragement. "I would think by now you'd know better. What if he had waited out here and grabbed you and taken you off with him?"

She indicated the doorman. "He would have saved me."

"He isn't always here. He might have been called away as you came out," Eric worried. "Or this

216

Jiri might have lured you further into the shadows of the street before attacking you."

Gale looked sheepish. "I'm sorry."

"You don't know how to take care of yourself," was his warning.

"I'll do better in future," she promised.

"I sincerely hope so," the young reporter said. "As it is, you seem to hurry into every trap set for you!"

She protested, "His coming here wasn't a trap to catch me. He was here for some other reason. As soon as he saw me he rushed out and vanished."

"Let's be thankful for that. If we want him later I'm sure we'll be able to find him."

"I hope so," she said.

"Time for bed," he told her. "Especially since I may need you to meet those people early in the morning."

"I know," she said wearily and made her way in through the door again.

As they walked toward the elevator, its ornate bronze door opened and two people stepped out. She could not help but notice them. They were deep in a serious conversation as they passed, and neither seemed to notice her. The man on the left was short and stout with a small mustache and wearing a dark suit and Panama, evidently European of some nationality. The other man wore a white robe and flowing white headdress. He was more than six feet tall, with a narrow, cruel face, a long hooked nose, and small, nervous eyes. And he had no right hand; in its place there was a dangerous-looking steel hook!

She gave a small gasp and turned to see the two leaving the hotel by the revolving door. Then she turned to Eric and in a nervous voice, asked, "Did

217

you see him? That has to be Sheik Sidi Abdullah."

"And you happen to be right," Eric admitted.

"What do you suppose he was doing here?" she asked as they got in the elevator.

"Everyone comes here," he said. "It is a center for all sorts of business dealings."

"Then he was likely here on business," she said. "Would that mean that Revene is staying here?"

"Not under his own name, certainly," he said. "It's possible—anything is—but he rarely stays in hotels."

"So we're not likely to find him unless he comes looking for one of us," she said bitterly.

"It's just about that," he admitted as the elevator halted at their floor and they got off.

Eric saw her to her room and made sure all was right within. Then he took her in his arms for a good night kiss. She responded warmly even though she knew she might still be another man's wife. It seemed all her feelings for Paul had evaporated in her love for this brilliant young Englishman.

"I shall be in touch with you as early as I can," was his promise as he left.

She undressed slowly, thinking of the night's events and what tomorrow might bring.

When she sank into an exhausted sleep her dreams were of Paul and her first days in Casablanca with him. In her nightmare she fought with him and ran out of the chateau on to the white sandy beach. She was rushing along the beach when out of nowhere there appeared the sinister figure of Revenel. The arms smuggler came toward her with a sneer on his cruel face. Then he seized her and despite her screams began to tear off her clothes until she was left naked. Then he hurled her down on the sand and sadistically raped her!

She wakened to her own screams and sat up in bed, perspiration oozing down her temples, her lovely eyes wide with fear as she stared into the shadows of the dark room. Nothing stirred and as her heart gradually eased its pounding she realized she had been having a series of nightmares. She gave a deep sigh and sank back on her pillow.

She must get away! That was her one determination. Back in New York she might recover from this nightmare, and no one would bother her about missing briefcases or anything else. Back in the security of the house of her aunt and uncle she could regain her peace of mind.

She was reluctant to leave Eric. Especially in such a danger-filled situation. But he was used to taking care of himself and would know how to cope with his enemies. Exposing such people as Revene was his profession. She could not ask him to give it up.

With luck they might be together again in New York. If all went well they could be married there. She knew her aunt and uncle would like him. But any such move was a long way off. Not until she knew whether Paul was alive or dead, dare she try to make plans for a future with Eric.

Closing her eyes, she slipped back into a restless sleep which lasted until the morning. She opened her eyes to sunshine streaming into the room and quickly rose to wash and have her breakfast. She went downstairs to take her breakfast in the dining room of the old hotel and she was seated there when she had an unexpected visitor.

"May I intrude?" a familiar suave voice asked her.

She glanced up in surprise to see the hawk-faced Carl Revene seating himself at the table across from her. He was nattily dressed in a cream suit and white shirt with a crimson bow tie.

She said, "What do you want?"

He raised a slim, deprecating hand. "Do go on and enjoy your breakfast."

She stared at him in dismay. "You do not encourage my appetite."

"I regret that," he said, with seeming sincerity. "Since I so much approve of you."

"What are you doing here?"

"I have been an overnight guest of this hotel," he said. "Just as you have."

"So Sheik Sidi Abdullah was here for a meeting with you," she said, remembering the one-handed sheik she'd seen emerging from the elevator the previous night.

Revene smiled in his smooth fashion. "I'm really only here to talk about you."

"I should call the manager and have him turn you over to the police!"

"For what?" he asked mildly.

"Kidnapping for one thing," she said. "Rape for another."

"I think you might have difficulty proving either charge," was his assured reply.

"You think yourself above the law!" she said with some anger.

He looked amused. "It would be better to say that I know the courts in this unhappy land. The police and the law are most inefficient."

"They must be, or vultures like you wouldn't flourish here," she retorted.

"Let me remind you that your husband was my associate."

"I'm not proud of that!"

"Nor am I," Revene said with mock sorrow, "since he proved himself a traitor."

"I'm sure you deserved it!"

"That is a matter on which I know we could never agree," he said in his same friendly fashion. "I understand you have been the means of causing the death of one of my valued customers, Sheik Ali Yusuf."

"He brought about his own death," she said.

"So you say," he commented. "I'm not altogether sorry since I have lately entered into a new agreement with his brother. And they were not at all friendly to each other."

"Please go!" she told him.

"In a moment," he told her. "Let me say what I have come here to say."

"What?"

He showed embarrassment. "You are so direct! I'm a man of some sensitivity."

"Not when it comes to the business of murder," she told him.

"You do me an injustice," Revene said unhappily.

"I think not!"

"What I wished to say, is that I have come to care for you deeply," he went on. "My physical experience with you left me with a hunger for your charms. I have offered to marry you."

"I consider myself dishonored by your offer."

He stared at her. "What a pity!"

"You know how I feel!"

"I hoped you might change," he said, with another sigh. "Well, I suppose I must face the ugly fact that you do not appreciate me. But on to other matters. Until you change your opinion of me I shall be sadly forced to limit my association with you to a mere business one."

She said scornfully, "I have no business with you."

"I'm sorry," he said in a soft voice as he leaned across the table. "You have forgotten something?"

"What?"

"A certain briefcase."

She gave a weary groan. "Are we back to that again?"

"We are. When are you going to return it to me? Your husband stole it from my office."

"I know nothing about it."

"I have reason to believe otherwise, dear lady," the hawk-faced man insisted. "I do not wish that case to fall into other hands."

"I cannot help you," she said firmly.

His cold black eyes held a cruel light in them as he inquired gently, "Not even to save your husband's life?"

11

She gasped and then said, "Paul is dead!"

Revene's smile was a sneer. "You'd like to believe that, wouldn't you? Especially since you've found your London reporter friend."

"How dare you!" she exclaimed.

He raised a placating hand. "Your pardon! I did overstep propriety. Only let me tell you, my dear Mrs. Cormier, your husband may not be as dead as you seem to believe. We have reason to believe that he is alive and still here in Casablanca."

"You're lying to me," she accused him. "Trying to make me do your bidding by telling me Paul is alive and in danger."

The hawklike face of the millionaire displayed cold disdain. "I would not stoop to such tricks, I assure you. And let me also assure you, should your husband be alive, he is truly in danger."

"From you, no doubt!"

He shrugged. "From me and certain others with whom he has done business. Yet there may be a way to protect him."

"I know," she said bitterly. "Give you the briefcase."

"You have stated it exactly."

"I do not have it. I have never had it," she said angrily. "Will you never accept that?"

"I'm afraid not," he said, his eyes fixed on her coldly. "I beg you to think it over. For both your sake and that of your husband."

"I can't help you!" she protested.

He stood up. "And I very simply do not believe that. But have it your way." He nodded slightly with an icy smile on his lean face. Then he turned and strode out of the dining room.

She sat there stunned by the encounter. It took her a little time before she could resume her breakfast. And when she did she had little appetite for it.

If Jiri had escaped, why not Paul? She must face it, her husband was probably hiding out somewhere and carrying on his own illegal deals in opposition to Revene. And the missing briefcase had a great deal to do with it all.

In her opinion, if there was a briefcase, it was still in Paul's hands . . . assuming that he was alive. Apparently he had this valuable collection of official papers which could spell embarrassment for some of the representatives of the powerful nations. And if she knew her husband, he meant to use the papers to blackmail these men.

She finished breakfast and went back up to her room to think it all over. If Paul were still alive she would do all she could to try and free herself from him.

At the same time she did not wish to see him come to harm at the hands of someone like Revene and his gang. She was still Paul's wife and owed him some loyalty. If he were alive she would do all she could to help him out of the trouble into which he'd managed to get himself. But after that she would face him frankly with the news she wanted a divorce.

She was pacing slowly up and down in her bedroom, lost in these thoughts, when there was a knock on her door. It was Eric. He seemed in a good mood. Coming in to join her, he kissed her and with his arm around her began to talk.

"I'm later than I expected but I've had a busy morning," he explained.

She said wryly, "So have I." And she told him about her conversation with Revene.

Eric stood facing her and listening intently. When she'd finished, he said, "I don't like the sound of it!"

She worried, "Nor do I. And it tends to make me think that Paul may only be in hiding."

"It's possible," Eric said, sounding far from convinced.

"What have you managed this morning?" she asked him.

His handsome, tanned face showed a weary smile. "I felt I'd managed a good deal until you came along with your own surprises."

"Do tell me!" she implored him.

"We are to have luncheon with the British Consul," he informed her. "And while your consul is ill and cannot attend, he is sending his associate, a bright young man from Boston."

"Oh? What time do we meet them?"

He took out his pocket watch and studied it. "We are due there in about twenty minutes. Can you manage it?"

"I think so," she said. "I'll just change into something a little more elaborate and wear a hat."

Eric studied her with admiring eyes. "You look perfect just as you are!"

"I must dress properly," she insisted.

His eyes showed amusement as he suggested, "Do you still have your harem costume?"

She took him by the arm and led him toward the door. "I have heard quite enough," she said. "You wait for me downstairs in the lobby."

The British Consulate was an important-looking building in a busy section of modern Casablanca. Two of Her Majesty's armed guards stood on duty at either side of the entrance gate to its courtyard and gardens. Eric had to produce proper credentials before they were allowed to go on in.

They walked up a palm tree-lined gravel walk to the entrance door of the white stucco consulate building. There they were greeted by a pleasant young man who informed them he was Colonel Hudson's secretary and led them down a long corridor with fans whirling from the ceiling to a conservatory-type room with a row of windows overlooking the consulate gardens.

Impressive, monocled Colonel Hudson greeted them there. He was red-faced and hearty British in manner. He showed a smile on his broad face and said, "So this is the young lady. I'm delighted to meet you, Mrs. Cormier."

"It was kind of you to invite us," she replied, offering a white-gloved hand to him.

"Not at all, ma'am," the big man in the white linen suit said. "Come in and meet Mr. Adams, from your consulate."

He led them into the room which had been furnished as a dining room and they were introduced to a graying, sanguine-faced thin man with a decidedly nasal New England accent. He shook hands with Gale and Eric and told them, "I'm Richard Adams from Boston. I'm representing our consul here today."

"I have often visited Boston," she told the thin man in the gray suit. He had a sort of all-over gray, reserved appearance. "I enjoyed the city very much."

Richard Adams looked pleased. "We Bostonians are loyal. Perhaps you met some of my family. We have a place on Beacon Street."

"I have visited on Beacon Street," she told him. "But I do not think I met any of your family."

Richard Adams' thin, wrinkled face revealed interest. "I hope you may one day meet them. I'll give you the address before we leave."

Eric asked him, "Do you expect to be serving in Morocco for long?"

"It is difficult to predict," Adams said. "I could be sent to a different assignment at any time. I would like to return to the United States when I can. A post in Washington would be much to my liking."

"Why not London, Mr. Adams?" Colonel Hudson asked in his good-natured, bluff fashion.

"That would surely be my second choice," the lean Mr. Adams said with professional courtesy.

"Well said!" Colonel Hudson laughed. And to Gale and Eric, he said, "I trust you both enjoy shellfish. I have chosen a particular dish which my chef does very well."

"I'm fond of shellfish," she told him.

"And so am I," Eric agreed.

"What about you, Mr. Adams?" the British Consul asked.

Richard Adams revealed a careful smile. "As one brought up on the Cape Cod scallop, I confess to a weakness for shellfish of any kind."

"Excellent!" Colonel Hudson said. "We are all in agreement. So on to the gin and tonics, and I'll tell

Mrs. Cormier something about our gardens before we gather at the table."

He led her out a door on to a balcony and, gin glass in hand, pointed out the high points of the gardens. The gardens were guarded on the outside by tall walls of great stone beauty and color. In these walls were inserts, fantasies in iron which gave both protection and beauty. In the garden espaliered trees spread out their arms in rows like a waiting corps de ballet. A fountain tossed arcs of water high and caught it in a red marble basin. Rose trees were the high spot of the lovely scene, trimmed neatly but not stiffly. Flower beds were edged with box, but spilled over. This spectacle of varied warm colors contrasted with the background of cool plaster walls and several robust cedar trees.

"It is lovely," was her opinion.

"Thank you," the bluff Colonel Hudson said, his face glowing with pleasure. "And now let us sit down to luncheon."

The food and service were perfect, as she had expected them to be. All during the meal the Colonel kept the conversation tuned to the lightest of subjects. He discussed events in London and the peccadilloes of the aging Prince of Wales. After that the Colonel and Richard Adams compared opinions about the weather of Morocco and agreed it was perhaps the best in the Middle East. Gale listened to it all and occasionally offered an opinion when asked for it.

Across the table Eric gave her a sly smile to indicate he was also enjoying the manner in which the friendly British Consul was directing the conversation. It was not until they were having their coffee that any hint was given that this was anything but a purely social event.

Then Colonel Hudson looked at her earnestly and said, "My dear, Mr. Simms has told me all about the trying experiences you've had. I must say you've shown considerable courage and are to be commended."

She felt her cheeks burn at his sincere compliment. She said, "I fear I have been little more than bewildered. It is Mr. Simms who showed great courage by rescuing me in the desert."

Colonel Hudson nodded. "I have heard the story. These Sheiks are getting completely out of hand. The Sultan does not seem to realize the seriousness of the situation. And the French appear to prefer to ignore the danger."

Richard Adams spoke up in his nasal fashion, "I think the French are behaving in this ostrichlike manner on purpose. They want an excuse to make Morocco a protectorate. So they plan to let things come to a boiling point, with the Sultan overthrown. Then they will take over."

"Exactly what we think," Colonel Hudson said soberly. "In the meanwhile we are living in a period of great disorder. It is most difficult for our nationals to carry on business with this country."

"Agreed," Adams said. And he glanced toward Gale to add, "I must apologize that one of our citizens should be given the treatment which you have suffered. It is a black mark on us. But we are almost powerless here."

Eric Simms suggested, "You are telling us that citizens of Britain, the United States, or any other country do business here at their own risk. That there is no protection for them."

"I regret to say there is very little," Colonel Hudson admitted. "Here in these peaceful surroundings it is hard to believe. But you have learned it the hard way, Mrs. Cormier."

"I have," she said.

Eric asked, "Would you say the malicious influence of such an organization as International Ventures goes beyond what is happening here in Morocco? That this firm represents an international danger?"

Colonel Hudson replied, "Yes. My government firmly believes this to be the case."

"And mine," Richard Adams agreed. "But thus far we have been able to do little to restrain Carl Revene. He has become very rich and powerful."

"Not to mention his henchmen, Peter Hall, Edmund Walton, and all that foul crew," the Colonel said with an angry note in his voice. "I fear your husband was one of them, Mrs. Cormier."

"I found that out too late," she replied.

Eric said, "Now they are hounding her about a missing briefcase, which her husband supposedly hid away somewhere."

"I have heard about the briefcase," Colonel Hudson said. "In it are papers dealing with some of the arms transactions. Names on these papers belong to people in high places who made the transactions possible. It could create chaos in world political circles if these names were revealed."

She said, "And that is why they are so desperate to get them?"

"Yes," the British Consul said. "In the hands of a man with no scruples it would be an excellent blackmail weapon."

Gale said, "I expect that my husband planned to use it in that manner. He told me he meant to break with Revene. That was only shortly before his death in the launch explosion."

Richard Adams and the bluff Colonel Hudson exchanged knowing looks and the American said, "Mrs. Cormier, there are reasons to think your husband may have escaped death. That he may now be in hiding somewhere. And probably with the briefcase in his hands."

"I begin to believe that possible," she said, and went on to tell them about her encounters with Jiri and how he always ran from her. And of her visitations by what had seemed like the ghost of her husband.

Colonel Hudson heard her out and then said, "I agree with you, Mr. Adams. I'd say there is at least a fifty-fifty chance your husband is alive."

Adams took up the thread of conversation by saying, "We also have a second problem. While we have been trying to deal with Revene and curb his operations, another mystery figure has moved into the field of running illegal munitions."

Eric Simms showed interest. "What is his name?"

"We don't even know that," Colonel Hudson admitted. "We only know he exists. And that he is giving Revene some strong competition. We have hopes the two may engage in a private war and eliminate each other. Thus ridding us of both of them."

"It is easy to deal with the underlings once the head men are eliminated," Adams said in his cautious way.

Eric asked, "Who are the principal customers for these illegal arms?"

"Sheik Ali Yusuf was one," Colonel Hudson said. "We know from Mrs. Cormier's account of things that he is dead. But there is his brother Sheik Sidi Abdullah, the most powerful and dangerous of all. And if this Jiri and your husband escaped in the launch explosion, Mrs. Cormier, there is a strong likelihood that Sheik Abdul-el-Krem is also still alive and ready to cause trouble. But that is sheer speculation."

"There may be others with whom we're not familiar," Richard Adams pointed out.

Colonel Hudson gave Gale a concerned look. "The proper thing for you, Mrs. Cormier, is to return to New York as soon as you can."

"I completely agree," she said.

The Colonel went on blandly, "But that would not help us. That is why I'm going to ask you to consider remaining here in Casablanca for a little while longer."

Perplexed, she stared from one to the other and asked, "May I inquire why?"

"You have every right to ask," Colonel Hudson told her. "I'll allow Mr. Adams to explain a few things to you."

The thin, proper Bostonian looked embarrassed. He said, "I agree with the Colonel that you ought to go back to the United States. But there is a chance you can offer a signal service to your country here, and that is why we have invited you to lunch with us."

"I knew it wasn't to discuss the racing season," she said with a tight smile.

Richard Adams said, "When you arrived here you lived in a house by the beach owned by this Revene. Lease papers show your husband rented it from him for a period of a year with an option to buy it."

"He didn't tell me that," she said with surprise.

"We have the documents," Adams said smoothly.

"So with your husband deceased, the lease of the house reverted to your name," Colonel Hudson explained.

"I don't want it!" she protested. "It is a gloomy, awful place."

"It has an evil reputation," Colonel Hudson agreed. "And I think Revene used this to his advantage. First, in buying it cheaply, and secondly, using it as a cover-up and headquarters for his criminal operations here."

"Without question," the thin Adams agreed.

"The house has been unoccupied since you left it," Colonel Hudson informed her.

"Since I was kidnapped by Revene aboard his yacht," she said with some bitterness.

"Truly unfortunate," the big man agreed. "None of the others have used the house and presumably are living somewhere else, perhaps aboard the *Siren* with Revene."

"I think that altogether likely," Eric said.

Richard Adams addressed her again. "Your husband had a brother, Benjamin."

"Yes, I met him," she said.

"He lived here in Casablanca for several years and more than once was in trouble with the authorities. Were he and your husband on good terms?"

"Not really," she said. "Though he did come to visit us and we went to his studio once. He was an artist. He planned to do a portrait of Paul and give it to us for a wedding present. Of course he never did."

"Oh?" Adams showed interest.

"I went back to his studio in the medina and found it deserted. An old man staying there told us Ben had been stabbed to death and the woman he was living with had fled. Everything had vanished, including all his paintings."

The lean member of the American Consulate staff nodded. "I'm not surprised that he came to a violent end. He was an inveterate gambler. He sustained big losses several times, which he was unable to pay. He made enemies in the medina underworld."

She suggested, "Isn't it odd that his body was not found?"

Colonel Hudson smiled grimly. "Not in Casablanca, dear lady. Men, and women also, vanish here every day and are never heard of again."

"There are many places to dispose of unwanted bodies," Adams agreed. "The local police authorities cannot hope to keep up with the homicides."

Gale said, "What do you want of me?"

"A direct question," Richard Adams said with a wan smile. "It deserves a direct answer. We would like you to help us get more evidence against Revene and this other mystery competitor who has suddenly come upon the scene."

She frowned. "How could I do that?"

Adams eyed her unblinkingly. "Very easily. By going back to the chateau on the beach and living there for a while. You would be the bait to attract Revene and the others."

Eric gave her a warning look across the table. "Think about it, Gale. It could be dangerous."

She considered the suggestion. "But it would land me in the middle of things again," she explained. "They're bound to come after me, looking for that briefcase."

"We would hope so," the jovial Colonel Hudson

admitted. "In that way we may be able to bring them into the open where we can deal with them."

Eric rose from his table and went around to stand by her. Looking down at her, he said, "I brought you here at the request of these gentlemen. And I must admit I had some idea of what they had in mind. But you are in no way obligated to cooperate with them."

"I realize that," she said quietly.

"Let that be clear," Adams said in his nasal twang. "We do not wish to force you to do anything against your will."

"Certainly not," Colonel Hudson said, adjusting his monocle. "If you decide against our suggestion nothing more will be said."

"And I shall at once arrange a passage for you to New York," Adams told her.

She sat back in her chair with a sigh. "I will be leaving here not knowing whether my husband is still alive or not."

"That is the situation at the moment," Adams said.

"A nasty bit of unfinished business," Colonel Hudson agreed.

She stared at the two men. "You wouldn't ask me to stay alone in that house?"

"Not at all," Richard Adams told her. "We would arrange for you to have companions. And they would be specially chosen by us."

"Would I have police protection?" she asked.

"To a degree," Colonel Hudson said. "We have had a limited promise of support from the Morocco police officials. But no uniformed officers or military can be conspicuously posted in or around the building. That would scare these bounders off and defeat the whole purpose of the plan."

Eric asked the two, "Who would her companions be?"

"We have considered carefully," Adams said. "And we think one should masquerade as a servant to do the cooking and generally look after the house. We have an ideal man for this task."

"Who?" she wanted to know.

"We will call him Hassan," Richard Adams said in his wary fashion. "Suffice to say he is a giant of a man, an officer of the Casablanca police but not well known enough to be recognized. He would be well armed and able to summon additional help when it might be needed. We would also arm you."

Colonel Hudson broke into the conversation, saying, "Let me assure you this Hassan is no ordinary man. He has the reputation of being strong and resourceful. The Moroccan authorities chose him specially for us."

"Who else?" she asked.

"Someone to keep you company," Adams said. "And at the same time someone who you can help. I refer to Mademoiselle Madeline Leduc, the daughter of the balloonist who was killed during your desert rescue."

Gale was surprised. "Have you spoken to her of this?"

"Yes," Adam said. "She is grieving for her father and quite alone here. She is willing to enter into any scheme which may bring about the downfall of those directly responsible for her father's death."

"She speaks excellent English," Colonel Hudson chimed in. "And she seems a most pleasant girl, though understandably now in a depressed mood."

"I understand she was returning to France," Eric told them.

"She was," Adams said dryly. "Then we discussed this plan with her and she volunteered to be part of it."

Gale listened to the discussion, finding herself filled with indecision. She wanted nothing more than to get back home. Yet she disliked leaving Morocco without knowing whether Paul was still alive. Also, she felt some guilt in the accidental death of Professor Leduc. If his adolescent daughter was prepared to risk her life to trap Revene it was not beyond the limits of reason to expect her to also take part in the plan.

Eric suggested, "Perhaps you'd better sleep on the matter. Give your answer tomorrow."

She glanced up at him. "Will I also have your support if I agree?"

"Naturally," he said. "But I'm answerable to my paper. This story is happening all over Morocco. I could be sent to some remote village within an hour."

"But Casablanca will remain your headquarters?" she said.

"Yes," he agreed.

She turned to the two older men and in a quiet voice said, "It seems you have me in a position where I cannot well refuse to help you."

"So you will return to the chateau?" Colonel Hudson asked eagerly.

She nodded. "Yes."

Richard Adams' lean face showed pleasure.

"You are doing your country a service, Mrs. Cormier. I may say, even contributing to world peace."

"Without a doubt," Colonel Hudson told her emphatically. "Revolution here could spread through the Middle East and within a short while involve several world powers. If we can halt this traffic in illegal munitions, we may be able to keep the peace here and everywhere else."

She asked, "When do you wish me to move in?"

"Tomorrow?" Adams suggested.

"Very well," she said. "I shall remain at the hotel for tonight."

"A carriage will come for you tomorrow," Adams said in his precise way. "Hassan will be at the house to receive you and live in as your servant and bodyguard."

"What about Mademoiselle Leduc?" she asked.

"The carriage will call for her later and bring her to the chateau," the prim Bostonian said. "I have it all arranged."

"So it would seem," she said with irony.

He looked embarrassed. "I could have changed the plans quickly had you decided against helping us."

Colonel Hudson went on to say, "One thing, no matter what happens it must not be known that we are behind this scheme. At least not until it has been brought to successful completion."

"I see," she said.

Eric asked, "What liaison will this Hassan have with the Casablanca police?"

Adams said, "The commissioner of police will make men available whenever Hassan contacts him."

Eric looked doubtful. "Do you think that good enough?"

"It is the best we could manage," Colonel Hudson apologized. "Things are a bit grim here. Factions are at each other's throats at every political level. Even accomplishing this much wasn't easy."

"I can understand that," Eric said. "Yet as I see it, Mrs. Cormier will, with Mademoiselle Leduc, be taking a substantial risk."

Bostonian Adams spread his slim hands. "I will not deny that. Yet considering the fact she does not know her husband's fate, and this may surely settle the truth for her, it is a gamble which she is well advised to take."

Eric asked her, "Do you feel that way?"

She gave him a solemn look. "I think I should make an attempt to go through with it. If I find it too trying I can always give up."

"You have our promise of that," Colonel Hudson said at once.

"Then it is agreed," she said, rising. "If you gentleman have no further need of me I'll go back to my hotel."

The older men rose at once and were loud in their praise of her. They escorted her and Eric to the door of the consulate, shook hands, then vanished inside. Gale and Eric walked out past the guards to their waiting carriage.

Gale raised her parasol to protect them from the midday sun as they rode through the wide streets of the new city.

Eric said, "Those two had it all set out, didn't they?"

Looking at him, she said, "Yes. I think they were sure I'd agree from the start."

"Apparently so."

She sighed. "They realize I have to know the

truth about Paul. And they also have guessed that I have a score to even with Mr. Carl Revene."

"He's a dangerous one to take on," Eric warned her.

"I know that," she said. "Up until now everything has gone pretty much his way. But there is bound to be a change. I want to be there when the tide turns against him."

Eric promised, "I'll do all I can to help you."

"I know you will."

"It may not be all that easy," he continued. "I've already postponed assignments outside Casablanca. I can't go on doing that!"

"I don't expect you to."

"This could be dangerous for you," the young man worried. "Revene is bound to come after you."

"I will have Hassan," she pointed out.

They returned to the hotel and he saw her up to her room. He promised, "I'll be back in time to take you to dinner at seven."

She smiled. "I'll look forward to your return."

"We can talk more about this scheme then," he said, still troubled about it. "You can always back out, you know."

"I know," she said. He kissed her and then left while she went on inside.

She rested during the hot part of the afternoon but was awake again as five o'clock came around. She then rang for a maid and explained she wanted to take a bath before dressing.

The elderly Frenchwoman was devastated: No portable tub was available at the moment. There was, however, a room on every floor especially for bathing. By a miracle it was unoccupied at the moment and she would prepare it for her. The woman left to look after this chore and Gale laid out a fresh change of clothing on her bed.

Wearing only a dressing gown, she stood by the window staring at the busy traffic outside the Empress Hotel and thinking about the morrow and her return to the sinister house by the white sands and sea.

It was a troublesome, wicked business and she wished she had never been involved in it. Now that she had fallen in love with Eric Simms, she only wished to find Paul to make a break with him. Her love for her husband had been killed by his deceit and coldness toward her.

There was a knock on her door and the elderly maid entered again with some large bathtowels on her arm. She said, "Your bath is ready, Madame. I will show you the way."

She followed the old woman down the hotel corridor to an ell, and in the ell was an open door to a bathroom. There was a large iron tub on legs which lifted it about six inches above the ground. There was a step by the tub to facilitate climbing in. Along one wall was an open three-paneled screen which could be used as a place to dress and undress. Jugs containing extra water were available and there was a stool and a battered dresser without a mirror. Such was the bathroom facility offered on the fourth floor of the Hotel Empress.

The maid placed the towels on the dresser and stood by. "Does Madame wish me to assist with her bath?" she asked.

Gale smiled and said, "No. I can manage very well." And she gave the old woman some coins she'd placed in the pocket of her dressing gown.

"Merci, Madame," the elderly one said, taking

the coins. She pointed a gnarled finger at a buzzer near the door. "If you wish help, just press the buzzer and a maid will come."

"I'll remember," she said. "Thank you." And she let the maid go out and then bolted the door for privacy.

She tested the water and found it too hot, so she lifted up a jug of cold water and poured some in. Testing the water again she found it suited her. She made sure there was soap and then removed her dressing gown and flung it over the screen. The pleasantly warm water was delightful as she stepped into the huge tub and settled down in it to lather her shapely body.

It amused her to think the great iron tub was almost large enough to swim in. After an initial lather she lay back in the tub and luxuriated. It had been worth all the trouble of rounding up the maid and making the trip down the hotel corridor. At least at the chateau she would have her own private bath once again.

Realizing that quite a little time had elapsed, she forced herself to get out of the tub and began toweling herself vigorously. At last she stood there with her naked, lithe body tingling with a feeling of well-being. She reached out to take her dressing gown from the screen and in doing so she inadvertently caused the screen to fall forward!

She gave a startled gasp, for standing concealed behind the screen was a familiar figure—the scarfaced bandit who had been with Revene on the yacht and who had taken her prisoner in the medina. There was a grin on his ugly, scarred face as he stepped toward her, a menacing-looking dagger in his hand!

"You!" she said in a taut voice and she tried to don her gown to cover her nakedness.

He reached out with his free hand and snatched the gown from her frightened grasp, leaving her standing naked and terrified before him.

He advanced with the dagger held out, and as she tried to dodge away from him he caught her and placed the tip of the dagger at her throat.

"One sound from you and it is over," he told her.

"Please!" she begged him.

An expression of lust crossed his ugly face as he held her close to him. "I can see why Sheik Ali wanted you for his harem even if you are an infidel," he said with a thickening of his voice.

The sting of the dagger on her taut throat made it impossible for her to offer the slightest resistance as she remained there naked in his grasp!

12

Suddenly there was a knocking on the door and the voice of the elderly French maid came from outside, "Has Madame completed her bath? I have another party waiting."

Scarface was all menace as he told her in a hoarse whisper, "Answer her!"

Somehow she managed, "In just a moment!"

"Thank you, Madame," the maid said and then she could be heard retreating down the corridor.

Scarface held her close to him. The foul odor of his breath disgusted her. "Another time!" he said in the same hoarse whisper.

Then, still keeping her in his grasp with the dagger on her throat, he backed up to the window which the fallen screen had hidden. She saw that the bottom sash had been raised open. As he backed close to it, he nimbly twisted his body and vaulted over the sill. In the next moment he was gone!

Trembling, she covered her breasts with her hands and ventured to the window sill to see that just a story below it there was a fire escape. That was how the desert gangster had managed to gain access to the bathroom and lie in wait for her. But how had he known she would be there?

Shakily, she went back and picked up her dressing gown and put it on. Then she lifted up the screen and put it in place as another knock came on the door.

A male voice asked in a British accent, "Will you be long?"

Still shaking with fear, she unbolted the bathroom door and emerged into the corridor. She was confronted by an indignant grizzled colonial British type who eyed her rather savagely and said, "You should remember, Madame, this is not a private bathroom but for the use of us all!" Having delivered himself of this he stamped angrily inside in his threadbare dressing gown with his towels over his arm.

Gale felt she might have laughed under other circumstances but it had been too close a call. She passed the little French maid hurrying down the hall toward the bathroom.

The maid looked relieved. "Ah," she said. "So the Major has managed to get in!"

"Yes," Gale said in a small voice and continued on to her room.

There another surprise awaited her. The room had been ransacked, her carefully laid-out clothes tossed to the floor. Every dresser drawer had been opened and gone through. The closet door was open and clothes hung in it were now on the floor. Even the mattresses had been lifted up roughly while someone searched the room.

Then she understood. Someone had been in the corridor when she'd summoned the maid to get her bath ready. They had notified Scarface to post himself in the bathroom and keep her there while they

245

ransacked the room. He had intended to rape her, she was sure . . . Thank heavens the Englishman had wanted a bath!

She slowly went about picking up her things from the floor and restoring some order to the room. And it struck her that she was really no more safe in this hotel than she would be at the lonely beach chateau. There was no haven for her in Casablanca.

When Eric knocked on the door at seven o'clock she did not let him in until he'd identified himself. And then she opened the door to him and told him the whole story.

The young newspaperman looked shocked. "I think you should reconsider. Leave the country. Go back home."

"I think it's too late for that."

"What do you mean?"

Her eyes met his. "Paul involved me too deeply. They're sure I know where that missing briefcase is if I don't have it myself. What makes you think I'd be safe in New York?"

Torment flared in his expressive eyes. "You're right! Revene has agents everywhere! He'd send a cable ahead and there would be someone waiting at the New York docks to follow you."

"Exactly," she said. "Oh, Eric, will I never be safe?"

He crushed her to him as if his arms could lock out an army of assassins. "If any harm comes to you I'll never forgive myself."

"It has nothing to do with you."

"I took you to the consulate today."

"That was only a late development in a pattern which was already set," she said. "You merely gave them a chance to ask me to cooperate with them."

"You don't have to."

"I want to," she said. "Now let us go down and have our dinner. I'm over most of my terror and I'm famished."

He smiled at her. "I say it again, you are a most remarkable young woman!"

Dinner was a pleasant interlude. And when it was over they strolled in the gardens under the stars for a little. Eric was in a strangely subdued mood.

She told him, "Don't be so dejected. It's not the end of the world."

"No," he agreed. "And I've inquired about this Hassan. They couldn't have selected a better man to protect you. I worry less knowing you will have him close by. And I think you will like Madeline Leduc."

"I'm looking forward to meeting her," she said.

As they continued strolling along the gravel path in the refreshing night air, he told her, "I'm almost sure she is doing this without the permission of the French Consulate."

"Why?"

"The French are playing their own game in this," he explained. "They want the sheiks to rebel and the country to have a revolution. It will give them the excuse they've been waiting for to take control."

"You really think that?"

"It's true," Eric said. "That is why they have so long closed their eyes to what is taking place. They'll let Revene and whoever his competitor may be run their illegal munitions into the country, just so long as it works in their favor."

"You're saying the responsible French government is actually encouraging revolution and the death of hundreds of innocent people?"

He nodded grimly. "There are times when governments believe themselves to be in the right no matter how wrong they are. This is one of those times with the French government."

"So they would not approve of Madeline trying to help catch the gun smugglers?"

"No," he said. "You must understand there is a great deal of politics involved in all that is happening here." And he took her inside and to her room.

She slept badly. Once she wakened to the darkness of her room and was sure she heard someone stirring about. She lit the candle on her bedside table and held it up to throw a soft glow over the dark corners of the room. There was no one there. It had been her imagination. She blew out the candle, but lay awake for a long while.

Morning came and with it pouring rain. The kind of downpour one encounters only in a tropical climate. Her head was aching and she rose in a properly dejected mood. Not even a good breakfast with strong tea downstairs made her feel any better. She trudged back to her room and slowly began packing for the move she was supposed to make. But she had no heart for it.

Then early in the afternoon Richard Adams appeared. He wore a rain cape over his suit, explaining, "I felt this to be something I had best oversee myself."

"I'm glad," she told him. "I wondered who you might send."

He saw her luggage packed. "You are ready?"

"Yes," she said with a wry smile. "It seems a suitable day to journey to that depressing chateau."

He raised his eyebrows. "I understand it has not been all that pleasant for you here."

"Eric told you?"

"Yes."

She said, "That convinced me I have to work with you."

"I agree," the Bostonian said. "With Revene as your enemy you have to attempt to defend yourself."

Richard Adams had the baggage taken downstairs to the waiting closed carriage. They ducked out the entrance door and into the vehicle. Then they were driven off in the direction of the beach.

As they rode along, he said, "I will take you inside and introduce you to Hassan. Then I shall go pick up Mademoiselle Leduc."

"I'm looking forward to her company." She paused. "Her father was a pleasant man and seemingly very clever."

"A specialist in lighter-than-air craft whom the French government sent here. They will sorely miss his genius."

"I owe my life to him," she said.

"It gives you a bond with Madeline Leduc," he suggested. "Also she hates this wicked group as much as you do. And is as anxious to see them brought to justice."

LeClaire House with its castlelike white stucco turrets looked sinister on this rainy day. The carriage drove into the courtyard and almost at once the front door was opened by a giant of a smiling black man. He wore loose-fitting trousers and a white shirt open at the neck. A gold medallion of some sort hung about his neck on a golden chain.

He had a friendly face, gleaming white teeth, and sharp eyes. He greeted her warmly, "Welcome, Madame Cormier!" And then he helped the driver with her luggage.

All was familiar, if rather threatening, inside. The place had no pleasant memories for her. Richard

Adams stood by as she supervised the bringing of her luggage in and seeing it carried upstairs to the room which she had occupied with Paul.

A sensation of pain shot through her as she stood in the doorway of the room and remembered her happy expectations when she had first come here as a bride. How differently it had all turned out.

The giant Hassan put her bags down and left the room. She and Adams stood there alone. She said, "I really loved Paul once. I had so many hopes for us. All dead now!"

His sharp eyes fixed on her. "You have come to hate your husband?"

"Yes. I almost hope he is dead."

"You really mean that?"

She felt her cheeks burn. "No. I suppose not. But there is no question of loving him or wanting to go on being his wife. He has chosen a criminal life and brought me into it."

"I fear that is so," the prim Bostonian agreed. "But if he died in the launch explosion he paid for his crimes."

"If he did," she said. "I'm becoming more and more convinced he's alive."

"Perhaps he may be," he said. "I have a great respect for instinctual feelings, especially those of females."

She could not help but ask him, "Are you married, Mr. Adams?"

It was his turn to look flustered. "No," he said. "I am a confirmed bachelor. In a career of this sort it is better. I have seen too many family problems with members of the State Department."

"I asked because you seem to have a good understanding of women."

His smile was thin. "I pride myself on being able to understand people."

"That is a true gift," she told him. "It should be most valuable to you."

"Thank you," he said. "Now, if you do not mind, I will go along. I must get Mademoiselle Leduc."

After he left she began to unpack and it was only then that she noticed that the bags which had been packed for her and taken to Revene's yacht had been returned here to her room. She went to them and opened them to find most of the clothing she had brought from New York. She was fascinated to find them brought back.

She went downstairs and found Hassan busy in the kitchen. The big black man greeted her with one of his warm smiles. "Can I help you in any way?" he asked.

Gale smiled in return. "I think so. Can you tell me who brought my bags back here?"

"The luggage in your room?"

"Yes."

He looked surprised. "It was here when I arrived. I thought it had been here right along."

"No," she said. "It was . . . removed for a while."

"I'm sorry, I don't understand."

"It's all right," she said. "Revene had them. Probably he or some of his men brought them back here expecting I would one day return for them."

"Yes, Madame."

She sighed. "And here I am. Do you like this house?"

Hassan shrugged. "It makes no difference to me. Better than the police barracks where I normally live."

"Have you been in the police long?"

"Since my youth," the big man said proudly. "I preferred it to being a soldier or a blacksmith."

"From what I've heard you made a wise choice," she said. "They say you are a most competent police officer."

"I have yet to prove myself in Casablanca," he admitted. "But perhaps I will here."

"I don't doubt you'll have the chance," she said. "Revene is persistent."

"I shall be ready," Hassan said, patting his hip, and for the first time she noticed that he wore a revolver in a leather case on his hip. It hung from a leather belt which he wore loosely at his waist. "Revene and his like are vultures preying on the greed of misguided leaders among our people. The Sultan's reign is corrupt, but the way of revolution will not be a solution here. The French are waiting. They will one day take over, and we will become mere slaves."

"You really think that?"

"I do. We will be subjected to their rule until the day when blacks rise up in Africa to demand their own and battle the white man rather than fight among themselves. Then we will know salvation."

Gale was impressed. "You really do have strong political views!"

"I cannot be blind to what is happening," the giant Hassan said quietly.

"I hope it goes well for us here," she said. "And that we shall be able to defeat Revene."

Hassen looked grave. "That would also be pleasing to me. But do not be deceived. He is a man of strength and resources."

"I know that."

"Powerful in high political places."

"I'm aware of that also," she said with some bitterness.

Hassan eyed her with sympathy. "I have heard your history and also that of Mademoiselle Leduc. You both have endured much, with your experiences being the more difficult."

"Which reminds me," she said. "Mr. Adams told me I would be armed to defend myself."

"Of course," the giant black police officer said. "I have been waiting for the moment to discuss that with you."

"I'd say it was at hand."

"Yes," Hassan said. And he moved across the room to what looked like a stew pot on the back of the big stove. He took the lid off the pot and fished inside it with a huge hand. He brought out a small, vicious-looking pistol with an ivory handle. "This was to be yours," he told her.

She accepted it and weighed it in her hand. "Is it loaded?"

The big man nodded. "Yes. It is ready for use. It has a small safety catch which I will show you."

She watched as he showed her how to use the catch. Then she asked, "Does it matter that I'm not an expert shot?"

Hassan smiled. "That is not expected. The pistol will be mainly a deterrent. No one but a fool would take a chance even with an inexperienced woman shooting at close range."

She held it. "It's not going to be a burden. It will fit somewhere in most of my outfits."

"I'm sure it was selected as being practical," the policeman said.

She turned to leave and then paused to ask, "Do you actually know how to cook?"

"A little," he said. "Until something happens, I will attempt to offer you reasonable food, though nothing fancy."

Gale smiled. "We're not in a position to be choosy. If I want anything done to my special taste I can come down and cook it myself. The same will likely be true of Mademoiselle Leduc."

"The kitchen will always be open to you," was his promise.

She went back to her upstairs room and with a renewed enthusiasm went about unpacking the rest of her things. The pistol she placed in a pocket of the skirt she was wearing. It gave her some small feeling of confidence.

About a half-hour later she heard the carriage returning to the windy, rain-swept courtyard. And she went down to meet Madeline.

Richard Adams stood there with his Panama in hand and the rain trickling down his black rubber cape. At his side was a delicate-looking, attractive girl only a few years younger than Gale. The girl had long, curly black hair, sparkling black eyes and small, even features. She was a beauty and not what Gale expected from having met only her stout professor father.

When they were introduced they exchanged kisses on the cheek. Gale at once took Madeline's flowing cloak-coat, which was drenched with rain. "I'll have this hung up to dry," she promised.

"How good of you," Madeline replied in perfect English. "You are almost exactly as I pictured you."

"And you surely live up to my expectations," she replied with a small laugh, holding the dripping coat over her arm.

Madeline glanced about the shadowed room and said, "It is too early to tell about the house. Especially on such a dark, gloomy day."

"I'm afraid it tends to be rather dismal at all times," Gale said. She gave the wet coat to Hassan who at once went to the kitchen to see about drying it. Richard Adams had been standing back quietly once the girls had been introduced.

Now he spoke up in his nasal New England way, "There is no need for me to remain longer. Mrs. Cormier will have you shown to your room, Mademoiselle. I must return to the consulate."

Gale asked him, "Will you not remain with us for a drink?"

"Thank you, no," the prim Bostonian said in his quiet way. "But I shall be calling by regularly to see how you are making out. And do not hesitate to notify me in the event of an emergency."

Gale smiled wryly. "I'm afraid that most of the urgent situations so far have happened too suddenly for me to have any warning. Let alone warn anyone else."

Adams accepted this bleakly. "We can only hope that it will be different in the future." And he made his way to the door.

Gale saw him out and then returned to Madeline. She said, "I fear Mr. Adams is somewhat on the precise side."

"I would call him a cold, old stick," Madeline told her with an impudent smile.

She laughed. "You have a good command of English."

"I traveled almost everywhere with my father. And we spent much time in the United States and in England," she said.

"Good! My French is really rather poor."

Gale gave the girl a choice of the remaining rooms upstairs and she chose one almost directly across the hall from her. Hassan had accompanied them upstairs and he put Madeline's luggage down in the room.

Gale told him, "That will be all for a while, Hassan."

The giant black bowed. "Yes, Madame. I shall always be in the kitchen when I'm not working anywhere else in the house."

Madeline smiled and said, "Thank you for the help."

"It is my duty, Mademoiselle," he said.

She shook her head. "Not really! You're a police officer and rather important. Mr. Adams told me."

Hassan's big face revealed his pleasure. "My background in police work is not supposed to be discussed while I'm on this assignment."

"It's no secret to us," Madeline told him. "Or speaking for myself, I wouldn't be here."

"I can join in that," Gale said.

Hassan bowed again. "I shall try to live up to the confidence you ladies are showing in me." And he went out and down the stairs.

Madeline said, "I think I'm actually going to like it here. Hassan is marvelous, isn't he?"

"He is," she said. "I feel much more secure. He'll also give you a personal weapon for your protection. I got this a little while ago." And she brought out the pistol and showed it to the dark girl.

"It has a lethal look," Madeline said with a tiny shudder and gave her back the weapon after examining it.

Gale put it back in her skirt pocket. "We are not

here on a lark," she said. "You will do well to arm yourself."

The pretty, dark girl was at once solemn. "You are right. Our business here is dangerous." Her eyes met Gale's as she went on, "You were with my father when he was killed, weren't you?"

"Yes."

"He didn't suffer, did he?" the question was put anxiously.

"No," she said. "I think he was probably stunned, and so drowned without ever knowing what was happening to him."

Madeline listened attentively, then she said, "I'm glad. He was a brave man. He could have met any kind of death. But he deserved a good one."

"It was a tragedy, of course," Gale said with sympathy. "He was so good and capable and brave."

The French girl sighed deeply and turned from her a little. "I was very, what you call broken, after I heard the news. But then my sorrow was replaced by anger. Anger at these wicked men who are making fortunes from the illegal munitions business without a thought of killing those who threaten them."

"I know."

Madeline turned to her again. "So I agreed to come here with you. Be bait for these monsters. Perhaps we can turn the tables and be their undoing!"

"I would like that very much," Gale said.

The other girl eyed her soberly. "Your husband brought you here?"

"Yes," she said bitterly. "Kind of him! I think he's dead. But whether dead or alive I shall always despise him for the kind of life he chose."

"Your dilemma is more heartbreaking than mine,"

the French girl said. "I have only a father to avenge. What if your husband should return alive?"

"I will divorce him as soon as the opportunity allows," she said.

"Not easy," Madeline commented. "But then neither is any of the other things we face. If we fail . . ." The girl shuddered. "I understand that of the Moroccans, Sheik Sidi Abdullah is the most cruel. He is also the one most liable to lead the revolution against the Sultan."

"I briefly met his brother Sheik Ali," Gale said. "I can only say I'm relieved that he is now dead."

She then left the young girl to unpack, certain she had been blessed with a lively and intelligent companion. The consulate people had chosen well.

Just before dinner time there was a knock on her door. It was Hassan. He informed her, "You have a visitor, an English gentleman, Mr. Simms."

She was delighted. "Eric!" she exclaimed. "He is a dear friend of mine! A newspaperman and someone to be trusted. He will always be welcome here!"

Hassan nodded. "Yes, Madame."

"Tell him I'll be down at once," she said. After Hassan had gone to deliver her message she went across to Madeline's door and knocked on it.

Madeline, in a dressing gown, opened the door. "Yes?"

"I wanted to let you know we'll be having a guest for dinner," she said. "Eric Simms, the newspaperman who . . ."

The young girl smiled. "Of course. I have met him before. He came to my father to take him to the desert."

"Yes." And who, like herself, had survived the crash that had killed Leduc.

"I liked him," the other girl said, "And I'm sure he means a great deal to you."

She blushed. "Yes. I'll admit to that. Do come down when you're dressed."

"I won't be long," she promised.

Eric took Gale in his arms and kissed her. "I'd have been here earlier but things have been happening."

"They have here, also," she said. "Madeline Leduc has arrived."

He raised his eyebrows. "She's charming, don't you think?"

"I do," she said. "And she seems fond of you. Perhaps I ought to be jealous."

Eric laughed. "She's special, but rather young for me I'm afraid."

Gale smiled up at him. "For once age is on my side. Tell me your news!"

"There was an attempt to assassinate the Sultan today."

"So, it's beginning!"

"Luckily it was a failure," Eric said soberly. "If it had been a success the whole country would be in chaos. The streets of Casablanca and every other city in Morocco would have been full of rioters!"

"Was news of the attempt suppressed?"

"Yes," he said. "I wasn't allowed to file a story on it. The authorities may give me permission later, but not yet."

"What happened?"

"He was walking to prayers when a man rushed out of the bushes in the royal garden and brandished a gun at him. The man declared, 'Death to the tyrant!' and fired. But before he properly took aim, the bullets of the Sultan's bodyguards had cut him down. The Sultan escaped with a shoulder wound."

"Has the would-be killer been identified?" she asked.

He gave her a meaningful look. "Yes. One of Sheik Sidi Abdullah's men."

"And Revene is supplying the arms to Abdullah." Eric nodded. "Correct."

Their conversation was interrupted by the arrival of Madeline, animated as usual. The three of them enjoyed an excellent dinner supplied by Hassan. The big man was clearly happy when Gale made a point to congratulate him.

After dinner it was Madeline who made the suggestion, "Let us go to Chez Paris for a little."

"I don't know the place," Gale said.

Eric smiled. "It is in what might be called the French Quarter of Casablanca. But not the best area; in fact it borders on the slums of the medina. But it is known for its excellent food."

"And music and dancing," the dark and lovely Madeline said enthusiastically. My father dearly loved it. And always when I go there I feel better. I have an idea his spirit somehow haunts the place."

"Would you like to go?" Eric asked.

"I don't know," she said. "Is it still storming?"

Madeline went to the window and came back quickly with the report, "The rain has ended! It would do us all good to have some fun."

Eric laughed. "Very well. You girls get ready and I'll go out and find us a carriage."

It was a quarter-hour drive to the Chez Paris. The streets were again beginning to fill with people now that the rain had ended. As Gale descended from the carriage she saw gas lamps burning over the entrance of the night club and posters in vivid colors on the wall at either side of the doorway. The posters showed gorgeous women laden with beads and glitter and only a few wisps of veiling.

Madeline had seized her arm and was assuring her, "It is the best dancing place west of Cairo!"

Eric escorted them inside. The club was crowded, mostly with Westerners, and French seemed to be the prevailing language. A four-piece orchestra played Western dance numbers and the floor was almost continually filled.

Eric found them a table near the dance floor and they sat down in the smoke-filled room as the waiter stood silently by for their orders. They each selected a different drink and the waiter went off to get them.

Gale shouted across the table to Madeline, "It's so small and noisy."

"I like it that way," the dark girl said mischievously.

Eric asked Gale, "Would you care to dance?"

"I suppose we should," she agreed. And they went out to join the other couples on the crowded floor. Madeline smiled encouragement to them from her place at the table.

Eric said, "She is something of a character."

She laughed. "Young and lively."

"Yes," he said. "But I think there is something more. I have an idea she feels her father's death much more than she has let on."

Gale considered this as they danced. "You may be right. She is almost too animated."

"Exactly," he said. "It's not normal."

"It's too bad," Gale said. "I feel sorry for her. I shall have to try and help her. But living in constant danger in that house will be no medicine for her. Dance with her next, please?"

The music ended and they found themselves on the other side of the floor away from their table. They pushed their way through the crowd and when they reached the table were astounded to find it empty. The drinks had been brought out and Madeline's was seemingly untouched.

"Where can she be?" Eric worried.

"Perhaps she felt ill," Gale suggested and looked about the place for some sign of the girl. There was a veranda which ran across the back of the club over the entrance door. A narrow flight of stairs led to it and as she raised her eyes she had a flashing glimpse of Madeline vanishing through a doorway leading from the balcony.

Eric also saw her at almost the same moment. He said, "She must be ill. I'll go to her!"

"No," Gale said. "It might be better if I went to her. I can send for you if I need you."

Eric looked upset. "Very well!"

She left him and again had to push her way through the crowds in the smoke-laden room. The orchestra was starting up and dancers were moving back onto the floor once again. She hurried up the steep, rickety stairs and arrived on the balcony breathless.

Then she made her way through the doorway and found herself in a murky hall. From the other end of the hall she heard a girl's voice alternately sobbing and pleading. She listened and had no doubt it was Madeline she heard!

She moved silently down the dirty, dark hallway to an open doorway from which the sobbing had come. Very carefully she edged toward the door so she might look in without being seen from the inside. And what she saw shocked and disgusted her!

Madeline was there still uttering whimpering sounds with her bare arm stretched out. Meanwhile a stout man was bending over her arm with a hypodermic needle in his hand.

The stout man plunged the hypo into her arm and the girl gave a tiny moan. Then he withdrew the needle and straightened up so Gale was able to see his evil, smiling face. It was Peter Hall, Revene's henchman!

13

Gale lost no time deciding what to do. Reaching into her skirt pocket she felt the reassuring touch of the ivory-handled pistol. She quickly drew out the pistol and entered the room with it pointed directly at the stout Peter Hall.

The fat man stared at her in surprise which at once turned to rage. "What are you doing here?" he demanded.

"I might ask you that," she said coldly. Madeline's back was to her, and the girl seemed dazed, or unconscious.

Peter Hall stepped toward her menacingly. "This is none of your business!"

"Keep back!" she commanded him.

The fat man sneered at her derisively and said, "You won't use that toy!" And he came straight at her.

She pressed the trigger. A shot rang out and Hall staggered back with a shocked look on his bloated face. At the same instant Madeline seemed to become aware of what was going on and ran to her. Gale took her by the arm and rushed out with her as the fat man still stood swaying a little with a rush of blood showing on the front of his soiled linen jacket.

Madeline allowed herself to be dragged along

like a rag doll. Gale hurried along the dark corridor as quickly as she could, praying that the pistol shot had not been heard in the noisy room below.

No one seemed to take any notice of them as she led Madeline down the narrow, rickety stairs. A wave of relief swept over her as she saw Eric elbowing his way through the crowd toward them.

As he reached them, he asked, "What is it?"

"I'll explain later," she said. "We must get her out of here at once."

"Of course," the young reporter said. He took the other side of the near-collapsed Madeline, and they made their way to the door. He halted only to thrust a wad of franc notes into the hands of the headwaiter with a request that he take care of their bill.

Outside, Eric quickly found a closed carriage and within a few minutes they were on their way back to the chateau with Madeline, barely conscious, leaning heavily against Gale.

Eric, seated across from them, asked, "What is wrong?"

"She's drugged!"

"What?"

She nodded soberly. "I went upstairs just in time to see Peter Hall giving her an injection of some sort . . . I suspect morphine."

"Is she—I don't think I understand. Isn't morphine to kill pain?"

"Yes, but one becomes dependent on it. My father—I'll tell you later. The important thing is that Madeline seems to be addicted to it. Probably that's why she was so nervous and determined to go there tonight. Hall threatened me and—oh, Eric, I shot him!"

"A fine situation!" Eric said with a hint of despair in his voice.

They reached the chateau and helped Madeline up to her bedroom. The dark girl stretched out on her bed and closed her eyes. She was sleeping peacefully.

"How long will she sleep?" he asked humbly.

"A quarter- to a half-hour more if she responds as most people," she said, looking worried.

"It's a dreadful business," he commented, staring at the sleeping girl. "Dare we leave her?"

"Yes," she said. "She'll come to herself in a little while and feel very well. That is, until the craving for the drug returns."

"I don't understand," he said again. "I know that morphine is a derivative of opium—but people either smoke opium, or drink it as laudanum. Morphine is used medically, isn't it?"

"Yes," she said sadly. "And in many ways it's a blessing. Say you were run over by a carriage, were badly hurt and bleeding. A doctor would give you an injection of morphine, and your pain would stop— for a while. And he'd give you another, then, and still another. And after a while your wounds would heal, but you'd still need the morphine. If you tried to stop you'd be in a different kind of agony. And you—like my father—might decide that death was better. . . ."

There was a silence. At last Eric reached out and drew her to him. "My poor darling," he said tenderly. "I didn't know."

She rested her face against his jacket. "They've done this to her deliberately. But why?"

They left the girl on the bed and went back downstairs. Eric said, "Their plan has to be to use the girl some way. By getting her addicted to the drug they expected to control her. She would do their bidding as long as they supplied her with the evil stuff."

"So having her here with me is particularly dangerous!"

"Yes," he agreed. "I'll have to contact Richard Adams without delay."

"He should know," she agreed.

Eric gave her a direct look. "Do you think you killed Hall?"

She shook her head in despair. "I don't know. He was still on his feet when we fled. But his coat front was covered with blood."

The young reporter compressed his lips. "So it could be bad, or merely a minor wound."

"You'll hear if he dies, won't you?"

"I think I can find out," he said. "Sometimes they keep these things mysterious so they can better pounce on you."

"I think the shot caught him in the shoulder," she said, trying to visualize the scene. "It happened so quickly."

Eric took her in his arms. "You're still trembling!"

"Yes," she admitted in a small voice.

"You mustn't lose your nerve at this point," he said earnestly. "You must work harder than ever to save yourself and Madeline."

She remembered, "Hassan was to give her a gun to use to protect herself."

"That has to be canceled," Eric said.

"I'll call Hassan," she agreed.

They summoned Hassan from the kitchen area where he had his room and Eric told him, "We've just made a grim discovery. Miss Madeline is a morphine addict. She has been getting supplies at the Chez Paris."

Hassan listened intently. "That is possible," he said in his deep voice. "Chez Paris is a place where people go for opium, morphine, cocaine. A bad business."

"I don't know how she was trapped into it," Eric went on. "But it changes things."

"I understand," Hassan said.

"She may have to be sent away," Eric told the black man. "In any case she is not to be armed. And until we do something about her I ask you to be on your guard. Ready to help Mrs. Cormier."

The big man looked concerned. "It is too bad."

"It surely is," Eric agreed. He glanced at his pocket watch. "It is late but this matter is urgent enough for me to call on the American Consulate tonight. Adams must be informed. He will advise Colonel Hudson at the British Consulate in his own time."

"What will I do?" Gale asked.

"Just carry on until I return with or without Richard Adams," Eric said tersely. "I'd better be on my way."

She saw him to the door and then returned to the living room as a ghostly-looking Madeline slowly made her way down the stairs to her. The lovely French girl descended every step slowly, seeming to pause a second on each one. Then she crossed the big room to face Gale.

Madeline's face was deathly pale. She asked her, "Where has Eric gone?"

She said, "To see Richard Adams."

"About me?"

"Yes."

Madeline looked distraught. "There is no need to make this fuss! It's not that important!"

Gale eyed her sadly. "You know it is. I saw you tonight when that man plunged the needle in your arm and gave you that drug. You'd been pleading with him for it!"

268

Madeline's composure crumpled. She began to sob as she turned away and sank into the nearest chair. "Oh, Gale, I'm so sorry!"

Gale went to her and touched a sympathetic hand to the sobbing girl's shoulder. "How did you get into this awful business?" she asked.

Madeline didn't reply at once but as she brought her sobs under control, she said, "I take laudanum for my stomach. It hurt when I worried about my father. When he went away, I had a premonition... So when Mr. Hall said he had a better medicine than laudanum, I tried it. It was wonderful. I didn't hurt and I didn't worry. Until the medicine wore off. But Mr. Hall was so kind—he arranged that someone would be at Chez Paris to give me the injection when I needed it."

"Peter Hall? But why...?"

"He'd been a doctor back in England, he told me, before he retired."

"And?" Gale asked tautly.

"It became a nightly thing," Madeline admitted. "Then I knew suddenly that I could not do without the drug. That I was dependent on it. I told him."

"What did he say?"

"He smiled and said not to worry, that was the way he'd planned it. And he would always supply me with the drug if I did as he asked."

"And after that?" Gale said.

"One night soon after, he asked me to submit to him in a physical way," Madeline said, her head down and her voice low. "It was disgusting but I went through with it. I had to have the injection."

"How did you think you'd manage when you came here?"

Madeline looked up at her unhappily. "I told myself I could break myself of the habit. That I would be all right with someone to help me. But I couldn't stand it. That is why I suggested we go to the Chez Paris."

Gale said gravely, "That visit has cost us dearly. Do you know I had to shoot Peter Hall to get you out of there?"

Fear shadowed Madeline's lovely face. "I knew something had happened. I was so confused! Did you kill him?"

"I don't know."

"He's vicious! He'll try to revenge himself on you if he does live," Madeline warned her.

She shrugged. "It makes no difference. If not him, then Revene."

"Oh *mon Dieu*," Madeline whispered. "What will become of us?"

Gale looked at her for a long moment. At last she said, "We'll find a way."

Madeline gave her a tragic look. "You won't be able to trust me! When the craving starts to gnaw at me tomorrow I'll lie to you, cheat you, anything!"

"Wait until we hear from Eric," was Gale's reply. "He's gone to see Richard Adams."

"At this hour?" Madeline said, as if she'd not comprehended it when Gale had first told her.

"Yes. We all realize this is an emergency," Gale told the other girl.

It was almost an hour later when Eric returned with Richard Adams. The men came in and joined Gale and Madeline in the living room.

Adams had never looked sterner. Facing Madeline, he exclaimed, "How could you do this damnable thing to yourself?"

Gale quickly went to the thin Bostonian and told him, "It happened through her worry for her father. You must try to understand."

Richard Adams gave her a reproving glance. "You must let me handle this my way, Mrs. Cormier, if you please."

She shrugged and moved back to join Eric in the shadows by the door. Adams asked the distraught girl a number of questions and drew the same information, or at least most of it. Madeline did not tell the consulate official that Peter Hall had forced her to give herself to him, but all the rest matched what she'd told Gale.

Richard Adams relented a little as he heard the facts. He turned to Gale and Eric to inquire, "Are there any criminal depths to which this Revene gang will not sink?"

"I think not," Eric Simms said fiercely.

Adams told Madeline, "The problem is what to do with you."

Distressed, she said, "I will go. I will not burden you further."

"That is not the answer," the lean man snapped. "You know too much! You are a part of our plan. I cannot simply let you walk out of here and back into the hands of Revene's crowd."

Gale spoke up, "She has to be helped."

"That will not be easy," Adams said. "But getting her morphine will, I think." And he turned to Madeline again. "If I agree to help you, will you promise to be obedient to Mrs. Cormier in everything?"

"Yes, yes, if I can!" Madeline said miserably.

"What do you mean by that?" Adams snapped.

"I'm addicted. I can't answer for what I will do when the craving comes again," Madeline whimpered.

Richard Adams' lean face showed disgust. "There is only one way," he said. "I will have you treated by the consulate doctor. He will come here every day and give you enough morphine to steady your nerves.

But each day giving you a little less until at last he has you completely off the drug."

Gale was much heartened by Adams' words. She said, "I think that is an excellent idea!"

The lovely French girl looked up at them gratefully. "I'll do anything! Anything!"

So it was arranged. Later, while Eric sat talking with Madeline, Gale saw Richard Adams on his way. She accompanied him to the door where they paused for a moment before he went out to his waiting carriage.

"A word of caution," he said in a low voice. "This plan has pitfalls."

She stared at him in the shadowed doorway. "Oh?" She hadn't thought he understood.

"There are bound to be some withdrawal symptoms as the dosage of the drug is reduced."

"You're saying this might tempt Madeline to try to escape and give up the treatment?"

Adams nodded. "She must be watched. That difficult task will fall on you."

"I understand. The damage has been done."

"If she should give trouble or suddenly vanish, you must let me know at once," Adams told her.

"I shall," she promised.

Richard Adams left and she went back and joined Eric and Madeline. The French girl was talking hopefully and was full of plans for her cure. It would not be easy to be put off guard, Gale realized, but other moments were bound to come when the lovely Madeline might change dramatically.

Madeline went up to her room first, and then it was time for Eric to leave. He seemed more than usually concerned about her.

"This twist in events has upset me," he confessed

at last. "Rather than being a help to you Madeline is going to be another danger."

"The consulate doctor will give her an injection tomorrow," Gale pointed out.

"I know," he said. "But you must be especially careful. If Peter Hall is alive he will have a double reason for hating you. And you can be sure he'll try to even up the score."

"We'll know soon enough," she said.

"Maybe too soon," was his wry reply. He kissed her good night and left with a promise that he would return sometime during the next day. She went on up to her room and saw that there was no light showing under the door of Madeline's room, so she could assume the girl had happily gone to sleep.

She slowly prepared for bed, trying to convince herself that she was only in minimal danger. Hassan was down below within call and ready to defend her.

Her thoughts turned to Paul. Was he really alive? Had he also been introduced to opium? That might explain why when she had seen him he'd looked more like a ghost than a human. It was a frightening thought!

She fell asleep with her mind a turmoil; nightmares came. She shot Peter Hall. His startled expression was large in the phantom screen of her nightmare. The features loomed huge over her and so did the sight of his bloodstained jacket. She saw him staggering toward her and tried to push him away, tried to scream, but her voice froze. The cries of terror caught in her throat!

She awoke with a start, dripping with perspiration as she stared into the darkness. Sitting up in bed she tried to calm herself, tell herself it was nonsense to be upset by a ridiculous dream!

Suddenly she heard it—a kind of sliding sound

which she couldn't identify. She waited: In the following moment she heard the creaking of a floorboard. At the same time she was filled with a sense of not being alone in the dark room.

Her first thought was of Madeline. She called out, "Madeline, are you there?"

She waited a moment for a reply. But there was none. Again, she called, "Madeline, speak to me if that's you!"

Again, no reply. But there was another sound, a kind of shuffling that suggested someone was painfully making his way toward her. She gazed into the dark with fear-stricken eyes and saw a male figure gradually emerge from the shadows. The figure came close to her and now she was able to make out the face!

"Paul!" she gasped at the sight of her husband's pale, emaciated face.

"Gale!" Her name came in a hoarse whisper.

"Paul, you *are* alive!"

"I'm in torment," came the hoarsely whispered reply. "You must find the briefcase and leave it for me."

"I don't know where it is!" she protested.

"Jiri!" he whispered, his face expressionless. "Find Jiri! Get the case!"

"Paul!" she said tensely. "What have they done to you?"

"I'm their hostage," he whispered.

"Paul, you must tell me more!" she insisted.

But already he was vanishing into the shadows. And after a moment there was no sign of him. She sat staring into the darkness with disbelief. Then she fumbled to find the candle on her bedside table and with trembling hands lit a match and touched it to the candle. Then she held it out to study the room. To all intents it was empty of anyone but herself.

She put the candle down and lay back against the pillows. Had it been part of her nightmare?

She left the candle burning for comfort and, as dawn came, her eyes closed from sheer weariness and she slept again. This time her sleep was deep and she did not awaken until the sun came streaming into her window.

She quickly got up and went to the door and picked up the water jug which Hassan had dutifully left outside in the corridor for her morning ablutions. She had just placed the jug on the commode when the sun struck something on the floor, catching her eye! Something golden!

With a tiny cry she crossed over to the object and held it up in her hands. The object she was holding was an engraved gold cigarette case which she had given Paul as a wedding present! He had always carried it with him! And now he must have left it as a token of his visit the night before!

A visit from a living Paul or from his ghost? She could not help but speculate. Had this golden case lain beneath the surface of the harbor and been rescued from this dark place by her husband's phantom hand?

It seemed much more likely that Paul was alive and a hostage of the scoundrel who had employed him. Unquestionably Revene had caught him in traitorous deals and was now making him pay. The price for his release was to be the immensely valuable briefcase! Of which she knew nothing!

The golden case made her face the fact that the husband she had come to regard with hatred was still alive. She had fallen in love with Eric so easily, thinking herself to be free. Now her weakling of a husband was entreating her to rescue him and save his life.

It was a dilemma which she had not thought to face. And which was beyond her solving. She put the case on her dresser to show it to Eric and Richard Adams and began washing and dressing. She had just put on her dress and was finishing with her hair as the knock came on her door.

"One moment!" she called, and placed the last amber hairpin in the bun at the base of her neck. Then she hurried to the door and opened it.

The huge Hassan stood there looking upset. He indicated with his hand, "The door to Miss Leduc's room is open and she is not there."

"Are you sure?"

"Yes, Madame," the big man said.

"Let me see," she replied quickly and ran across the hall to the girl's room. Hassan had surely been right. The room was empty and there was no sign of her having slept in the bed. Gale looked and saw that the girl's things were still there. She must have fled with only the clothing she wore.

Hassan was standing in the doorway. "I did not hear her leave!"

"Nor did I," she said. "But she's gone!"

"The drugs," Hassan said gravely. "They do strange things to the mind."

"I'm sure they do," Gale agreed. "She must have been afraid we'd cut her down drastically on the drug she was taking. Even though Richard Adams promised that wouldn't be so."

The black man said, "With drugs there is no reason!"

"I must let Richard Adams know at once!" she said.

"I will find a messenger," Hassan said.

"No. You mustn't waste time doing that," she

told him. "Go to the United States Consulate yourself. Find Mr. Adams and let him know what has happened."

Hassan looked unhappy. "But I cannot leave you here alone without protection."

"It's bright daylight," she said. "I'll be in no danger. In any case I'm expecting Mr. Simms to come by and see me."

The black man considered. "You will keep the door locked while I'm away?"

"Of course," she said.

"And you will open it to no one but Mr. Simms?"

"You have my promise," she said.

He sighed. "Then perhaps I shall risk it. I shall return as soon as I have delivered the message."

"That's the main thing now," she told him.

"Your breakfast is ready and set out for you," Hassan told her as he prepared to go downstairs and start on his errand.

For a while all she could think of was the disappearance of the French girl. If Madeline fell back in the hands of the Revene gang she would be kept on drugs and victimized until she was beyond being saved. It was a horrible thought but she knew that Madeline's probable end was the utter degradation of being sold to one of the Arab brothels in the street of cages. She must be rescued at all costs. Gale realized she must somehow seek out the elusive Jiri and get the sought-after briefcase! She would gladly trade the briefcase to save Madeline's life.

But then what of her husband? What of Paul? Did she not at least owe him the chance of redeeming himself by building a new life? And she decided that if the contents of the briefcase were valuable enough, it might be that she could bargain for the release of both Madeline and Paul.

Then she would let Paul know that their marriage must be ended. She had lost her trust in him and at the same time found true love with someone else. He would have to understand that. She could never take him back as a husband.

Madeline had made the ultimate error in running off in this fashion. It made the entire situation most difficult. And there was a very real chance that the unfortunate girl might come to her death before anything could be done to help her. Gale lingered over her breakfast but ate little.

A carriage arrived at the door and someone knocked to enter. She approached the bolted door cautiously and called out, "Who is it?"

"Eric!" The reply came in a voice so familiar she could not doubt it. Her heart gave a bound of relief and she hurried to the bolted door and opened it.

Eric, in a fresh gray suit, looked relaxed and handsome. He smiled and said, "You are being cautious this morning."

"Yes," she said, closing and bolting the door after him.

"Don't misunderstand," he said, "I thoroughly approve." And he took her in his arms for a kiss.

She pushed him away. "Eric, there's more trouble!"

His eyebrows raised. "What now?"

"Madeline has run off!"

"When?"

"Sometime in the night," she said, with an unhappy gesture of her hand. "I didn't hear her go. Neither did Hassan."

Eric looked shocked. "What a mad thing for her to do? It may cost her dearly!"

"I know."

He was grim. "She's likely gone straight back to

the Chez Paris looking for more dope. Did she know you shot Hall?"

"Yes."

"There are probably others who have supplied her with drugs as well as him. There are plenty of agents in the medina. She may not have gone near the Chez Paris but headed for the medina."

"That is so dangerous for a girl," she said.

Eric sounded pessimistic, "She's too drug-crazed to think of that!"

"I've sent word to Adams."

"Good."

"I had Hassan go," she explained. "That's why I was so slow about answering the door. He told me not to let anyone but you in and to make sure it was you before I unbolted the door."

"Hassan told you right," Eric said. "But I can't think why you let him go personally with the message. You should have had him send it by someone else."

"It was too important," she said. "Someone else might have dallied along the way."

Eric looked doubtful. "I suppose there is some argument there. But I don't like your being here alone."

She gave him a wan smile. "I'm not alone. You're here!"

"But I can't stay," he said. "Something big is breaking at the Sultan's palace and I'm supposed to be there. All the other foreign correspondents are probably there now. The Sultan has some sort of political announcement for us."

She said, "You can leave. I'll be all right alone. You don't have to stay here on my account."

He didn't make any move to go. "I have time yet," he said.

"Are you sure?"

"Yes," he said. "I've made some inquiries in the right places and I can't find out anything about Peter Hall being shot to death. So I'd say you can rest easy that you merely put a bullet in his arm or shoulder."

"Which only means he's alive to be a threat to me," was her reaction.

"I'm afraid so," he said.

"There's something else," she told him. "Something I must tell you."

"What?"

"I almost put it out of my mind with all this confusion about Madeline," she said. "But my husband is alive!"

He eyed her incredulously. "What gives you that idea?"

"I saw him again last night. He came to my bedroom."

Eric said, "I don't think it's anything more than a bad dream. You've had them continually in this house. It's a place of hauntings."

"No," she said. "This was Paul. He spoke to me."

"Spoke to you?"

"Yes. He said he was being held hostage and that if I could get the briefcase and give it to Revene he'd be freed."

"A bad dream!" Eric said with disdain.

"No," she said. "I have proof. I gave Paul an engraved gold cigarette case as a wedding gift. When I got up this morning it was on the floor where he'd stood last night. He left it for me as a token the experience had been real."

Eric stared at her. "I'd like to see it," he said.

"It's on my dresser in my bedroom," she said. "Come up and I'll show it to you."

Gale hurried upstairs with a cynical Eric at her side. She said, "I know you don't want to believe me!"

"I'm not all that happy to know your husband is alive."

"What difference? I mean to leave him anyway."

"Thanks," he said. "But I think you dreamt the whole business."

They reached the landing and she walked ahead to her room and went directly to the dresser. Eric was on her heels. She halted by the dresser. "It's not here!"

"I don't think it ever was!"

She turned to him unhappily. "Eric, you must believe me! It was here! I put it on the dresser myself."

"Then where is it?"

"I don't know!"

He pointed out, "There's only been you and Hassan in the house since Madeline ran off. Do you think he stole it?"

She was indignant. "He wouldn't do such a thing!"

"Then where is it?"

"I don't know," she said in an anguished tone. "I must have put it somewhere else."

"Where?"

"One of the dresser drawers." She began opening them all and vainly searching them for the missing gold case.

Eric said, "I'm afraid you lose this round."

"You refuse to believe me?"

"There's no case," he said. "Produce it and I'll say you didn't have a bad dream."

She began looking about the room, on the top of the commode and the bedside table. "Give me time. I'll find it."

Eric glanced at his pocket watch. "Sorry, darling. I can't stay any longer or I'll be late for the Sultan's announcement." He started out.

Following him, she said, "I will find it and then you'll believe me!"

"Of course I will," Eric said, descending the stairs in a hurry with her at his heels. "And until Hassan returns don't open this door to anyone."

"I won't," she promised. "When will you be back?"

"As soon as I get my story and have time to file it with the cable people," Eric said. "I'll rush back as soon as I can."

She bolted the door again after he left and stood there in a state of confusion. She knew she had put the golden case on the dresser. Maybe she hadn't looked in the right place, maybe she'd accidentally brushed it off on to the floor when she'd heard the news about Madeline's running off. She had been extremely upset.

She went up to her room and knelt on the carpet in front of the dresser and searched underneath it for the missing gold case. There was no sign of it.

She got to her feet and was about to turn away from the dresser when she saw something on it she hadn't seen before. A torn scrap of notepaper with a message penciled roughly on it, "Find the golden case on the rooftop." It must have been put there while she was seeing Eric on his way!

14

Staring at the slip of paper, Gale decided that it bore out the stories that the chateau was honeycombed with secret passages. It was evident that this must be true. Hence, the sudden appearance of Paul last night and his equally quick disappearance. Now someone had entered the house by a secret passage despite all their vigilance and had taken the gold cigarette case while she was downstairs talking to Eric.

Whoever had taken the case was now waiting for her on the rooftop. Why? Was it a trap? Or was it someone with a message for her, perhaps from Paul? She debated the risks of keeping the rendezvous and it seemed to her she must chance it.

She took the ivory-handled pistol from her pocket and released its safety catch. Hassan had cleaned and reloaded it, so it was ready for use again. It had proved invaluable before and she would not have considered going up to the rooftop without it.

Cautiously she made her way to the upper floor of the castlelike building and saw the final, narrow stairway which led to an opening in the roof. The trapdoor was significantly open to indicate someone was up there waiting for her. She waited at the bottom of the stairs for a few seconds, aware that she might be advancing into great danger.

But her curiosity impelled her to make her way up the steps and out onto the asphalt and gravel surface of the flat roof. The sun blazed down on her, and she could see no one.

As a precaution she drew the pistol from her skirt pocket and advanced slowly with the weapon kept at the ready. She scanned the turrets at the four corners of the rooftop and could see no one. Yet the open trapdoor suggested that someone was up there.

Using her free hand to shade her eyes from the blazing sun, she called out, "Where are you?"

There was no reply, but she thought she heard a footstep on the gravel surface of the roof directly behind her. Before she could manage to turn she felt the prod of a knife tip in her back.

A familiar cold voice ordered her, "Drop that pistol!"

"No!" she said.

The knife tip penetrated her skin and made her cry out. At the same time she let the pistol drop. "You daren't!" she exclaimed.

"Turn around," he ordered her.

She turned and found herself looking into the threatening face of the fat Peter Hall. The fat man's left arm was in a sling from the bullet wound she'd inflicted on him. In his right hand, pointed at her, was a businesslike-looking dagger.

She asked tautly, "What do you want?"

He laughed softly. "I think you know!"

"I don't have the briefcase," she protested.

"So you say!"

"It's true," she said. "And I'd never give it to you

in any case after what you have done to Madeline."

"You wasted your time trying to save her!" the fat man said with relish.

"What kind of fiend are you? What have you done with her now?"

Peter Hall gloated. "She's where you won't find her."

"What did you do with that cigarette case?"

"It served its purpose," he said. "I recognized it was like the one your husband had."

"It is the identical one!"

"You think so?"

"I know!"

"I doubt it," was his mocking reply.

"It had his initials on it! I gave it to him!"

"In that case he gave it to someone else," the fat man jeered at her. "But that's not important. What is going to happen to you is."

Fear had been coursing through her from the moment she'd had to drop the pistol. She eyed it on the ground not all that far from her and wondered if she might dash for it and use it. But the chances seemed against taking the risk.

"What do you want with me?" she asked.

"You'll find out," he said. "Now walk over to the side of the house nearest the street!"

"Why?"

"You tried to kill me. I have a way of paying people back!"

"You can't blame me for defending myself and trying to save that poor girl!"

He ignored her, and jabbing again with the point of the dagger, said, "Move on!"

She halted so that she could see the cobblestoned streets four tall stories below. It made her dizzy to stand so close to the edge. She protested, "I daren't go any further!"

"Just a little!" he goaded, and she felt the dagger tip break her flesh again and cried out as she was forced on until the toes of her tiny white slippers showed over the edge of the roof.

"Look down!"

"No!" she said, desperately afraid if she did she would become dizzy and fall.

"Either you topple over of your own accord or I shove you," the fat man hissed in her ear. "You are going to have a nasty accident no matter which way it happens!"

"Please!" she begged him.

"What about the briefcase?" he asked. "I'll trade your life for it! You'll never get a better bargain!"

Before she could answer she heard a wild, animal-like cry from far behind her. Her tormentor also heard it as he moved back in a startled gesture. She heard the thud of heavy footsteps coming toward them and then Hall shoved her in the back. She screamed as she fell forward into the street far below!

She saw the street rushing up toward her and then something happened to break her fall. She felt a tug from behind and heard the ripping of cloth and in the next instant ready hands grasped her about the middle and dragged her back onto the surface of the rooftop, where she lay moaning for a moment.

She opened her eyes and saw Richard Adams standing above her. He leaned down and took her by the shoulders again and hauled her a further distance from the roof's edge. At the same time an enraged Hassan grappled with the fat Peter Hall for the dagger. Hall managed to stab the big black man in the side!

Panting furiously the fat man drew back, crouching with the dagger still on the ready. The giant Hassan stood with a stunned look on his face as the blood from his wound began to pour down his left side.

Watching them all like a cornered mad dog, the panting Hall kept the dagger at a threatening angle and warned, "Don't come near me! Not any of you!"

Hassan stood very still for about three seconds. And then with a wild roar of rage he bore down on the fat man and with a stunning show of strength lifted the wriggling man into the air, the dagger now impotently cutting swaths in nothingness as Hall screamed in fury and fear!

In an almost graceful and deliberate movement the giant black man held him over the roof's edge and then let him drop. Another wailing scream issued from the doomed man's lips and barely ended before the thud of his body sounded from the cobblestones below.

Hassan, bleeding profusely, gazed down at the street with an expression of utter contempt on his broad face. Richard Adams hurried up to him.

"Are you badly hurt?" Adams asked.

"No," Hassan said, breathing heavily. "It is a flesh wound. Not dangerous!"

"Good!" Adams said. "It must be attended to." Then he bent and retrieved the dagger which had dropped from Peter Hall's hand just before he'd been dropped to his death. The consulate official said, "We better keep this. It will make it easier for the authorities to accept the story of Hall's suicide."

Hassan nodded. "Yes, sir."

Adams came back to Gale and helped her to her feet. "What about you, my girl?"

"I'm all right," she said. "Though my skirt is badly ripped!"

"You can be thankful it was of stout material," Adams told her. "It was all that stood between you and death. When I snatched at it I had no hope of saving you from going over. Too close for my liking!"

And for the first time she realized that he was also in a state of shock. She said, "You and Hassan arrived in the nick of time."

"It took us several minutes to decide where you were," he said. "Finally we narrowed it down to the rooftop, and the open trapdoor showed that we were right."

They made their way downstairs. Richard Adams had his carriage driver go fetch the Moroccan police and enlisted a native to stand guard over the body until the police arrived. Then he helped her clean and bandage Hassan's wound. It was only a superficial one but the big man had lost a surprising amount of blood. When the wound was dressed, Hassan went back to his quarters.

Adams told her, "It will be easier if we stick to a story that Peter Hall came here and for some unknown reason jumped to his death. Suicide will be a more simple explanation."

"Someone may have seen the struggle up there," she reminded him.

"I think not," the precise Adams said. "It all took place very quickly, and fortunately the street was empty at the time."

"Your driver must know."

"He is a trusted consulate employee and will not say anything," Adams assured her. "You may be thankful that we've settled a score with at least one of them. Hall would never have rested until he revenged himself on you!"

"He already has Madeline back in the hands of the gang again," she lamented.

"I know," Richard Adams sighed. "I came as soon as Hassan brought me the news."

She said, "You must institute an immediate search for her."

"I will," he said. "I'll enlist the help of the local police in the search. But you must know it will be difficult."

"Yes, I know," she admitted.

The thin man faced her in the shadowed living room, cool and peaceful after the blazing sun of the rooftop. "I'm sure they'll take her where she'll be safely hidden. Perhaps on Revene's yacht."

"The *Siren*," she said. "Do you know whether it is docked in Casablanca?"

"It's certainly not docked here, but it may be only a short distance away. Revene is clever enough for that. The rumor is that he has a munitions depot in Turkey and regularly crosses the sea to land his illegal cargoes over here."

"In Turkey?"

Richard Adams nodded. "Yes. It's another country filled with corrupt officials. As our secret service has it, the Turkish officials order more munitions than they require and then make a stupendous profit by giving it to Revene in resale. And he then doubles that price and sells the stuff to the renegade leaders here."

"In other words they make an easy source of supply for him," she said.

He nodded. "The French government is aware of it along with our own people and the British.

The French seem to be allowing it to happen. They want the witless Sultan off his throne so they can take Morocco over as a protectorate."

Gale and Adams were still in conversation when the police arrived. He sent her upstairs to change her clothes. By the time she'd finished the police had left. She was thus spared any questioning.

Joining a cool Adams in the living room again, she asked, "Did they seem suspicious?"

"If they were they didn't show it," he replied. "Most of the Westerners here are a scraping from the bottom. There are a great many suicides and murders. They accepted Hall's suicide as just another one in a long list."

"They took the body with them?"

"Yes. They have a sort of morgue. If the body isn't claimed, it will be buried within twenty-four hours."

She worried, "Revene will be furious when he hears. Hall was one of his chief henchmen."

Richard gave her a sharp look. "He was, indeed. Along with Walton and your husband."

"Yes, I know," she said unhappily. "There is something I must tell you." And she recited again the appearance of Paul in her room.

After she finished, Adams said, "You're certain the gold case was the one you gave him?"

"Yes. It was engraved with his initials."

"And it was taken from your room by Hall and a note left, luring you to the roof?"

"The note will be on my dresser."

"I don't question it," Adams said impatiently. "But you ought to have told me about this earlier."

"I was too confused."

"Hall must have had that gold case on him."

"I would say so," she agreed.

Adams frowned. "There's no chance of our finding it now. If the fellow I had guarding the body didn't take it, the police certainly have. They regard whatever they can filch in that way their just bounty."

"I'm sorry," she said.

He shrugged. "It really makes no difference. I mean, beyond corroborating your story. So we must accept that Paul Cormier is alive."

"Yes."

"And he told you to seek out this Jiri, who was the chief associate of Abdul-el-Krem. Which means that he is also alive and has this important briefcase."

"He seemed to be in a strange, tormented state," Gale said.

"No doubt Revene is holding him hostage and punishing him for attempting to double-cross him."

"Then that would mean there was someone with Paul last night," she said. "Someone I didn't see, hiding behind him in the darkness ready to put a bullet through him if he made a wrong move."

"That is most likely," Adams agreed.

She grimaced. "You and Colonel Hudson seemed sure there would be developments if I came back here. And you've surely been proven right."

"I regret the ordeal you've suffered," Adams said awkwardly.

"I've not been hurt," she told him. "But what about poor Madeline?"

"That evil situation had begun before we brought her here," he said.

"That is true," she was forced to agree. "If you hadn't brought her here you might never have found out about her drug addiction. She must be found before more harm comes to her!"

"I know," he said. "I will do everything I can."

He then called Hassan and told him not to leave Gale alone under any circumstances. Then he left, promising to send her word the moment he heard anything concerning the vanished Madeline. She rested for a little, and shortly after she wakened, Eric arrived back.

He said, "I've seen Adams and heard all about what happened here."

She smiled solemnly. "I can hardly believe it now."

"I made a mistake in leaving," he said with a frown. "When I think how near you came to death..."

"You had your work to do."

"I could have gotten the information from someone else," Eric said with a sigh. "The Sultan was in high form. Now he claims the renegades are attacking Moroccan ships and sinking them."

"Is he suggesting that revolutionaries have a navy of their own?"

Eric nodded. "It sounded like that! Actually he's mad. He says the marauder is invisible and his ships are sunk without seeing who their attacker is."

"It does sound mad," she agreed.

"I think it's simply a wild rumor," Eric said. "The French are ignoring it. But I understand the British are having part of their Middle East fleet in this area for maneuvers shortly, and Colonel Hudson in an effort to placate the Sultan has offered to notify them of this phantom marauder and ask them to keep a sharp eye out."

Gale said, "They couldn't interfere in any case."

"No," he said. "But if they see anything suspicious, they could report it."

"Richard Adams says that Turkey is involved in supplying the munitions to Revene. So it does begin to have international aspects."

Eric eyed her seriously. "It is my bet, if that briefcase everybody wants really exists, it has something implicating the Turkish officials in it."

"That could well be!"

"If the papers became available it would end the illicit trade for at least a short while," he said. "The officials would lose their posts and not be able to cooperate with Revene any longer."

"We must try to find Jiri," she said.

"Because your husband asked you to?"

"No. Because he must have that briefcase and we can use that to bargain with if we have to. Try to exchange it for the lives of Madeline and Paul."

Eric said, "I'm concerned about Madeline. I can't say that I'm sympathetic to your husband."

"We must do this the proper way," she insisted. "I would always feel guilty if I deserted Paul now. But when this is all settled I will tell him that our marriage is finished. That I love you."

He took her in his arms. "It's impossible to win an argument with you," he said and kissed her gently.

The following afternoon he joined her for an excursion to the medina. It had been there that Jiri had once come to her aid, when she and Paul had been attacked. This made it seem a logical place to begin the search for him.

Eric was a reluctant partner to the adventure. He said, "You should remain in the chateau. It is dangerous enough there but you run all sorts of risk on the outside."

"I'm not going to stay there as a target," she said. "I'm going after them rather than have them go after me."

They were riding in a carriage which Eric had hired and were slowly making their way through the crowded traffic of the city's busy streets. Ahead lay the gates of the medina.

They left the carriage outside the gate and began making their way along the narrow streets. Some of the streets were so narrow, the houses, leaning outward, almost touched at the rooftops. They passed a group of three men and a woman seated before a storefront of brasswares playing cards, gambling intently. The men were real desert Berbers with daggers at their belts, flowing turbans, and big leather purses slung over their shoulders. The woman wore a brightly colored print dress with jeweled necklace, silver bracelets, dangling earrings, and her hair was bound in an elaborate coiffure. A thin veil covered her face from the bridge of her nose downward.

As they moved on, she said, "They looked like desert men."

"They were," Eric said. "The same as the Berbers of Sheik Ali."

"What is the difference between Arabs and Berbers?" she wanted to know as they left one narrow street for another.

"The Berbers are the original people of North Africa. The conquering Arabs drove the Berbers from the coastal plains into the mountains and desert. The Berbers became Moslems, but they still hate the Arab city dwellers."

Gale paused for a moment and said, "Over to

the left there is a short street where Paul's brother had his studio before he was killed."

"The place was empty when you went there before," Eric remembered.

"Let's stop by again," she suggested. "There was an old man living there. He may be able to tell us where to find Jiri."

Eric shrugged. "We can try if you like."

They went on until they came to the doorway of the house in which Ben Cormier had his studio. The door was ajar as usual and they went inside. The first surprise was that the studio looked much as it had when she'd first visited it with her husband. Her brother-in-law's paintings were displayed against the walls as before, several piles of them, leaning one on top of another.

She gave a small gasp. "I don't understand. The paintings are back again."

She went over and began inspecting the paintings more closely and found they were the same ones she had seen earlier. There was something ghostly about the sudden reappearance of the paintings. She repeated, "I don't understand."

Eric said, "I'd say we are wasting time here."

She rose from inspecting the paintings and said, "No. I don't think that." She was going to add something else when she was shocked into silence by the appearance of a figure in the doorway of the studio. None other than the late Ben Cormier.

Sleazy-looking as usual, with rumpled, soiled clothes and a stubble of beard on his face, he stood there smiling at them—an extremely live ghost.

"Gale!" he said pleasantly. "I'm glad to see you!"

She stared at him in dismay. "You're dead!"

"Dead?" Ben looked at her innocently.

Eric said impatiently, "We were given to understand you had been murdered. The result of a gambling quarrel. When Gale was here last, the studio was empty."

Ben chuckled. "And the old man living here told you I had been murdered?"

"Yes," she said. "Why do you find that so funny?"

"Because he followed my instructions to the letter," her brother-in-law said.

She gasped. "The whole thing was a lie!"

"I'm afraid so," Ben said apologetically. "You are right in saying I was in serious trouble through gambling. I had to hide out until the people I owed money to left Casablanca. Then I returned from the dead."

Gale was stunned. "I never questioned what the old man told me."

Ben gave her a wise wink. "That is because you and my brother would prefer to believe I was murdered."

"Don't say that!" she protested.

"Sorry," he said. "I was speaking for old Paul rather than you. He didn't have your scruples."

"Paul is still alive," she said. "He came to me at the chateau last night."

"Never," Ben said with his usual jaunty confidence. "I happen to know the launch Paul was in blew up and there's bits and pieces of him at the bottom of the harbor."

"Not Paul," she said bitterly. "He somehow survived and so did that fellow Jiri."

Ben rubbed his chin. "You're not pulling my leg?"

"About a thing like that?" she asked incredulously.

Eric said, "There are sound reasons to think

Paul Cormier is still alive. A search is still under way for him."

"I still say he's dead," Ben told them, "but you never know. I'm here and alive, as you can see."

Eric placed an arm around Gale and said, "Bear up! It will soon all come to an end."

"I wonder," she said, still gazing at the contented Ben with awe. "I understand the police are looking for you."

"Only to confirm my death," Ben said. "And I don't propose to give them any help in that."

"You're willing to be put down as dead?" she asked in amazement.

"I'm not interested in what people think about me."

She turned to Eric and asked, "What do you think about it all?"

"At least let me make some good of my resurrection," Ben Cormier said. "Let us share a drink and mourn Paul."

"And if he's not dead?" she said.

Ben's smile was instant. "I shall be much disappointed."

"You've simply come back here and set up shop after having given it out that you'd been killed by someone to whom you owed money?" Eric said.

"That sums it up nicely," Ben agreed.

Eric said, "Have you heard anything about Paul?"

"No," Ben answered. "My brother and I did not have any mutual friends."

Gale said, "There must be someone!"

Ben considered for a moment, then he told her, "I did know the fellow called Jiri. But he also died in the launch explosion."

"We're not sure about either," she said. "This Jiri used to live here in the medina, or at least he stayed here somewhere. Do you know where?"

"Certainly," the resurrected Ben said. "He lived in the house of his cousin Fazi. In Little Goat Street, only a short distance from here."

This brought Gale to the alert. "Does this cousin still live there?"

"To the best of my knowledge," Ben Cormier said. "He's a strange old fellow. Bit demented about his religion. But then I think most Moslems are mad."

Eric added, "Just as they class Christians in the same way."

Ben spread his hands. "I'm a tolerant man. Do not make me out a bigot. My lady friend is a Moslem. You must wait and meet her. She is out shopping."

Gale said, "I'm afraid we haven't time to wait. But I will return."

"I count on it," Ben said warmly. "Are we not part of the same family?"

Eric asked him, "Will you point out the direction of Little Goat Street?"

"Of course," the artist said. And he went to the street with them and pointed to the left. "Over there," he said. "Take the third alley and it will lead you directly into Little Goat Street. But I think you are wasting your time. You'll get no help from Fazi. He hates all Westerners."

"We'll have to try," Gale told her errant brother-in-law. "I must find out if Jiri is alive and where I may locate him."

Ben's smile was malicious. "I'd suggest the bottom of Casablanca harbor." And he stood laughing at his own joke as they moved on.

"It begins to look as if all the people we believed dead are alive," Eric said bitterly.

"I doubt it," she said wryly. "I have no questions about Sheik Ali."

"That's another story," Eric said as they came to the alley which Ben had promised would lead to Little Goat Street.

They came out into a narrow street which seemed devoted to shops of various kinds. They passed the quarters of a bicycle repair man, then a vendor of patent medicine sitting on his haunches chanting his wares. They went by this squatted graybeard to pass some little girls, with babies strapped to their backs, playing hopscotch. One of them accidentally bumped into a vendor with a high pile of oranges in front of him, sending the oranges in every direction. She ran off, the vendor shaking a fist at her and cursing her vehemently.

They asked a little boy where the house of Fazi was and the child at once pointed to a ramshackle building ahead on the left.

Gale was jubilant. "We've found him, just like that!"

"Don't count on it," Eric warned her as they pushed ahead to the open doorway of the old house.

They paused before the doorway and suddenly from inside there came the sound of a drum being beaten in a monotonous fashion. They exchanged glances and Eric led the way inside. The room was small and evil-smelling and in a far corner a black man in turban and dirty robe sat squatted at a drum. He continued to pound it and ignored them.

Eric stood before him and asked, "Is this the house of Fazi?"

The black man halted his pounding on the drum to eye them both suspiciously. Then in a deep voice, he said, "It is."

Gale stepped up beside Eric and said, "We have come to ask your help."

The black man sneered. "I do not help infidels."

"We are friends," Eric told him. "And we will pay you well for cooperating with us."

Ignoring the stench and the old man's unfriendliness, she told him, "Jiri was a friend of ours. We know he was your cousin."

He stared at them and then slowly got up and came closer to peer at them. "You knew Jiri?"

"Yes," she said. "We wish to talk with him."

The black man rolled his eyes. "Who talks to the dead?" he demanded.

Eric said, "We are almost certain he escaped death in that launch explosion. That he is alive."

The man regarded them with scorn. "It is true that all infidels become mad under the power of our sun."

"Believe us," Gale said. "We want your help. We will pay you well."

The man's eyes glistened greedily. "You wish to hire my services?"

"Yes," Gale said.

Eric gave her a warning look. Then he told the wrinkled black cousin of Jiri's, "We will pay you a reasonable sum if you will take us to Jiri."

Fazi speculated on this. Then he said, "I will accept five pounds of British notes now and five more when you greet my cousin."

Gale at once said, "Agreed!"

Eric gave her another warning look. "Are you satisfied with our bargain?"

"We have no choice," she said. "Give him the first five pounds. I'll repay you when we return to Casablanca."

Eric frowned and dug in his trousers' pocket, "It is not the money. I'm not sure that he means to play the game with us."

Fazi was now smiling and fawning on them. "It is agreed?"

Eric handed him five crisp one-pound notes and said, "That is all you get until we are face to face with Jiri."

Fazi snatched the bills from Eric and used his clawlike hand to stuff them away in his robe. He said, "It shall be done, but we must wait for a while."

"We paid you what you asked for," Eric said with some anger. "Why must we wait?"

"You do not understand," Fazi said. "In a very short while my cousin will enter this room."

Gale showed surprise. "You are expecting him here?"

"Yes," the black man nodded.

Eric frowned. "You pretended you believed him to be dead."

Fazi bowed low and smiled, "My good friend, that was before you showed yourself one to be trusted."

"Meaning what?" Eric asked.

Fazi made an apologetic motion with one of his clawlike hands and said, "I was afraid for my cousin. Often he has been in trouble with the white authority. I did not wish to betray him."

"And all the while you were expecting him?" Gale said.

"It is true," Fazi said, with a nod. "He always comes to see me about this time of day. We smoke and have coffee. You must let me prepare the coffee, and you shall join us in a friendly fashion."

Eric said, "I'm not thirsty."

Gale gave him a meaningful glance. "I think we should drink with Fazi and his cousin as proof of our honesty."

The black Fazi smiled and eyed her with admiration. "What a wise woman! It is a pity you are not veiled! You have the wisdom of a proper follower of the prophet!"

"Thank you, Fazi," she said warmly. "Prepare the coffee and we will join you."

"At once," Fazi said bowing. "You will excuse me!" And then as he went out through an entrance covered by a ragged curtain, he paused to tell them, "Allah is great!"

As soon as he'd gone Eric turned to her and said, "I don't like this at all!"

"But we're about to meet Jiri!"

Eric said, "I'm almost ill from the stench in here and I'm not at all as convinced by what that fellow says as you seem to be."

"I know it's stuffy in here but we can't hurt his feelings. We need only sip a little of the coffee, and it may be quite good."

"I doubt it," Eric said worriedly. "What I want to see is Jiri coming into this room."

They were interrupted by the old man's return with a tray bearing the coffee urn and tiny cups. He offered them a warm smile and said, "I will pour for us and when Jiri enters he will see he is among friends."

He carefully poured cups for them and for

himself. As he gave them their cups, he said, "The coffee is sweet and rich. Done in the fashion of my tribe."

Gale took hers and sipped from it. "It's actually very pleasant," she said.

Eric was frowning but he also tried it. He smacked his lips. "Sweetish!"

"That is our manner of preparation," the old man said, beaming at them.

Gale sipped some more of the potent brew and it tasted even better than before. She was about to tell Fazi this when her head began to reel and she felt as if she might collapse!

15

With difficulty she focused her eyes on Eric and was terrified to see his handsome face go slack. Suddenly he let his coffee cup drop, then he crumpled on the floor in front of her. She glanced in the direction of the watching Fazi and had a blurred impression of a gloating smile. Then she could hold back the confusion no longer and felt herself falling down into a velvet darkness.

Her first awareness was of a steady pounding! She turned restlessly and fretfully tried to remain asleep. But the throb of motors continued and a stench of oil filled her nostrils. She opened her eyes to semidarkness and discovered she was stretched out on a bunk in a tiny, shadowed area. And now the throbbing became louder and seemed to dominate everything.

A cruel-looking hook swayed above her and she wondered if she were going to be hung from it like a section of beef. Then she saw that the hook had an arm and the arm, a body. A grim, brown-faced man in red and white turban and brown robe stood staring down at her. He had a small Vandyke beard and mustache, and his eyes were filled with hatred.

"How do you do, Madame Cormier," he said in an accented voice.

She stared up at him in fear, instinctively knowing he was the enemy. "Where am I?"

The character with the hooked nose and Vandyke beard seemed to relish the question. He said, "You are at the bottom of the sea!"

She moaned and crossed a hand over her eyes as she sought to remember. They had been looking for Jiri and . . . She raised herself on an elbow and accused him, "Fazi drugged us! There was something in that coffee!"

"Of course there was," the robed man said suavely. "A potent sedative, which I must say worked very well."

"Fazi tricked us!" she groaned. And then she asked him, "Who are you?"

"I have been waiting for you to ask," he said and bowed. "I am Sheik Sidi Abdullah, chosen to be the leader of this unhappy land."

"I've heard about you," she said. "You are the brother of Sheik Ali."

"Sheik Ali was my brother," the man grieved. "Also he was murdered by infidels. An act which rid me of an undesirable relative."

"You two were rivals," she recalled.

"Now I alone will bring freedom to my country," he observed, his eyes gleaming fanatically.

"Where is my friend?" she asked.

"On a similar bunk in another area. You are my prisoner," Sheik Sidi Abdullah informed her. "A hostage of the people's movement. We will never know peace until you Westerners and the foolish Sultan have been forced out of our blessed land."

He made her angry and she sat up despite her aching head to tell him, "You will release me at once."

"Where do you propose to go?"

"Anywhere but here," she said. "What is this foul place? Some cellar in the medina?"

The bearded man looked delighted. He said, "No, Madame Cormier, you are, as I told you, at the bottom of the sea, in a submarine operated by my group."

She stared at him in disbelief. "A submarine?"

"Of the same type used by the Turkish navy," he told her. "In fact, my men were trained for this operation by Turkish naval officers. This is one of the one-hundred-sixty-ton steam-driven submarines built by the British and sold to the Turkish navy in 1887. Now three years later I have full possession of this one. It cost me a great deal of money but it shall win me the revolution!"

And then the pieces all came together for her. It was truly a submarine, and no doubt it was at the moment resting at the bottom of the sea. She'd heard of the notoriously corrupt Turkish officials. They had been daring enough to turn one of their submarines over to Revene at a high profit and he, in turn, had managed to get a queen's ransom for it from the desperate Sheik Sidi Abdullah.

She said, "So Revene got this for you."

The Sheik smiled and said, "I would prefer not to discuss the matter. But we have done well. In the past weeks we have sunk much of the Sultan's fleet and we shall keep at it untill Morocco is on her knees."

She recalled Eric's story of the Sultan announcing that some invisible craft was decimating his merchant vessels. It seemed he hadn't been so mad after all.

She said, "What do you want of us?"

He made a gesture with the hand which ended in a cruel steel hook. "Why do you ask me the question? You know what I seek. The briefcase! The one your husband had!"

"I don't have it."

"You lie."

"Say that as much as you like," she told him. "I do not know anything about the briefcase. I was searching for it when Fazi drugged me."

"Ah!" Sidi Abdullah said. "So you are aware of its importance."

"Only because so many people have tried to get it from me."

"It would be wise if you found some memory of it," the sheik warned her. "As soon as I have it in my hands, you will be released."

"I simply can't help you!" she protested.

Sheik Sidi Abdullah eyed her with disdain. "You will change your mind. I have ways to make people talk." And he held the steel hook, which served as a hand, before her.

She leaned back. "Don't threaten me!"

"The hook cuts deeply and can do much damage in a moment," the sheik said in his smooth fashion. "You have such a lovely face it saddens me to consider damaging it."

The great trouble was she believed him. He did mean to mutilate her face unless she talked. Terrified, she suddenly wanted the presence of Eric.

"I must see my friend," she insisted.

The sheik showed interest. "You wish to discuss this with him?"

"Yes," she said, willing to say anything to get to Eric and see that he was all right.

"Very well," Sheik Sidi Abdullah said. "It is a reasonable request. It should be a man's decision. A woman is clearly too weak to deal in such matters. I will take you to Mr. Simms."

"When?"

"Now, if you like," the sheik said. "You will walk before me."

She got up from the bunk and was more than ever aware of the submarine's throbbing engines and its slight motion. He propelled her along a gaslit corridor. Along the way they passed bearded, robed men at various operating posts of the very modern machine. An incongruity!

They came to another small ell where Eric was dejectedly seated on a bunk like the one which she had occupied. He glanced up when he saw her arrive followed by the sheik.

He stood up, his head almost touching the iron roof, and taking her in his arms, said, "You're all right?"

"Aside from an aching head."

"I have that too," he agreed. And glancing at the sheik, he asked, "I want to know when we're to be released?"

The sheik smiled humorlessly. "The lady and you must decide that. I am a man of understanding, so I shall leave you two alone. But remember there is an armed guard at either end of the corridor. They have instructions to shoot if you attempt to leave this area."

"How kind of you!" Eric said angrily to the back of the departing sheik.

She looked up at Eric. "What are we going to do?"

He said forlornly, "You know where we are?"

"In a submarine."

"A submerged submarine," he said with a groan. "I knew that trying to find Jiri was a mistake."

"It can't be blamed on Jiri. It was his cousin Fazi who turned us over to the enemy. But it isn't all that important now," she said. "What I want to know is how do we escape?"

"That is an unanswerable question," Eric told her. "Sit down. The motion of this thing won't bother you so."

She sat on the bunk and he sat beside her. She said, "As usual, Sheik Sidi thinks I know where that briefcase is."

"I imagine the Turkish officials who helped him get this submarine are wild to have it," was Eric's opinion. "Their names and the agreements must all be in the case."

"I told him I knew nothing about it. And like the others, he doesn't believe me."

"And he threatened to torture you?"

"Yes," she said. "How do you know?"

He grimaced. "He used the same tactics on me. He is not all that subtle."

She said, "I feel we have no chance this time."

"We are cut off from everyone," he agreed. "But they have to surface every so often for supplies and fuel. We must somehow try to stall him off until we do surface. Then try to escape."

"He is too smart to allow that."

"We'll have to be smarter. Though when I think

how easily that Fazi took us in, I'm not too sure about it," he added with angry despair.

They sat in gloomy silence for a little—the heavy throbbing of the submarine's steam engines and occasional distant voices crying out in Arabic the only things to break the quiet. She knew that much, if not everything, that Eric had said was true. They had walked straight into a trap and it was the worst fix in which they had found themselves to date.

She debated what she might tell the sheik. She would have to lie and somehow make it seem like the truth. This might at least give them the time they needed.

She said nothing of her plan to Eric. She decided it might be better if he at first thought she was telling the truth. In that way she would get an honest reaction from him. This would make her own lying seem all the more convincing. Now she began to work out some details to make the story plausible.

She assumed, for no particular reason, that it was daytime though it was hard to say on the submarine. Some time went by and a sullen youth brought them some pieces of meat, bread, and water. It was the sort of fare served in prisons but she knew there probably was no better food stocked on the underwater craft.

Eric gave her a worried glance after the Arab youth had taken their dishes away. He said, "We must try to think of some plan to escape."

"I have been thinking of one," she told him quietly.

"What?" he asked.

"You'll find out soon," she promised.

Sheik Sidi Abdullah returned to stand over them. He asked her, "Well?"

She looked up at him. "If I give you the information you want, will you free us?"

"I will," the man with the steel hook said.

She hesitated for a moment and then said, "Very well. I will tell you. But you must release us."

A crafty look came to his bearded face. "Only when I have the case in my own hands will you be released. But you have my word!"

"That is not a fair bargain," she protested.

"It is the only one you'll get from me, Madame," the sheik told her.

Eric gave her an anxious look and advised, "I don't think you should tell him anything. He'll trick you."

Abdullah drew himself up in a dignified fashion and told them, "I am a prince of the desert. Of royal lineage. Soon I hope to be Sultan. My word is my bond!"

She pretended to be impressed by this though she knew him to be a scoundrel who would think nothing of going back on his word. She turned to Eric and said, "I believe he really means it!"

"Don't be a fool," Eric said desperately. "He doesn't hesitate to take hostages and threaten them with torture; why should we accept his word about anything?"

"I must try, at least." Turning to Sheik Sidi Abdullah, she said, "I'm going to trust you. Put my life in your hands."

"You may do so with an easy mind," the sheik said, bowing.

She clasped her hands and gazed down at them. "The briefcase is in Casablanca."

"Where?" the sheik asked eagerly.

"Paul gave it to me the night he was said to be

killed in that launch explosion. He told me it was valuable and asked that I find a safe hiding place for it."

"Go on!" the impatient sheik ordered.

Eric gave her a look of anguish. "You shouldn't tell him anything. It is bound to turn out a mistake."

"I'm sorry, Eric," she replied. "I've made up my mind." And she quickly glanced up at the sheik with anxious eyes. She asked him, "You know the chateau?"

The sheik said, "Revene's house by the water."

"Yes. Paul and I lived there before all this happened."

"I know the house," Sheik Sidi Abdullah said.

"I was left alone with the case and knew I had to locate a good hiding place," she continued. "I took the stairway to the wine cellars and down there I found a small room. A kind of steward's room where one could select the wine and even taste it if he wished."

Sheik Sidi Abdullah said, "I know the room you mean."

"Then it should all be easy for you," she said.

"Indeed?" he asked.

"I stood in the steward's tiny room and looked up and saw there was a trapdoor in its ceiling. I opened the trapdoor and found a dark interior where valuables might be concealed. And that is where I placed the briefcase."

The Arab leader stared at her suspiciously. "This is no trick, you swear?"

"I promised I would tell you where it is and so I have," she said.

The sheik nodded. "Very well. We shall put in to Casablanca and when I have the briefcase I will set you and this man of yours free."

"I am in your hands," she said meekly.

The sheik left them and a few minutes afterward the submarine's engines were turned to full speed. The passage of the big ship through the water was choppy. It was evident her story had made the sheik change his plans.

Eric gave her a worried look. "Why didn't you tell me you had the briefcase?"

She whispered, "Because I haven't got it."

"You haven't?" he lowered his voice to a whisper. "Why that story then?"

"You know why," she said. "To give us time."

"He'll be enraged after going to Casablanca and not finding the case. He'll have us tortured and killed."

"He was going to do that anyway."

Eric shook his head. "We have a nice outlook."

Hours passed and they were kept confined in the small ell off the submarine's main corridor. Then Sheik Sidi Abdullah came to them with two evil thugs at his side. He gave them orders in Arabic and the two at once went about binding Gale and Eric at both the ankles and wrists.

"We shall be at dock while I go in search of the case," he said. "I cannot risk your trying to escape."

"You ought to be freeing us rather than doing this!" Eric said angrily.

The sheik gloated over him. "You will not find me making the mistakes the others have."

They were left completely trussed up and then ignored. No one came near them. However, most of the submarine's crew were busy at their posts. The big ship slowed its speed once again and they had the sensation of rising to the top of the waves. This was confirmed almost at once by its rolling like a small craft in the rough water. Down below it had been fairly quiet.

"We're riding on the surface," Eric told her. "We must be entering Casablanca harbor."

"At least we'll be near land," she said.

Eric gave her a despairing glance. "A lot of good that will do us, with us bound in this way."

"I agree it looks bad."

"It will look a good deal worse when he returns in a rage without that briefcase."

"I had to do something," she protested. "You said we should fight for time."

Eric's angry expression relented and in a gentle tone, he said, "How can I blame you? You did what you thought best. I'm only sorry your story won't help us."

She made no reply. She knew that their chance of escaping had been reduced to almost nil. The sheik had not been wrong when he'd claimed himself a crafty adversary. It seemed she had told her elaborate lie for nothing.

But even realizing this, she was visited by a wave of optimism which didn't make sense. A small voice within told her they would, in spite of everything, survive.

Loud bells rang; there was a clamor of new machinery working, and the wave-tossed craft came to an extremely slow speed. She could almost picture them maneuvering it to a place by a deserted dock. In the darkness of night they could tie up and not be noticed. Before dawn they could quickly slip out again. It was certain that Sheik Sidi Abdullah must have brought his pirate submarine in to Casablanca on other such nights.

All motion stopped but a gentle swaying. There

was only the hum of the machinery kept under steam but with the pressure greatly reduced. Arabic was shouted back and forth and there seemed to be a great deal of moving about by the crew.

She whispered, "We must be docked now. The sheik and his men will soon be leaving the ship."

"But we are still his prisoners. Hopelessly so," Eric reminded her.

"I know," she said. "We must do something to attract one of those left to guard us. Perhaps we can bribe our way out of this."

"With what? Promises? Hardly! My Arabic isn't all that good and we have no cash on us. All we're liable to get for our efforts is a bayonet tip in the ribs."

She said, "You've noticed their guns are of the latest type and equipped with those evil-looking bayonets."

"Revene deals only in the best," Eric said grimly.

"I keep worrying about Madeline and whether she is all right," Gale said unhappily.

"At this moment you need not worry about anyone but us," he said grimly. "That ought to take all your time!"

She made no reply to this. The flurry of activity aboard the submarine seemed to slow down. It became fairly quiet on board the underwater craft. The stench of oil diminished, as if some opening allowed fresh air to enter the craft while it was docked.

Gale glanced at Eric, trussed up and miserable at the other end of the bunk, and felt sorry for him. True, her position was just as hopeless. The minutes went by and she tried to judge how long it would take the sheik to reach the chateau on the beach and find her story a lie.

It all depended on how far this dock might be from the modern part of the city. Again, it was likely that he had selected a deserted dock somewhere on the outskirts rather than in the perpetually busy harbor. This meant they would have extra time before he and his men returned. She judged that the whole thing might take up to two hours. Not long when it might mark their life expectancy!

She closed her eyes in apprehension and it was only a gasp from Eric which made her open them. Standing before her as if materialized by some genii was the brown-skinned Jiri. The man in the red fez made a signal for them to say nothing. Then he knelt and swiftly cut the bonds first at Eric's ankles and wrists, then hers.

All her hope came bounding back. She gave Jiri an inquiring look and he motioned for them to follow him. They did so and the first thing to startle them was a guard on the floor with a knife buried deep in his back.

They followed Jiri in stepping over the dead man, and she marveled at how quietly the guard had been brought down. They had heard nothing. Only a little distance further they saw another of the sheik's men sprawled out by the controls of the submarine in a grotesque position and surely dead.

Jiri halted by a metal ladder which went up into a turret. He then climbed up the ladder and she followed after him with Eric in the rear. In a moment she emerged from the submarine to breathe the fresh night air and see the stars overhead. Never so welcome a sight!

Eric was at her side. Jiri clambered up onto the dock first and then assisted them. Strangely, there was no sign of guards on the dock. She assumed that the sheik had been so confident of their helplessness he had left the submarine with only two men to guard it. Jiri had silently and quickly put them to death. She had not overestimated him.

Jiri raced along the wharves and they followed after him. Not until they were at least a mile away from where the submarine was docked did he slow his pace. Then he took them into what seemed an abandoned shed.

As they stood there in the darkness, striving to catch their breath, she finally gasped, "How did you know where we were?"

Jiri replied, "My wicked cousin Fazi bragged about taking your money and turning you both over to Sheik Sidi Abdullah for six golden sovereigns."

Eric said, "And you knew where the submarine docked?"

"I found that out later," Jiri said, "from one of Abdullah's men who believed me to have shifted to their side. I knew where the submarine would dock but I did not know when."

"So?" she said.

"I found a comfortable place to hide and waited," Jiri told her. "It was good fortune that brought the evil craft in sooner than I expected. I was told Abdullah sometimes only came to Casablanca at five-day intervals."

She said, "It came in tonight because I told Abdullah the briefcase he was looking for was in the chateau."

"You could not have told him that," Jiri protested.

"Why not?" she asked.

"Because I have the briefcase in hiding, and it is not at the chateau," Jiri said.

"I knew it," she exclaimed. "That is why we went

looking for you. I had some sort of visitation from my husband. And he told me to find you and get the briefcase for him."

Jiri spoke in a taut voice, "But Madame, your husband is dead. Drowned when the launch exploded."

"You were also said to be on that launch and dead," she said. "But you are alive."

"It was arranged I should not go, so I could be the keeper of the briefcase," Jiri explained. "When your husband and Abdul-el-Krem went aboard that launch, they took a man who was dressed like me and resembled me. He is the one who died with them!"

"But my husband seemed to know you were alive," she said. "And he knew you had the briefcase. He begged me to get it."

Eric spoke up, "It was obviously someone pretending to be Paul."

"I can't believe the likeness could be so true," she demurred.

"You've always said this phantom figure had a ghostly look," Eric reminded her. "So you've never really seen it at close range."

"No," she said.

Jiri spoke up, "Someone is playing the ghost to trick you, Madame. I wish that your husband and Abdul-el-Krem were still alive; I would know better what to do."

"What do you mean?" she asked.

"Our cause was sacred to us," Jiri said. "Your husband supplied us with arms when Revene gave his support to Sheik Sidi Abdullah and Sheik Ali. For that your husband was murdered by a bomb planted in the motor launch. And our leader Abdul-el-Krem with him. Now our group has broken up and we are finished."

Gale said, "I think much could be accomplished to stop Revene in his illegal arms deals if that briefcase is placed in the right hands."

Jiri said sternly, "If I could destroy this Revene by doing so, I would gladly hand the case over to you."

"I will give it to the American Consulate," she promised. "And along with the British Consulate there will be some sort of joint official action."

"Have they told you this?" Jiri asked.

"Yes," she said. "That is why I remained in Casablanca to be a bait for Revene and his associates in a hope of bringing them to justice."

"It shall be done, Madame," Jiri said. "You shall have the briefcase. But first I must get you both to the city in safety."

"How do you propose to do that?" Eric asked.

"Further along the way there is a covered wagon with produce in it, much like the ones which regularly bring food into the city. There will be room for you two to hide in safety."

Gale said, "How can we thank you?"

"It is a sacred trust," Jiri told her. "Your husband was our friend and helper."

After making sure there was no one in sight, they left the shed and hurried on to a nearby narrow street where the wagon was waiting, as Jiri had promised. He spoke to the driver and then told them to get into the back where the covering would hide them.

Eric asked, "Where are you going?"

"Back to the medina," Jiri said. "I have many things to do."

She said, "When will you bring me the briefcase?"

"As soon as it is in my hands," Jiri said. "I gave it to another for safekeeping. It will take a little time to get it back. My friend is not always in the city."

"It's urgent," Eric told him. "Every day counts."

"I do not think it should take more than two or three days at the most," Jiri said. "My friend makes trips into the desert but he always returns quickly."

He saw them safely into the covered wagon and instructed the driver to take them to the British Consulate. Eric had requested this, as he felt they might be offered more safety there. And Colonel Hudson could notify Richard Adams and have him join them.

As they crouched in the wagon, Eric worried, "Do you think we can trust him?"

"He went to a good deal of trouble for us," she reminded him. "He could have been killed."

"True," Eric said. "Yet I wonder if we'll ever see that briefcase. Too many people want it."

"I think Jiri will do his best."

"A knife in the back could finish him as easily as the next man," he reminded her.

She shuddered. "Don't say such things!"

"And Abdullah will be in a nasty mood after he ransacks the chateau wine cellars and finds nothing."

"I know," she agreed.

"On top of it all this is one of the roughest ways to journey across the city I know," Eric said with a groan as the giant wagon wheels struck another rough spot in the road.

She could only agree. And when the wagon took them into the driveway of the consulate she was more than grateful. She and Eric scrambled out of the back of the wagon to be at once confronted by two threatening British soldiers with their rifles pointed at them.

"Here now!" One of the soldiers challenged them. "What are you two doing here?"

"British citizen and newspaperman," Eric told him. "This lady and myself are friends of Colonel Hudson. Here on important business!"

"They don't look like friends of the Colonel's," the second soldier said as they kept their rifles on them.

"They bloody well don't!" the first soldier agreed.

At this point an officer stepped out of the entrance of the consulate and came briskly to the little group. He asked the first soldier, "Now, Hawkins, what is the bother here?"

Before Hawkins could answer, Eric spoke up, "They don't think that I and Madame Cormier are friends of the consul."

The officer stared at him and then recognizing him, said, "Simms! Of course! The newspaper fellow!" And turning to her, he said, "Madame Cormier! Both the Colonel and Mr. Adams have been at their wits' end since you vanished. Mr. Adams is inside with the Colonel now."

Within a few minutes they were seated in Colonel Hudson's office having drinks with the old man and Richard Adams.

"Confounded good luck that you elected to come here," Colonel Hudson said. "Adams has been with me most of the evening."

Standing by the Colonel, Richard Adams was in a grim mood. "It was most unwise of you and Mr. Simms to go questing in the medina on your own. I would never have given you permission to do it."

Gale said triumphantly, "But in spite of everything we have come up with valuable information and we've had a promise from Jiri that he will bring the briefcase to me."

"I hope that he keeps his word," Adams said. "And as for your other information it is anything but welcome."

Colonel Hudson adjusted his monocle. "Ghastly business! To think that madman Abdullah is roaming about the Mediterranean with an armed submarine!"

"Built in England and originally sold to the Turks," Eric said. "What a story it will make!"

The Colonel gave him a disapproving look. "It may make a big story one day, young man. But for the moment I impose silence on you. This is too grave a political situation. You must give me time to cable my superiors and receive their advice on how to act before I can allow you to file the story."

Eric was on his feet, upset. "That is hardly fair, sir. After all I have risked to get the story."

Richard Adams snapped at him. "As I see it, this young woman was the one who instigated the adventure. You merely accompanied her. And it was through her friend, Jiri, that you were rescued. Not by your own efforts."

Eric looked startled. "Then I'm to be censored?"

"Only as long as need be for official permission to print the facts," Colonel Hudson promised. "I want the world to know what is going on just as well as you do. But we must first make up our minds how to act against these pirates: Abdullah with an armed submarine and Revene with a powerfully swift and armed yacht."

Gale asked, "What about Madeline?"

The stern Adams sighed. "I regret to say we have not found her."

"Most unfortunate," Colonel Hudson said with a frown.

"I think so, gentlemen," Gale said. "Especially as you two men were responsible for her joining me in a dangerous enterprise."

Adams said, "We did not introduce her to drugs!"

"No," she said. "I'll grant you that. But I know she has no one else who cares. We must somehow save her."

"We shall leave no stone unturned," Colonel Hudson said. "I promise you. Now what about you?"

"I shall return to the chateau," she said. "I still have a role to play there until Revene is brought to justice. Hassan will protect me."

"Hassan is not there," Adams said. "He has been back at police headquarters directing the search for you. But I will have a message sent to him and he will return."

Eric asked her, "Do you think you dare return to the chateau? You sent Abdullah there on a wild-goose chase to find the briefcase in the wine cellars."

"He will be gone by now, I'm sure," she said.

"We can tell when we get there," Richard Adams said. "I'll call on the Colonel to supply us with a few armed men in case of trouble."

"Gladly," the Colonel said, rising.

There were two carriages. Adams, Gale, and Eric rode in the first one along with their friend, the young officer. The second one held four heavily armed soldiers.

All too soon they came within sight of the chateau. She studied it against the starlit sky and with a tiny shudder said, "Back home!"

"I trust all our visitors have come and gone," Eric said.

They drew up by the entrance and it was open. The lock had been rifled by Abdullah and his men and they'd not even bothered to close the giant doors. All was quiet with no hint of anyone around.

The young officer with his men searched the upper regions of the house and found nothing. Then they went down to the wine cellars with Adams, Gale, and Eric following. They crossed the dark region with the young officer showing the way with a lantern.

He was in the cellar ahead when he cried out, "Something here!"

They all crowded in and the sight which greeted them brought them to stunned silence. Gale thought she might faint. Hanging from a rafter was the grotesque figure of a robed man, his eyes bulging and his tongue protruding in death! The face, despite its distortion, was known to her. It was the face of Jiri's cousin, the double-dealing Fazi!

16

Eric escorted Gale back upstairs. In the meantime Richard Adams supervised the British officer's cutting down of Fazi's frightening corpse, and the soldiers carried the body out of the house. Later the soldiers restored some order to the litter of destruction in the wine cellar.

Adams came upstairs to tell them, "I'm afraid a great deal of wine is missing and many bottles smashed on the floor."

Gale grimaced. "I'm not concerned. It belonged to Revene."

The prim Bostonian said, "Sheik Sidi Abdullah took you at your word. He tore away almost all the ceiling in the wine cellar before he gave up his vain search for the missing briefcase."

"At least the ploy saved us," she said.

Eric gave her a knowing look. "He balanced the account by hanging Fazi on the scene. Since it was Fazi who turned us over to him in the first place."

Adams asked her, "Are you still willing to remain here for a little?"

"Yes," she said.

"Very well, then," Adams said. "Until Hassan

returns I'll leave these soldiers on duty here. They should offer you any needed protection."

"I must disagree," Eric protested. "I'm sure there are secret entrances and passages here, spots the soldiers cannot have knowledge of or guard."

The dour Adams said, "If you feel so worried, Mr. Simms, why don't you remain here for the night as an extra precaution."

"I will," Eric said promptly. "But I'm no more competent than your soldiers."

Adams asked Gale, "Do you still have the pistol Hassan gave you?"

"Hardly," she said. "I miss it."

"I will see you are provided with another tomorrow," the Bostonian said. "Meanwhile, I doubt if there will be any more problems tonight."

"I hope not," she said. "I'm much too weary to face up to new trouble."

Richard Adams then turned to Eric and sternly reminded him, "You will obey Colonel Hudson and make no attempt to publish any information about the renegade submarine."

"It seems I haven't much choice," Eric grumbled.

"Diplomacy must be served," Adams told him. "We are in a delicate position here. And unfortunately the French, for reasons of their own, do not mind if it gets worse."

Adams and the British officer left a little while later but the four soldiers remained at various points of the grounds to guard the house. To all intents she was as safe as she might expect to be.

When they were alone Eric took her in his arms and after kissing her, said, "Have I ever told you what a remarkably brave lady you are?"

"I don't know," she said. "You can tell me again if you like. I enjoy hearing it."

His eyes regarded hers tenderly. "The trouble is that I'm so much in love with you! It frightens me to have you take the risks you do."

"So far we've survived," she said with a smile. "And I love you more than you can imagine."

Still holding her in his arms, he said, "Jiri assured us your husband is dead."

"Everyone thought Jiri dead, but he is alive."

"He explained that," Eric said. "He was never in that launch, so he missed the explosion. But your husband and Abdul-el-Krem were in it. And so they died."

"Perhaps," she said worriedly. "How do you explain the several times I've seen Paul since? His whispered pleading with me to get the briefcase."

"The ghostly encounters?"

"If you want to call them that."

"I'm not sure," he said. "Either your nerves have played tricks on you or they've found someone who resembles Paul and are having this fellow play the ghost to terrify you and get you to do their bidding."

Gale considered this and said, "You may be right. I don't know. The face seemed to be Paul's and yet it didn't."

"Undoubtedly some look-alike made up to scare you."

"You could be right," she worried. "But surely if I remain here long enough the truth will come out."

"Providing you are not murdered by these scoundrels in the meanwhile," Eric said angrily.

"I'll not worry tonight," she smiled. "I'll have you beside me."

Still holding her in his arms, he stared at her and asked, "Does that mean literally beside you?"

She nodded. Her eyes bright and her cheeks a soft crimson. "I think it is time," she said.

"Past time," Eric said intensely. "I thought of it while we were prisoners on the submarine, knowing that we were soon to die . . . It seemed so damnably unfair!"

In a sense the grimness which had marked the beginning of the night was swept aside. A romantic Eric carried her up to her bedroom in his arms and after gently kissing her once again, left to allow her to prepare for bed.

She was so caught up in the excitement of their love that all else was excluded from her mind. When she had undressed and donned a flimsy dressing gown, she went to the window and stared up at the large full moon and the stars reflected on the dark ocean. Tonight all nature was deceptively placid.

Eric came into the room a short time after. He was naked to the waist as he stood with her a moment at the window. She glanced at his lithe, manly body and thought of all they had braved together and now they were about to share a new experience.

He smiled at her and led her over to the side of the bed. Gently he removed her dressing gown so that she stood naked before him in the shaft of moonlight which cut across the room. He tossed his trousers aside to face her nude for the first time. Then he lifted her in his arms and tenderly placed her on the bed and lay down beside her.

Gale recalled little of their lovemaking except that it was completely satisfying and joyously right. When at last they had expended their love, they lay close and fell asleep with their arms around each other.

Morning came and with it the burdens of another day. Eric had to leave directly after she had made breakfast for them. While he could not file the story about the submarine, he had several other matters to look after. Their parting embrace was indicative of the warm, new relationship between them.

It was a warm sunny day and she felt so relaxed and happy that she spent a little time sitting on the patio under a large colored umbrella to protect her from the sun. But she soon began to worry about the unfinished problems facing her. She was terribly concerned about Madeline, positive that Revene and his villainous crew would use the French girl's addiction to enslave her further.

Hassan returned just before noon. The big black man was in radiant good humor. "You managed to get away from them, Madame," he said. "It was very smart of you."

She laughed. "I'm sure that Sheik Sidi Abdullah will try to make me pay for it."

Hassan scowled. "He is an evil man. But he had better not venture too far."

"You are back to guard me for a while?"

"Yes," Hassan said with some pride. "I have sent the soldiers back to the British Consulate."

"I'm sure you can cope as well as any four of them," she said. "I shan't soon forget how you saved my life on the rooftop here. Is your side healing well?"

"Very well," he said. "I have no pain from it at all."

She said, "I think Mr. Simms will be staying here most nights from now on. He's been very upset about my safety."

"That is a good thing," Hassan said soberly. "Mr. Simms knows this country and its people."

She had not time to ask Hassan about another weapon before Richard Adams arrived. He joined her in the sun and eyed her with interest.

329

"Considering the ordeal you've gone through, you look positively radiant today," was his comment.

"I rested well last night," she said, afraid that she was blushing.

"Utter exhaustion, no doubt," the prim Bostonian said with his usual tact. "And of course the knowledge that Mr. Simms was close by must have helped."

"It did," she agreed, without explaining quite how close she and Eric had been.

The stern Adams dusted a speck off the knee of his white linen trousers and said, "There are a number of questions I wish to ask you."

"Of course," she said. "I'll tell you anything I can."

"Colonel Hudson has notified the British naval group holding their maneuvers just off the Casablanca shore of the presence of the renegade submarine. They are familiar with its design since it was British-built and they'll be on the lookout for it."

"Can they take any action against it?" she wondered.

"Not officially," he said. "It might create an international incident. The difficulty being that the French may be secretly encouraging this Abdullah financially in his madness. They wish to see Morocco in an uprising so that they may step in."

"I should say that is likely to happen soon."

"It is inevitable," Adams agreed. "All we can do is hope to hold the timetable of revolution back."

"You would rather see the country independent than a protectorate of France?" she said.

"Our governments would prefer that an independent guardian be appointed to end the troubles of this unhappy state."

"The kidnapping of Eric and myself was surely an illegal act, equal to piracy on the high seas," she said. "Why can't the British take action on that basis?"

"Colonel Hudson has cabled London and is waiting for a reply concerning that," Adams said. "Eric is a British citizen and the reporter for an important paper."

"What about Revene?" she asked. "I'd be willing to bet that poor Madeline is a prisoner on his yacht."

Adams said, "We have to catch Revene in the act, so to speak. Thus far it has not been possible. If we could get our hands on that briefcase with the contracts and names of the various parties conducting transactions with him, we could build an excellent case against him."

She said, "It exists. I know that. And Jiri has given me his promise to turn it over to me."

"Can this Jiri be trusted?"

"Yes," she said. "He is loyal to the memory of my late husband. It seems Paul was selling his group munitions as opposed to Revene, who was dealing with Sheik Ali and Sheik Sidi Abdullah."

"Your late husband?" the prim, dark man said. "Do you now feel Paul Cormier is dead?"

She blushed. "Jiri swore that he was."

"But you claim to have been visited by him?"

"Under ghostly conditions," she said. "I now think I was duped by an impostor pretending to be Paul."

"The appearance would have to be almost identical to deceive a wife," Adams said, his keen eyes fixed on her. "I do not see how they could produce such a look-alike."

She realized his argument was good and tried to explain, "These visitations were always in the night. The room in utter darkness. And I was most struck by his strange pallor. I was too upset to be able to judge critically. It is possible that the likeness was not as great as I imagined."

"It would seem so," Adams said dryly. "I find it odd that earlier you appeared convinced your husband was alive and now you seem equally anxious to think of him as dead."

"I'm sorry," she said, flustered. "It is how I feel and mostly because of what Jiri told me."

"Much depends on this Jiri, it would seem."

"Yes."

"Will he resent the fact that his cousin Fazi was hanged here in the cellar as a direct result of your deceiving Sheik Sidi Abdullah?"

"He will not care. They were enemies."

"I see," the consulate officer said. "Now let us get back to your husband's half brother, Ben Cormier. He was reported murdered."

"It was a deliberate hoax to evade his paying gambling debts," she said. "Now the people to whom he owed the money have left the country, so he felt free to return to his studio once more."

"A thoroughly undesirable character."

"Paul always felt so," she said, "but I have found him helpful enough and pleasant when he wishes to be."

"He directed you to the dwelling of the late Fazi?"

"Yes."

"And Fazi had contact with Abdullah," Adams went on. "I think I should talk to your brother-in-law and see if he cannot give us more information about these rebels."

Gale said, "I think he'll cooperate if he can."

"Shall we try him?" Adams said. "Every clue we can get may bring us nearer to rescuing Madeline."

"I'll be glad to take you to him," she said.

"Fine," he said, rising. "It would be best if you introduced me as a friend of Mr. Simms, perhaps another newspaperman."

"If you like," she agreed.

"Then we will go to the medina as soon as you are ready," he said. "My carriage is waiting outside and will take us as far as the gates."

They left a few minutes later and made the now familiar journey from the new city to the old. Adams talked to her along the way, mostly of Boston and his hope to return there soon. She paid little attention to the palm-lined, crowded streets.

She wasn't even paying much attention to the sober Adams. She was thinking of Eric and how much she loved him. She was certain that the consulate official guessed about the previous night. But she was in no way ashamed. As soon as this terrible business was at an end she and Eric would be married in the most proper fashion. Meanwhile, their bond was as sacred to them as any marriage vows.

They left their carriage and began walking to the old city. A troop of youngsters in scarlet costumes edged across their path and put on an acrobatic display. Richard Adams threw them a few coins when they'd finished.

He told Gale, "I can't resist these street beggars. Would you believe that when I was a boy I could do cartwheels such as they did?"

She smiled. "You're still slim and athletic."

"Lean for a man past his prime," Adams said with a bitter smile.

Another beggar, an old white-bearded fellow, pushed his way through the passersby to plead before them. He was stooped and emaciated and his arm was in a plaster cast. Again Adams thrust some coins in the withered hand.

As they continued on Adams told her, "That cast likely was first put on as a fake. So he could beg. But by now I'm sure the arm beneath it has truly withered into uselessness."

She asked, "Why do the men wear turbans or fezzes?"

He said, "No Moslem will wear a brimmed hat, the brim would prevent the wearer from touching the ground as required in prayer prostrations. Men who haven't prayed in years will still refrain from wearing a brimmed hat!"

They made their way down the narrow streets toward the obscure alley where Ben Cormier had his studio. They passed a shop before which stood a very battered old man with a raw sheepskin over his arm. It gave off a rank smell. Adams shook his head, but the old man said something in Arabic, some plea or blessing offered them if they would buy. Adams got rid of the old merchant by thrusting a coin in his hand.

They reached the alley where the studio was located. She said, "This is where it is."

"I trust we'll find him there," Adams said, as they walked together down the hilly, cobblestoned surface.

"There is an old man who lives in the back," Gale said, pointing out the graybeard she'd talked with before. He was standing outside the doorway of the studio talking earnestly to another old man in a white turban. This man held a string of turquoise beads in one hand and fingered them as he talked. Then he bowed and gave the traditional sign of farewell, a handclasp and then each hand placed on the breast. The old man who was a stranger to her moved on, while the graybeard stood with his head slightly inclined until the other, presumably of higher status, had vanished down the alley.

Gale went up to the old man and asked, "Do you remember me?"

He gazed at her with bleary blue eyes and said, "You are related to the infidel Cormier."

"Yes," she said. "We wish to speak with him."

The old man shrugged. "It is not my affair."

"We mean no harm," she said quickly. "It is a friendly call. Is he inside?"

"Look for yourself," the graybeard said.

"Let us go in," she told Adams over her shoulder and the prim Adams followed her inside.

She gave a gasp of disbelief! The studio was as empty as the second time she had visited it. All the paintings and every sign of habitation gone.

She turned to Adams, "I don't understand!"

"This is the place?"

"Yes. I'm sure of that."

"There's no one here," Adams said, looking around. "You said he'd returned."

"So he had!"

The graybeard came shuffling in and stood gazing at them with disdain. "The medina is a dangerous place for infidels."

Gale went to him. "What happened to Ben Cormier?"

"The desert men came in the night. There were arguments and much talk. By the morning everything had vanished and the infidel as well."

Gale turned to Adams, "It looks as if Abdullah got here first."

"No doubt Fazi told him about Cormier before Abdullah had him hanged."

"I expect so," she said. "It would seem we have another one to rescue."

335

"With hopes of rescue dimming as time passes," Adams said with a frown.

"We might as well move on," she said. "We will get no more information here."

They went back outside and stood together in front of the doorway of the ancient house. Adams seemed to be pondering something.

He suddenly asked, "Can you direct me to where Fazi lived?"

"Yes," she said. "It's not far from here."

"Perhaps we might pick up a clue there."

"We might," she agreed. "Jiri may even have returned with that missing case."

"Possible," he agreed. "Surely worth a try."

So they went on through more narrow streets and alleys, ignoring the din and appeals of the shop owners, the veiled, secretive women, and the men in their turbans and fezzes.

They finally reached the street in which Fazi had lived. And as they came up to the doorway of the house, Gale had a strange feeling of uneasiness.

She asked Adams, "Should we go inside?"

"I think so," he said. "I'm armed."

"I'm not."

Gale could not shake off her fear. Perhaps because she had seen the hanged Fazi. She stepped into the shadows of a large room.

Without warning a robed figure came out of the darkness and rushed toward them. She cried out as the robed one pushed her aside and then hurled Richard Adams against the wall. The Arab vanished into the street after the violent encounter. She was still stunned as she turned to her companion and to her horror saw that he'd been wounded.

Adams' lean face was pale and he was clutching his side as he slumped down onto the rough wood floor of the empty room. She knelt by him and frantically cried, "Mr. Adams!" And then she saw the stiletto protruding from his side and the blood oozing from the wound.

"Stand up!" The order was sharp, delivered in a hard, familiar voice and came from behind her.

She rose slowly and turned with fear shadowing her lovely face to find herself confronting a figure from the past. Edmund Walton, Revene's henchman, whom she'd not seen since that night on the yacht. Walton who had killed his attractive mistress, Diana.

She said, "You!"

His wolfish face was made to seem more so as he revealed his yellowed teeth in a nasty smile. A revolver pointed directly at her, he said, "Did you think I was dead like the rest?"

"I didn't know! I don't care!"

"You'd better," he said. "You have only me to look after you now."

"Help him!" She indicated the silent, huddled figure on the floor.

"Don't worry about him," Walton jeered. "You have enough worries of your own!"

"He'll die if he isn't helped!"

"Let him!"

"You can't mean it!" she pleaded.

His reply was a cynical glance. Then the robed man came back into the room and Walton called out to him in Arabic. Before she could put up any fight or even realize what was happening, the robed man came up behind her and placed a rag over her nose and mouth. She recognized the sweet taste of chloroform! She fought to free herself and resist the fumes but she was no match for the sinewy Arab. He held her there until the fumes blacked her out.

She stirred and the sound of distant music came

to her. Confused, she opened her eyes and found herself in a small room stretched out on a cot. The room had a single table with a lighted candle on it and a window with panes thick with dirt and iron bars nailed across it on the inside.

She groaned and stared up in time to see Walton come into the room. She gave another small moan and attempted to sit up.

Walton said, "Don't strain yourself! You're staying right where you are!"

She looked at him angrily, feeling nauseated, and knowing her clothes and hair were unkempt. "Where have you brought me?"

"Not important," he said with another sneering smile.

"What about that man?" she asked, meaning Adams.

"He's dead!"

"I don't believe you!" she protested, sickened and terrified.

"He died almost right away," Edmund Walton gloated. "But he did us a good turn, delivering you to us."

"That was hardly his intention," she said, fumbling with her hair and smoothing her wrinkled dress.

"You never did like me," Walton remembered.

"You murdered Diana!"

"That is what you say," he said sharply. "I say she was struck down in the street by a thief."

"Just like the man who struck down Richard Adams! Hired by you!" She noticed the music again as she finished saying this and it was familiar enough for her to exclaim, "I know now! We're upstairs over the Chez Paris."

338

"Don't worry yourself about it," he said in his mocking fashion.

"Why have you brought me here?"

"Someone wants to talk with you," Walton said.

"Who?"

"I'll tell him you're awake and he can speak for himself," Walton told her. He went out and closed and locked the door, leaving her alone with the distant music pounding far below. She got up and went to the window to find the iron bars were as solid as they looked. She rubbed the dirt from the panes of glass and stared downward. She had a blurred vision of rooftops.

She moved away despondently, thinking how soon she had managed to get herself in trouble again after being rescued from the submarine. She had felt sure that venturing into the medina with Richard Adams would be safe enough. He was armed and an official of the United States Consulate. She ought to have known better!

Eric would be shattered and enraged. As a result of her indiscreet move, Richard Adams was now dead, if Walton had told her the truth, and she had little doubt that he had. And she was once again in the power of the gang looking for that lost briefcase. And she could not envision Jiri coming to her rescue another time.

A key turned in the door again and it opened to reveal an immaculately clad Carl Revene in a brown linen suit and Panama. He came to her with a smile on his cruel hawk's face.

"I was sure you'd become lonesome for me," was his opening remark.

She stared at him with disgust. "I hoped never to see you again."

He chuckled in his suave manner. "Only because you felt unable to trust yourself with me. You succumbed to me once and seemed quite happy about it."

"You raped me!" she charged him.

"You were not unwilling," Revene said. "But that is not important at the moment."

She looked at the confident, well-dressed figure with his diamond stickpin, knowing he was nothing but a gangster, a purveyor of misery and death, careful not to let his own slim, manicured hands be involved in any of the filthy deeds.

She said, "You have gone too far this time!"

He arched an eyebrow. "You think so?"

"Yes," she said. "You have wounded or killed a member of the United States Consulate, along with kidnapping me. You cannot possibly escape without punishment."

"I have managed thus far."

"You will be wise to free me," she said. "You could use my goodwill when you're in court."

His smile was maddening. "We're a long way off from that."

"Maybe not as far from it as you think," she said. "At this moment both the United States and British consulates are waiting for advice as to how to act against you. The murder of Richard Adams will only make them move more swiftly."

"It does not matter," he said. "My business here is almost finished. But for one thing. The briefcase your husband stole from me."

"I do not have it!"

Revene said calmly, "Perhaps not. But you have met Jiri. You know it exists and where it is. I learned that much from Abdullah, though you chose to trick him."

"I could not tell him where it was since it is not in my hands," she said.

"Are you worried about your friend Madeline?" he asked, his eyes gleaming maliciously.

"I am," she replied. "What have you done with her?"

"She is on my yacht, enjoying herself," Revene said with a smirk. "She gets her injections of morphine every day, a larger dose now, and she has become my mistress. She is, you see, quite willing to pay for the price of her pleasure. But I will have no trouble including you in my little harem!"

"I'll kill myself first!"

"You may mean it," Revene said easily. "But you will not be given the opportunity." And without warning he came toward her and, seizing her by the arms, kissed her savagely.

She pushed him away fiercely. "Let me go!" she cried.

"Little tiger!" he laughed and struggled with her.

She fought as she never had before and managed to get her right hand free and use it to claw the side of his face. Her nails went deep and the flesh rolled back in tiny swirls as blood began to flow from the scratches. He uttered a loud oath and let her go. He staggered back and placed a white handkerchief to his torn cheek.

He said nothing as he backed out of the room but there was a vicious gleam in his eyes which sent fear shuddering through her. She knew she had touched his vanity, perhaps his greatest weakness.

She waited, not daring to think what might happen. Again she went to the window and again she realized there was no means of escape from the room except by that one door. She was standing by the window when the door was flung open and an enraged

Carl Revene came back into the room. He was hatless and his cheek was still bloody from the scratches inflicted by her fingernails.

It took her a moment to see that he held something in his right hand! A whip of the sort she had seen the native drivers use in the caravans, short of handle and long of lash! Such whips often had a lash eight or ten feet long! Now he let the whip uncurl.

She retreated to the far corner of the room. "No! No!"

His reply was a loud oath and then he moved forward and lifted the whip high and let its lash hit her about the waist! The pain made her scream and stagger. This blow had barely fallen before there came another! She groaned and tried to dart to the other side of the room but he cried out in anger and struck her with the long snake of the lash once more.

Now she was on her knees. "Please! You'll kill me!"

But there was no pity in him. The lash struck her three more times and then she collapsed unconscious on the rough floor.

She had no idea how long she lay there. It was still dark outside the window when she came to and stared about her in a dazed state. Her entire body ached from the lashing she'd received. Slowly and painfully she dragged herself over to the cot and up on to it. But there was little relief for her; the welts where the whip had hit her seemed to be getting more painful as the hours progressed. She lay there sobbing and staring up at the dirty ceiling.

Toward dawn she fell asleep. She wakened again after it was daylight when an elderly native brought her water and a dubious-looking mixture on a plate. She could not eat but she eagerly drank the water.

Her entire body, including her arms and legs,

were stiff and it hurt her to move. She examined some of the welts and found that the skin had not been broken though the black and blue spots were swelling. Revene had known how far he could go without killing her.

The key turned in the door again and Walton came in with a look of cruel amusement on his lined face. "So you are on your feet again?"

"Gloat!" she said. "It suits your craven nature."

Walton shrugged. "You have no right to look for sympathy. You brought that beating on yourself."

"It was worth it to draw blood from him."

"You may not think that before he's done with you."

She said, "He daren't kill me. He needs that briefcase too badly."

Walton gave her a wise look. "There are some things worse than death."

She knew this to be true but she wasn't about to let him relish her fear. She said, "I'm not afraid. And you can tell your Mr. Revene that!"

"I can't tell Revene anything," Edmund Walton said. "He's gone back to the yacht."

"Are you going to keep me here?" she demanded.

"No," he said. "We're taking you to the yacht as well. Revene thinks some fresh ocean air is just what you need."

Gale said, "If you would help me escape I'd give you full credit for it."

"With who?"

"The court!"

He laughed. "I'll never be in court. Nor will Revene. You have a lot to learn!"

"I can't believe you'll continue to get away with your evil," she told him.

"Well, you don't have anything to say about it,"

he told her. "Let me explain how we're going to move you to the yacht."

She turned her back on him. "I don't want to know."

The thin man went on, "We had a death here last night. One of the girls died of some kind of fever. She's to be taken out for burial today. Moslems are very strict about these things."

"What has that to do with me?"

"We've made other arrangements for the girl to be taken to the cemetery," he said with a grin. "We're going to put you in her plain wooden burial box and have the box carried out as if you were being taken to the cemetery. But at a certain corner the coffin bearers will head for the docks."

"You wouldn't dare!" she protested.

"It's all arranged," he said with another of his evil smiles. "Prepare yourself. In a few minutes you're going to be a dead girl."

17

Gale watched with growing horror as two natives came into the room carrying a narrow wooden coffin. They removed the top from it and she saw it was empty.

Walton gave an order in Arabic to the men and they quickly bound her wrists and ankles. She knew it was useless to struggle. She could only hope that later on she might do something to free herself.

As she stood there bound and waiting, Walton went over to her with a cloth in his hand. "We can't afford to have any screaming," he said with a sour smile. "And this could make you edgy."

"What are you going to do with me?"

"Nothing serious for the moment," he said. "We're taking you to the yacht. And just in case some of your friends may be watching this place, we wish to get you out quietly."

She told him, "You'll pay for all this."

"You paid a little for your actions last night," he jeered at her, indicating the welts she'd received.

Then he quickly placed the cloth in place and tightly gagged her so she could utter no sound. Rendered helpless, she was lifted by the two natives and placed in the coffin. Then they set the cover in place.

The feeling of claustrophobia was overwhelming. She began to perspire from fear and her own gathering body heat in the coffin. She assumed there must be at least small air holes drilled in it or she would soon suffocate!

Suppose they had forgotten or overlooked this in readying the coffin for her? Panic followed on fear as she twisted and tried to raise herself out of the coffin but to no avail. She had not enough freedom of movement and she was only making her general condition worse!

She decided that it would be best to relax as much as possible under the circumstances and so use as little air as she could.

Now she had the sensation of the box being lifted and swung about. Shortly after, it was tilted back so that the blood rushed to her head in a startling manner. Then, fortunately, it reached a level once more. She assumed that she had been carried down the stairs and was now about to be taken out into the street.

After she had been set down for a moment, she was aware of street sounds, a tiny bit of fresh air, and the uneven jogging of her pallbearers as they carried her along the cobblestoned street.

She lay very still to preserve her remaining strength and in any case her body was still too sore from the whipping Revene had given her to allow her to struggle much. What did he have in store for her aboard the yacht? She dare not think about it!

All at once she was aware of distant cries coming nearer—the sound of shouting and something pounding over the cobblestones. Then, suddenly, the coffin was hit by a strong force and sent flying.

It struck the street with agonizing force. Then the coffin rolled over and the top popped off, leaving her staring up at the sky. All about her there was a clamor! Amid the angry shouting the black face of a member of the Moroccan police patrol peered down at her in the coffin. He registered shock and vanished, only to appear again a few moments later with a second officer. She pleaded to them with her eyes to set her free.

Her pleading did the trick. Within a few minutes they had untied her and removed the gag from her mouth. Her first words were, "Please take me to the British Consulate."

The black officer who appeared to be the senior of the two said, "A runaway horse and carriage broke up the procession!"

"They were kidnapping me," she said, standing by the coffin and for the first time realizing that a circle of enthralled native onlookers had gathered about her. It was not every day they saw someone rise from the dead.

"Your pallbearers have vanished? Are you English?"

"I'm American but I have been working for the British Consulate," she said. "Colonel Hudson, the consul, will vouch for this." She did not want to be taken to the police station or the American Consulate. She did not know whether Richard Adams was alive or dead and no one else at the American Consulate knew her.

The red-fezzed police officer was in a quandary. "It is very distressing," he said.

"Just take me to the British Consulate," she insisted. "I'm sure they'll be grateful to you."

He eyed her doubtfully. "It is perhaps right I should first take you to my superiors."

"The consulate will get in touch with them later," she said. "It is urgent that I see Colonel Hudson."

The black man conferred with his fellow police officer for a few minutes, and then having come to a decision, they summoned a carriage. She got in it with them and heard them direct the driver to the British Consulate.

Colonel Hudson proved a true diplomat. He congratulated the two policemen for bringing her in, promised that he would mention it not only to their superiors but he would praise them highly in a letter to Queen Victoria. The two left glowing and convinced they had done the right thing.

The Colonel took her into his private office, had her sit down, and poured her a brandy. As he handed it to her, he said, "My dear, what a terrible ordeal you've been through!"

She sipped the brandy and smiled weakly. "I must look a sight."

The Colonel chuckled. "Feminine vanity! The truth is you don't look all that bad, but you should."

"And I'm still suffering from a whipping which Revene gave me," she told him.

Colonel Hudson's normally kindly face turned purple with rage. "The scoundrel! Something has to be done about him!"

"Now, with his yacht and Abdullah's submarine, he can move about almost at will," she pointed out.

Colonel Hudson paced back and forth behind his desk. "We have to move so slowly. It is most frustrating. And now I'm at a disadvantage with Adams in hospital."

"Then he's alive?" she exclaimed happily.

"Yes," he said. "The wound was a bad one but he is going to recover."

"That is the main thing."

"The problem is that he is out of it all now when I most need his advice and help."

She asked, "Is there anyone else at the American Consulate who can replace him?"

"I don't think so," the Colonel worried. "I'll let him know you're safe. He's not well enough for visitors, but I'm allowed to see him for about five minutes every day."

"What about Eric?"

Colonel Hudson smiled. "I have already sent a message to his office. He should soon be here to escort you to the chateau or, if you are afraid, to a hotel."

"I'll risk the chateau again," she decided. "All my clothes are there. And I have Hassan to guard me. And Jiri has promised to bring the briefcase to me there," she went on. "If I went to a hotel, he might not be able to find me."

The stout Colonel sank down into the chair behind his desk and, adjusting his monocle, picked up some papers and read to her, "Her Majesty's Mediterranean Fleet has been advised of a pirate submarine at large and a threat to normal shipping. Several merchant vessels have fallen prey to it. Orders are to locate the craft in question and bring it to the nearest port."

She listened and said, "That should accomplish something."

He put the papers down and sighed, "I hope

so. It is a difficult business. As is the matter of the yacht."

The door of the office burst open and it was Eric. He at once embraced her and then chastened her for going back to the medina. "You should have known better!"

She chided him. "You begin to sound like a husband."

"I care as deeply for you as any husband could! I've been nearly out of my mind with worry!"

"I'm sorry," she said.

Colonel Hudson approached them both and took each of them by an arm, saying to Eric, "Don't nag the poor girl, Simms. She has had a most awful time."

The Colonel assigned them one of his carriages and they were soon on their way to the chateau. Gale sat back and wearily recounted all that had happened to her, as Eric listened with increasing anger.

"I'll show that Revene something about a whip if I ever get my hands on him," he said in a rage.

"I've survived," she said. "The worst pain of it is over now."

"And you're still willing to return to the chateau? To go on with this?"

"I have no choice," she said. "The best hope of bringing Revene to justice is to get that briefcase."

Eric shook his head. "I thought newspaper people were the only mad ones."

"I would be mad to give up after all this."

He sighed. "Maybe you're right. I shall remain at the chateau with you."

She gave him a roguish look and said, "I'm

afraid I won't be a good bed partner until the whip welts have healed."

Eric turned beet red. "I wasn't thinking of that!" he protested. "I'll stay in another room!"

Hassan was pleased to welcome them. But he warned, "Things have been happening which I do not like."

"What sort of things?" she asked the big black man.

Hassan frowned. "Footsteps and no one to make them," he said. "I have heard footsteps above and when I went up there I could not find anyone. This house has too many secret passages."

Eric said, "Prepare the room across from Madame Cormier for my use."

"I will do that, sir," Hassan said.

"And let me have another weapon," she said. "I feel very lost without something to defend myself."

"I have a pistol like the one I gave you before," Hassan told her. "I will get it for you. It will be best since you already know how to use it." And he left them.

She went upstairs and after a bath and a change of clothes felt much better. Eric had returned to his office but promised to be back later.

She went down to seek out Hassan in the kitchen and he gave her another ivory-handled pistol, a twin of the first one. She placed it in the pocket of her skirt and said, "I feel better now."

"You look very well for all that happened," Hassan told her. "You must be very careful here, though. Besides the footsteps there have been moanings. Down here and also above."

"Moanings?"

"As if someone were in agony," he said solemnly. "And then one night I saw a face."

"What sort of face?"

"The face of a white man, pale and tormented," Hassan said. "It seemed to float in the air and then vanish."

"I have several times seen that same face," Gale told him.

"It is a phantom face, Madame, almost bluish white in color."

"It's the same," she agreed. "It is the phantom face of my husband. And whether he is alive or dead I don't know."

"Was he not killed some time ago?"

She shrugged. "We all assumed that. But Jiri is still alive and he was also thought to have died in the launch. It is possible my husband still lives."

"And that could explain the footsteps?"

"Yes. He may well have been coming and going, searching for me."

"I still do not like it, Madame."

Gale went up to her bedroom filled with foreboding. There would be more visitations at the chateau, she knew.

So much had happened in the past few hours that she felt as dazed as she was stiff and sore. It was a relief that Richard Adams had survived the knife wound, anyway.

The question of Ben Cormier intrigued her. She could not imagine why Paul's ne'er-do-well brother had vanished again. It made sense the first time, but now she was confused. Had Ben perhaps swung over to Paul's enemies? Or was it fear that had made him vanish for a second time? Or had something really happened to him? Perhaps the gamblers had returned and had taken him hostage. Such things happened.

She stretched out on her bed and tried to rest but sleep would not come. At last she went downstairs and out on to the patio. She stared out across the water and saw a yacht moving by which looked to her suspiciously like the *Siren*. She went in to see if she could find a pair of binoculars but there didn't seem to be any in the mansion.

Eric returned in time for dinner and they went into the living room to have their coffee. It gave them a leisurely chance to discuss the incidents of the day. She particularly wanted to talk about Ben Cormier.

She asked, "What do you make of Ben's second vanishing."

"Those gamblers he feared may have caught up with him."

"I suppose we'll never know," she said.

Eric smiled at her wryly over his coffee. "Whyever he did it he must have had a strong reason."

She said, "Could he be in with Revene?"

"I don't think it likely," he said. "And speaking of Revene, everyone is in a sweat at knowing a renegade submarine is loose and threatening shipping. No telling what that mad Abdullah will try to do."

"I agree," she said.

"And we received a story on the cable today about a warship owned by Chile being sunk by submarine attack. Which gives an idea what they can do."

"Perhaps Colonel Hudson will be able to get the navy to do something about it."

"It's damned unfair that he won't let me file my story." Eric sounded aggrieved.

"You must admit the story would cause extra alarm. More people would know here and all around the world as the story spread."

"I gave in," Eric said.

"I'm sure you won't regret it," she told him. They moved about the house the rest of the evening discussing their plans for the future. Eric had decided he would apply for a transfer to the New York office. She was already anxious to introduce him to her aunt and uncle.

She showed him letters from them concerned about her plight and asking for her to come back home. She folded up the letters and said, "I have not told them why I've stayed on so long or the near escapes I've had. They know of Paul's death but the only aspect of that which worries them is that I've been left alone."

Eric touched her arm gently. "Not completely."

She smiled. "I haven't mentioned you and Hassan. I know they'll like you."

"I hope so," he said. "Since they didn't approve of Paul."

"They were right about him," she said. "It's just that a young woman deeply in love for the first time is impossible to reason with. I wouldn't listen to anyone."

"You'd better listen to me now," he warned her. "No more wandering to the medina. Let them take the chances and come here. That was the agreement."

"I know," she said.

It grew late and he escorted her to the door of

her room and tenderly kissed her good night. He said, "If anything upsets you, just call me."

She promised that she would and went on into her bedroom, positive that she would be all right. Her weariness had come back tenfold and she lost no time in undressing and getting into bed. She gave only scant thought to the hazards of the phantom appearing before she dropped off to sleep.

She was awakened by her name being whispered close to her ear. She came awake with a start and saw only darkness. Then at the bottom of her bed the pasty bluish face materialized in the darkness.

Sitting up in bed, she gasped, "You again!"

"Yes!" The same hoarse whisper.

She said, "I have only to cry out and help will come."

"You need no help with me," the hoarse whisper told her. "I mean you no harm. I only ask your aid."

"If you're talking about the briefcase Jiri hasn't given it to me yet. I don't know where it is."

"I must have it!" the phantom with Paul's face said hoarsely. "My life depends on it!"

"Paul!" she exclaimed. "Is it you, terribly ill and changed, or a ghost?"

"I can be saved," he said in the hoarse whisper. "You know that. And you know what must be done."

"I have seen Jiri only once," she said.

"Seek him out again!" the phantom said in that ghostly whisper. And then the face vanished.

"Where are you?" she asked.

No reply came. She reached feverishly for the matches and lit the candle on her bedside table. In the glow of the candle she could see the entire

355

room, if only somewhat dimly. There was no sign of the figure which had pleaded with her only a few seconds earlier.

She stared into the shadows. Once the phantom had left a token—the gold cigarette case. She got up and searched the room but there was no token this time.

Any thought of sleep was out of the question. She left her room and encountered Hassan in the corridor outside her door. He had a gun in his hand.

He said, "I did not expect to find you wandering about, Madame."

"I can't sleep," she said.

"I have been making the rounds of the house," the black man said grimly. "I heard those footsteps again. They seemed to come from up here."

"Yes. It was the phantom. He disappeared. I'm going in to wake Eric."

"It can't have gone far." Hassan hesitated in the dark hallway. "You will be all right?"

"Yes," she said, her hand on the doorknob.

"I will go upstairs and look." Hassan moved on with the tiny lantern in one hand and the gun in the other.

She tapped on Eric's door and called out his name. But there was no answer. After doing this twice, she began to feel uneasy. She tried the doorknob and it turned easily. Slowly she entered the dark room, which seemed to have an eerie silence about it!

She made her way to the bed, her eyes now more accustomed to the darkness, and called out, "Eric!"

Almost at the instant she spoke she saw that the bed was empty, the clothes thrown back as if

356

he had suddenly been awakened. Panic rising, she noticed that a door leading to an adjoining room was open. She hurried across the dark room to the doorway.

"Eric, are you in there?" The fear in her own voice served to increase her panic.

The adjoining room was another bedroom, and she could not imagine why he would be in there. Slowly she advanced into the room and then stumbled over something, and she knew that it was Eric stretched out on the floor.

She knelt down and cried his name and tried to rouse him. Her fingers touched his temples and she felt a warm, sticky mess—blood! Eric's blood! Someone had struck him down after luring him into the room. She sprang up and ran back out through the other room to the corridor where she'd last seen Hassan!

She screamed the big black man's name. "Hassan!"

And then she saw him! Coming slowly down the stairs with Edmund Walton behind him, holding a gun to his back. Hassan was now unarmed and someone else came behind the two carrying the lantern. It was Carl Revene!

The strangely assorted trio came closer to her as she stood there frozen with fear. The look of pain on Hassan's shining black face was hard to bear. He said nothing, but it was evident he had been taken by surprise and could not believe it.

"Finish him!" Revene crisply told Walton.

To her horror, Walton fired into the big black body at close range and with a loud cry Hassan threw up his arms and fell face forward on the floor—a circle of blood, growing larger every moment, showed on his back.

Now Revene advanced to her. "If you're smart you'll give us no trouble!"

"Monsters!" she cried.

"Grab her!" Revene told Walton. "We don't want to waste any time here! There may be other guards."

"Come on," Walton said savagely, and gripping her fiercely by the arm, pushed her down the stairs ahead of him. They went all the way to the cellar and then out a door she didn't know. A door which led to the beach.

Outside, Revene took hold of her other arm and the two men propelled her toward the water's edge, where she saw a small boat with a man in it waiting.

When they reached the boat she was practically thrown into it. Revene and Walton followed her with Walton still holding a gun in his hand. The thought of her own pistol still under the pillow in her room made her feel ill.

The man at the oars strained and the shore soon was far in the distance. She saw the outline of the chateau against the sky and prayed that both Eric and Hassan might live. If Eric died she would have no reason for living.

Revene was seated so that he could gaze down at her in the bottom of the boat where she lay. "Sorry we couldn't give you time to bring some more clothing. But I like you in your nightgown!"

"You're mad!" she told him.

"I have been called far worse than that," he said airly. "And I would remind you that you have brought this trouble on yourself."

"How dare you say that?" she lashed out at him.

"You have refused to cooperate with me from the very start," he told her. "Now you will have no choice."

She did not reply and he began conversing with Walton in low tones. She was unable to tell what they were talking about but felt it might concern her fate. The lights of the big yacht at anchor drew closer. She wondered if she would see Madeline! And if the French girl would be in any state to help her.

Rough hands lifted her up onto the deck. She stood there shivering, her hands across her breasts, shamefully aware of her thin nightgown, which was much too revealing for this situation.

Revene took her by the arm again, saying, "You ought to know your way about the ship. You were here before."

She told him, "I still don't have the briefcase!"

"We can discuss that in the morning," he said tersely. "Just now I'll put you in my cabin to spend the night with an old friend of yours."

They had reached the cabin door and he unlocked it and shoved her inside. Then he locked the door on the outside and walked back along the deck, leaving her a prisoner in the big cabin with its lantern hanging from the middle of the ceiling. As first she thought she was alone and then the door to the smaller room off the cabin opened a crack as someone peered out at her.

She cried, "Madeline!"

The door opened a little further and she saw a bedraggled Madeline in a dirty-looking dressing gown which was too large for her. The pretty

French girl's lovely hair was matted and filthy. Her face even had a soiled, gray look, and she had lost a great deal of weight. The only recognizable thing about her was her large eyes. Still lovely, though strangely dulled.

Gale rushed over to her. "Madeline! Don't you know me?"

The dejected creature who had once been the vivacious Madeline nodded slowly. "Yes," she said, in a low voice. "Yes, I know you!"

Heartbroken by what she was seeing, Gale placed an arm protectively around the girl. "You look ill! Come and sit down!"

Madeline let herself be led over to the bunk, where they sat side by side. Then the drug-sodden girl stared at her and asked, "Did you come for me?"

"Do I look like it?" she asked. "I was kidnapped from the chateau and they struck down Eric and my guard."

Madeline stared ahead into nothingness. "I should not have left the chateau. You would have helped me."

"Of course we would have," she said. "And we will once we get free of this monster!"

The French girl shook her head. "There's no hope of being free again."

"What have they done to you?" Gale said despairingly.

"I feel very well," Madeline said. "He gives me all the morphine I ask for and more than I need."

"You can't feel well," she said. "You're being slowly killed! You have lost weight and your appearance has suffered in only a short time."

"I feel very well," Madeline repeated, parrot-like. "It is like floating peacefully along. Just like a dream. As long as he doesn't keep me waiting for it."

"You must fight it!" she told the girl. "You must refuse to take the drugs when he brings them."

Madeline showed a strong emotion for the first time. It was fear. "No," she said, her voice rising, "I can't do that! I must have it!"

"Listen to me," she pleaded. "Try to stop using the drugs, if only a little at a time. Otherwise you'll die!"

"It doesn't matter," the girl mumbled.

"Has he abused you?"

Madeline gave her a jeering glance. "Of course he has! And so have most of the others! I'm the ship's prostitute!"

Gale sat shocked and silent. She finally said, "Very well, if you won't fight for yourself, I'll fight for you."

Madeline clutched her with a clawlike hand and pleaded, "Don't let them cut off my supply. I'll die!"

"I won't do that," she said. "But somehow I'm going to get us off this ship."

"I had dreams of that," Madeline said brokenly. "When I first came aboard. Now I know better."

"They've broken your spirit."

"I even had a plan," the girl said. "But as long as they gave me the stuff it didn't seem worth trying."

"You mustn't give up," Gale said. "Neither must I. We will find a way to escape, no matter what."

"Escape where? Into the ocean?" Madeline asked.

"There has to be a way," Gale told her with a confidence she didn't feel.

"I'm tired," Madeline said, and almost at once slumped down onto the bunk in a strange sleep, marked by her heavy breathing.

She pulled the girl further up onto the pillow and in a more comfortable position. She was sure that the French girl would sleep until morning.

The cabin had grim memories for her. It was here that Revene had raped her. And for a time she had been afraid she would never escape. But she had. And what she'd done once, she could do again. Only this time there were two of them. She could not desert Madeline in her dreadful condition. She had expected Madeline to be changed, but this was a mere wasted shell of the girl she had known. Gale gazed at her sheer nightgown and began rummaging in the cabin to find more suitable clothing.

In the closet she found several dresses and selected one which she could wear for daily use. It was fortunate that she and Madeline were about the same size. She laid the dress on a chair back and went over to the other bunk and stretched out on it. After a little she fell into a light sleep.

She awoke to the throbbing of the ship's engines and saw that the bedraggled Madeline was already standing by one of the portholes staring out.

Gale raised herself up and said, "We're on our way somewhere."

Madeline gave her a nervous glance. "Yes. Farther out to sea. He only went near shore last night to get you."

"Did he tell you that?"

"Yes. He boasted about it."

"He was sure of himself," Gale said grimly as she got up. "Do you mind if I borrow one of your dresses?"

"Borrow them all," Madeline said with a shrug. She indicated the shabby dressing gown, "This is all I need."

She slipped on the gown and then went over to the girl. "You frightened me last night! I couldn't seem to reach you at all!"

Madeline smiled crookedly. "I'd just had the needle. I don't think so well right after."

"You must not go on taking drugs," Gale told her.

"I'm waiting for him to come now," Madeline told her. "I've been pacing up and down here while you slept."

"No!" she said.

Madeline shook her head. "You don't understand. Once he kept the drugs from me for three days to torture me. I was so sick I thought I would die. I'm finished, you have to accept that. I can't live without the needle."

The key turned in the cabin door and then the door was opened. Revene came in with Walton at his side. The gunrunner patted Madeline on her emaciated cheek, and smiling, said, "You've been waiting for me, honey?"

"Yes, yes," the French girl said eagerly. "You are late this morning."

"Never fear," Revene said with amusement. "We'll begin your day the way you like it." And turning to Walton he said, "Fix her up!"

Walton removed a hypodermic from his side pocket, and taking Madeline roughly by the arm, went to the other end of the cabin.

Revene stood in Gale's path.

"You fiend!" she cried.

"I do what I must and no more," he said. "And I advise you not to cause me any additional trouble!"

"You're slowly murdering that poor girl!"

"She is having a wonderful time," he said mockingly. "Ask her!"

"I'll save her from you somehow," she promised.

Revene laughed scornfully. "It might be a wiser idea for you to consider saving yourself."

"What does that mean?"

"I intend to have the information about that briefcase from you," he said. "Either you give it to me willingly or I will reduce you to this girl's state and you'll tell me whatever I ask. It will be interesting to see how long it takes before *you're* begging for the needle."

18

Gale heard his cold announcement with a surge of fear. She knew he was completely capable of the vicious deed which he threatened. The evidence was the degraded state of poor Madeline. She turned to see that, following her injection, the girl had slumped into a leather chair. Madeline's eyes were closed.

Edmund Walton's cruel, thin face displayed a menacing smile as he pocketed the hypodermic and made his way by her to the deck. His manner seemed to suggest that she would be his next victim.

Revene still stood facing Gale, and now she said to him with all the evenness she could manage, "You will never reduce me to her state!"

Revene smiled smugly. "Don't count on it! Drugs can twist the brain in remarkable ways."

She said, "As soon as I'm missed an alert will go out to find me. They know you're in nearby waters on your yacht."

"I have excellent hiding places for both you girls," he assured her. "They can search the *Siren* from stem to stern and not find you."

"I see," she said quietly.

"Further, I'm not going to argue with you anymore," he said. "You know what I want. If you will turn it over to me I will allow both of you to return to Casablanca. Not that there's much future for her!" He indicated Madeline with disdain. "I'll give you three hours. Then you'll be tied up and given your first morphine injection. By the end of ten days you'll be like her, begging for it!"

"At least I'm prepared," she said, refusing to give him the satisfaction of showing her fear.

"You had better be," Revene said. "And don't count too much on your friends for help. Adams is dying in hospital, Hassan is dead, and so is Eric Simms!"

"I don't believe you!" she cried.

He laughed. "It makes no difference to me. I simply don't want you to build on any false hopes. I'd much prefer to have this settled and be rid of you."

With that he gave her a curt nod and went out and locked the cabin door again. She gazed after him in despair, knowing that he had meant all he'd said. She wouldn't let herself believe that Eric was dead. Revene would not have been so quick to tell her of the death if it were true. He was deliberately trying to undermine her courage. She did think Hassan was dead, his wound had been terrible. But the last word she'd had about Richard Adams was that he was recovering.

She now turned her attention to Madeline, coming out of the first shock of the injection. It was at this period, when she was fully sustained by the drug she had come to depend on, that she was alert. Closer to her normal self.

Gale went and knelt by the French girl. "Are you somewhat better now?"

"Yes," Madeline said dully. "I'm all right."

"He's threatening me with all sorts of dreadful things unless I tell him where the briefcase is and I don't know. He says he'll force me on to the same drugs he's giving you."

Madeline's eyes opened wide in terror. She whispered, "Don't let him do that! Don't let anyone do that to you!"

"I don't see how I can escape. Unless I somehow kill myself."

"I wish I had the courage to do that," Madeline said dully.

She decided to take the big gamble now that she seemed to be able to communicate with the drug-sodden girl. She said, "Last night, you were rambling. You told me you'd had an escape plan and then you gave it up. You lacked the courage!"

Madeline looked frightened. "Did I say that? It's not true!"

Gale insisted, "I think it is. You don't need to be afraid to tell me. I'll keep your secret."

The girl's eyes moved nervously about the cabin, her lovely face was gray. In a whisper she said, "You mustn't ever tell anyone. I have a gun!"

She gasped. "Where did you get it?"

"Revene forced me to go to the crew's quarters and let them all rape me! They were all very drunk and careless. One of them put down his gun before he lay with me. He passed out right after, and I took the gun and hid it in my folded-up dressing gown. When I put it on later I managed to keep the gun covered and next to me. They were too drunk to notice as they brought me back here!"

Gale was both horrified and elated by the story. "Where is the gun?"

"I have it safely hidden," Madeline said. Then she began to whimper, "If they find it they won't give me my injections and I'll be sick again. I couldn't face that!"

She placed an arm around the trembling girl. "There'll be no risk of that. If worse comes to worst, I'll shoot you and turn the gun on myself. But first we must keep it nearby to use when we can. We must make at least one attempt to escape before we give up hope."

"You can't escape," Madeline told her. "Even if we managed to kill one or two of them we'd never get off the yacht!"

Gale said grimly, "At least we might rid the world of Revene and his murderous friend, Walton. Get me the gun!"

"Dare I?" Madeline hesitated.

"Do it for your father's sake if not for ours," Gale urged her. "It was Revene who indirectly caused his death."

Madeline stared at her a moment and then said, "All right. But you must promise to kill me if they turn the tables on us."

"I swear," she said.

Madeline went over to her bunk and lifted up the pillow. She opened the end of it and reached far inside the pillow filling and produced a small wicked-looking gun.

Gale at once took it from the frightened girl and gave it a close examination. She noted with satisfaction that it was small enough to conceal on her. She also saw it was enough like the pistol she'd had to be easy for her to use.

Gravely she told the other girl, "Now it is merely a matter of waiting for the right opportunity."

"Out here in the middle of the sea? What opportunity can come?" Madeline forlornly argued.

"You never know," Gale said. Though she realized all too well what the girl was saying was correct.

Madeline settled down to a drugged sleep for a while. Gale knew the pattern. When she came out of the sleep she would begin to be restless, and this restlessness would advance toward hysteria until she was given another injection of the drug. She had no idea how much the girl was taking now, but it had to be more than a daily shot to wreck her health so.

She went to the porthole and gazed out at the distant horizon. There was no sign of any other craft. For a moment she felt despair. Revene would destroy her as he had so many others. But at least he would not gain the briefcase, she reminded herself with grim satisfaction. What would have happened if she knew where it was? Would she have been strong enough to stand up against Revene, knowing she could have her freedom for the case? She might have decided to make the deal. Even then Revene would likely have gone back on his word and kept her hostage.

She was standing by the porthole thinking these things when all at once the *Siren*'s engines became silent. The yacht no longer moved swiftly through the water. She heard some loud talk from the deck.

She opened the porthole a fraction. It was then she heard the word, "Submarine!" coming from Edmund Walton as he hastened to join Revene on the deck only a little distance from the cabin where she was a prisoner.

The two men were now at the rail watching for something in the water. Others of the crew began to join the group at the rail and jabber excitedly in Arabic.

Then Revene said loudly, "Over there! Look!"

She studied the water before her, but could see nothing. The group at the railing, however, seemed to grow more excited. She strained her eyes and at last spotted a sharp pole, black against the blue water, then the outline of the conning tower appeared, and finally the full hull of a submarine! It was Sheik Sidi Abdullah coming for a meeting with Revene.

There was much loud shouting and confusion on the deck as the submarine came nearer. The engines of the yacht were started again and slowly the elegant craft was maneuvered alongside the submarine. Lines were thrown down and it was made secure to the yacht.

As Gale watched, a ladder was dropped down over the side of the *Siren* and within a few minutes several of Abdullah's men came scrambling up the rope ladder onto the deck. And then Abdullah himself came over the rail. He and Revene shook hands and moved away out of her sight.

It had been an amazing sight. Here were the two chief plotters together, with the submarine and yacht side by side as Abdullah and Revene conducted their evil business. She knew that this situation dimmed her hopes of escape. Now there would be twice as many enemies to deal with. She paced up and down the cabin worriedly.

One of her chief fears was that Abdullah would come to her, perhaps take advantage of her in some cruel way. She was sure Revene would not interfere.

Suddenly bedlam broke out on deck once again. Her curiosity aroused, she went to see what it was. Steaming up on the horizon, she saw, and advancing at a good speed, was one of Her Majesty's warships. A flood of hope went through her! She prayed that the warship would note them and lose no time bearing down on them.

She ran to the bunk and shook Madeline until she was awake. "A British warship," she exulted. "Coming toward us."

Madeline eyed her dully. "Other warships have come close by."

"I have a feeling this one might save us," Gale said.

She filled Madeline in with the business of the submarine having come to the yacht for a meeting. Even as she talked they watched from the porthole and saw Abdullah and his Arabs hurry over the side to return to the submarine. The lines were drawn back and the ladder pulled in. Then the submarine began to move. And now the process was reversed with the entire hull being in sight for a few moments, then the conning tower only, and it vanishing at a fast rate. At last only the black rod of the periscope was in view.

"They're getting away!" Gale cried in dismay.

But the warship was quite close now. So close she could read the name *Ensign* on its side. The submarine had taken a course directly to the right but for some unknown reason abruptly changed course and moved to the left instead. This placed it almost directly in the path of the big warship.

Madeline said, "I think the submarine is going to try to sink the ship."

"I doubt Abdullah's men are equal to the Royal Navy," Gale said, but she watched with growing dismay.

There was a loud outcry from the deck as a truly incredible event took place. The submarine surfaced a little, seemed to waver, and then crossed directly before the keen bow of the *Ensign* as it cut swiftly through the big waves. The ship visibly cut into the submarine, and there was a spread of foam on the sea as the submarine sank down out of sight.

"Finished!" Revene cried in anger. "The fools sent her straight across the bow of that warship!"

There were other cries of dismay and the next thing she heard was Walton asking, "What now?"

Revene sounded worried. "They'll board us for questioning."

The great warship had swung about in a remarkably small circle for so large a craft. Now it had come to a halt and a longboat with a half-dozen men was being lowered.

"Hadn't we better make a run for it?" Walton asked.

"And end up at the bottom of the sea like Abdullah," Revene said with disgust. "We can't run away from a ship like that. Our only chance is to stay here and bluff it out!"

"What about those two in there?" Walton demanded.

"Take them below to the hiding place; they'll be safe enough," Revene said. "I'll stay out here and watch what is developing. Take a man and get them out of sight. The French one won't give any resistance, but watch the other one!"

Gale swiftly turned to Madeline and said, "They are coming for us! This is the moment!"

"No! I'm too sick and weak! I can't!" Madeline protested.

She backed up against the wall close by the cabin door with Madeline crouched beside her. The key turned and then the door was thrown open and

Walton came rushing in with an Arab crewman beside him.

Gale did not hesitate. She shot at Walton and caught him full in the face; his features became a bloody pulp and he fell. She fired again immediately and caught the Arab under the arm and he went down. She knew the shots would be heard and they must get out of the cabin at once.

"Come!" she pulled a lagging Madeline after her as they crossed over the two on the floor and emerged on the deck. "To the railing!" she hissed.

Revene was about fifteen feet away. His cruel face took on an expression of surprise as he saw them. Gale hesitated. Then, as she saw him lift his gun, she fired. Revene staggered.

She urged Madeline to the railing, "Come! We have to jump!"

An expression of horror crossed the drug-ridden girl's face but she managed to join Gale in scrambling over the railing. Just as they dropped, a shot rang out from above. Gale was sure it must be Revene shooting at them and waited for another, which would surely hit her.

She landed in the water and sank below for a moment, but the shot never came. As she surfaced, she saw Madeline come up for a moment and then go down again. She swam to her, crying out encouragement, but by the time she reached the spot the girl was gone.

Sobbing, she struck out away from the yacht and within a few minutes she was being lifted into the longboat. A young officer bent over her and said, "Mrs. Cormier?"

"Yes," she said between chattering teeth. "The other girl!"

"I know," he said. "We'll find her."

It was then she collapsed and she did not regain consciousness until she found herself in a bunk in the warship's hospital. A serious-faced brown-bearded man in uniform sat by her.

He said, "I'm Macready, ship's surgeon. You've managed well in spite of a dreadful ordeal."

She sighed and closed her eyes, only to open them again. "Where is Madeline?"

"The other young woman?" the doctor said. "I fear she was drowned. Actually, first shot and then drowned. Her body couldn't be found."

Tears formed in Gale's eyes. She said, "She found the gun. If it hadn't been for her we'd never have made it!"

The bearded doctor said, "Rest for a while. Captain Rodney will be down to see you shortly."

The doctor had a warm broth brought for her and she sipped it and felt better. Then she was joined by the young officer she had first seen in the longboat.

He stopped beside her and smiled. "You have a remarkable amount of spunk, Mrs. Cormier."

"Thank you for rescuing me," she said.

"All in line of duty," he said, and then frowned. "Sorry about the other young lady."

"She was my friend. A wonderful girl."

"Also kidnapped by Revene?"

"Yes," she said. "What happened on the yacht?"

Captain Rodney looked grave. "Revene is dead from a bullet wound, which I believe you inflicted."

"Yes," she said in a low voice.

"Also his second in command, Walton. The Arab is alive and not seriously wounded. We have taken the yacht in tow and we are bringing her back to

Casablanca. We found a large cargo of illegal arms on board."

"And the submarine?"

"Gone with all on board," Captain Rodney said. "A pity, she would have made a prize! But the fools operating her ran her directly in front of us."

"I saw it," she said. "So we are on our way to Casablanca?"

"We'll be there in a few hours. Colonel Hudson alerted all ships in the fleet as soon as your kidnapping was discovered."

Tensely, she asked, "Do you know about the others? Eric Simms, the newspaperman?"

"I spoke with him before leaving," Captain Rodney said with an understanding smile. "He was not hurt badly. But very worried about you."

She murmured a prayer of thanks. "And Hassan?" she asked.

"Dead, I regret to say."

"I was afraid of that."

Captain Rodney said, "Your dress is being dried. It will be ready for you when we dock. In the meanwhile you must rest."

The *Ensign's* communications officer had sent the momentous word of her rescue and the details to Casablanca. So when they docked Eric was there waiting for her. Captain Rodney escorted her down the gangplank and politely bade her good-bye. Then she was in Eric's arms.

Laughing and crying at the same time, she said, "I was sure I'd never see you again."

"I was nearly out of my mind with worry about you," he told her.

"Revene said you had been killed."

"That sounds like him," Eric said grimly. "His

obituary has been received with delight by a good many people."

"What about Hassan?"

"The poor chap was killed instantly."

"I thought so," she said. "He was so excellent at his work. I'm only thankful he did not suffer."

"There was no chance of that," Eric said. And then he added sadly, "So Madeline is gone."

She gave him a knowing look. "It may have been for the best. She was so far gone in her addiction I doubt she could have been cured."

Eric said, "There are a lot of loose ends to tie up."

"I know," she agreed. "For one, that briefcase is still missing."

"Where do you want to go?"

"Back to the chateau."

He stared at her. "After all that has happened there?"

"Yes," she said. "If I hope to see Jiri again that is where he is most likely to come."

"As you say," Eric said. "I have a carriage."

In the carriage, she asked, "How is Richard Adams? Revene said he was dying."

Eric shook his head indignantly. "Not a bit of it! I'm happy to tell you that Adams is out of the hospital and active again. He helped plan your rescue with the help of Colonel Hudson."

It was Colonel Hudson who sent her two servants from the consulate and a guard of four military men to watch the chateau. And after she'd enjoyed a good night's rest, Eric brought word that the British Consul and Adams planned to have a meeting with her early in the afternoon.

It was a pleasant reunion. And after all the expected comments had been made, it was Richard

Adams who brought up the matter of the briefcase.

"We have eliminated Revene and his gang from the scene," he told them all. "But we have failed in one thing. We have not put our hands on the briefcase with its invaluable papers."

Colonel Hudson sighed. "Perhaps it will never be found."

"I disagree," Gale said. "I know that Jiri has it, and if he is still alive, he will one day bring it to me."

"*If* he is still alive!" Eric said. "The chances are against it."

Richard Adams' lean face expressed concern, and he said, "The fact is, there is still one member of the gang at large. From all we've been able to find out, he was the liaison man with those financing the illegal arms-running."

"And, as such, a key figure," the British Consul said.

Adams continued, "He is still at large. And you may be sure he wants that briefcase more than ever now. His whole future is in it. With it, he can build a new organization to peddle arms; without it, he is in grave danger of arrest. Certainly so, if it falls into our hands."

Eric spoke up, "Who do you think this man is?"

Colonel Hudson looked embarrassed. He spoke apologetically to Gale, "I hate to say this, dear lady; you have cooperated with us so marvelously. But all suspicion points to your late husband, Paul Cormier."

She tried to hide her distress. "In which case he is not my late husband, but very much alive."

Richard Adams nodded. "I'm afraid that is the truth."

Eric said, "Gale means to divorce Paul Cormier, if he is alive."

"Without a question," Adams said, "the danger is that Paul Cormier will seek out this Jiri and get the briefcase from him."

"It's possible," she said. "Jiri regarded him as a friend. But he also assured me Paul died in the launch explosion."

Eric spoke up bitterly, "Which only means he was deceived like the rest of us."

Colonel Hudson asked her, "Will you remain here a little longer in the hope that some of this may come to light?"

"I must," she said. "I have to know whether Paul is alive or not."

"Good," the Colonel said. "The staff I sent you will remain and so will the guards."

Adams was on his feet. "You have done both our governments a great service. The consul is sending a long account of your bravery to Washington."

"Hardly bravery, Mr. Adams," she said. "I foolishly and impulsively made a marriage which brought me into this criminal underworld."

Life at the chateau became calm, although the violence Gale had known there haunted her. She also mourned for Madeline and Hassan. And now it seemed likely that Paul was alive. That still didn't tell her why he acted and looked so strange when he had made those midnight visits to her. She could only wonder if there would eventually be a final visit which might solve some of the problems?

Eric had to report to his office after dinner. He felt safe in leaving her alone since the four soldiers guarded the house in three shifts.

Gale was in her bedroom writing a letter to her aunt and uncle when a tap came on her door. The maid came in and told her, "There is a man downstairs requesting to talk with you. The soldiers tried to send him away but he made a fuss. So they have him down there."

She frowned. "A man?"

"A native," the maid said. "A brown man in a red fez."

She felt a bound of hope. "Jiri!" she exclaimed, and rushed by the woman and down the stairs.

It was a sullen Jiri who stood between the two soldiers. And the first thing she noticed was the briefcase which he firmly clutched.

She told the soldiers, "It is all right. He is a friend of mine. I'd appreciate it if you left us alone."

One of the soldiers tipped his cap. "We'll be just outside if you want us. You need only call."

"Thank you," she said. And the two went out.

Jiri stood there staring at her. "You have made a most miraculous escape, Madame Cormier."

"Yes."

"And Revene is dead," he said.

"He was your enemy as well as mine," she reminded him.

"I have many enemies," Jiri said. "That is why I dared not venture here before."

She indicated the briefcase. "You have kept your word and brought it to me."

"Yes," Jiri said. "You may do with it what you like." And he passed the heavy case over to her.

"What about you?"

"Tonight I vanish into the desert."

"Why?"

"My group is scattered, and a new revolutionary leader is taking over. His first task will be to eliminate any of us who might be rivals. I have had enough of it."

"So?"

"Perhaps I will go to Algiers and then to Egypt," Jiri said. "I hear there are opportunities for English-speaking natives in Cairo."

"I hope so," she said. "And I wish you well."

He bowed. "Thank you, Madame."

She said, "One other very important thing. Do you believe my husband is still alive?"

Jiri shrugged. "After so many happenings I could believe almost anything. I do not think so, but I cannot swear to it."

He left and she found herself with the briefcase of papers which had so frequently nearly cost her life. They had come to her in a most casual way, without any effort on her part, except being there to receive them. She summoned one of the soldiers.

"This briefcase must be delivered at once to the British Consulate," she told him. "Colonel Hudson must personally receive it. It is most valuable. Do you understand?"

"Yes, Madame," the soldier said. "I'll take it to the Colonel at once."

She was in the living room waiting when Eric returned about an hour later. She smiled and said, "I think we should celebrate. Whiskey and sodas are suggested."

Eric laughed, "Very well, if you say so." He made the drinks and brought her one.

She raised her glass. "To the briefcase! I received it tonight."

He gaped at her. "When? How?"

She told him, ending with, "And it is now in Colonel Hudson's hands, so you'll have some big stories to write when the important names come out."

Eric shook his head. "Don't count on it. This is an affair between governments. They'll have heavy censorship on it for a while. Perhaps forever."

"At least Colonel Hudson has the papers."

"Yes," Eric said. "That leaves only one mystery. Is Paul still alive?"

"I asked Jiri," she said. "He wasn't sure."

"Which leaves us exactly where we began," Eric said with a groan.

"Enjoy your drink," she told him. "It is bound to turn out well."

"I'm glad you think so," Eric said, sounding doubtful.

He had taken to sleeping in the room across from hers again. And on this night of celebration it was late when he kissed her good night at her door. She went inside and prepared for bed quickly, relieved that the briefcase had been found and delivered to the proper authorities.

She slept soundly and so she did not awake until the phantom touched her shoulder. She opened her eyes and when she saw the pale, anguished face of Paul bending over her in the dark she let out a small cry!

"Be silent!" the phantom whispered.

"Paul?" she questioned the ghostly figure.

"You knew I would return to you," he said. "You have the briefcase. Jiri brought it to you today."

"Yes."

"I must have it," the phantom whispered hoarsely and anxiously. "Where have you placed it?"

"I don't have it!"

"You lie!"

"No," she protested, "I sent it to Colonel Hudson, the British Consul."

"Liar!" the pale face of Paul came closer and he slapped her hard, stunning her.

Before she could reply, her door burst open and Eric appeared, a gun in one hand and a candle in the other. The phantom swung and she saw a gun in his hand.

"Eric! He's going to shoot!" she screamed.

Eric fired as she spoke. The phantom did not return the shot. Instead he staggered to the foot of the bed, held on to the brass post for a moment and then fell down onto the floor!

Gale was on her feet. In the glow of the candle she had seen the phantom's black-clad figure. Now she cautiously advanced toward the fallen figure to view his face.

The man was flat on his stomach and Eric knelt by him and slowly turned him over. Gale saw his face and gasped. It was not a face but a white, painted mask! A mask which so resembled Paul's features she could hardly credit it.

Eric gave her a quick glance and then removed the man's mask. Revealed was the face of Ben Cormier, Paul's half brother. The slight movement seemed to revive him and he opened his eyes and stared up at them.

"Game is over," he managed with great difficulty. "Made mask of Paul! Almost worked!" His eyes closed and his head fell to one side.

Eric took a sheet from the bed and covered him. He turned to her, "We'll call the police and Colonel Hudson. End of the story!"

She shook her head. "Not the end, the beginning!" And she stepped into his waiting arms.

PULSE-RACING, PASSIONATE HISTORICAL FICTION

LOVE'S TENDER FURY
by Jennifer Wilde (81-909, $2.50)

Over 2.5 million copies sold! This is the enthralling story of an English beauty—sold at auction like a slave—who scandalized the New World by enslaving her masters.

THIS LOVING TORMENT
by Valerie Sherwood (82-649, $2.25)

Born in poverty in the after math of the Great London Fire, Charity Woodstock grew up to set the men of three continents ablaze with passion! The bestselling sensation of the year, boasting 1.3 million copies in print after just one month, to make it the fastest-selling historical romance in Warner Books history!

CARESS AND CONQUER
by Donna Comeaux Zide (82-949, $2.25)

Was she a woman capable of deep love—or only high adventure? She was Cat Devlan, a violet-eyed, copper-haired beauty bent on vengeance, raging against the man who dared to take her body against her will—and then dared to demand her heart as well. By the author of the bestselling SAVAGE IN SILK.

SAVAGE IN SILK
by Donna Comeaux Zide (82-702, $2.50)

Born of violence, surrendered to the lust of evil men, forced to travel and suffer the world over, Mariah's only sanctuary lay in the love of one man. And nothing—neither distance nor war nor the danger of a wild continent would keep her from him! A dazzling historical novel as exciting as love itself!

DARE TO LOVE
by Jennifer Wilde (81-826, $2.50)

Who dared to love Elena Lopez? She was the queen of desire and the slave of passion, traveling the world—London, Paris, San Francisco—and taking love where she found it. Elena Lopez, the tantalizing, beautiful woman—was she too dangerous to love?

ROMANCE...PASSION... ADVENTURE...

KASHMIRI PASSIONS
by Clarissa Ross (82-839, $2.25)
Across the British Empire she fled casting off the violent embrace of an Indian Prince... Escaping the marriage bed of a lecherous English lord... To India... where adventure awaits her, a new identity can be drawn about her like a cloak, and sweet forgetfulness can be attained in other arms!

JOURNEY INTO FIRE
by Patricia Wright (81-525, $2.50)
He was a musician trained as a murderer. She was a dedicated surgeon. Together they survived imprisonment and torture, war and betrayal, in a novel that sweeps across half a century of Russian history—a love story shaped by an undying passion and a ruthless destiny.

TO THE OPERA BALL
by Sarah Gainham (82-592, $2.25)
Who is he? This airman Rolf. How did he come to be at the Opera Ball, to enchant the beautiful young heiress Leona and to lure her away with him? He is the child of a love affair, as romantic, as passionate and yet as different from his liaison with Leona as darkness is to light, as the dance of death is TO THE OPERA BALL.

WARNER BOOKS
P.O. Box 690
New York, N.Y. 10019

Please send me the books I have selected.
Enclose check or money order only, no cash please. Plus 50¢ per order and 20¢ per copy to cover postage and handling. N.Y. State and California residents add applicable sales tax.
Please allow 4 weeks for delivery.

_____ Please send me your free mail order catalog

_____ Please send me your free Romance books catalog

Name_____

Address_____

City_____

State_____Zip_____